When You're Home

Abby Millsaps

ebook ISBN: 978-1-7370947-0-8
Paperback ISBN: 978-1-7370947-1-5

Edited by Joanne Machin
Cover Design by Cover Couture www.bookcovercouture.com

To my husband, David—

I have loved you since the night you offered to share your secret pizza with me.

It's always been you.

Prologue

TORI

Tori knew she'd find him out here. She felt his eyes drilling into her as soon as she stepped over the broken spot in the fence that connected their yards. Rhett's long, toned body was spread out on a pool chair. Her eyes scanned the length of him unnecessarily. She already knew the angles and contours of his form by memory. He was barefoot, wearing nothing but a pair of jogger sweatpants even though it was early spring in Ohio. He had probably planned to climb into the hot tub after he texted her. He clearly hadn't expected her to actually come over.

"Are you sure about this, V?"

Tori walked toward him, steeling herself and finding the courage to close the gap between them. Her chest tightened with anticipation as her eyes continued to adjust to the dark. She could just start to make out his features. *Chill*, she scolded herself. She hated the way her body betrayed her in his presence. She needed to keep it together long enough to lay a few ground rules before anything happened tonight. Tori swallowed hard, willing her voice not to shake as she answered his question.

"Oh, I'm sure," she confirmed. Two and a half years apart was long enough.

Rhett had never stopped pursuing her, not really. They had dated all throughout high school, then she broke up with him before college. They had fallen into a miserable pattern anytime he was home in Hampton: They would hang out, and he would play the part of the platonic, protective best friend. But eventually he'd get frustrated at the reminder of what they once were, and he'd shoot his shot. Sometimes it was just a cocked eyebrow and a suggestive smirk. Other times it was a lingering, heated pause before he told her goodnight. Tonight's attempt came in the form of a suggestive text.

Tori usually resisted his advances. Every now and then, she flirted back and teased him, but only when she was feeling lonely. She had never actually reciprocated until tonight.

Tonight she wasn't teasing. He had texted her a few hours after they got home from their shifts at Clinton's Family Restaurant, just like she assumed he would. And tonight she actually responded to his advances. Now she was here, standing in front of her ex-boyfriend on a frigid March night, curious to see just how much of her resolve had dissipated.

"Why now?" His question cut through the night, snapping her attention back to the moment. He lifted his arm toward his head, running his hand through his dark, wavy hair. His voice was deeper than normal. She knew he'd been drinking. She also knew he was laying there and questioning everything. Rhett was way too analytical to just go with the flow: He'd been like this since they were kids. He needed to understand the rules to whatever game they were about to play. He needed to know how to win.

"Don't question this," she insisted, sauntering over to him. She watched for his reaction as she approached, but he didn't move a muscle. She was going to have to make the first move. She joined him on the lounger, spreading her legs wide to straddle his lap. As soon as their bodies connected, he sat up and circled his arms around her waist. She purposely lined up her core with his erection. She let her fingertips brush the outline of his bare stomach. Rhett sucked in a sharp breath in response to her touch.

"Because this? Whatever this is between us? I miss this. I miss us together." Tori shifted her hips forward, applying the slightest edge of pressure against his groin. She knew he wouldn't be able to resist the contact. It was a tease as much as it was an invitation. Her body practically vibrated because of the proximity. One quick movement, one ragged breath or deep exhale, and their lips would touch.

"What are you saying, V? You want to get back together?"

There was hope in his voice. Tori knew she had to nip that in the bud. She shook her head slowly, letting the hair that had fallen out of her messy bun brush against the tops of his shoulders.

"We can't. You know that, and you know why," she reminded him. "But I still want you."

Emboldened by the solidness of his erection between her legs, she found the dip of his collarbone with her mouth. It was one of her favorite spots on his body: the deep valley on either side of his neck where tight shoulder muscles gave way to soft, delicate skin. She couldn't resist breathing him in, inhaling the familiar scent of salt, sandalwood, and a hint of something spicy. Something distinctly Rhett.

When he didn't respond, Tori squeezed her thighs against his lap for emphasis, just in case he needed a bit more clarification about what she was asking for tonight.

His body tensed underneath her, and she prepared to be ejected from his lap. She knew he wanted more than she was willing to give him. After everything they'd been through together and apart, would this offer be enough? Would he say yes to just tonight?

Rhett wove his hand into the hair at the nape of her neck, then pulled her head back to stare into her eyes. "You know you can have me anyway you want me."

Tori's vision had adjusted enough to the darkness that she could see the desire in his gaze. His blue-grey eyes were stormy, his hunger palpable. His answer was written all over his face: they were doing this.

Were they really doing this?

She didn't know how they could stop if they started back up, but she also felt powerless to the wanting that coursed through her body whenever she was around him. It had been two and a half years since they had been together, and it was evident Rhett hadn't just gotten over her when he went away to college like she assumed he would. She had no idea how this was going to work, and she knew there was a good chance they were both going to get hurt in the end, but she was willing to risk the pain if it meant they could be together tonight.

Prologue

Rhett

"Tori…" Rhett groaned, flopping back onto the mattress and letting out a long exhale to try and steady his breathing. He raised his arm to his forehead and let it rest across his eyes. An anxiousness started to creep back into his mind despite the explosive orgasm that had just ripped through his body. He still couldn't believe this was really happening. It was almost too good to be true.

After almost three years of floundering in the friend zone, he had somehow convinced the love of his life to be with him again. Well, maybe that was an exaggeration. They weren't technically together, and Tori had been upfront with him that this was all temporary. First she said it was just for the night. Then she insisted it was just for the weekend. But they had spent the last seven days entwined in each other's arms, and that in and of itself was a miracle in his mind.

Rhett shoved off the bed and headed into his en suite bathroom to take care of the condom. He tied it off, tossing it into the trash can before washing his hands. *Good riddance*. They never had to use condoms in high school because Tori had an IUD and they had been each other's first and only. He was annoyed they were necessary now.

Condoms aside, the last week had still been better than anything he could have dreamed up. They spent their days working alongside their friends at Clinton's, then they spent their nights wrapped up in each other's arms in his bed. But tomorrow was the last day of spring break, and that meant whatever they were doing was about to be over.

He was dreading it. He didn't want it to end, but he didn't know how to broach the subject with her either.

Rhett walked slowly back to bed. Tori had taken up residence in the middle of the mattress and was spread out like a starfish, her dark blond hair fanned out behind her. Her eyes were closed, but he knew she wasn't sleeping. She had a mischievous smile on her pouty, swollen lips.

This girl, Rhett thought to himself affectionately. He loved so many things about her: the way she lit up like a firework when he challenged her. The way she cared for her dad and the kids she volunteered with at camp. The way she prided herself in her independence. The way she could be so open and warm when she wasn't pushing him away.

She was the love of his life. For Rhett, it had always been Tori. He knew his feelings weren't unrequited. They were clearly still attracted to each other, as proven by the multiple orgasms they had doled out over the last week. The connection between them was undeniably deeper than physical attraction. Her excuses for why they couldn't be together were just that: excuses.

He lowered himself down onto the bed to join her, mindful not to disturb her blissed-out state.

"*That* was my favorite," she professed as she rolled over to close the space between them. He eagerly pulled her into his arms. What he wouldn't give to make this last a lifetime...

"I'm glad you liked that. I really like making you come," he whispered as his lips found the crook of her neck. She leaned into him, all soft and malleable in his arms. He loved the way the curves of her body molded under his touch. He couldn't let himself get distracted now, though. He knew this was probably the best opportunity he was going to get to broach the subject of what was next, so he needed to take his shot.

"I think we need to talk," he blurted out, running his hand from the nape of her neck all the way along her spine to her low back. He really did want to talk to her, but he also couldn't keep his hands off of her. There was a low-key frenzy humming in his body that he was constantly trying to satiate. It was like his brain still didn't believe him that this was really happening. *Two and a half years apart had been way too long.*

Tori let out a loud breath. It was a mix between a groan and an exasperated sigh.

"Hey, don't do that, V. Don't shut down on me. This last week has been incredible, but I have to go back to school tomorrow. I want to talk about this, to figure out whatever it is we're doing. Are you into this?"

"Everhett, you were just inside of me, so yes, I would have to say that 'I'm into this.' You knew the answer to that without asking. There's nothing to talk about or figure out. It's not gonna happen."

"Umm, I hate to break it to you, beautiful, but it kind of did just happen," he teased as he swept his hand lower and pinched her ass. "Twice."

She squirmed in his arms, then raised her head to look at him. "You know what I mean," she insisted. "We're not going to get back together. I'm not going to be your girlfriend."

The pain of her rejection didn't even register in his mind. Being turned down by Tori had become commonplace over the last few years.

"Well, Victoria Thompson, today must be your lucky day. I don't expect you to be my girlfriend. I don't want or need a girlfriend. In fact, I've been girlfriend-less since you broke up with me before college."

"And that, Everhett Wheeler, is the whole damn problem," she countered, stroking the tips of her fingers against his chest. He shuddered in response to her touch. *Two could play that game.*

"Is that so?" he questioned as he shifted his weight on top of her. He pushed up quickly, catching one of her nipples with his teeth as he pinched the other one between his fingers. She let out a hiss followed by a soft moan in response to his touch. *Oh yes. Two could definitely play this game.*

"The only reason you don't have a girlfriend right now is because you aren't looking for a girlfriend," she accused as she writhed below his tongue. She kept trying to make her case as he kissed along the curves of her breasts. "You're charming and smart and hot as hell. Any girl would be lucky to date you. I think the reason you don't have a girlfriend is because you're holding out for me to change my mind about us, but you can't keep doing that. This isn't going to happen again." She muttered the last part softly, almost like she didn't believe it herself.

Rhett read her cues and continued to move down her body, burying his face into the dip of her waist. He licked the soft skin beneath each breast and continued to pinch and tease her nipples. He pinned her hips in place with his own as she tried to arch her back.

When he reached the apex of her thighs, he placed each of his hands on the inside of her legs and held her open. The tips of his fingers just barely grazed her center. He licked along the crease of one thigh, intentionally teasing her as he withheld what she really wanted. Tori tried to buck her hips in response, growling in frustration when she realized he was holding her steady.

He peered up at her from between her thighs. "You were saying something about this not happening again?"

"Okay, okay! Fine, you made your point. Maybe this will happen again, but it's not going to happen again without clear boundaries," she huffed, slightly breathless.

"So what do you propose?" Rhett asked huskily. He was trying in earnest not to forfeit the negotiation. They were onto something, hovering on the brink of something new. But she wasn't the only one affected by the proximity of his face to her clit. He was so hard right now, so eager to please her.

"I don't want this to be over, but I also don't want either of us to get too attached," she murmured, trying again to lift her hips and make contact with his mouth. Rhett smiled at her eagerness.

"We both know you're not going to get too attached, V," he muttered before he finally gave in and ran his tongue gently through her folds. Tori sighed and appreciatively tugged on his hair. He flicked the tip of his tongue against her clit several times before closing his mouth around it and sucking. He continued to lick and kiss her core as he slowly slipped one finger into her sex. He had already made her come twice that day. Now that she was satiated, he wanted to savor her. He took his time massaging her from the inside, basking in the closeness she was finally allowing to blossom between them. He would spend all day buried inside this woman if she would let him.

"I want you," she moaned.

Rhett stilled. He wasn't sure if she meant she wanted him physically because of what he was doing to her body at the moment, or if she was continuing the conversation. He glanced up at her again, hoping for clarification.

"Damnit, I want you." It sounded like an admission more than anything. "So if you promise to not get too attached... and if you promise to keep doing this..." She gave him a pointed look and raised her hips again toward his face.

Was this really happening? Did she just admit she wanted to keep this going between them? He smiled so wide he felt his cheeks begin to tingle.

"I'm addicted to you, V. I went two and a half years without a fix. I'll agree to just about anything if we can keep doing this when we're together, so yes, I promise not to get too attached."

"Give me your phone then," Tori demanded, hoisting herself up on her elbows. She dug her heels into the mattress to move away from his mouth.

"Wait, what? Are you being serious right now?"

"Yes, I'm serious. Hand me your phone. I have an idea."

Rhett groaned in protest but reached over on the bedside table to give her what she wanted. He tossed her the phone without unlocking the screen. She knew his passcode by heart.

"I feel like I should be insulted that you'd rather play on my phone than let me play with you," he teased. He kept his tone light, but he was curious. He still didn't understand what she was doing.

"Oh, we'll be resuming the regularly scheduled programming momentarily," she informed him with a salacious smile. "But I just had an idea about how we could make this work, and I need to set it up now before you can fight me on it." She stared intently at his phone for a minute before continuing. "You, Everhett Wheeler, are about to venture into the world of online dating."

"What?" he groaned. It was his turn to push up off the sheets and join her at the head of the bed. "What the hell, Tori? I don't want to do any of that swipe right shit." He made a half-assed attempt at reaching over and grabbing his phone from her hand, but she swatted him away.

"No worries. You don't have to do a thing. I'll set it all up for you. We both know I can probably make you sound better anyways." She stuck her tongue out playfully. Rhett shifted closer and pressed his mouth against hers. She squealed in surprise from the contact but pulled away quickly to focus on her task.

"Tori, I'm serious. I don't think I want to do this."

"Well, do you want to do *this*?" she asked him pointedly.

He knew what "this" meant. He nodded without missing a beat.

"Then you need to date other people. I feel like this could be the best of both worlds, Rhett. I don't want to be your girlfriend or be in a relationship with you," she explained.

"Ouch."

"No, not ouch. There's no point in being in a relationship with an expiration date. I won't do it. This wouldn't have worked a few years ago, but we're older now. I think we can handle hooking up without getting too attached. Here's the deal: we can be together when you're home if you find someone else to be with when you're at school."

A few beats passed as he processed her proposal. He didn't like anything about the idea except for the fact that it meant he got to keep sleeping with her.

"Tori, this is ridiculous," he protested. He needed to find a flaw in her plan. "You can't really expect me to try to date someone else then come home and be with you? There's got to be an easier way."

"Fine," she clipped. "If you think this is ridiculous and you don't want to do it, then we aren't doing this." He knew that tone. She was digging her heels in now. Any hope for an alternative plan had officially vanished.

"Tori," he half-heartedly protested again, but he already knew he was going to follow her lead. She had given him an opening. Granted, it was a paper-thin pseudo-opening that came with strings attached, but it was still an opening. It was more than she had given him in the last two and a half years, and he wanted her any way he could have her.

"Fine," he relented.

"Fine?"

"Yeah, fine. I accept your ridiculous terms. I'll find someone to date, or hell, I'll find lots of people to date, if it means we can be together whenever I'm home."

"You have to follow through, Rhett." Her words were solemn, the look in her eyes pleading for him to take her seriously. Her sincerity surprised him. He wondered if maybe she was worried about more than just him getting attached if they kept hooking up when he was in Hampton.

"I will, I promise. I wouldn't lie to you, beautiful. You know that."

"Then you've got yourself a deal, Wheeler." She smirked, her expression playful once again.

"Hey, just a heads-up. I've got a lot of trips home planned for the rest of this semester."

"I wouldn't expect anything less from you."

Rhett couldn't believe this was happening. Leave it to Tori to shock the shit out of him. He hadn't expected this turn of events, but he wasn't mad about it, either. Well, maybe he was a little mad about having to date someone else, but he could deal with that later. He was already trying to think through his schedule and figure out when he could come home next. Before his thoughts could wander too far, another idea presented itself in his mind. The idea quickly blossomed into a desire that took root in the deepest part of his soul. He didn't know if he could even suggest it without revealing his truth, but he knew he had to try.

"Hey, I've got my own idea for your consideration," he proposed, reaching over to twirl a strand of her hair. She was still typing on his phone, her nose scrunched up slightly as she peered at the small screen.

"What's that?" she asked without looking up from the device.

"Let's both get tested before we're together again so we don't have to use condoms."

Tori looked up from the small screen, bewilderment etched on her face. Rhett held his breath as she processed his suggestion. He knew what he was asking, but he didn't care if she saw through him to the heart of his request. If he could only have her sometimes and on her terms, he wanted to be as close to her as possible. He wanted as much of her as she was willing to give. After another breath, her whole face illuminated with a smile.

"Oh, you definitely have yourself a deal."

Hell. Yes.

"Enough talking," he declared then. "Can you please stop downloading apps on my phone so I can go down on you again?"

She held his gaze as she tossed the phone onto the other side of the bed and shimmied back down into his sheets. Rhett didn't know how they'd gotten here, but he wasn't going to question it. She was his, sort of, sometimes, as long as he followed through on the arrangement. He would worry about the dating thing later. Right now, he only had two things on his mind: making her come for the third time that day and figuring out when he could come home and be with her next.

CHAPTER 1

3 YEARS LATER

He shot up in bed, his head swimming thanks to the exuberant amount of Jameson he had chugged from a sports bottle earlier that night. He blinked hard, trying to clear out enough brain fog to remember how to shuffle one foot in front of the other.

His bare feet hit the thickly carpeted floor. *That's right.* He was at his parents' house in Hampton. The plush carpet conjured up the details from earlier that day as memories flitted across his consciousness.

The mail strewn across the countertop of his apartment.

The accusatory look in her eyes.

The screaming match that ended with him grabbing his jacket and car keys.

The final words he threw back at her (*"I'll never not do this!"*) before slamming the door.

The relief that settled in his body as soon as he put the Prelude into reverse and peeled out of the parking lot.

Rhett lazily walked into the bathroom, his eyelids heavy with sleep and overindulgence. His hand groped for the panel of switches, flicking on the one farthest from the door to illuminate the small light above the sink.

He reached for the corner of the window shade out of habit. A quick glance out the bathroom window confirmed what he subconsciously already knew: Tori was still awake.

He'd heard her car pull up the driveway to the house directly behind his parents' house around ten thirty. It must have been a slow night at work. That tended to happen on Fridays in the dead of winter in Ohio. He felt a tingle run through his spine when he heard her voice raise up two octaves to call Penny back inside the house. It took every ounce of willpower in his body not to call out to her across their backyards. He had purposely left his cell phone inside the house for the same reason. He had tried to ignore the hum of her proximity the rest of the night as he sunk chin-deep into the hot tub and nursed his sports bottle alone.

Rhett's head felt less cloudy after he washed his hands. He turned to exit the bathroom but not before stealing another peak out the window. The little curtains that hung above the windows of the Thompsons' garage were pulled shut, but that didn't matter. He could still see her in his mind's eye. She was probably squatting low over a canvas, her hair secured to the top of her head in a massive bun, her favorite black leggings taut against her ass.

Rhett flopped back onto his bed, feeling the queen-size mattress creak under the weight of his six-one frame. He wasn't going to fall back asleep anytime soon if he kept thinking about Tori's ass. Exhaling, he reached for his phone and pounded out a quick text. Annoyed with his lack of restraint, he threw the phone down next to him as soon as he hit send.

Ev: Why are you still awake?

He knew it might be hours before Tori even saw the message. She got so in the zone when she was painting. He loved the way she could get lost in a canvas, mixing different colors and blasting the same music they'd been obsessed with since high school on the old five-CD stereo in the garage. She didn't get to paint very often between work and classes. He felt a brief pang of guilt. Maybe he shouldn't have interrupted her with a text. He should have just stuck to his original plan and called her in the morning.

The phone buzzed next to him. The serotonin rush that accompanied her reply banished all feelings of remorse as he swiped up to unlock the screen.

V: Why are you home?

Rhett scowled. What the hell was he supposed to say to that? Maybe the whiskey wasn't as metabolized as he wanted to believe. He clearly hadn't thought this through. It wasn't a holiday or anyone's birthday. Tori knew damn well he would have told her if this was a planned visit home. He had no real reason to be back at his parents' house this weekend, and yet here he was.

He considered lying for about two seconds.

"Damnit," he muttered to himself. He wouldn't lie to her. Even if he could bring himself to do it, the repercussions weren't worth her rage. Tori would call his bluff so fast his head would spin. She had a secret temper that only reared its head when she knew she was being deceived.

Rhett flipped the phone over and over again in his hand, contemplating how much to tell her. Was he really going to recount all the details of his fight with Chandler? That was going to get awkward fast, considering the fight was about Tori.

Frustration got the best of him as he typed out a version of the truth he hoped she would accept.

Ev: I just needed a break.

He held his breath and squinted at the bright phone. He watched for the three little dots to appear on the screen, willing her to reply to his vague response. How much could he get away with not saying tonight? His eyes grew heavy as he laid in bed, waiting, one hand holding the phone above his head, the other arm splayed out across his bare chest.

Rhett had all but given up on hearing back from her when the phone vibrated in his hand. He fumbled with the device and almost dropped it on his face as he desperately tried to swipe up.

V: Ledges tomorrow? Lia said she would cover my lunch shift.

Rhett let out an extended breath to steady his heartbeat. Anticipation washed over him when he finally let himself inhale.

He hadn't seen Tori in more than three weeks. Just the promise of being with her tomorrow made him feel lighter. Eagerness mingled with relief as he smashed down his pillow with his fist before sending his reply.

Ev: Yes please. Can't wait. Goodnight, V.

CHAPTER 2

Tori

Tori stared down at her phone and reread his text. The part of her brain that wasn't consumed with anger felt a bit of smugness. If Rhett was home tonight, that meant something had happened with Chandler. He wouldn't up and leave Easton for any other reason, not without letting her know. She felt like she had won some sort of contest she didn't even know she was competing in.

She knew he was home almost as soon as she got back from work. She noticed the lights from the hot tub when she went to her room to change her clothes. It could only be him. She could just barely make out his body slouched deep in the water, the blue and purple lights dancing across the surface. The Wheelers had gone to their lake house in Michigan for the weekend. Rhett's mother, Anne, had texted her that morning to give her the heads-up, just like she always did.

The hum in Tori's body confirmed her suspicions. She hated that she was so physically attuned to him. That was definitely Rhett in the hot tub.

She considered putting on a bathing suit instead of her painting clothes when she stripped down to her underwear and piled her hair on top of her head. Her shoulders ached from serving a huge party at Clinton's earlier that night. Every single person in the party of twelve ordered double beverages: a Coke and a water, a Coors Light and a water, and so on and so on. Dipping into the Wheelers' hot tub would immediately dissolve the tightness in her upper back.

That's not the only thing that would dissolve. She knew her resolve didn't stand a chance in close proximity to that man. It would be a matter of minutes before she was eagerly closing the space between them and straddling Rhett's lap if she let herself go over there tonight.

She banished the idea on principle. She wasn't going to go skipping across the backyard and through the broken fence to join her friend-with-benefits without even so much as a courtesy call. Rhett came home to Hampton without telling her. He had some explaining to do.

"You just needed a break," she muttered to herself, walking back to the folding table she had set up to spread out her paint supplies. She had spent the first few hours in the garage prepping canvases for the art therapy class she was teaching next weekend. There were already thirteen kids registered for her workshop through the New Hope program. Maggie, the volunteer coordinator, said it had the highest registration rate out of all the offerings that month. Tori recognized at least half the names on the sign-up list. She was looking forward to seeing some of the kids she had grown close with at last summer's sleepaway camp, but her heart ached prematurely for the new faces who would show up to the workshop. Project New Hope offered monthly grief therapy programs and a summer sleepaway camp for bereaved kids who had lost one or both parents. Tori had been a participant for years before aging out and starting her role as a volunteer.

Once all the canvases were prepped, she moved on to work on her own art for the night. She was just about to thin out a gorgeous patina teal paint when Rhett's first text had come through, but she was determined not to let his late-night interruption stop her from finishing her new piece.

"Shit!" she muttered as she accidently poured too much floetrol into a mixing cup. She was furious with herself as she inspected the almost-overflowing container. Could she somehow salvage it? Paint thinner was expensive, and she would be missing out on a lot of tips tomorrow by giving up a weekend shift. Lia had already texted her back and committed to working for her. Her best friend had even refrained from making judgmental comments when Tori admitted she was giving up the shift to spend time with Rhett.

What did that man think he needed a break from, anyways? His expensive off-campus apartment and his fancy business MBA program? His gorgeous girlfriend with her impossibly long legs and perfectly curated social feed? The full-time job with benefits at his granddad's company that he'd walk into after graduation?

Tori bit down on her lower lip, working it back and forth as she tried to conjure up a frustration that just wouldn't stick. She was surprised by his unexpected visit to Hampton, but that surprise dissolved into anticipation when she thought about seeing him tomorrow. Her eagerness to see him ratcheted tenfold as soon as his text came through and confirmed he was home. The yearning she usually pushed deep into the back of her mind was threatening to spill over like the overflowing cup of paint in front of her. There was a visceral longing for Rhett that lived right under the surface of her skin.

Home.

Rhett was home for the weekend, unexpectedly, and he wouldn't tell her why. Or at least he wouldn't tell her over text.

She turned back to her mixing table, defeated. She knew she wouldn't be able to focus on anything else tonight. She gathered up her paints and pour cups, carefully screwed on the caps, and folded up the disposable tablecloths. She stashed away her supplies on the one garage shelf she claimed as her own before heading inside the house.

"Goodnight, room," she muttered under her breath as she flicked off the lights in the garage, reciting a line from one of the books her mother used to read to her when she was a little girl.

"And goodnight, Ev," she added toward the direction of Rhett's parents' house.

CHAPTER 3

Tori

She adjusted her sherpa pullover and tightened her ponytail as she practically skipped down the stairs the next morning. It was early —really too early to be up for someone who had stayed up until almost four a.m. last night—but her body was buzzing with so much anticipation she couldn't sleep any longer. She pivoted right at the landing and headed for the kitchen.

"Morning!" she called in her dad's general direction as she ducked her head into the fridge in search of coffee creamer. Paul Thompson was seated at his favorite spot at the kitchen table, the crossword puzzle from that day's paper spread out in front of him.

"Good morning, sweetheart." The words came out barely louder than a whisper. He was deep in concentration, his brow furrowed. The frown deepened the prominent wrinkles in his forehead.

"What's the clue?" she asked, assuming he was stumped.

"Idle!" he exclaimed a moment later, grinning to himself triumphantly as he penciled in the letters.

Tori poured coffee into one of her mom's favorite Christmas mugs, her back turned away from her father. She hadn't had the heart to put the mugs away with the rest of the Christmas decorations last month.

"Rhett's home," her dad announced. It was more of a statement than a question.

"Mhmmm," she murmured in reply, not wanting her dad to know that she wasn't expecting to see him this weekend. Or that she had ditched her shift at the restaurant today to be with him. She took her time pouring creamer into her coffee, watching the milky liquid swirl and transform the dark cup.

"I heard him get in around nine o'clock last night. I thought the Wheelers were in Michigan this weekend?"

Tori pulled open the fridge door harder than necessary. The condiments on the door rattled against each other as she set the creamer back inside. Steeling her expression, she settled her eyes on her almost overflowing cup of coffee and slowly made her way to the table.

"Yes, Anne texted me. They left yesterday afternoon."

"What in the world is that boy doing home then? He just went back to Easton for the start of the term..." He trailed off, letting the thought linger as he scowled at the next clue on the page. Tori puffed out her cheeks and blew out a slow breath, hopeful that the conversation was over before it really started.

She took a long sip of her coffee, smiling to herself as she lowered the mug she knew her mom used to love. What she wouldn't give to be sitting at this table with both her parents right now. It had been twelve years since her mom passed away. Tori had officially lived more of her life without her than she had with her.

Her dad had tried his hardest to stay whole for her, "tried" being the operative word. Tori had put in the work to navigate her own grief, but she knew an unrelenting pain still harbored deep inside her dad. He was the shell of the man she remembered from her childhood, his life decimated into a pile of grief and stress when he lost the love of his life.

Years of therapy had helped Tori to recognize that she had lost two parents when her mom died. Her mother was dead, and her father would never be whole again, not unless he put genuine effort into working through his pain. Some days she felt like she was the only reason he still had any will to live. After years of suggesting and then eventually begging, she knew it was unlikely her dad would ever seek help in navigating his own grief. He was the only one who could do the work. She was just a bystander to his slow and unconscious self-destruction.

A satisfied grunt snapped Tori out of her thoughts as her dad filled in another answer. She reached down into the side pocket of her workout leggings for her phone, hitting a button to illuminate the screen. 9:04 a.m. *Rise and shine, Everhett Wheeler.*

Tori smiled to herself as the anticipation of the next few hours played out in her mind. Her dad was wrong—Rhett had not just recently gone back to school. It had been twenty-six painstakingly long days since he had been in Hampton. Since he had run his hands through her hair. Since he had made her breath hitch as his lips and teeth met the hollow of her neck.

She opened the lock screen on her phone and shot off a text.

V: Are you up?

Her phone buzzed less than five seconds later.

Ev: Yep. You coming?

V: Hopefully.

She hit send, punctuating the text with a winky kiss face.

"Say hi to him for me," her dad interrupted her dirty thoughts. Tori wiped the grin off her face and sheepishly looked up from the phone screen.

"I will." She locked eyes on her dad and felt a surge of gratitude for his ability to not pry into her personal life. It had taken several years and a few tense moments, but he had learned not to get too inquisitive about the details of her relationship with Rhett.

"Are you working anymore this weekend?"

Guilt scratched at the surface of Tori's excitement for the day ahead. She had already ditched her shift for today, and there was a good chance she would be begging Lia or Cory to cover her Sunday shift, too. She did some quick math in her head and tried to visualize the spreadsheet labeled "February Expenses" she had saved on her computer upstairs.

"Lia and I traded a few shifts this weekend, but it's fine. We are all paid up until the fifteenth," she explained, offering a tight smile meant to reassure him. "Plus, Mike posted the new schedule last night, and I'm on all weekend of Valentine's Day."

He stayed quiet for a moment, then returned Tori's tight-lipped smile and nodded. "Sounds good, sweetheart."

She handled their finances. She paid the bills and budgeted their monthly expenses. As long as she made enough at the restaurant to cover the groceries, utilities, Internet, and their phones, her dad's job at the local auto parts store covered the rest. She had insisted on taking over the responsibility after she graduated high school and it became clear to her that they were living paycheck to paycheck. They were still living paycheck to paycheck now, but they usually had a bit more breathing room at the end of each month.

Her dad had a good job as a mechanic at an auto shop before her mom died, but the balancing act of being a single dad to a preteen girl drowning in his own grief proved to be too much. He was fired less than a month after they buried her mom.

Tori used to get angry when she thought about the cruelty of firing a man who had just lost his wife, but nowadays she was grateful he wasn't still putting in fifty-hour weeks of manual labor. Working part-time at the auto parts store was the better fit for her aging father, and she was happy to contribute. They were a team. They had an unspoken agreement to make it work no matter what. Even though the house was too big and the taxes were too high, they would do everything in their power to keep the house her mom had made into a home.

"Will you take care of Penny for me this afternoon, Dad?" Tori asked, smiling sheepishly over her mug as she finished her coffee. "Rhett and I are going to the Ledges, and I don't want to take her in case it's icy on the rocks."

"Sure thing, sweetheart," he replied, any tension from their little money talk already dissipated. "Be careful out there. And text me if you won't be home tonight," he added, quickly ducking his head back into the paper to avoid making eye contact with her.

"Thanks, Daddy." Tori kissed the top of his head on the way to the sink. After quickly rinsing her mug and loading it into the dishwasher, she headed for the back door. She zipped up the top of her pullover and shoved her feet into her hiking boots before trekking across the yard.

She let herself into the Wheeler house through the sunroom door. She knew without testing the handle that the doorknob would give; Rhett always left it unlocked for her when his family was out of town.

She knocked her boots against the rug before slipping them off. A light dusting of snow had fallen after she finally fell asleep last night. She could just barely see her footprints where they started at the broken spot in the fence that connected their yards.

She inhaled, taking in the earthy scent of the various plants Anne was storing in the sunroom for winter. She glanced past a particularly tall fiddle leaf tree toward the built-in bar in the corner. The Jameson was pulled out and left askew against the regiment of bottles lined up against the wall. That confirmed her suspicions about why it took him so long to finally text her last night.

Tori made her way into the main house. Everything had been left neat and tidy; Anne obviously did a once-over before they left for their cabin in Michigan. Maddie's backpack was the only element out of place. It was thrown over a kitchen chair and left open like she had to grab something quickly before running out the door.

She kept walking, her wool socks catching against the hardwood floor every few steps as she made her way to the staircase. She took the stairs two at a time, making a sharp left at the top. To this day, she wondered what the Wheelers were thinking when they gave Rhett the bedroom closest to the stairs. It was ridiculously easy to get in and out of without disturbing anyone else in the house.

She didn't bother knocking, instead pushing the heavy oak door with enough force to make it clunk into the doorstop. Her eyes raked over Rhett's room. The dark navy walls and mahogany bedroom furniture scratched all the happy places in her brain as she took in the familiar scene. Rhett wasn't in his bed, but the sheets were askew. She inhaled, letting the notes of sea salt and sandalwood linger before she started to feel heady.

"Hey, V." A deep voice knocked the breath out of her as she spun around to see him standing at the entrance of the attached bathroom, one arm thrown up as he leaned into the door jamb. Damn. He looked so good. She had missed him so much.

"How long were you standing there watching me?" she demanded, her eyes narrowing. She could barely contain the smile that threatened to take over her entire face.

He threw up both hands in mock defense. "I was in the bathroom when you came in!"

She took the opportunity to let her eyes roam his body. He was naked, save for the charcoal boxer briefs that hugged his thighs and sat low on his hips. He had the broadest shoulders, and she loved the little dips of his collarbone, the hollow at the base of his neck. His chest was well defined with lean muscle, and the definition in his stomach tapered in, creating deep, delicious grooves just above his hips.

"Are you going to come over here and greet me properly?" Rhett smirked, breaking her trance. She had no idea how much time had just passed as she made her sultry assessment of his body.

"You look like a cat about to pounce," he taunted her. His voice had dropped a full octave. She knew what he was doing. Teasing her, testing her. Willing her to go to him and close the circuit of the electric connection that ran between them now.

"Shhh!" she insisted, slowly shaking her head. She wasn't done. Her eyes made their way back to the taut inlines of his hips. The sharpness of his muscle definition combined with the dark happy trail that led from his navel to below the band of his underwear was like her own personal siren song...

"Victoria."

It wasn't a suggestion this time or even a plea. Her head snapped up at his command. His eyes locked on her, holding her in place as he willed her to finally look at him. His irises had gone dark, and his head bobbed slightly as he took in ragged, uneven breaths.

"Tori, please." Softer this time, his words came out barely above a whisper. She was across the room before she even realized her feet were moving. She immediately laid both hands on his midsection.

"Whoa there!" he yelped. "You're frozen!" He pulled away from her the moment her hands brushed against his chest.

"Oh! Sorry! I didn't even realize I was cold." She started to rub her hands back and forth before Rhett encased them in his own, raised their joined hands to his mouth, and exhaled. Warmth spread from her fingertips to her core, sending a full-body shiver down her spine.

"Yeah, I didn't realize that would be possible either after the way you just eye-fucked me." He pulled her into his body and gave her a playful swat on the ass.

He must have just gotten out of the shower, Tori thought to herself as she felt heat radiate off his skin. They both leaned into each other for a few more beats.

"Hi," he whispered, pulling back slightly and looking down at her. It was a sincere apology and a hopeful prayer wrapped up in one word.

"Hi," she replied, nuzzling her face into his chest in an attempt to reassure him that she wasn't upset about this unexpected weekend visit. This was their thing. They could say so much—share so much between them—with just a few words or a single glance. Ten years in and out a relationship together would do that.

"Missed you," he muttered into her hair, tightening his grip around her body. Tori breathed him in, savoring the warmth of his bare chest underneath her cheek. She didn't need to look up to know the sharp lines of his jaw were set in a hard line.

Just because she wasn't mad at him didn't mean she wasn't curious. What the hell was he doing here? What was he so tense about? It felt too early in the morning and too early in the weekend to get into anything just yet. She pulled back in time to see him wipe the sullen expression from his face.

"Is that what I owe the pleasure of this visit? You missed me so much you just couldn't stay away?" Rhett said nothing, instead squeezing her tighter. She rested her cheek back against his chest, allowing him to hold her for just a little longer than normal. He obviously needed the comfort, and she had missed him so damn much.

Something shifted as they continued to embrace. Tori felt herself respond to him. It wasn't a choice; it was an unstoppable reaction. Her body softened. Her resolve dissipated. The teasing and playfulness she had felt earlier evaporated to make room for something more, something deeper. She inhaled, breathing in his scent, letting the proximity intoxicate her.

She finally lifted her head, knowing what would happen when she glanced up. Permission granted, Rhett's mouth was on hers. He was hungry, almost frantic, as he gripped the base of her neck and pressed his lips into hers. His other hand moved down her back, settling right at the base of her spine. He used that hand to pull her against him even tighter. He was the anchor, but they both knew she wasn't going anywhere. Tori rolled her hips forward, connecting the lower halves of their bodies as he groaned. His tongue teased her, seeking entrance. She willingly let him in.

No one kissed like Rhett. He used his mouth to worship her, oscillating between sweet, tender promises and urgent, heated demands. Every kiss was a confession, every touch an invitation home.

She recognized the familiar-but-still-sultry passion in the way he kissed her, but there was something else there today, too. Something unidentifiable. Something that almost felt dangerous. He was home unexpectedly, and the desperation behind his kiss confirmed her suspicions: something wasn't right.

"Hey." She reluctantly broke the kiss and pulled away from him. He didn't stop kissing her, instead moving down to work over the pulse point on the side of her neck.

"Ev." She tensed, dropping her hands to her sides. Disengaging would get his attention.

"Hmmm?" he asked, his forehead coming to rest on hers. He released her body slowly, untangling their limbs and shifting his weight back a few inches.

"Are you okay?"

It wasn't so much of a question as it was a recognition: Tori was telling him she saw him, that she saw right through him, and she knew something was wrong. He didn't say anything. He didn't even open his eyes as he continued to rest his forehead on hers.

"How can I help?" Worry doused the heat that had been building between them. Rhett was usually so in control. It was unnerving to see him this way.

"Well, that was helping." He bent down to kiss her softly again as he opened his eyes. Maybe she was reading too much into things. If he was capable of joking right now, it couldn't be that big of a deal. She needed to chill and just wait for him to tell her whatever it was he needed to say.

"I'm sorry." He exhaled, blowing out a long, slow breath. "I don't think I realized how much I missed you until I saw you standing in the doorway just now." She knew he missed her. She could feel his erection through his boxer briefs as he shifted his hips toward her and pulled her in for another hug.

"We've gone a lot longer before, you know," she reminded him, returning his hug. Just because they had gone longer without seeing each other didn't mean it had gone well. Tori had lost track of time since the start of the new semester at school, but he was right: More than three weeks had passed since he'd gone back to school after winter break. Usually by the time she started to really miss him, he had already sent her a calendar notification with the dates of his next trip home. That was Rhett. The planner. The doer. Mr. Consistent and Mr. Dependable. He was the steadiest, most reliable person in her life.

He gave her a tight smile, then bent low again to kiss her on the forehead. He placed his hands on her shoulders as he guided her backwards toward his bed, depositing her on top of his rumpled sheets before ducking into his closet.

Okay then.

Tori wasn't expecting him to pump the brakes on what they both knew was inevitable. He was home. They had the house to themselves. It was weird that he wasn't already on top of her. She decided to follow his lead, though. They still had the whole day ahead of them. She scooted herself further up the mattress and crawled under the covers as she waited for whatever was going to happen next.

CHAPTER 4

Rhett

"Go ahead and make yourself comfortable." Rhett chuckled as he watched her arrange herself in his sheets. *Damn*. She looked so good lying in his bed. What he said had been true: He had missed her over the last three weeks. More than usual, more intensely than he had in a long time. Yesterday's showdown with Chandler may have been the catalyst for him coming home to Hampton this weekend, but something told him he would have ended up here soon regardless.

"You know I always do. I would invite you to join me, but I have some questions before we proceed." She wagged her eyebrows as he walked all the way into his closet.

"Such as?" he called back from inside the closet.

"Do your parents know you're home this weekend?"

"Nope," he replied automatically, surveying his T-shirt stack. "Hey, have you been swiping more of my shirts? I've got like three options left in here."

"Don't try to change the subject," she replied too quickly. Busted. "I thought I was the one asking the questions."

"Fair enough. Proceed."

"Does your best friend know you're in town?" she asked.

Rhett stepped into a pair of joggers and pulled them up before moving to stand in the doorframe. He knew she meant Jake, and the answer was technically no. "My best friend is lying in my bed right now, so yeah, I think she knows."

Tori rolled her eyes as he wandered back into the closet. He still needed to find clean socks, a base layer, and at least a hoodie if they were going hiking today.

"What are you doing in there?" she asked. He couldn't see her now, but he could hear her rustling around in his sheets.

"V, I know you don't have any qualms about being naked in public, but there's no way I'm going to the Ledges without clothes." He peeked his head out of the closet and shot her a teasing grin. The look on her face was more than skeptical, though. He watched as realization passed over her expression.

Tori toyed with the corner of his sheets, running her fingers back and forth over the navy fabric. "You left Easton so fast you didn't even bring a bag with you." It didn't come out as a question or even an accusation. Her observation was spot on.

"Everhett... What happened?" Her voice was dripping with concern. He stepped further into his closet to delay answering her right away. He could feel her gaze boring into the back of his head, willing him to turn around and face her. He still wasn't ready to explain the details of his blowup with Chandler. Hell, he didn't even fully understand how everything unfolded or where things stood with his girlfriend back at Easton.

"Did you break up with Chandler?" Tori pushed. Her eyes scrutinized him as he emerged from the closet with a sweatshirt in hand.

"No," he answered firmly, watching her face for any sign of a reaction.

"Okay, good." There was no undercurrent to her response.

"Good?" His cheeks flushed at her lack of reaction. What would she have said if he'd said yes? What would she dare say to him if he had actually ended things with Chandler?

"Yeah, Rhett. Good. Really good. I see the pictures she posts of you guys. You look happy. That's all I've ever wanted for you."

He turned away from her again, silently fuming. How dare she act so nonchalant about the stupid arrangement she had set for them. Tori knew damn well what would make him happy. He was happy right now, in this moment. Here. With her.

He hated the current state of their relationship, or lack therefore. The friends-with-benefits arrangement she had proposed three years ago was still going strong, but it never felt like enough for him. He had tread so lightly for so long, playing the game by Tori's rules, doing whatever he could to keep her in his orbit. But now that he was in his final semester of his MBA program, he felt the imminent threat of an expiration date overshadowing what he wanted most in life.

"Are you hungry?" Rhett asked as he finished dressing, his mind still racing. He paused at the edge of the bed and looked over at her. Her gaze was even and steady. She knew he was frustrated, but she was letting him have his moment.

Rhett exhaled sharply. He was home now. She was here with him. He needed to switch gears if they were going to make the most of their time together today.

"Yes, I'm starving." She smiled up at him, catching his hand and bringing his knuckles to her lips. He knew she was trying to soothe him, to silently smooth over the jagged edges of frustration radiating off his body. "Let's get Jersey Bagels on the way to the Ledges."

"You got it, beautiful." Rhett felt an ache in his stomach that didn't have anything to do with hunger. It was the familiar yearning that tended to creep in when he was alone with her. What he wouldn't give to climb into bed and stay there all day, holding her, making love to her, just being with her.

She said she wanted him to be happy. All he wanted was her.

CHAPTER 5

Tori

"I'll take a plain bagel, lightly toasted, with butter," Tori rattled off her usual order over the plexiglass divider at Jersey Bagels, "and he'll have two asiago cheese bagels, toasted, with plain cream cheese." She felt Rhett's hand find the small of her back as she turned on her heel and headed to the beverage cooler.

"What's your pleasure?" she asked, biting down on her bottom lip while reaching for her favorite unsweetened iced tea. His eyes landed on her mouth and stayed there. He wordlessly lowered a hand between their bodies, letting his fingers brush against the front of her workout leggings. Tori stilled, not leaning into his touch but not pulling away, either, curious to see just how far he would try to take it. A single finger caught in the waistband of the black fabric and pulled, dipping into her pants and grazing the top of her underwear. Tori cast her eyes up to meet his and bit down on her bottom lip harder to prevent her face from giving anything else away. Her insides were quickly turning to molten lava, and he was barely touching her. Rhett let his finger linger there, teasing her, promising her what they would be doing later that day. He stood as still as a statue, pretending like he wasn't responsible for the wanton heat rising up inside her. She couldn't get enough of the way he looked at her, like she was all he wanted.

"Orange juice," he finally answered, taking another step and closing the space between them. His hip bones pressed into her midsection as he aligned their bodies, sandwiching his hand in place while that one single finger continued to tease. She could feel the air crackling between them. He bowed his head low but stopped a few inches from her lips, instead letting the tip of his nose brush against hers. His hot, minty breath washed over her.

Tori made no effort to pull away—she felt the same desire to be physically connected to him right now. It was like each point of physical contact was a pinprick that released a bit of the pressure building up between them. She wasn't sure how much longer this charade was going to go on, how much longer it would be before he told her the real reason why he was home, but she was grateful for his reassuring touches.

"Rhett Wheeler!!" A booming voice from across the room jerked them both out of their trance. Tori's head snapped up in attention as she looked for the source of the voice. It was coming from a guy about their age whose neck was as thick as her thighs. She didn't recognize him, meaning he was either someone Rhett knew from Archway Prep or Easton University.

Tori held her breath as she turned her back to Rhett, leaving him alone to make small talk with his friend. She grabbed his bottle of orange juice and headed to the end of the counter to pay. She smiled at the girl behind the register as she set down the bottles. Their bagels were already rolled up and sealed in a brown bag.

"Three bagels and these," she confirmed, unzipping her wristlet to fish out her card.

"That'll be $12.85," the cashier replied, accepting the card and inserting it into the reader.

"So what's going on with you now, man?" Tori overheard the meathead ask Rhett. She kept her ears perked, desperate for clues that would tell her if this guy was from school. Desperate, really, to know if he knew Chandler.

"Just finishing up my MBA at Easton. I graduate in May," he replied. She exhaled a sigh of relief. This guy wasn't from Easton, which meant he didn't know Rhett had a girlfriend. It didn't matter whether he had seen any of their drink cooler shenanigans. They were safe.

"Hey, I've gotta go, but it was good running into you." Rhett slapped his friend on the shoulder before walking away. He reached the checkout counter in three strides, right as she collected her debit card and grabbed their food.

"Let's go," he instructed, his voice an octave lower than normal. He placed his hand on her elbow as he guided her toward the exit. Did he think that was a close call, too?

He pushed the bagel shop door open and held it for her while pulling out his phone with his other hand. They walked to his car in silence. Tori felt her phone vibrate against her thigh as she opened the passenger door. She climbed into the bucket seat and reached for her seatbelt. The entire car shifted when Rhett lowered himself into his seat.

It was hard to believe he still drove this tiny thing after all these years. His parents had gifted him a new Audi for his sixteenth birthday. That car lasted six months before Rhett and his best friend, Jake, totaled it on Archway's campus. Rhett wasn't even supposed to be out that night, and he and Tori had been drinking a little before Jake called him for a ride. But Jake was in trouble, desperate really, and Rhett couldn't not go to him. He made it to campus okay, but things went sideways when they tried to drive home. They were both hospitalized. Rhett had been hurt worse than Jake. The whole thing was a mess, and the boys should have gotten into more trouble than they did, but both their families had enough money and influence to make the situation go away. There was no legal trouble in the end, but there were still consequences.

Rhett's dad refused to buy him another car. It was impossible for sixteen-year-old Rhett not to have access to a vehicle after experiencing that level of freedom for half a year. He took matters into his own hands and started working as a dishwasher at Clinton's Family Restaurant the week after the accident. Tori was hired as a server a few weeks later. By his seventeenth birthday, he had saved up enough cash to purchase a 1994 Honda Prelude that her dad promised to help him get up and running. They spent months working on the car together, mostly because Rhett had to go paycheck to paycheck to save enough for all the parts they needed.

He could have traded the Prelude in for a newer car by now, especially because he had access to his trust fund and was already working part time for his granddad's company, but he just kept dumping money into the Prelude. She knew that working on the car with her dad gave him an excuse to come home to Hampton more often than necessary. The whole situation was very on-brand for Everhett Wheeler. He held onto things for as long as possible. He had never been good at letting go.

Tori placed both drinks in the cup holders before pulling out her phone. A notification at the top of the screen alerted her to the $12.85 he had just sent to her account.

"You know I can afford to buy bagels," she snapped at him, annoyed but also impressed that he was attentive enough to know the total without having to ask.

Rhett stuck the key into the ignition and checked his mirrors as he put the car in reverse. "Nuh-uh." He shook his head. "No way. We're not going there, beautiful. You get to make a lot of rules for us, and I don't say a word about them."

Tori snickered.

"Well, not usually, anyways," he amended. "I play by your rules, and I rarely question you. This is a hard line for me, though. We're not going to argue about money this weekend," he declared with finality. “Besides,” he added, softer. “I know you’re missing out on a lot of tips today because of me.”

Tori’s chest swelled with appreciation. She was okay letting him take care of her in this way, knowing he had a financial safety net in place she couldn’t even begin to wrap her mind around.

She reached over and rested her hand on his thigh as they waited for the light to turn green. “Thank you,” she offered quietly, abandoning her hostility. He grabbed her hand just as the light changed and lifted it to his lips, placing a kiss on the tips of her fingers. She felt the heat of his breath linger on her skin as he dropped her hand and took the turn, heading west for their favorite spot in the Cuyahoga Valley National Park.

CHAPTER 6

Rhett

They drove to the Ledges in comfortable silence, listening to music and eating their bagels. There was an ease to being with Tori that he appreciated more than usual today. He felt so much more in his body when they were together.

Rhett climbed out of the vehicle and lifted his hands over his head to stretch. As much as he loved his car, driving four hours on I-71 all tensed up in a bucket seat last night had done nothing for his back.

He glanced around and noticed there were only three other cars in the parking lot. They would have the trail and overlook practically to themselves. He raised the hood of his sweatshirt and pulled the drawstrings of his hoodie tighter to brace against the cold February air. The compacted snow crunched under his boots as he continued to shift his feet and roll out his neck.

"We haven't been here in months," Rhett grinned. "Do you want to do the trail or just go to our spot?"

"I'm afraid it's going to be icier than we thought," Tori mused, taking a cautious step out of the car. "I feel like by the time we get through the meadow, I'll be happy to just go to our spot."

"Come here," Rhett demanded then. She closed her door and circled the Prelude to his side. He pulled her into him and held her close, sinking into the physical contact he had been craving since they left his house. "I'm happy we're here. This was a really good idea," he whispered into her hair. She shifted to move out of his arms, but just like earlier he resisted letting her slip away. Tori relented and exhaled, leaning into him with more of her weight.

Anyone who saw their embrace would think they were together. *Good*, Rhett thought to himself. Tori was his, and he wanted everyone else to know it. She didn't usually let him hold her like this in public. It was one of the many rules she carefully crafted as part of their arrangement to keep him from getting too close. He hated the rules, but he still played the game. Given the choice between a casual friends-with-benefits relationship with Tori and no relationship at all, there wasn't any question in his mind. He would do just about anything to be with her in some capacity.

Rhett knew that his love for Tori was not unrequited—it was anything but. Why else would she have come back to him after breaking up with him before college? He knew how other people looked at her. He'd seen it with his own eyes when she was waiting tables at Clinton's. She was desirable but approachable, effortlessly sensual and genuinely kind. She could have anyone she wanted, yet she kept coming back to him. Or at least she had for the last three years. All that was about to change in the next few months.

Now that Rhett was in his final semester, it felt like they were racing toward a finish line he had no desire to cross. Graduation meant the official start of his career at his granddad's company, NorfolkStar Transport. It also meant he would be moving at the end of May. There wasn't a path forward for them after he moved to Virginia: Tori had made that abundantly clear when they started their arrangement. It wasn't possible to have a long-distance relationship with someone who refused to be in a relationship in the first place.

"Okay, enough! Are we here to hug or to hike?!" Tori exclaimed, finally trying to push away from him. When a shove against his chest proved ineffective, she poked her fingers into his armpit, surprising him and making him recoil against her tickling.

"Let's go, Wheeler." She took several steps toward the path to the meadow but reached her gloved hand back for him.

He caught up with her in two strides. A few loose pieces of gravel crunched underneath his boots as they made their way from the car to the expansive meadow that separated the parking lot and the trailhead.

They walked quietly at first, each concentrating to find their footing in the snow. Some patches proved to be unyielding and easy to traverse, but every now and then, they would hit a deeper-than-expected spot of soft powder and sink in. The only sound around them was the amplification of their own breathing.

"Do you remember the summer before junior year of high school when we came out here to stargaze?" Rhett asked, glancing down at Tori as they continued across the snow-covered meadow.

"Um, yes. That was literally top ten for me." She looked back at him like he was obtuse.

"What?! You never told me that!"

"I don't think you've ever asked me about my top ten list before," she countered, smiling up at him.

"Please remind me in as much detail as possible... What was so great about that night?"

"Nope. You brought it up first. You tell me what was so great about that night." Tori gazed up at him with that sultry look in her eye. Was this a test? Rhett racked his brain, trying to recall the details of one of their many, many outdoor escapades from high school. They were halfway across the meadow now, their breathing in sync.

"All I remember is you climbing on top of me and riding me into oblivion. The sight of your body against the stars in the sky..." Rhett had to adjust himself through his joggers thanks to that memory. "Is that what you remember?" he tried, worried he didn't pass the unexpected pop quiz.

"Yes," Tori nodded, "partially." She gave him a sly smile.

"Partially?"

"Yes. I remember setting out our blanket and thinking we were completely alone. I remember getting on top to ride you. And I remember how my whole body felt like it was on fire even though I was topless and you had my skirt hiked up. But I also remember thinking I heard someone. Or, more likely, two people. They probably had the same idea as us. I don't think we were alone that night," she confessed.

"It was too dark for me to see anyone, but I figured if I could hear them, then they could probably hear me." Tori had a satisfied smile on her face that told him she was getting excited just thinking about the sordid memory. "I remember being particularly loud that night because I liked the idea of someone hearing us. I came so hard..."

"You never told me that!" Rhett exclaimed, laughing, as amused as he was surprised by her confession.

"Well, I thought at the time that you would freak out. I didn't want to ruin our night. Then later I just kept thinking about it... about how wet I got knowing they could hear me. I wasn't about to tell my seventeen-year-old boyfriend that I got off because I knew other people were listening to us have sex."

"I should've known!" He laughed again, pulling her into his side affectionately. "You've always been loud for me, and that's exactly how I like it." He shamelessly inhaled the scent of rosemary and mint of her shampoo before kissing her temple.

Rhett loosened his grip on her and glanced up. They had reached the end of the meadow where the expanse narrowed into the trail. He felt a strong sense of resolve settle over his body as he decided this was it.

"Here we go," he said just barely above a whisper, more to himself than to Tori. He knew what he was about to say—what he was about to confess and put on the line—and he had no idea how she was going to respond.

CHAPTER 7

Tori

They had first visited the Ledges years ago when the Wheelers decided that they should all participate in a fall hiking spree together. The spree involved visiting different local trails and completing at least eight hikes from the designated list. Peter and Anne Wheeler dragged Rhett and his little sister, Maddie, to a different location each Saturday afternoon, insisting Tori join them since her dad typically worked on Saturdays. Rhett's parents thought they were providing a wholesome outdoor experience for their kids. Little did they know they were just giving Tori and Rhett ideas for places where they could go and be alone together as soon as Rhett got his driver's license.

They both loved coming out to the overlook at the Ledges. Slabs of rock gave way to a vast nothing. There was a two-mile trail looping through the cliffs and caves, carved out over time by the perpetual flow of water against earth.

Even without the lingering nostalgia she felt for this place, the Ledges felt like sacred ground. On a clear day, you could stand on the edge of the overlook and see all the way to Cleveland. The treetops formed a canvas that changed with the seasons. By February there was a blurred softness to the edges of the thousands of branches that reached up toward the sky, desperately seeking the sun.

There was also a bit of danger to the Ledges. There was no fencing along the overlook, no safety net to separate visitors from the drop-off. There was enough space along the flattop rocks for people to spread out, but there were lots of roots obstinately growing through the quartz and shale rock formations.

Rhett helped her find her footing, glancing back periodically to make sure she was okay. As soon as their boots hit the flattop rocks, he dropped her hand.

Tori smiled to herself as she thought about the last time they had brought a hammock out here. They had strung it up away from the main area, between two V-shaped trees. She glanced over at Rhett, curious if he was also thinking about their gravity-defying escapades from last summer. But he wasn't looking at her. His gaze was cast toward the overlook, his face set in a deep scowl. She saw a hard line of determination in his eyes.

Oh, we must be doing this now, she realized. She had let herself get so wrapped up in the nostalgia of visiting the Ledges and being with Rhett that she hadn't noticed him tense up.

Tori stopped where she stood and gave him the space he clearly needed. Rhett kept moving forward toward the edge of the overlook. Now that she was paying attention to his body language, the message was loud and clear: He was agitated. She felt her own heart rate pick up in response to his vibe. Usually she loved how attuned her body was to his energy, but this was not one of those instances.

He stopped a few feet in front of her, still facing forward. There was a good fifteen feet between him and the end of the Ledges, but Tori felt uneasy seeing him so keyed up near the edge of a cliff.

"Chandler opened up my mail yesterday," he said. He spoke slowly and clearly, probably to avoid having to turn around and look at her. Tori stood frozen in place. She hadn't expected him to just start talking without any prompting, especially not after the way he had avoided the topic all morning.

"I had done all the grocery shopping and restocked the fridge when I got back to Easton after winter break. She said she wanted to double check the totals so she could send me her half." His tone didn't waiver, but he paused for a few breaths before speaking again.

"She saw the charge for the flowers I sent you on the twentieth."

When Tori inhaled, the icy air hit her lungs with a dull throb. *Shit.* Chandler was probably pissed. *Shit shit shit.* Of course she would be pissed. Why would anyone in their right mind not be pissed to see expensive flowers on their boyfriend's credit card statement that he'd sent to someone else? Who the hell even opened credit card statements anymore?

Tori's mind was spiraling as she forced herself to inhale again. The white calla lilies Rhett sent her were not supposed to be a romantic gesture, but they were an act of love nonetheless.

Anne Wheeler started the tradition of sending her flowers on the first anniversary of her mom's death. Rhett took over the responsibility when he went away to college. He never forgot, and she knew Anne didn't have to remind him. Over the last six years, the flowers felt even more significant since January 20 was usually around the time he had to go back to school after winter break. The annual delivery was a comfort she looked forward to and cherished, especially when she was deep in her grief.

"Chandler freaked out," he continued. "I tried to explain to her what the flowers were for. I don't think it was just about the flowers, though. It felt like something snapped between us. She started asking questions, making accusations. Obviously, a lot of them were true." He gripped the edges of his hoodie and jerked the hood off his head in agitation. He was radiating tension, a man literally on the edge.

"She just stood there, holding the credit card statement, screaming at me, demanding to know if we were sneaking around." Rhett paused for several beats. "And not for the first time since we started this whole arrangement, I didn't want to lie anymore. I came so close to telling her everything, Tori. I'm so fucking sick of pretending to not be in love with you."

Tori inhaled, trying to suck in as much cold air as possible to distract herself from the tears welling up in her eyes.

"Chandler called me out. She said I needed to be done with you. That us—whatever this is—it can't go on if I want to be with her." He finally turned around to face her. She tried to look away, to look at anything but him. Her mind was racing, her heart pounding. So much of what they shared was only possible because Rhett had Chandler in his life. The thought of that ending struck a harrowing chord against her heartstrings.

His voice went flat as he finally caught her gaze. "So that's why I'm home this weekend. She freaked out, and now I'm freaking out. Because I know damn well you won't be with me if I'm not with her."

Tori blinked hard, quickly wiping away the tears from her eyes with the hem of her pullover. She didn't even know why she was crying. She had come to terms with their arrangement three years ago. Hell, she had set the terms of the arrangement.

She refused to be in a committed relationship with Rhett because of her past and her future. She was hell-bent on protecting him, on ensuring he didn't throw away the most vibrant version of his life just to be with her. She knew what her future entailed. She also knew what Rhett's life should look like five or ten years from now. There was no intersection between the two.

Her mom was diagnosed with breast cancer at twenty-eight. They found it during her postpartum checkup, just six weeks after Tori was born. It took two years of brutal treatment to rid her body of the disease. Then, nine years after her first battle, cancer came back with a vengeance for round two. When Tori was eleven years old, her mom was diagnosed with stage four ovarian cancer. A second cancer, a second threat silently raging inside a woman who wasn't even forty years old. There were so few options for treatment by the time they caught it. Hospice started coming to their house that week. Her mom was gone two months later.

"She was just so young." That was the phrase Tori heard over and over again following her mother's death, first at calling hours, then at the funeral. The sentiment still echoed through her encounters with neighbors and acquaintances years later. It was a whisper that haunted all her waking days, a promise that sent her spiraling during sleepless nights.

To combat the inevitable, she went for a series of benchmark scans twice a year as part of an aggressive screening protocol. The screenings were part of a multi-year research study she qualified for based on her genetic history. Those scans were a lifeline, but they also served as a regular reminder that she couldn't dream of anything long term for her life. She planned things six months in advance, one scan at a time, her eyes always on the finish line of preventative surgery. First, she would graduate from Holt State University, then she would get a full-time job with great health care benefits. Her goal was to have both a preventive bilateral prophylactic mastectomy and a risk-reducing salpingo-oophorectomy before she turned twenty-seven. The surgeries would eliminate the increased risk factors lurking in her DNA. As long as she stayed focused on school, she could graduate in two more years then have the surgeries before she reached the age her mom was when she was first diagnosed.

When Tori thought about the possibility of a long-term relationship with Rhett, she knew it was a nonstarter. She would never have kids. Aside from being physically unable to do so after the preventative surgeries, she refused to pass on the risks associated with her gene pool. She loved him and his family too much to subject them to years of medical drama coupled with the promise of not carrying on the family name. Her shortcomings did not need to be their disappointments. The baggage that weighed her down was hers to carry alone.

"You told me you guys didn't break up?" she finally replied, her words coming out as both an accusation and a question. She felt the panic starting to rise in her chest.

"We didn't. At least I don't think we did. I don't know where things stand, I guess. Goddamnit, Tori! Didn't you hear what I just said? I don't want to do this anymore! I don't want to be with her. Chandler is a nice girl... but she's always been a means to an end." Rhett took two steps toward her.

Tori shook her head violently. What the hell did he think he was doing? This was not part of their arrangement.

"For me, the end is you. It's always been you," he confessed, softer but with determination in his eyes.

She gave herself a silent minute to find her calm. She watched the side of his face contort as he worked over the inside of his cheek, glancing down at his own feet to avoid making eye contact as he waited for her to respond. He was clearly anxious, as he should be. He knew damn well what he was doing right now, scratching at the scar tissue that stretched over her deepest wounds. After another minute, Tori tested out his name on her lips, willing her voice not to waiver.

"Rhett," she started, "you know why it has to be like this." He still didn't look up at her. She felt like she was scolding a small child.

"I'm no good for you. I'm never leaving Hampton. I'll never have kids. It's not fair for you to not live the life you deserve to live." Tori felt her lip quiver, but she bit down hard to stop it. She knew if he sensed any weakness in her delivery, he would pounce on the opportunity to try and trap her.

His face twisted into a pain-stricken grimace at her rejection. But that didn't stop him from pushing. "I know you're scared, V. We can't predict what the future will hold. But I want to be with you, no matter what happens, no matter how long we get. There's nothing I want more than you." He took another step forward, testing her.

She knew he would give it all up for her: his dream job, the possibility of having children, the hope of growing old together. But the pressure of being enough for him—of being his everything, of being his whole world—was too much. She knew that regardless of how much time they had together, it would never be enough to fill in the craters of grief she'd leave for him one day.

She had watched her father shatter. She now lived with a husk of a man, a human stripped down by years of unprocessed grief. She had practically raised herself because of it. That couldn't be Rhett's future. She wouldn't do that to him. She wouldn't do that to his future children.

The earnest expression on his face as he waited for her response reminded her so much of the twelve-year-old that had comforted her at her mom's funeral. Her only happy memory of that day flooded back to her then: Rhett's lanky preteen arms wrapped around her, the scent of his middle school body spray assaulting her nostrils as his steady breathing filled her ears.

The memory from her mom's funeral was the reality check she needed. Earnest expression be damned. She couldn't entertain the notion that she and Rhett could have a real relationship. She wouldn't. Not when she knew damn well how it would end.

She already knew how the rest of the conversation was going to go: She would refuse to be in a committed relationship with him and threaten to end their arrangement. Rhett would get angry but insist he could hold his head above the water and not get too attached. Their arrangement would stay intact. Nothing would change. And because she wasn't stronger, she would let herself believe she wasn't going to break him in the end.

"We're almost done." She spoke evenly, a coldness lacing her voice now that she had found her resolve. "We both know there's a time limit to this—to us. You don't get to change the rules now that the game's almost over," she sneered, forcing a sharpness to her tone that she never used with him.

"I guess it's up to you whether we're done right now or whether we keep this going until you leave for Virginia in the spring." She delivered her ultimatum with a cool sense of clarity.

"Tori, please. Just think about it? This doesn't have to end. We can do long distance. We can at least try and see what happens. It has always been you. It will always be you." The ache in his voice drilled into her with an unexpected pain.

She couldn't think about it. There was nothing to even consider. She responded to his question without hesitation.

"No." Her answer came out as a whisper. She stared past Rhett's head toward the overlook, noticing how the cell phone towers off in the distance blinked in an unhurried rhythm. "No," she stated again, louder this time. A small part of her heart wept at her declaration. She honestly didn't think she could say anything else without breaking down.

Seconds, minutes, maybe even hours passed as they faced off in silence. He was standing close enough that she could feel the white puffs of his breath crest over her head, but she refused to look him in the eyes. Panic started to rise in her chest as she realized this could be it. This could be the day that he finally had enough. This could be the day that he finally walked away. One of them would have to end it eventually. She always figured it would be her, and she definitely hadn't counted on it happening today. But if Rhett decided this was it, she needed to let him go. She loved him too much to cling to him and pull him under.

"Please don't hate me because of this," she whispered, finally breaking the silence. She made no effort to wipe away the tears that flowed freely down her cheeks.

Rhett moved in closer, resting the palm of his hand on her tear-streaked face. He bit down on the inside of his cheek and stared right into the deepest parts of her soul. He shook his head back and forth so softly she barely realized he was moving at all. She didn't miss the tears welling in his eyes.

"No part of me could ever hate any part of you, beautiful." He pulled her close and kissed her forehead, not once, not twice, but at least a dozen times. Each kiss was an apology, an acceptance of the reality of the situation as they held each other and grieved what would never be.

Something shifted between them as they embraced. Maybe it was acceptance, maybe it was forfeiture, or maybe some combination of the two.

"But that's bullshit if you think we're done now. We're not over yet," he added as he hugged her tighter.

Tori let him hold her. She was broken. Decimated. It was selfish to lean into him, knowing she would be the one to walk away in a few months. But that still didn't stop her from seeking the comfort he so generously offered now.

She crept her hands under the fabric of his hoodie, feeling the sharp edges of the muscles of his back. She buried her face into his armpit and wafted in his scent for comfort. He held her close and let her feel the rise and fall of his chest, just like he had all those years ago on the saddest day of her life. Tori cast her gaze toward the overlook as they hugged, this time finding a tree she hadn't noticed before. One sad, defiant evergreen rose out of the winter brush, offering the only sign of life along the edge of the Ledges.

Rhett eventually found her chin and tilted it up, giving her a chaste kiss. She responded to his mouth by returning the kiss and deepening it. She was anxious to ease the unnerving energy between them, to smooth things over for now, while they still had time. In the end, he may never forgive her for it, but Tori offered up everything she had to give him right then: her body and her heart, but only when he was home and only for a few more months.

CHAPTER 8

Rhett

Rhett turned onto Sunset Drive and crept toward the Thompsons' house. He was scared out of his mind to let Tori out of the car. Between his cliffside confession and her outright rejection, she was a definite flight risk. This could be the last time he'd see her this weekend.

He pulled into the driveaway, instinctively looking around for Paul. The garage was closed, so Rhett assumed they were alone. Had he gone too far at the Ledges? He hadn't outright begged her to be with him like that for a long time. She had shut him down with such certainty. She didn't even offer an explanation, although it wasn't really necessary, considering they had been having different versions of the same argument for years. He put the Prelude in park, then turned to face her.

"Are you going to paint tonight?" he asked, testing her determination to stay away from him now that his relationship with Chandler was in question.

It was a farce to let Tori believe that being with Chandler changed his feelings for her in any significant way. Tori assumed he was happy. Satisfied. Stable. But Chandler was just the distraction that reminded him to not text Tori so much, to show some restraint when he desperately wanted to drive back to Hampton every single weekend. Being with Chandler had only ever felt like settling.

Tori unbuckled her seat belt and reached for his hand.

"Rhett, you're home. I don't love the reason for it, and I'm annoyed that you lied to me by omission about why you left Easton in the first place, but you're home. And when you're home, you're mine."

His heart swelled with relief. She was pissed, but she wasn't so mad she was going to shut him out completely. At least not yet.

"I'm going to shower and hang out with my dad and Penny for a bit," she continued. "I'll come over after dinner."

He squeezed her hand in confirmation. "Sounds good. Bring your bathing suit," he whispered.

"Why would I need my suit?" She looked genuinely puzzled as she moved to exit the vehicle.

"Um, so we can go in the hot tub?" Rhett scoffed, wondering what she was playing at. She knew damn well what he had in mind for tonight. Side glances and comforting words could only offer so much reassurance. He needed to feel her—to be buried deep inside her—to know they were really okay. He knew from the way she clung to him at the Ledges that she needed it, too.

"Oh, Ev. You know I don't need my suit for that."

With her flirtatious admission, Tori opened the door and climbed out of her seat. She peeked back into the car to give him one last mischievous smile, offering hope for the rest of the weekend after several tense hours. Then she turned on her heel and sauntered up the driveway. He didn't take his eyes off of her until she disappeared into the side door of the garage.

Rhett felt like he was existing outside his own body. He couldn't get comfortable. He couldn't slow his racing mind. All the feelings he stirred up at the Ledges were still swirling around him, prodding at the discomfort he had created.

He spent the rest of the afternoon flopping listlessly from the couch to his bedroom, then back to the couch again. He tried to watch SportsCenter, then changed the channel to some wilderness survival show. Nothing held his attention. Once it started to get dark, he decided he better eat. He warmed up leftover meatloaf and mashed potatoes he found in the fridge, hoping it was something his mom had made recently. He took his food out to the sunroom and grabbed a low-ball glass from behind the bar. He poured a healthy draw of Jameson, then threw in a couple ice cubes.

Rhett settled into one of the bar stools, his back to the Thompsons' house. He wasn't going to sit around waiting for the first sign of her like some lovesick puppy. He still had a few shreds of pride left after today's brutal shutdown.

His phone buzzed in his pocket. He reached for it, hopeful it was Tori sending him an ETA. Chandler's picture illuminated the lock screen instead.

Chandler: I'm so sorry about yesterday. I overreacted. I sat in the apartment making assumptions for almost 2 hours before you got home. I didn't even give you a chance to explain.

Rhett stared at the screen. A ball of guilt settled in his stomach as he thought about what an asshole he had been to her over the last twenty-four hours. He hadn't even sent her a text to tell her he was okay after he stormed out of the apartment.

Chandler was a senior majoring in fashion merchandising with a minor in marketing, on track to graduate in May when he graduated with his master's. They spent most weekends together, going out for date nights on Friday nights, then staying home and watching football or basketball on the weekends. He didn't mind her company, and she came from an upper middle-class family, so he didn't have to worry about her motive for being with him. She wasn't a low-maintenance girl by any means, but she had kept their relationship low-maintenance.

Rhett considered himself a decent boyfriend (aside from the fact that he had been in love with someone else for the past ten years). He knew he wasn't as emotionally available as Chandler would like him to be, but he sent her funny texts to tell her he was thinking about her, and he always paid when they went out together. He had mastered the art of taking pictures of her for social media even though their mutual friends teased him. He let her practically live at his apartment this year even though she was technically a commuter student and could drive to campus from her parents' house in Wetherington.

All of that had been enough for a while. He had a good time with Chandler when he wasn't thinking about Tori. He knew she put more effort into their relationship than he did, but that was her choice. Plus, they had never had a conversation about being exclusive. That was another caveat he carved out for himself—if Chandler didn't feel compelled to ask, he wasn't about to admit that he was also sleeping with Tori. They had somehow made it almost three years together avoiding The Talk. Maybe that's why their fight last night had been so explosive.

Chandler had treaded lightly around the topic of Tori for the last three years. She knew enough about his childhood and their friendship to respect that they had a history. She seemed to accept that Tori would always be in his life. Yesterday was the first time she had verbalized the thoughts that Rhett feared would bubble up to the surface one day.

Chandler: Rhett, please just tell me you're okay. I don't even know where you are. Are you coming home tonight?

Her second text jolted him out of his own head. He sighed, resigning himself to the fact that he owed her a response.

Rhett: Hey. I'm sorry about yesterday. Really sorry. I'm in Hampton for the weekend. I'll be back on Monday and we can talk then.

Chandler: Okay. Tell your family hi for me.

He grimaced. He knew better than to say anything about his family not being home this weekend. He wasn't about to throw a match in the gas tank.

He closed out his texts and repocketed his phone, confident their conversation was over. He had to hand it to Chandler: She knew when to back off and leave him alone. That was one of the reasons it was so easy to stay with her—she never asked for too much, always toeing the line between attentiveness and acceptance.

He felt her approach before he heard her. Turning his head, he spotted Tori crossing the pool deck and heading for the sunroom door. He hopped up to greet her. They reached the door at the exact same time. He felt her pull the handle out as he pushed the door open for her.

"Tori, I'm so sorry about earlier..." he started. She was in his arms before he could continue, her lips frantically seeking his mouth. He felt her nails scrape against the back of his neck as she pulled him in and kissed him hard.

He returned her kiss in stride. This was exactly what he had been craving all afternoon. He needed to feel her to know that they were okay. He ran his tongue against her lips, coaxing her to open her mouth. Then he captured her bottom lip between his teeth and bit down. She whimpered in response, his name coming out in a soft moan. They stood there kissing for what felt like hours, apologizing and seeking mutual comfort from each other. She must have needed the physical reassurance that they were okay, too.

Rhett felt a tug in his core as they continued to savor each other. He shifted his weight to better align his body to hers. He wove one hand into the hair at the nape of her neck, using the other one to grab her ass and pull her close.

She smiled under his lips as his erection pushed into her stomach. She was wearing a thin navy sundress as a cover-up even though there was a dusting of snow on the ground. He bent his knees slightly to reach down, his roaming hand searching for the hem of her dress.

His hand skirted over her bare thighs and ass cheeks, brushing against the fabric of her bathing suit bottoms. He dipped a finger along the crook of her ass and sent a quiver through her body. He loved the way she reacted to him, the way she responded to his touch. He found the end of one of the ties on her bathing suit and pulled. Tori's breath hitched in response to the sudden exposure as her bikini bottoms pooled on the floor beneath her.

"I thought you said you didn't need a bathing suit tonight?" he teased, breaking from her lips to kiss her neck. When she didn't respond, Rhett pulled back to check her reaction. His confidence had been shaken since coming back from the Ledges. There was a tentativeness to her gaze. *We're not out of the woods yet*, he thought to himself. Would he be walking on eggshells all night?

"Tori, I am so sorry about earlier," he apologized again as he rested his forehead on hers. He removed his hand from under her dress so he could wrap both arms around her body, willing his sincerity to flow through her like osmosis.

"It's okay. We're okay," she assured him in a determined voice. "We don't need to talk about it anymore this weekend. Or ever."

Rhett recoiled at her declaration. So her acceptance of his apology was conditional. She'd forgive him for earlier, but only with the assurance that he wouldn't bring it up again. Did he dare push her right now? He wasn't done pursuing Tori. He would never be done pursuing Tori. He was in love with her, and he had been for the last ten years. Yet it felt like the only way forward tonight was to succumb to her wishes, as usual.

"Okay," he whispered, nodding his head in agreement. *Okay for now*, he amended silently to himself. "Are you hungry? I can heat up more leftovers?"

Tori glanced past him to the half-eaten plate on the bar.

"Ohhhh, Anne's meatloaf!" she exclaimed with a hint of regret. "I already ate with my dad. Just give me a little bite of yours."

She hopped up onto the seat Rhett had previously occupied. He circled around the deep mahogany wood countertop and stationed himself behind the bar.

"Drink?" he asked. He knew she wouldn't want anything, but he still offered. Tori rarely drank—maybe half a glass of wine at a restaurant or a few sips of his beer during a game. Limiting alcohol was all part of her master plan to outmaneuver cancer.

She shook her head but still lifted his glass and sniffed.

"So it's a Jameson kind of weekend?" she asked. He gave her a sheepish smile. She obviously knew he had been drinking last night, too.

She cut into the meatloaf with the side of the fork he had been using, taking a big bite into her mouth.

"Ohhhh my gosh," she moaned in pleasure. "I love your mom's cooking." She went in for another forkful before she was finished chewing the first bite.

"I thought you already ate?" He spread his arms wide on the bar, leaning over to get closer to her. He felt himself start to harden as he watched Tori chew. How could the sight of her eating turn him on? His body and his mind had no chill when it came to this woman. "Gimme a bite."

Tori held out the utensil and offered it to him. Rhett didn't take his eyes off her as he leaned forward and claimed it with his mouth.

"So Tori Thompson," he started as he finished chewing, "we've got the whole night ahead of us and the whole house to ourselves." He raised his eyebrows suggestively. "However shall we pass the time?"

"You already know you're getting laid tonight, Wheeler." She grinned and matched his playful tone. Relief washed over Rhett's body as he let her words sink in. Worry and hesitation were replaced with a jolt of eagerness he hadn't allowed himself to feel until that moment. He couldn't wait to get her naked. To be inside her. To make her come.

"Yeah, but I want to hear you say it. Where, exactly, am I getting laid?" He felt his dick grow harder just thinking about the night ahead.

"I was thinking hot tub and bedroom," she suggested, holding up two fingers for emphasis. She moved her pointer finger to her mouth and inserted it, biting down hard and arching one eyebrow.

"You're trouble," Rhett moaned. He had no interest in finishing his dinner now, but he knew he was going to need the energy if they were going for two or more rounds tonight. He grabbed the fork from Tori's hand and shoveled the rest of the meatloaf into his mouth in three bites.

"Wait, do you have to work tomorrow?" he asked between mouthfuls.

Tori sighed.

Shit. This was going to put a major kink in their plans.

"Technically, yes. I could probably get Lia or Cory to cover for me again, but I haven't ask them yet." She looked at him apologetically. "I meant to text them this morning but then got distracted. When I got home this afternoon, I wasn't sure what to do. I figured maybe we could both use a little space..." Tori ran a finger along the grooves of the front of the bar as she left her words linger between them.

"Hey." Rhett reached across the bar and took her hand. "Hey," he said louder this time, willing her to look up. "We don't need space. I don't want space. We are okay, Tori. I promise."

She still didn't meet his gaze. *Too much, too soon,* he thought to himself. He could insist they were okay all he wanted. It didn't change that fact that he could still feel her trying to get him to loosen his emotional grip. It was a familiar feeling, really: Tori slipping through his grasp as he aimlessly fumbled to hold on to any part of her she'd let him have.

They sat in awkward silence for several seconds. He regretted being on the opposite side of the bar, unable to physically connect with her as he felt her fading away.

"Listen, I don't want you giving up another shift for me this weekend. How about I drive you in tomorrow and we can hang out at work?" He hoped that changing the subject would snap her out of her trance.

"No, that's silly. I don't want you just sitting around Clinton's all day. I'm working open until three."

Rhett let out a sigh of relief. At least she had responded to him. He could work with this.

"Tori, I want to. I'll hang out with Jake at the bar. You won't even know I'm there."

She side-eyed him as he waited for her response. "You know you're going to end up working, right?" He knew that. As soon as their boss, Mike, or any of their Sunday regulars saw him, he would be behind the bar making Bloody Marys.

"That is a risk I am prepared to take. Okay, it's settled then," he announced before Tori could argue with him. "We're going to work together tomorrow. What time do you have to be there?"

"Six thirty," she replied with a grimace. He held back any reaction to her admission, not wanting to deter her from their newly cemented plans.

"You better set your alarm now then, V. We've got"—he paused to pull out his phone and check the time—"eight hours until rise and shine. And you better believe I plan to make the most of all of them," he added, circling back around the bar to meet Tori where she sat.

"Hot tub time?" he asked suggestively, getting as physically close to her as the barstool would allow. She spread her legs wide and scooted her ass to the edge of the seat, lining herself up with his body.

There she is, he thought as he watched the spark return to her eyes.

"Hot tub time," she replied with a sly smile.

CHAPTER 9

Tori

She crossed the sunroom to scoop up the bikini bottoms Rhett had relieved her of within seconds of walking in the door. Had she really agreed to going in to work together tomorrow? *I'm in trouble,* she thought as she slipped her bikini bottoms back on and tied the loose side securely in place. She liked to think she was running the show when they were together, but Rhett was a commanding force against her willpower.

She made her way over to the storage chest, pulling her sundress off in the process. The Wheelers kept their hot tub storage cupboard as well stocked as the sunroom bar. She opened the cabinet door and reached in for two fluffy robes and a stack of towels, then set them on the loveseat near the door.

Rhett sauntered back into the sunroom from the kitchen. Tori ogled his bare chest as he approached. He had the most delectable neck she had ever seen on a man. His prominent Adam's apple contrasted against the hollow of his throat and the sharp definition of his collarbones. She loved to run her tongue through the peaks and valleys of his well-defined upper body.

Her eyes darted to his hands as they reached for the drawstring on the inside of his joggers. Suddenly he glanced up at her and frowned.

"Wait, did you put your bottoms back on?" he asked, mock annoyance lacing his voice.

"I did. Figured I should make you work for it after what you put me through today." She kept her tone light. The accusation was sharp enough on its own.

Rhett stilled. He stood frozen in place, but his eyes began to roam her body. *Ohhh, he came to play.* The whole scene felt like déjà vu as she recalled how she had eye-fucked him that morning in his room.

Warmth gathered in her core as she took a steadying breath. They both knew what was about to happen. It had felt like this for ten years. Their attraction. Their connection. A magnetic current was pulling them into each other's orbit. Together, they were an unstoppable force.

Tori was certain her string bikini top and bathing suit bottoms would catch fire if he kept his eyes on her much longer. All he had to do was tell her to undress. She stood there expectantly, ready for it. Wanting it. Needing it to forget the heaviness of the day. But he didn't tell her to undress. In fact, he didn't say anything. He just continued to assess her body with his searing blue-grey eyes.

She started panting softly as they stood in a stalemate in the sunroom. Her fingers grazed below her bare navel without conscious thought. Rhett's eyes grew heavy as he followed her fingers, watching her hand move slowly across the cool fabric of her bathing suit. Her hand landed between her legs, pressing down on her aching mound through the material. She moved her fingers across her center a few times, teasing herself, then squeezing her thighs together in response to her own touch. She let out a quiet moan as she applied a bit more pressure. Without thinking, she moved her other hand and started undoing the side of her bikini.

Rhett made a deep, throaty sound of objection. "Nuh-uh. Leave. Them. On," he demanded, stretching out each word for emphasis.

She squirmed at his command, arousal coursing through her body. She squeezed her eyes shut to keep from losing her cool.

"Let's go," he breathed into her ear. Tori's eyes shot open at the proximity of his voice. Not only had he crossed the room without her realizing it, now he was also naked. His dick pressed into her hip, urging her to turn into him for a few seconds before he stepped away and stalked toward the door. It took every ounce of self-control not to reach out and touch him as she followed him outside.

"How hot do you want it?" he asked, his voice dripping with innuendo. He reached down to grab the handle of the hot tub cover to pull it back. Steam immediately rose off the surface as the heated water mingled with the freezing February air.

"Turn it all the way up." She didn't care that their banter sounded like the opening lines of a porno. She could barely form coherent thoughts after that standoff in the sunroom.

Bubbles erupted from the jets as purple and blue lights danced under the surface of the water. The water was scalding already, and goosebumps cropped up over her entire body on contact. She lazily moved away from the stairs to make room for Rhett. She turned around just in time to see him step in.

His perfect, hard dick jutted out in front of him. She couldn't get enough of the way he stood so confidently before her. She could look at his body all damn day. He noticed her staring and smirked. Without breaking eye contact, he reached down and gave his penis a slow stroke, running his thumb over the tip to capture the moisture already visible on the end.

He slowly lowered himself into the hot tub and perched on his usual seat to the right of the stairs before beckoning for her to join him. Two curled fingers and a knowing glance—that's all it took for him to dominate the moment. Tori felt her body move through the water before she even fully synthesized what was happening.

Once she was within arm's reach he caught her, pulling her into his body but turning her around so her back was against his chest. She settled in between his legs and felt herself go soft. She molded her body into his and relaxed into his arms. His mouth found her earlobe as his hands began to explore. She could feel his rock-hard erection pressed against her bum, perfectly in line with her ass.

The ache between her legs was already overwhelming. She rolled her hips back along his dick, craving more contact. She lifted herself up slightly and realigned her body even closer to Rhett's. If she wasn't wearing bathing suit bottoms he would already be buried inside her. She reached down and wrapped her hand around his dick, shifting herself forward so the tip aligned with her center.

Rhett let out a hiss of approval. "You a little eager tonight, V?" he whispered into the shell of her ear. Tori kept her hand wrapped around him as she pressed his length against her own bundle of nerves. She wasn't as focused on jacking him off as she was on using his body for her pleasure.

His hands made their way up her arms and over her chest. He stayed above the fabric, using the purchase of the cloth to create extra friction against her breasts while kissing her neck from behind. He pinched and teased her nipples into stiff peaks. The combination of his demanding touch and the scalding water short-circuited her brain as her body registered the sensations as both pain and pleasure.

His mouth on her neck. His hands on her breasts. His dick pressed against her. It was all too much and yet somehow not enough. She needed more, and she needed it now.

"That feels so good," she encouraged him, breathless. She tried to turn around to kiss him, but he just pulled her in tighter against his chest and held her in place.

"Stay," he whispered in her ear, holding her in place. "Let me do this for you, beautiful. I want to make you feel so good."

There was no way she was going to fight him on that. He continued to caress her, picking up the pace as her body responded to his touch. Every time he kissed her neck, she felt a warm, tingly sensation in her sex. She grinded her hips back on his lap, matching the pace of his hands and his kisses. All the tension of the day unraveled with his touch. This is what she wanted. This is what they needed. She involuntarily bucked her hips back into him again, harder this time, desperate for more.

Apparently, that was the sign Rhett had been waiting for. He used one hand to hold her close, bracing her against him as the circulating water threatened to pull her away. His other arm hooked under her from behind, forcing her to spread her legs wide. They were alone and surrounded by a privacy fence, but the position still made her feel exposed in the best way.

"If I take these off again, do you promise to leave them off this time?" She could feel his fingertips already working at the knot of her bikini bottoms.

"Promise," she panted, reveling in the warmth of the water and the heat of her mounting arousal. She felt him smile against the side of her face. He had the first knot undone in seconds before moving to the other hip.

The moment she was exposed, he pressed his entire hand against her, palming her and claiming her. His fingertips pressed into her clit while his palm rested firmly against her entrance. He held her like that for a breath, and then another. The anticipation of what he would do next nearly sent her spiraling. Finally, he began to move his fingers, working her clit with the same deftness he had used on her nipples.

Tori's mind went blank as she lost herself to the rhythm of his hand. He knew just where to stroke and exactly how hard to press to bring her climax to the surface. She clenched her thighs together at the first signs of her building orgasm.

"Not yet," Rhett ordered, his voice heavy with desire. He moved his hand away as she whimpered. She ground her hips back into him again, trying to gain purchase against something, anything, to meet the need between her legs.

He lifted her off of him and stood up in one motion. She whipped around to face him, agitated to have been snapped out of the moment. His eyes grew wide at the sight of her: she could only imagine how wanton she looked.

"I've got you," he reassured her with a devilish smile. "I have an idea I want to try." He turned her around again then gingerly guided her forward. Tori played along, excitement coursing through her body as she let him push her toward the side of the hot tub.

"Kneel down," he commanded. Tori fumbled slightly as she found her balance. She was kneeling on the seat he had just occupied, her upper body exposed out of the water. His hand slid down her spine, his fingers dipping into the crack of her bare ass below the water. His thumb lingered against her back door while the rest of his hand caressed her. The new angle sent a fresh jolt of wanting through her already primed body.

"Rhett, please," she begged as she squirmed against his hold.

"I said I've got you," he crooned into her ear before grazing his teeth against her earlobe.

Before she could sass him back, she felt him wrap a strong arm around her stomach. He lifted her body with ease and moved her a few inches to the right. When he lowered her back into the water, she gasped. He had lined her up perfectly with one of the jet streams of the hot tub. She almost came on contact.

"Is that okay?" he murmured into her ear as his fingers circled her opening.

"Yes." All coherent thought left her consciousness. She couldn't conjure up any other word to express her pleasure. "Yes, yes, yes." She moaned as he pushed two fingers into her at once, stretching and massaging the front wall of her core like he knew she liked. Within a minute, he had worked another finger into her, eliciting a deep moan of appreciation. He began to thrust in and out, mindful not to move her away from the stream of the jets for too long. She didn't know where to focus. There was pressure and pleasure building in every limb of her body.

"Rhett," she exhaled, unable to formulate any other words or make sense of what was happening. He continued to move in and out, building her up then withdrawing his hand for a few seconds at a time. Her mind went blank. Her other senses dulled. All she could feel was the water surging over her clit and Rhett's hand driving into her. There was only this. There was only him.

The buildup dragged on for a torturously long time before an orgasm ripped through her so hard one of her knees slipped off the seat. She didn't have enough awareness to care that she was at risk of drowning.

"Whoa, whoa there." Rhett caught her and moved her away from the jet stream. He steadied her body against his, supporting her weight with his arms. His touch was gentle and loving, a sharp contrast from the unrelenting force he had just used to make her come.

He chuckled into her ear, spinning around to sit back down. "Fuck, Tori. You are so loud." She had been so wrapped up in her own pleasure she hadn't realized she had made any sound at all.

She felt him move her body through the water until she was cradled in his lap. She rested her head in the crook of his neck and sighed. They sat in silence, save for the soft moans she let out every few breaths as she rode out the aftershocks of bliss.

There is only this, she thought to herself again. *There is only him.*

CHAPTER 10

Rhett

He hugged her to his chest, savoring the adorable little noises she made post-orgasm. He couldn't believe how hard she just came. Or how loud she had been. He had half a mind to wonder if her dad could hear her across their yards.

There wasn't time to worry about that, though, because Tori was super-charged from her climax and already eager for more. He felt her shift from soft and docile to a woman on a mission, pulling herself upright as she straddled his lap.

"That. Was. Incredible," she gushed between kisses. He was disappointed that she hadn't let him hold her for very long, but that disappointment vanished as he felt her reach below the water and wrap her hand around his dick.

"Seriously. I'm going to have to reorganize my top ten list after that." She smiled against his mouth as her hand started stroking him. He bucked his hips in response to her praise and her touch. Even though she was straddling his lap, she was high up on her knees, making it impossible for him to push against anything but her hand. She was in control as she continued to pump her fist underwater.

"You're not the only one with ideas, you know. Think you can handle a little ice?" Tori whispered, tugging on his lower ear lobe with her teeth before moving her mouth along his stubbled jaw. He loved how turned on she was and how easily she trusted him to get her off. Nothing made him harder than making her feel good.

She didn't linger on his jawline long, instead moving lower to the hollow of his neck and the outline of his collarbone. She nipped and kissed along the planes of his chest. She had established a rhythm, stroking him, pressing her body against him, and kissing him to a beat that only she could hear.

"I can handle anything you want to give me," he vowed, breathless from the different sensations she was inspiring throughout his body. He stilled his own thrusts to allow her to take over completely. He would let this woman do just about anything to him.

"I want you on the stairs," she instructed, releasing her grip to motivate him to move. Rhett didn't need to be told twice. He stood up quickly, the frigid night air sending chills down his spine as he made his way through the water.

"Up higher," she commanded when he tried to settle in on the lowest level. He hoisted himself up two more stairs, exposing his entire upper body and the tops of his thighs. His dick protruded out of the water as goosebumps erupted on his skin. He didn't know what Tori had in mind, but she better hurry up before he lost his erection to the February night air.

She was on him a moment later. She ran her hands along the backs of his thighs, lightly pulling on his balls under the water. She moved the other one to circle the base of his dick. She was kneeling two steps below him, gazing up in reverence. She took the tip of his penis into her mouth, using her other hand to stroke him just like he liked. When her lips lowered to meet her fist, his brain almost short-circuited.

Her hand on his balls. Her fingers curled around his shaft. Her tongue pressed against the underside of his dick. Her bare ass cresting the surface of the hot tub every time she bobbed down to take more of him in her mouth. Rhett thought he was going to lose his damn mind.

"Tori," he moaned, arching his back as he felt a familiar warmth start to build in his groin. He felt his balls draw up and his spine tingle. He knew he wasn't going to last long after making her come so hard, but he was still surprised by the swiftness and intensity of his mounting release. "Fuck, that feels so good. I'm close. Don't stop," he begged. He was at her mercy.

After another minute he couldn't hold back any longer. The only warning he offered was a guttural, drawn out moan. Tori knew what that meant. She knew what he liked, what he needed. She gripped his pulsating dick with one hand, then used the knuckle of one finger to gently press up behind his balls. She sucked hard as he came into her mouth in waves.

Rhett's vision went fuzzy. He felt his dick continue to pulsate in her mouth even after he was empty. When she finally released him, she looked up and smiled. He watched her swallow and felt an immediate pang of arousal return to his core. *She is unbelievable.* He was satiated in every sense of the word.

It took a few seconds to remember he was still sitting out of the hot tub. He pushed off against the steps and reached out for her in the water. Their bodies melted together, a tangle of arms and legs. She wrapped both her arms around his neck and shimmied her legs around his thighs, letting him hold her once again.

"That was mind blowing, V." He leaned in to kiss her, tasting the saltiness from his own release on her tongue. She returned his kiss at an unhurried pace. She moved from his lips to his throat to his collarbone then back again, savoring him and letting herself be savored in return.

He pulled back to admire her. He couldn't get enough of this woman. Her hair was hanging down in wet tendrils around her face, her eyes bright and filled with love. Her lips were swollen from sucking him off and kissing him so hard. He wished he could take a picture of her at this moment. He wished he could keep her like this forever.

"What are you thinking?" she asked, taking advantage of his distraction to move her lips from his face to his neck again. Tori continued to slowly nip and suck on his collarbone. He felt so wanted and desired by her. He refused to think about why it couldn't be like this always.

In any other situation, and on any other day, he might have found the courage to answer that he loved her. She knew it. They had both known it for years. But all the pain and rejection from earlier prevented him from saying anything along those lines now.

"I'm thinking I might need a power nap before we go for round two." He caught her gaze and noticed how sleepy she looked, too. It had been a long day for both of them.

"Let's go upstairs then," she whispered in agreement.

CHAPTER 11

Rhett

Rhett turned off and covered the hot tub, then made his way into the sunroom. Tori worked on closing the blinds while he locked the back door and gathered up their towels and clothes.

"Come on, beautiful," he instructed, letting his gaze linger on Tori's robe-clad body. "Let's go to bed."

He followed her into the house and up the stairs, smiling when she skipped the squeaky stair toward the top out of habit.

"I'm going to take a quick shower to get the chlorine out of my hair," she told him as they walked into his room. She started to untie her robe as she made her way to his en suite. "You can join me if you want," she offered over her shoulder before pulling the door semi-closed.

Rhett stared at the bathroom door for a few beats as he considered her proposal. But instead of joining her, he decided to get everything ready for the night. He set about turning down his bed and rearranging the pillows. He wandered into the hallway and grabbed an extra blanket from the linen closet, then he detoured into Maddie's room to steal a phone charger. He set everything down on Tori's side of the bed.

He glanced back at the bathroom door. He could hear the water hitting against the tile of the shower, and he could see the steam swirling around the bathroom through the slightly ajar door. As tempted as he was to join her, he quietly snuck out of the bedroom and headed downstairs instead.

He grabbed two water bottles from the fridge, then set to work programming the drip side of the coffee machine for five a.m. Satisfied he had thought of everything, Rhett quietly made his way back upstairs to his room. He found Tori's phone in the pocket of her cover-up. He plugged it into an outlet on her side, then grabbed his own phone and set an alarm.

He made his way into his closet and fished out a clean pair of boxers and sweats for himself, plus an old lacrosse club T-shirt for her. He hit the lights of the closet and turned around to find her staring at him from the bathroom door.

The sight of her soaking wet body wrapped in nothing but a towel —his towel—sent a spark of warmth through him. It didn't matter that they'd just spent the last hour naked together in the hot tub. He couldn't get enough of her.

"How was your shower?" He smiled.

"It was unexpectedly lonely in there," she replied, cocking an eyebrow. "Everything okay?"

"Yes," he responded quickly. "Of course. I just realized I forgot to do a few things downstairs. Come here," he prompted, lowering his eyes to meet hers. The last thing he wanted was for Tori to start overthinking things again.

She padded across the carpeted floor toward him. He wrapped her in his arms and held her body as close as physically possible. She melted into the hug and let herself be supported by him.

He recognized it immediately. After a day of stress and surprises, Tori had finally gone soft. Her armor was off. He leaned down at the same time that she lifted her chin to him, each searching for the other's lips. He kissed her gently, savoring her, committing this moment to memory. After ten years on and off, he had enough sordid memories to fuel a lifetime of fantasies. But it was moments like this, moments when she wasn't radiating tension or trying to push him away, that he cherished most.

He let his hand wander as he deepened the kiss, weaving his fingers through her soaking wet hair. He knew that she was raw enough right now that she would let him take care of her, and he intended to take full advantage.

"I'll go find a brush for you in Maddie's room," he offered when his fingers caught a tangle in her hair. She smiled against his lips and nodded. He ducked back into his little sister's room and found what he was looking for. Tori was just slipping his shirt over her head when he walked back into the room.

"Are you going to be warm enough?" he asked, handing her the hairbrush and running the back of his hand against her bare arm.

Tori rolled her eyes. "It looks like someone already got me an extra blanket, so I think I'll be fine." She obviously knew what he was up to, but she didn't call him on it or show any resistance.

"Alarms are on, coffee is set, and I got you a water," he ticked off. "Let's go to bed, beautiful."

He watched her crawl under the covers and make her way to the middle, wrapping the extra blanket around herself in the process. Rhett flicked off the bathroom lights, then the overhead light, casting the room into darkness before climbing into bed to meet her.

Their legs connected first, followed by their lips. He kissed her slowly and deeply. He was lost in the taste of her, in the feeling of her in his arms. They could spend the rest of the weekend in bed just like this, and it still wouldn't be enough.

Tori swiveled her hips. He could feel her bare lower half rub against the fabric of his sweatpants. She placed her palms on his bare chest: an invitation. He paused. He was up for it, but he knew she was exhausted.

"We can just sleep, V," he whispered to her through the dark. "I know we have to be up super early tomorrow." She dug her nails into his chest and ground her hips harder against him in protest.

"I know. I'm so tired," she admitted quietly. "I just need to feel you inside me tonight."

Rhett sucked in a breath at her confession. He had been so wrapped up in making her feel good—in making her come hard enough to forget all the bullshit from earlier in the day—that he hadn't realized they hadn't had intercourse. He couldn't leave her wanting. Tori never admitted to needing anything. He pushed down his sweatpants and boxers in one fluid motion, desperate to fill her request.

"Do you know how beautiful you are?" he demanded, finding the hem of the T-shirt she had just put on and lifting it over her head. "Do you have any idea what you do to me?"

Instead of answering, Tori took his lower lip between her teeth and bit down. She slipped her hand between their bodies and wrapped her fingers around his already-hard erection. She teased him with feather-light touches, her thumb rubbing back and forth along the crown of his dick. She grasped him tighter and pushed her hips forward, tracing the tip of his penis back and forth against her bundle of nerves. Another minute of this and he would be blowing his load before he could even get inside her.

"What do you want?" he croaked as she continued to use him like a joystick against her clit. He knew the answer, but he wanted to hear her say it. She was so soft and open to him right now. He needed to hear the rawness in her voice.

"I want you. I want you inside me," she purred. Her voice was breathy and filled with desire.

"Say it again."

"I want you, Rhett. I want you so damn much." Tori peppered his neck with kisses as she continued to rhythmically grind his length against her center. He felt her line him up. He was right there. He was so close. But then she stilled. "Do we need a condom?"

Rhett froze. He was very much aware of the underlying question that lingered between them. They had already talked about Chandler multiple times that day, but they hadn't talked about this. An unplanned trip home meant he hadn't made his usual detour to the quick clinic near campus. She must have noticed his distress because she shifted her weight and crawled up toward his ear.

"Hey, come back to me," she summoned. She released her grasp on his dick and ran her fingers through his hair. He could feel her breath warming the skin on his neck as she tried to comfort him. "It's okay. It won't change anything if we need it. You're still getting laid," she added with a smile.

Goddamnit. He froze for one second, and now she assumed he was barebacking it with Chandler.

He felt the weight of all the things they had dealt with that day. It was all so heavy. He decided he didn't want to put one more lie or omission between them, so he might as well just say it, even if she read too much into it or got angry with him.

"We're good. I didn't get tested before coming home, but I haven't had sex with anyone else since I was with you over winter break," he confessed. Something flashed in Tori's eyes—but it was gone so fast he couldn't tell if it was judgement, relief, or surprise. He knew his admission could backfire on him.

"Good," she responded, her voice laced with desire. "Because I need to feel you inside me right now."

Rhett slanted his mouth to kiss her and wrapped his arm around her torso. She didn't even have to reach down to line him up this time. His body took over, nudging her opening and willing her to let him in.

"Rhett," she sighed as the tip of his penis entered her. He moved his hand to her lower back and pulled her closer, deepening the connection between them and solidifying that, after a day of so many highs and lows, they really were okay.

CHAPTER 12

Rhett

"What is happening right now?!"

How could he possibly be this loud so early in the morning? Rhett wondered.

Jake looked from Rhett to Tori, then back again, doing a literal double take as they walked through the side door of Clinton's Family Restaurant. "Am I really seeing this?" Jake exclaimed, slinging his bar towel on his shoulder and making his way over to them.

"It's so good to see you, bro!" He pulled Rhett into a hug, his voice filled with sincerity.

"Bro code, though. Why didn't you text me and tell me you were coming in today?" Jake questioned before he pulled out of the hug.

"Wait a minute..." He squinted his eyes at Tori with a knowing look. "How long has he been in town?" Jake shot an accusatory glance at Rhett then quickly turned back to Tori.

When no one replied, he filled in the blanks for himself. "And now I know why I had Lia riding my ass all day yesterday when she wasn't even on the schedule," he muttered, circling back behind the bar and slapping down his bar towel before picking up a paring knife.

"You better get your ass back here and start cutting my celery, Wheeler. You owe me." He pointed the small knife at him for emphasis.

Rhett didn't have time to respond before the side door swung open again.

"Wheeler!" a booming voice called out in greeting as a blast of cold air entered the bar area. Rhett turned around to see his old boss outstretching a big, meaty hand. "I didn't know we were expecting you in today."

Mike Hobbs was a retired Navy SEAL turned small-town restaurateur. He had owned Clinton's for more than fifteen years and had recently bought the old Oak Barrel Tavern next door. He was a mainstay in the community and a constant presence at the restaurant. It was never a question of whether Mike was around. It was just a matter of whether he was in the back cooking, behind the bar pouring, or next door working on renovations for the new space.

Mike had taken a chance and given Rhett his first job washing dishes at Clinton's. He knew he was a spoiled asshat back then. He had been lazy and entitled and a cocky know-it-all to boot. He shouldn't have lasted two days on payroll, but Mike was much more interested in training him than firing him. Maybe it was the SEAL mentality, but he approached his staff with a "leave no man behind" attitude. Once you were part of the crew at Clinton's, you were part of a family for life.

Rhett shook Mike's hand and nodded. "It's good to see you, sir."

"What are you doing here, son?" Mike glanced over to Tori, essentially answering his own question. "Just home for the weekend?"

"Yeah, something like that." Rhett was anxious to change the subject. "Cool if I help Jake prep for brunch?"

"He owes me, Mike!" Jake interjected from behind the bar. Rhett wondered what sort of mood Lia had been in yesterday to make him so intent on collecting payback. Or maybe the real question was what had Jake done this time to deserve her wrath.

"I don't have you set up in the system for this pay cycle, Wheeler, but you do what you gotta do, and you make sure Jake splits tips." Mike clasped him on the shoulder one more time before heading toward the kitchen.

"Hey, and I better not catch you two in the walk-in cooler," he deadpanned as he looked between Rhett and Tori. "It's Sunday, so we're gonna be too busy to be down a server."

Tori rolled her eyes at Mike's admonishment. They hadn't been caught in the walk-in since high school, but it used to happen frequently enough that it was a deserved reminder.

Rhett watched as Tori tightened her ponytail and slipped behind the bar to clock in. She smiled at Jake and said something he couldn't hear. Jake smirked and replied to her, then gave her a playful side-hug in the process. Rhett smiled, reveling in the sight of two of his favorite people joking and having a good time together.

He pushed up the sleeves of his Henley as he joined them behind the now-crowded bar. "Have a good shift," he murmured in Tori's ear before she moved away from the clock-in station and started tying her apron around her waist. He couldn't resist reaching out and lightly brushing his hand over her hip, catching her fingers in his for just a few seconds.

Tori locked eyes with him, her free hand busy adjusting her uniform. She shook her head twice, before growling, "Behave," under her breath.

Rhett could barely hold back his smirk. "Always, beautiful." With a wink, he playfully smacked her ass, eliciting a yelp and a swat of her notepad.

"Wheeler!" Jake exclaimed in his best Mike impression, sounding equal parts annoyed and amused. "Chop chop... literally!"

Rhett washed his hands, then set to his task, expertly chopping long stalks of celery for Clinton's bottomless Bloody Marys Sunday special. He fell into a natural rhythm beside his best friend, relying on muscle memory to go through the motions of brunch prep.

"Alright, man, so what's going on?" Jake pulled down glasses from above the bar as he spoke. "Why are you home this weekend?"

Rhett bristled in response to the million-dollar question he just couldn't seem to escape. If this weekend had taught him anything, it was that he could not, should not, would not show up in Hampton unannounced ever again.

"I just needed a break," he grumbled, testing out the line he tried to use with Tori on Friday night. "It feels like the semester is flying by, and I honestly don't know how many more weekends I'll even be able to make it home."

Jake stayed quiet for a few beats, but he knew his friend well enough to know he had something on his mind.

"So what's been going on around here?" Rhett prompted, willing the conversation forward rather than waiting for Jake to pry.

"Same old same. Work. Sleep. Work out. Fuck. Repeat." Jake grinned as he ticked off his routine.

"And does all that fucking have anything to do with why Lia was riding your ass yesterday?" Lia was usually chill and even-tempered. Jake must have done something diabolical to earn her anger.

"What can I say? You and Tori aren't the only ones who know how to make good use of the walk-in fridge." Jake raised his eyebrows suggestively, leaving Rhett to fill in the blanks.

"Okay, Tori and I only ever made out in the walk-in, and that was in high school," Rhett objected. "Please don't tell me you and Lia boned by the produce? That's not sanitary, man."

He finished chopping and stacking the celery, then reached for the cans of tomato juice stashed under the bar. He methodically started opening them and dumping the contents into two different tubs.

"Well, Lia decided I wasn't worth her time anymore after New Year's Eve. She ghosted me, which is impressive considering we work together and I have to see her at least five times a week. I guess casual hook ups aren't everyone's cup of tea." Jake shrugged.

"So yesterday morning I was in the back doing inventory when Lia walked in unexpectedly. In my defense, she wasn't on the schedule when I checked it the night before, Tori was, so I had no idea she was coming in..."

Jake at least had the decency to cast his eyes down to the glasses he was rimming with black pepper and celery salt.

"And who, exactly, were you doing *inventory* with?" Rhett asked, knowing damn well his friend must have been caught in the act.

"Cory," Jake responded sheepishly.

"You're such a manwhore!" Rhett laughed then smacked him with his free hand. "Of course Lia's pissed if she caught you sucking face with one of her best friends at the place where you all work together."

"Like I said, we can't all be so lucky as to find ourselves in a no-strings-attached friends-with-benefits situation." Jake shot him a knowing glance.

Rhett scowled back at him. Jake knew damn well that he considered Tori so much more than a casual fling. But he also refused to explain their current relationship to his friend, hence the judgement in his tone. Jake was always trying to get a rise out of him about it.

They used to share all the details of their hookups, but the girl talk (and sometimes guy talk from Jake) came to a halt once Rhett and Tori started their current arrangement. Discussions about Tori were now strictly off limits, and he knew it.

"Don't go there, man. We're not talking about Tori. I know I always say that, but I really mean it today," Rhett implored.

Jake must have picked up on the desperation in his voice. He nodded once then changed the subject.

"Fine. We can talk about something else. Something way more important. A momentous occasion that we will both remember for the rest of our lives." Jake paused for effect—he could always escalate the drama in any situation. "Our grand finale Spring Break Bros Trip."

Rhett grinned at his best friend. He was also eager to make plans for next month. They had spent almost every spring break together since middle school, traveling with each other's families when they were younger, then setting out on their own adventures once they had access to a car. Over the years, they had road-tripped to Myrtle Beach, flown out to Vegas and Colorado, and just kicked it in Hampton and partied every night of the week when Rhett's parents went out of town. After last year's low-key trip to the Wheelers' cabin in Michigan, they made a pact that they would go all out this year for their final trip together.

"Alright, so let's nail down the timeline for that week. I want to make sure I put in my time off now."

He set the rimmed glasses aside and reached for one of the tubs Rhett had already filled with tomato juice. "You making spicy?" he asked.

"Oh, come on!" Rhett shook his head in disbelief. "As if Mike would let me back here without the unspoken vow that I'm in charge of the spicy Mary mix."

"You're such a cocky ass." Jake ribbed him in the side, then gathered up the ingredients for the mild Bloody Mary recipe. "Okay, so what's your schedule that week?"

"So there's a chance I won't have class the few days leading up to break, but it's not a guarantee. I have to meet for my practicum on Friday afternoons, so it's up to the professor if we meet that week or not. But," Rhett lowered his voice before continuing, "I'm taking Tori to the Karta Stella concert in Ann Arbor that Friday night for her birthday. She doesn't know yet."

Rhett scanned the restaurant for her then, his gaze landing smack on her ass as she reached across a booth to set out a jelly caddy. At that exact moment, she straightened up and turned around, locking eyes with him. If it was anyone else in the whole world, Rhett would have felt embarrassed or, at least, felt compelled to feel embarrassed. But not with Tori. He winked at her, but she just shook her head and rolled her eyes in return.

"Okay, so the first weekend's out?" Jake pulled his attention back to their conversation.

"Yeah, we'll head to the concert that afternoon or earlier if we can, then I plan to crash at the cabin instead of making the drive home on Friday night," Rhett explained. "My parents, Maddie, and a few of her friends are spending the whole week at the cabin, but they don't arrive until Sunday."

"So you'll be home by Sunday?"

"Yeah, the latest I'll be home is Sunday night. Do you want to hang in Hampton for a few days first? We've got tickets to the Sabres game for Wednesday, then the hotel in Niagara Falls is booked Thursday through Sunday."

"Abso-fucking-lutely. I'm thinking we go hard with back-to-back Jake and Rhett Parties just like the good old days. We'll host at your place on Sunday night, go for round two on Monday, and then we can sober up enough to drive to Buffalo on Tuesday."

"That works for me," Rhett nodded in agreement. "You handle the guest list, and I'll check the liquor supply at home before I go back to Easton."

He was relieved Jake didn't give him any pushback about not heading to Buffalo right away. Spending the first weekend of spring break with Tori then sticking around Hampton for a few extra days ensured they would get to spend a good amount of time together that week.

"Look alive, kids!" Mike hollered as he pushed through the kitchen doors into the main dining area. "Locks are turning," he warned, walking to the front of the restaurant to open for the day.

"You made the spicy, right, Wheeler?" he asked as he hustled past the bar area.

"Told ya," Rhett muttered under his breath as he sucker-punched his best friend in the chest.

"Yes, sir!" Rhett barked out for Mike.

Chapter 13

Tori

The Sunday shift at Clinton's flew by like it usually did, starting off steady as soon as Mike unlocked the doors, then really picking up after all the churches let out across town. Tori had been slammed with table after table, mostly families and large groups. She was fighting off fatigue as she shifted her weight from hip to hip, waiting for an older couple to decide whether to order the sausage gravy or the grits.

She took the opportunity to steal a glance across the dining room at Rhett, who had maintained his position behind the bar with Jake as promised. Every bar stool was filled, even at twelve thirty on a Sunday in their moderately conservative town. Tori had watched several regulars come in, notice that Rhett was working, and make a beeline for a seat at the bar. The boy had a magnetism to him that was undeniable. This town—and everyone in it—loved him.

He was currently entertaining the entire bar with some loud and boisterous story. He threw his hands up in the air, then wrapped one arm around Jake's shoulder as he concluded. Tori could hear a steady roll of laughter from the audience around him. She watched him as he worked, efficiently refilling everyone's water glasses and throwing in a few extra smiles and winks for good measure. He was so good at making people feel seen. It was more than just good manners. He had a gift for connecting and taking care of people.

As soon as Mr. and Mrs. Wishy-Washy decided to order both the sausage gravy and the grits, she mentally pulled herself together and took off for the point-of-sale station in the kitchen.

"Hey, V," she heard Rhett call out as she tried to discreetly press through the bar area unnoticed. Tori looked up to see him holding out a Bloody Mary, grinning at her.

"Clean rim, just the mix, extra spicy, and salty enough there's no way it'll make you have to pee," he responded to every single one of her protests before she could even open her mouth. His insistence on taking care of her was sweet at best, but suffocating at worst, especially when they had an audience. She silently cursed herself for letting her guard down last night. The man obviously thought he had a free pass to keep up the concerned boyfriend act today.

"Pass that to her, please," he instructed, handing the glass to a middle-aged woman still wearing her Sunday best. The woman eagerly took the glass from his hands.

"Here you go, dear," she muttered, following Rhett's direction without question while not taking her eyes off him.

"Thank you," she responded kindly to the customer.

"And thank you, overbearing bartender." Tori smirked as she continued on toward the kitchen. "Cheers!" she called back over her shoulder before she passed through the swinging double doors. She shouldn't have been surprised when a hardy round of "Cheers!" erupted behind her, followed by the swell of his laughter.

By the time three p.m. rolled around, she was a walking zombie. The restaurant was quiet now, save for a few stragglers at the bar. She knew most of the patrons were still there because of the surprise guest bartender hanging out with Jake. She made her way idly around the bar, using the back of her hand to hide a big yawn.

"Let's go home," Rhett whispered behind her, making her jump at his proximity. He deftly pulled on the strings of her apron and grazed her hip, just as he had done when they first arrived.

"You clocking out, too, Wheeler?" Mike asked sarcastically from the corner seat of the bar. He had finally emerged from the kitchen to eat a late lunch now that the afternoon crowd had dispersed.

"Yes, sir," Rhett replied earnestly. "I've gotta get my girl home to get some rest."

She stiffened at his words. He knew better than to say things like that at work. Everyone who knew them knew they were together-ish, but it wasn't something she liked to put on display. He must have picked up on her displeasure because he tried to amend the story on the spot.

"I convinced Tori to let me tag along today so we drove together. You know how chicks love the Prelude..." He trailed off with a casual shrug.

She couldn't help but crack a smile at that one. His two-door Prelude had a nonexistent backseat and the deepest bucket seats known to man; it was not the kind of car you used to impress a woman. His nostalgia for that old car knew no bounds.

"Alright, well, make sure Jake gives you your share of the tips before you go," Mike ordered, pointing a fork in Jake's general direction.

"Mike, please!" Jake chided from across the bar, holding a hand to his chest like he had just been stabbed in the heart. "Like I could ever hold out on my best friend! Besides, today's tips are all going in our Spring Break Bros Trip Fund. He woulda benefited from this money whether he showed up today or not."

"Are you ready?" Tori prompted. She knew if she didn't speak up, the guys would stand there shooting the shit all day, and she was having trouble just standing up at this point.

"Let's get you home," Rhett responded, finding the small of her back and guiding her toward the door.

"I'll text you later, man. Thanks for letting me crash your shift," he shot back at Jake as they made their way to the side door. They grabbed their coats on the way out, not bothering to stop to put them on. She couldn't wait to take a nice, long nap.

"Where are we going, V?" he asked as he opened the passenger door of the Prelude. He was around to his side a few moments later, lowering himself into the driver's seat and blasting the heat to try and warm up the car.

She considered his question. If he dropped her off at her house, their time together was essentially over for the weekend. She would end up taking a nap, making dinner for her dad, and getting sucked into schoolwork as the Sunday scaries set in. They had technically been together all day at work, but they'd barely had a chance to spend any time together, save for the few smiles they exchanged across the restaurant. She wanted more time with him.

"We're going to your house," she decided as she buckled her seatbelt and sank into the bucket seat. She glanced over at him and caught the earnest look of conviction in his eyes.

We're not over yet.

CHAPTER 14

Tori

She woke up in Rhett's bed for the second time that day. And just like that morning, it was dark outside when she peered toward the window through sleepy eyes.

"Hey, beautiful," he murmured behind her. She didn't turn around, instead shifting her body backwards into him and savoring the feeling of being in his arms.

"Hi," she replied, lacing his fingers through hers and bringing his knuckles to her mouth. She kissed his hand, lingering over each finger as she felt him move closer.

"How long was I asleep?" She hadn't realized how utterly exhausted she was until they were driving home from Clinton's. She was grateful they only lived six minutes away—she almost fell asleep in the Prelude.

Between her Friday shift and staying up late to paint that night, then staying up late with Rhett last night and getting up early for work that morning, she was bone-tired. She wouldn't have been surprised if he told her it was Monday morning.

"It's almost six p.m.," he informed her. "I know you said you didn't want to sleep past five, but I couldn't stand to wake you."

"It's okay," she reassured him. She hated how he was always so worried about doing the wrong thing around her. *You know he's like that because of you,* she reminded herself silently.

"Did you take a nap, too?" she asked, pushing her hips suggestively into him again. She felt his erection begin to grow beneath his joggers.

"Uh, not exactly," he admitted. "I was working on this..." Rhett trailed off as he gently pulled on her shoulder, prompting her to roll onto her back. She gazed up at the ceiling of his bedroom as her eyes adjusted to the dimly lit room. Enough light was streaming in from the bathroom and hallway to illuminate dozens of cut out ornaments hanging above them. Her eyes grew wide in wonder as she realized what she was looking at.

"Paper stars," she said breathlessly. There must have been at least fifty of them, each one taped to a small piece of ribbon and hanging above the bed at different lengths.

"Happy birthday, beautiful." He grinned as he held two pieces of paper in front of her face.

Tori grabbed the tickets out of his hand, squinting at them through the darkness. "Are you kidding me right now?!" she squealed.

"Not kidding. You, me, and Karta Stella. The show's next month in Ann Arbor, a week after your actual birthday, and we've got really good reserved seating. It's on a Friday night, so we can head to the cabin for a few days afterwards. Just the two of us," Rhett confirmed, answering her question before she even asked.

"Oh my gosh. This is fantastic!" Tori turned to face him. She could see him grinning even in the dark. "Thank you." She kissed him. "Thank you, thank you, thank you." She kissed him over and over again, deepening it each time she went in for more. She wrapped a leg around him, excitement and gratitude radiating through her.

Rhett tried to kiss her back, but she smirked against his mouth. She giggled when he tried again. Then she started laughing so hard it was impossible for him to kiss her at all.

"What's so funny?" he prompted, giving up on kissing her mouth and nuzzling into her neck instead.

"Do you remember the first time you put paper stars in my room?" He stilled at the recollection.

"I thought your dad was going to punch me. I was so damn nervous." Rhett groaned, referring back to how he asked her to prom years ago.

"He acted all on board when I explained the plan to him, but then when I went up to your room, he just stood in the doorway, watching me. I had to keep pretending I didn't know my way around while also trying to tape ribbon to the bumpy popcorn ceiling above your bed. I was sweating so hard I had to go home and take a shower when I was done."

Tori convulsed into a fresh fit of giggles. The thought of her dad not wanting high school Rhett to be alone in her bedroom... It was too much.

I love... she started to think before she squeezed her eyes shut in protest and rejected the phrase that crept into her mind. She refused to acknowledge her truth, or to give anything away to Rhett. She searched for something to say to distract from all the feelings trying to bubble to the surface.

"Was it worth it?" she wondered out loud. Her words carried more weight than she intended. Rhett exhaled against her neck, his breath warm on her skin, then bowed his head low in reverence.

"Tori, you're always worth it," he whispered.

She found his lips and let herself get lost in the way he kissed her, desperate to suppress anything else she may have been tempted to say.

Chapter 15

Rhett

Rhett: Maddie Girl! Are you guys driving back from Michigan tonight?

He shot off the text to his little sister once Tori had left for the night. He had tried to convince her to sleep over again, but she insisted she had schoolwork to do and that she had neglected Penny too much already this weekend. He knew she also didn't want his parents finding her in his bed when they got home.

The Wheelers bought into the "Chandler is Rhett's girlfriend" storyline (or at least his parents did, and Maddie graciously played along), but they all knew he and Tori were a thing, too. He refused to talk to his mom about the details whenever she pressed him on it, which wasn't often. But Tori was right to tread lightly where Anne was concerned. It was easier to keep things on the downlow and protect his mom from hoping they would be together in the long run.

Still. He hated watching her cross back over to her yard through the broken spot in the fence.

He considered pouring himself a drink but decided a clear head was the better option if he wanted to get in an early morning run the next day. He figured if he got up early enough, he could get some miles in, hang out with Maddie before school, and then drive back to Easton in time for his only class of the day at two.

Maddie: How did you know we were in Michigan?? Did Mom tell you?

He wasn't surprised by Maddie's response. He hadn't talked to her much this week, and he knew they hadn't talked about their weekend plans beforehand.

Maddie: Nevermind. Just checked Tori's social and saw a pic she posted from the Ledges yesterday. I'm guessing you're home?

Busted. But not really. He wanted Maddie to know he was in Hampton. She was one of the reasons he was staying one more night.

Rhett: I'm at the house now. I'm going to stay the night. I was thinking I could drive you to school tomorrow?

Maddie: I have conditioning at 7 am. Bleh. We're already halfway home... just wait up for me and we'll hang tonight?

He let out an involuntary yawn at the thought of trying to stay awake for another few hours.

Rhett: No promises. I got up at 5:30 this morning and worked the brunch shift at Clinton's. I'm getting up early to run in the morning anyways... just tell me what time you want to leave the house.

Maddie: If we leave by 6:30 we'll have time for coffee.

Rhett: Deal.

He closed out the text thread with his sister and shot off a separate text to his mom. He was surprised she hadn't already tried to call him in the two minutes since he told Maddie he was home.

Rhett: Hey Mom. I came home for the weekend and I'm at the house now. I'm going to stay tonight and head back to school after breakfast tomorrow.

He walked quietly through the empty house and made his way to the stairs. He checked to make sure the garage door was closed but didn't bother setting the security system. His phone vibrated in his hand as he hit the landing of the second floor.

Mom: Sounds great. Maddie said you're going to take her to school in the morning, so I'll have breakfast ready when you get home. Your father has a mid-morning flight so we can all eat together before you both have to leave.

Rhett: Sounds good. Love you, Mom.

Rhett flopped onto his bed and plugged his phone in to the charger. He shot off one more text as his eyes grew heavy, squinting from the brightness of the phone.

Ev: Good night, beautiful. I'll be home again soon.

It was a promise he needed to see written out for himself. He had to leave Hampton tomorrow, but he would be back home, back to her, as soon as possible.

"Rhett!" Maddie squealed and ran into his arms. She was dressed for conditioning under her unzipped winter coat, wearing fitted workout pants and one of his old lacrosse shirts that she'd cut the arms out of. And now he knew why there were so few T-shirts in his closet upstairs.

"Hey, Maddie Girl. It's so good to see you." He wrapped her up in a big hug. She was only a few inches shorter than him at five ten. Her body was long and lean like his, too, just with less muscle definition. She had light blue eyes in contrast to his stormy grey and straight blond hair instead of his wavy dark brown locks, but their resemblance was still uncanny. Now that she was older, people often asked them if they were twins.

"Here, let me take that," Rhett offered, reaching for her gym bag that was no doubt filled with the clothes and products she deemed necessary post-workout.

"Wait, why are we taking my car?" she asked as he loaded the bag into the trunk of her Lexus RX.

"I know you hate riding in the Prelude." He shrugged. "Plus, I'll be gone by the time you're done for the day. I didn't want to leave you stranded."

"Are you going to call a ride share to drive you home from Hampton High?" she smirked as she opened the passenger door and climbed in.

Rhett adjusted his seat and checked the mirrors before answering. "No, goober. I slept in longer than I thought I would this morning, so I'm going to run back."

"You're crazy, bro. It's like five miles from the school to our house, and it's less than thirty degrees outside right now." She hit the button to turn on both their seat warmers for emphasis.

"It's exactly three miles if I go past the elementary schools and cut through the park," he countered. He had run the route enough times to know the exact distance and time he was going for this morning. "Enough about my run, though. Tell me what's going on with you? How's conditioning going? When are tryouts?"

She slumped down into her seat and turned her head to look at him.

"It's fine. Coach has me leading everyone in the weight room for conditioning, so I feel good about my chances of making captain. Tryouts are right before spring break in March. It all seems sort of silly knowing I'm just a few months from graduating, though, you know? Like, why did I choose to do a spring sport this year?"

"Because you love it," Rhett replied automatically. "It'll be worth it, Maddie. I promise. Playing lacrosse my senior year is one of my best memories from Arch. Senior year just feels weird in general. You know everything is ending soon, and you start to just go through the motions with some things. Believe me, I'm sort of going through it again as I finish up my MBA. It's weird to feel like you have to say goodbye to some things and also get excited for what happens next."

"Yeah, I guess. These early mornings aren't as easy to get up for knowing I've already been accepted everywhere I applied, though." He smiled at his sister's nonchalance. He was so proud she had gotten into all six schools she had applied to for college.

"Are we stopping for coffee?" he asked as he approached the main intersection in downtown Hampton. He needed to know whether he should turn left at the light to park beside the coffee shop or turn right at the clock tower to head toward the high school.

"Yes, please. I need coffee. Want to just let me out and I'll run in and get it?"

"No way. I can easily find parking this early." He turned left and pulled into one of several open spots. "You stay in the car and I'll run in," he instructed, already unbuckled and opening his door.

He ordered Maddie's favorite double dirty chai along with a black coffee for himself. He only had to wait two minutes before he was back in the car, steaming to-go cups in hand.

"You're my favorite brother," Maddie quipped as she closed her eyes and savored the first sip of her drink.

"I'm your only brother, but I'll take what I can get, I guess," he teased. "Anything else going on with you? Who went up to the cabin this weekend?"

He turned the car around right in the middle of the road since there was no one else on the street this early. They sat idly as they waited for the light at the base of the clock tower to turn green. Rhett felt a wave of déjà vu as he realized he had been parking on this side of the green and walking with Tori into Clinton's at the same time the morning before. He had checked the posted schedule at work yesterday, and he was glad she wasn't on for breakfast again today. She'd get to sleep in since she didn't have classes until the afternoon on Mondays this semester.

"Chloe came up to the cabin with us this weekend, so that was chill. I'm trying to convince Mom to let me take a few people to the cabin without her over spring break, but so far, no dice. I'm pretty sure your high school antics ruined any chance I'll ever get at getting away with shit like that," she mused. Rhett smiled—she wasn't wrong.

"What's going on with you?" She turned the questioning back to him then. "How's Tori?" she asked, a weighty accusation to her question.

"She's good." He chewed on the inside of his cheek as he wondered how much to tell his little sister. "She didn't know I was coming home this weekend, either," he offered apologetically. He glanced over at Maddie as he made the turn on the road leading to the high school. "Chandler and I had a fight, and I just didn't want to deal with her drama this weekend."

"So you got in a fight with your real girlfriend and came home to her?" She filled in the blanks.

"Maddie," Rhett warned, lifting his left hand and running it through his hair in frustration. He hadn't told her about the fight with Chandler because he wanted an attitude about the situation.

"What?" I'm not sitting in judgement of your little love triangle, Rhett. I just worry about you sometimes. Whatever arrangement you two have doesn't seem fair..."

"Madison." This time it wasn't a warning. "Chandler and I have been dating for a few years now, but it's always been casual between us. I don't even think we'll stay together once I move to Virginia. What Tori and I have... it's just a lot of history, you know?" He trailed off, annoyed that he was trying to justify the situation to his little sister.

"That's all fine, Rhett. And what I was going to say before you cut me off is that none of this seems fair to you." Maddie glanced over and gave him a knowing look. "You know I love Tori like a sister, and I know she's not your real girlfriend, but I don't understand why not. It pisses me off."

"You and me both."

"What's going to happen between you guys once you move to Virginia?"

Rhett knew exactly what was going to happen. Tori had made that abundantly clear. When he moved, they were done for good. That was it. That was the end. It would be over—all versions of everything they ever shared. It was part of the original arrangement, and after this weekend's showdown, he knew she would stand firmly in her decision to walk away. He didn't know how he would let her go. Not in a few months. Not ever. But he couldn't think about the inevitable. Not when there was still time to try and convince her otherwise.

"Hell if I know," Rhett lied, turning into the school and heading toward the doors closest to the weight room. "Where am I supposed to park?"

Maddie pointed straight ahead.

"Look. I know you're just being protective, and that's sweet, but you don't have to worry about Tori. Her and I... we're solid. She tries to push me away sometimes, and we fight like an old married couple, but for me, it's always been her."

Maddie was quiet for a moment. She took a long sip of her drink before nodding.

"I know that, but that's what scares me. She has a lot of power over you, Rhett."

Rhett grimaced, silently agreeing with her acute assessment of his life. Sometimes he forgot she was only eighteen, then other times, like now, he couldn't believe she was only eighteen. Maddie was wise beyond her years when she wanted to be. He was glad he had stayed home to see her this morning.

Rhett finally broke the silence by pulling her in for a hug. "I love you, sis. Here, take your keys and have a good day at school." He hopped out of the car and made his way around to the trunk to fetch her bag.

"Thanks for the ride. And the coffee. And for staying home for me this morning." She grinned back at him, accepting the gym bag before heading toward the weight room doors.

Rhett took a minute to stretch out his hamstrings, using the car for balance. She was right—it was really cold this morning—but he knew he wouldn't feel it by the end of the first mile. He set off on the course he knew by heart, ready to lose himself on his run and be done thinking for now.

Chapter 16

5 Weeks Later

"Get your cute little butt up here, birthday girl!!"

Tori smiled as she closed her car door. She had turned off the headlights as soon as she pulled into Perry Farm, not wanting to disturb Lia's sleeping parents or the cows out in the pasture. She walked along the gravel driveway toward the first outbuilding. She knew without calling out to them that was where she would find her two best friends.

"I'm twenty-four years old today, you guys," she called up as she approached the ladder on the side of the pole barn. "At what age are we officially too old for this?"

Tori and Lia had been climbing up to sit on the overhang of the machine storage building since they were teenagers. The pole barn faced east, with the overhang extending away from the main house. They figured out in middle school that they could say they were going to check on the animals and disappear for at least a few hours without anyone coming out here to look for them. Many, many memories had been made over the years on the Perry Farm, a lot of them on this very roof.

"We'll never be too old to par-tayyyyy!" Cory shouted. Tori heard Lia shush him before dissolving into a fit of giggles. All three of them had left work at the same time tonight, but Tori wanted to go home and change before coming over. She hadn't realized her best friends would already be three sheets to the wind by the time she arrived.

She reached the top rung of the ladder and hoisted herself up onto the roof. *Seriously. We're getting way too old for this.* She didn't want to verbalize her concerns in front of Lia again. They each had their own hang ups about getting older. With each passing year, Tori got closer to the age her mom was when she was first diagnosed with cancer, and Lia got closer to her parents' retirement and her inevitable future of taking over for them.

The Perrys' cattle farm had been a fixture in Hampton for three generations. Lia would make it four. She was an only child, like Tori, held in place in a small town by the weight of her parents' expectations. Lia hadn't bothered going to college, much to the chagrin of the guidance counselors at Hampton High. She proudly skewed their post-graduation data. But what was the point, she always argued, when she knew her final destination would be right back where she started?

"Hey!" Cory greeted her excitedly. "How was your day, birthday girl?"

He shifted over a few feet to make room for her. Cory had been a surprise to both of them, a fast friend and the missing link they didn't know they were missing. He was the sunshine to Lia's misery and Tori's skepticism. It may have been Tori and Lia in high school, but it was the trio of Tori, Cory, and Lia now.

"Meh? Birthdays aren't really my fave," she reminded him, pulling her knees close to her chest as she settled in between her friends. The steel grooves of the pole barn's roof felt particularly cold through her leggings tonight. They usually didn't come up onto the roof until at least May.

"Okay fine, but that cake Mike ordered, you gotta admit that was incredible. Plus shots!! I've worked at Clinton's for two years, and

Mike has never given me free booze!" Cory was clearly tipsy, but this level of enthusiasm wasn't out of character for him. He really was this excited about everything, always.

Lia smirked but stayed quiet, sipping on the can of beer in her hand. No one offered Tori a drink, but she wasn't offended. They knew better than to waste their breath. She so rarely drank, and she had already turned down booze once earlier that night.

Cory was right: Mike didn't go all out for anyone else's birthday, yet for some reason, she was supposed to believe he had ordered her favorite cake from a bakery in Cascade Falls. They had all gathered around the bar and demolished the thing at the end of the night. Mike gave Jake the go-ahead to pour everyone a birthday shot (and then Jake took Tori's for her, because he was good to her like that and didn't want to put her in an awkward situation). The whole night was fun and celebratory, which she appreciated. It still didn't change the fact that she was another year older, another year closer to twenty-eight.

She let out an involuntary sigh. Lia wrapped an arm around her in unspoken understanding.

"What'd your dad get you for your birthday?"

"New tires." She smiled at her best friend through the darkness.

"That's practical," she muttered.

"I know." Tori shrugged. "But that's Paul."

"Well, we got you something together." Lia pulled an envelope out of her back pocket.

"You guys," Tori warned. "Seriously. I don't need anything."

"Oh, stop. We knew better than to buy you booze or bring any other party favors up here tonight. But you couldn't expect us to do nothing for our favorite girl."

Tori accepted the envelope as both of her friends watched and waited for her to open it.

"I'm not going to be able to see anything up here," she muttered to herself. It was true. The Perry Farm was on the far side of town, part of the original township, and there wasn't another house for at least two miles on either side.

"Just tell her what it is," Cory demanded.

"Fine," Lia relented. "We got you a salon gift certificate. I saw you weren't on the schedule next Friday or Saturday, so I assume Rhett has something special planned for your birthday?"

"Yeah, there are some plans," she admitted. It wasn't that she didn't trust her friends. But no one really knew the details of her arrangement with Rhett, aside from the fact that an arrangement existed. It was just easier to keep things separate from their friends when they had already blurred so many lines together.

"'Kay, you can be like that if you want. There's enough on the gift certificate for a haircut and a bikini wax, in case that's required for your secret plans."

Tori felt her face flush in the dark. She gave Lia a playful shove, forgetting for a moment that they were sitting fifteen feet off the ground.

"Victoria! Did you really just try to push me off the damn roof?" Lia was already laughing as she returned Tori's shove and looped an arm through hers.

"You know we love you. And we both just want you to be happy." Lia's voice was lower now, her tone more serious. "Happy Birthday, Tor."

Tori felt the blush in her cheeks deepen. She was touched by their gift and equally appreciative that they didn't push for more details about her plans with Rhett. She really did have the best friends.

"Thanks, guys. Seriously. I love you both." Tori linked her other arm through Cory's as a quietness fell over the trio. Cory and Lia sipped their drinks while they all listened to the soft moos out in the pasture.

"Okay, enough birthday talk," Tori finally broke the silence. "I feel like the three of us haven't hung out in ages. I need all the updates. Should we start with who's sleeping with Jake?" She knew Cory and Lia had both been with the guy in some capacity over the last few months, but she had no idea where things stood between any of them now.

"No comment," Lia replied automatically.

"That's not fair, Lia! Don't put me on the spot," Cory protested. "Your Jake baggage is way heavier than my Jake baggage. Honestly, mine's barely baggage. It's a carry-on. No, no, wait. It's the personal item you get to bring on the plane in addition to the carry-on."

"You're ridiculous." Lia laughed, taking another sip of her drink. "There's just not that much to tell." She shrugged, finishing her beer and crushing the can flat.

"So no one's hanging out with Jake right now?" Tori clarified.

"I'm definitely not," Lia replied quickly before continuing. "We had a thing going on around the holidays. I blame all the twinkle lights and ornaments Mike hangs above the bar. Jake just looked extra yummy and very much available a few months ago. But he's a fuckboy, and he's always been a fuckboy. I told him I didn't see us going anywhere long-term and he bolted." There was a sadness to her explanation. Tori knew there had to be more to the story.

"Aurelia," she sighed, pulling her best friend into her for a side hug. She squeezed Lia's shoulder softly before turning to Cory.

"And what says you, Mr. Personal Item?" Tori felt Lia smirk against her shoulder.

"I mean, Jake's hot. He's loud, and he's charming, and we all know he's secretly rich. He's like the rowdier, bisexual version of Rhett." Cory gave Tori a pointed glance. "He's been flirting with me on and off since last summer, then he finally made a move in the walk-in last month."

"You guys! Sitting on the roof. Making out in the walk-in cooler at work. These are things we are seriously too old for now!" Tori admonished them.

"Oh, we did more than just make out," Cory confessed.

"Uh, yeah. I walked in on it. Can confirm," Lia added.

"So let me get this straight." Tori turned to Lia first. "You were hooking up with Jake and pushed him away, then you walked in on him and Cory hooking up? Why aren't you two upset with each other about this?" she demanded. She knew Lia and Cory were close, but she also recognized she was the glue that held their little group together. Had they just been pretending to get along for her sake?

"I literally had no idea about Jake and Lia's... thing... when I hooked up with him," Cory defended himself.

"I knew he didn't know—I purposely kept it from him." Lia sighed. "No hard feelings from me. You can have him if you want him, Cor."

"No way, baby girl. I saw your face when you walked in on us. Jake's officially off limits for me now."

Lia sighed again. "I should have known better. I don't know what I was expecting, but I sort of hoped he would try harder after I told him I didn't see us getting serious. I think I wanted him to fight me on it... to fight for me," she clarified.

"You deserve someone who'll fight for you, sweetie," Tori confirmed.

"It is what it is. It's not like I'm ever leaving this town." She spread her arms out around her, indicating the fields and the cow pasture that made up Perry Farm. "And you know Mike's gonna end up making Jake the manager of Oak Barrel once the renovations are done. He's not leaving this town anytime soon, either."

"I won't get in your way if you want to try again with him," Cory said softly, reaching behind Tori's back to squeeze Lia's shoulder.

"Ugh," Lia moaned, dropping her head into her hands. "We should have brought something stronger than beer up here."

Tori smiled at her friends, grateful that even if they were technically too old to be drinking on top of a pole barn, they still pulled out all the stops for her birthday. The gift certificate had been nice, but being with her two best friends tonight was the gift she loved the most.

Tori pulled into her driveway a few minutes after midnight and breathed a sigh of relief. Her birthday was officially over. She turned down the volume of the stereo to a whisper before pulling out her phone.

V: Just got home. Can you talk?

Her favorite picture of Rhett—the one she took at the cabin a few years ago where he was mid-laugh—illuminated the screen a few minutes later.

"Hello?"

"Hey, beautiful. Happy birthday," he greeted her.

"Hey, you. Thanks for calling. Are you busy right now?"

"Nope, just out at a bar with a few of my buddies from class. But I stepped outside to talk, so I'm all yours now. How was your day?"

"It was good, actually," she said. She sounded genuinely surprised, but it was the truth. As far as birthdays went, this one wasn't horrible, and she still had the concert to look forward to next weekend.

"Oh yeah? What'd you do?"

"Nothing too crazy. I slept in this morning since I don't have Friday classes. I had to work tonight, but Mike ordered a cake from Della's Bakery, so everyone stayed after close to celebrate. Jake got the go-ahead to serve shots. It was fun."

"That sounds fun. I wish I could have been there." She recognized the sincerity in his voice. They hadn't communicated as much as usual over the last several weeks. This was only the second time she'd even talked to him on the phone since he went back to school six weeks ago. The space was necessary. She knew it would make it easier for him to mend things with Chandler and get their arrangement back on track if she kept her distance.

She may have been the one trying to hold back, but she hadn't expected to ache for him the way she did. It was hard to name all the emotions that had been coming up lately when she let herself think about Rhett. There was longing and a bittersweet sadness. Then there was also a streak of jealousy that surprised her. She had never been jealous before: It didn't serve her. She needed Rhett to maintain a relationship with Chandler to allow *their* arrangement to work. Maybe she had just been trying to push him away a little too much lately. She would finally be with him in a week. It was probably okay to be more open and honest with him tonight.

"I wish you were here too..." she let her admission linger as she traced the buttons on her steering wheel.

"You do?"

"Yeah, I really do. I miss you, Rhett." She swallowed hard. She almost couldn't believe she said that out loud. But it was the truth. "Although I guess you were kind of here in a way. I'm pretty sure Mike doesn't know what my favorite cake is or where to get it," she explained with a hint of sarcasm.

"Busted, huh?" She heard his smile through the phone.

"Busted," Tori confirmed. "That was really sweet of you, Ev. And totally unnecessary since we get to celebrate together next weekend."

"I know, but I wanted to do something special for you today, beautiful. I hate that it's your birthday and I'm not there."

"It's fine, Rhett. Really. I'm excited about our plans next weekend. It can be my birthday then, too, if it makes you feel better."

"Oh, you better believe I'm going to act like it's your birthday all weekend long. You, me, Karta Stella, and the cabin? It's about to be the best birthday weekend ever." Warmth spread through her limbs as she thought about all the ways they would get to celebrate when they were finally reunited. His promise galvanized her.

"Hey, I just noticed it's past midnight. Did you just get home?" Rhett's question interrupted her thoughts.

"Oh, yeah. I didn't realize it was that late either until I texted you. After we closed, I went out to the farm with Cory and Lia. They drank, I froze my ass off, but all in all, it was a good night."

"That's awesome, V. I'm glad you got to do something fun. I promise you next weekend is going to be epic. You're gonna be feeling allll the birthday love."

"Oh, I fully expect to be feeling all the love, Wheeler. We're staying at the cabin for the whole weekend, right?" she verified, a hefty dose of hopefulness behind her teasing tone. "I'm off Friday and Saturday, then I don't have to work until the afternoon shift on Sunday."

"Yes. You and me, beautiful, just the two of us at the cabin."

"It sounds perfect." She sighed.

"Hey."

"Yeah?"

"I really do wish I was there right now, V."

Tori bit down on her bottom lip. This would usually be the moment when she reminded him that their arrangement didn't allow for thoughts like that. But for some reason unbeknownst to her, her guard was down tonight. She didn't want to push him away. Maybe it was the nostalgia and slight dread of ticking off another year of her 20s. Or maybe it was the self-imposed distance she had insisted they maintain over the last several weeks.

The sentiment of what she said next didn't surprise her, but the fact that she actually said it to him did. "I really wish you were here, too, Rhett. Maybe next year we..."

A cacophony of sound came through the line then, almost like someone had turned up the volume in a small room. A peel of laughter came through the phone. The high-pitched noises definitely belonged to a woman, and Tori didn't need more than one guess to identify the source. She cringed as she thought about Chandler finding Rhett on the phone with her.

"Shit... hold on a second," he muttered, all but confirming her suspicions.

The swell of emotions she felt earlier started to crest to the surface again, this time led by the sharp pangs of jealousy. But this time she wasn't interested in exploring them; she was only interested in shoving them back down.

"No worries. I'll see you next Friday, Everhett," she said coolly. She ended the call before he even had a chance to say goodbye. She turned her car off and sat quietly, trying to make sense of her reaction. Another minute passed before her phone vibrated in her lap.

Ev: I miss you, beautiful. So damn much. I can't wait to see you. I'll be home soon.

She read his text again, memorizing the way it landed in her mind. She almost let herself feel the depth of his words, to unleash the wave of emotions she was trying so hard to temper. But then she reminded herself that Rhett probably had to delete the text immediately after sending it. That was all she needed to snap back to reality. Longing and jealousy still simmered below the surface, but they were no match for her resolve.

CHAPTER 17

Tori

Tori sat on her front stoop and checked her phone for the hundredth time that day. Rhett wasn't late, and she knew he couldn't control traffic on I-71 on a Friday afternoon. Still, her body was humming with anticipation.

They needed to get on the road soon. She wanted to leave before her dad got home and started peppering them with questions. He knew enough about their plans: She'd be with Rhett, and they'd be gone until Sunday. The fridge was stocked, and he was in charge of Penny.

She had spent the day prepping and picking up food for the cabin. She treated herself to a bikini wax and a haircut with the birthday gift certificate Cory and Lia gave her, then she made a baked pasta dish for her dad to eat all weekend. She packed and repacked her bag, obsessing over what she would need.

Much to her annoyance, Tori felt anxious about the next few days. She had spent countless weekends with Rhett. There was no reason to be this keyed up about seeing him. She ran her hands through her freshly cut and styled hair, focusing on how the straightened ends felt like silk between her fingers.

She heard the Prelude coasting down Sunset Drive before she could see it. The excitement running through her body cranked up another ten notches, her nerves on fire as she watched the red two-door car pull into the driveway.

She practically ran over to him before he could even put the car in park. *You have no chill today*, she scolded herself. She reached for his door handle as he unbuckled his seat belt.

Rhett looked up at her and grinned. He had the best smile. She loved the way his eyes lit up, the way his whole body looked excited to see her. He gracefully lifted himself out of the car, then his arms were around her.

"Happy birthday, beautiful," he whispered into her hair, pulling her in tight against his hard chest. She felt him nuzzle her neck and inhale. She wrapped her arms around him and squeezed in reply, melting into the solidness of the man standing before her.

"Shit, I missed you," he exhaled, working his hand into the hair at the nape of her neck. Tori stilled, relishing the feeling of being in his arms, but still acutely aware of their surroundings as she realized how easy it would be for Rhett to tilt her head up and kiss her.

"Hey, relax. You're good," he responded to the tightness in her body. How did he always know what she was thinking before she even spoke the words to him? "I know better than to try and kiss you out here for all the neighbors to see." He gave her a final squeeze before letting go. "But you know I would if I could," he admitted, his voice serious as he locked eyes on her.

"I missed you so much," she confessed, admitting out loud just how badly she had been aching for this reunion.

"Oh yeah? You can show me how much later," Rhett responded with a wink, wrapping his arm around her shoulders. *What twenty-four-year-old guy actually winks and gets away with it*?

"Everything here going with us?" he asked as he eyed the bags on the porch.

"Yep. Two bags of groceries, that case of water bottles, the cooler, and my bag," she confirmed, listing off everything she had packed for the weekend. "I've got the tickets in my purse," she added, snagging her crossbody from the front stoop.

Together they carried everything to the Prelude, and Rhett did a bit of trunk Tetris to make it all fit amongst the two large bags he had packed for himself.

"Geez, do you think we're going on a cross-country trip, Wheeler?" She scoffed at the sight of his two duffel bags.

"Can it, V. I had to pack for this weekend *and* for my trip with Jake, remember?" he said as he closed the trunk.

Tori rolled her eyes. "Oh, believe me. Every person in Hampton, Ohio knows about your Spring Break Bros Trip with Jake. The guy hasn't shut up about it over the last six weeks."

"Typical Jake. He's gonna have to wait his turn. I've got plans with my girl this weekend."

Tori bit down on her bottom lip and held back a little squeal of excitement. She wasn't sure what to make of all the joy and excitement she was feeling. Nothing had technically changed. But there was a barrier that had broken down when Rhett came home in February. She wanted him more now than ever, physically and emotionally. She planned to take full advantage of their time together this weekend, hoping to fill the empty chasm inside her that was much deeper than she cared to admit. She needed to get her fill now before he left for good.

"You ready for this, beautiful?" Rhett asked before climbing into the Prelude.

"More than ready," she responded without hesitation.

Once they were on the road, Tori reached over and laced her fingers with his, smiling and stealing side glances as she synced up her phone with the Bluetooth head unit.

"This is a seriously good playlist, V," he praised her as the next song began. She had arranged three hours of music for their drive, including lots of Karta Stella, plus some of their other favorites from high school, like Jimmy Eat World, Incubus, and Radiohead.

"Wow, thank you." She grinned at him, the proximity of their bodies in the small car top of mind. "That means a lot coming from a music snob like you."

"I'm not a music snob!"

"Ha! Don't even try to deny it." Tori rolled her eyes and readjusted herself in the bucket seat. "We left your prom early because you hated the DJ so much," she reminded him, raising her eyebrows for emphasis.

"That DJ played two Bieber songs in a row followed by a Nickeback-Pitbull remix, Tori. But it's sweet if you think that's why we left prom earlier than everyone else." He snickered, his tone shifting as he not-so-subtly adjusted himself in his seat.

The vibe in the car felt heavier after his admission. Tori smiled as she turned to Rhett and took him in. If she thought her body was humming in anticipation earlier, it was practically screaming at her now.

He looks so good, she thought to herself as she assessed his profile and drank him in. He had one hand on the wheel, and she watched him drag the other hand through his dark, wavy hair. He was wearing a fitted navy zip-up made of some sort of shiny moisture wicking fabric. The zipper was low enough that she could see the deep hollow at the base of his throat and just the start of the sharp edges of his collarbones. He was freshly shaven, his jawline smooth and supple.

She felt her breathing pick up just a bit as she let her mind start thinking about all the dirty, sexy things they were going to do this weekend. Six weeks apart was way too long. Tori ran her hands up and down the slick fabric of her faux leather leggings to stop herself from reaching over and touching him.

"What's wrong?" Rhett probed. He was so attuned to her; she couldn't even have a few naughty thoughts without him noticing.

"Nothing!" she insisted too quickly. "Just admiring the view..."

"Tori."

Her name came out low and gruff: a warning. She knew she was busted. She clamped her hands down in her lap once she heard the sound of her name on his lips. She watched as Rhett shifted in his seat again, groaning from the lack of space to stretch out and properly adjust himself.

She couldn't resist glancing down at his pants. Yep, he was definitely hard. She bit down on her bottom lip to distract herself from trying to do anything else with her mouth. She couldn't wait to get to the venue and be able to properly greet him. To kiss him. To push her ass into his erection. To run her fingers through his hair and along his waistband, to...

"Cut it out, V," he chided, shooting her a sharp side glance before turning his eyes back to the road. "We are not getting pulled over on the turnpike for indecent exposure, and I am determined to get you to this concert on time."

"Sheesh, Wheeler. Lighten up. I was just looking," she replied sweetly, resting her left hand on the center console.

"No. You were looking *and* thinking. I know how your mind works, woman."

She kept her gaze on him as he focused on the road.

"Tori!" He sounded equal parts despondent and amused. "Please don't look at me like that," he begged. He reached down, picked up her hand, and squeezed it.

She sighed and set her gaze back on the road. There would be plenty of time to do more than just think about touching him this weekend.

"Tell me about school," he inquired, obviously trying to change the subject and shift the mood in the car. "How did your portfolio review go?"

"It was fine," she responded, emotionless.

"Just fine?" he pushed back.

"Yeah, just fine. I mean, I passed. I've got enough credits now to be considered a senior, so this was the review where I had to finalize my degree path," she explained. "I've known since day one that I was going to get a BA in Graphic Design. That's why I picked Holt State in the first place."

"But?" Rhett added, assuming correctly that there was more to the story.

"But my advisor laid it on thick trying to convince me to go for the Bachelor of Fine Arts degree instead," she huffed.

"And that's bad because..."

She realized she was making him work too hard for this conversation. She silently chastised herself for taking out her irritation on him. It wasn't Rhett's fault she was still reeling from her advising appointment earlier that week.

"Because the BFA requires 12 extra credit hours on top of the regular bachelor's degree requirements," Tori explained. "I've been taking two or three classes a semester for the last six years, Rhett. If I stick with the BA, I'll be able to finally graduate in two years."

"Is the BFA the better degree?" he asked gently.

"I mean, yeah, technically. It's more studio-focused, which is what my advisor was pushing for after he saw some of the paint pours I included in my portfolio. But twelve more credits means at least an extra year of school for me... an extra year of tuition and a whole extra year before I can graduate and get a job."

That was the heart of the issue. In a perfect, cancer-free world, Tori would have loved to go for the Fine Arts degree. But an extra year of school would set her back a full year, and that wasn't an option. She wasn't willing to sit there and explain to the head of the department why she needed a full-time job with health insurance as soon as possible, so she just kept insisting she was fine settling for the BA.

"Tori, you're an amazing artist. If you want to go for the BFA, an extra year isn't going to derail..."

"Nuh-uh. This isn't a discussion. I know exactly what I want and what I need to do to get there. You have to be on my side on this," she begged, the request coming out more desperate than she had intended.

Rhett was silent for three beats. She could see his jaw moving as he chewed on the inside of his cheek, a nervous tell that meant he was holding back or carefully choosing his words.

"You're right. I'm on your side," he vowed as he reached over to take her hand again. He brought her fingers to his lips in a quick kiss.

Annoyance crept up with his admission. Did he actually agree with her? Or was he simply agreeing with her as a means of self-preservation? Guilt replaced the annoyance as she recognized how easy it was to get him to go along with anything she said. So much of their relationship was dependent on Rhett just agreeing with her and following her lead. Most times she was grateful he let her call the shots, but today she was agitated that he didn't push back or put up a fight.

Tori exhaled and decided she didn't want to stress over something as silly as Rhett being agreeable to her wishes. The weekend held so much promise between the concert and their two uninterrupted nights alone at the cabin. She wasn't going to let anything come between them over the next few days.

Chapter 18

Rhett

"We have arrived," he whispered as he pulled into an empty spot and put the Prelude in park. The show was supposed to start at nine, but Rhett was confident Karta Stella wouldn't go on right away, so there was no rush to get inside. He hastily unbuckled his seatbelt, anxious and horny after the three-hour drive.

"Come here," he demanded, reaching across the center console of the car to pull Tori close. When their lips connected his whole body tingled in response. She tasted like peppermint and vanilla. The scent of rosemary filled his nose as he wove his hands through her hair. All his senses seemed to awaken when he kissed her. For the first time in six weeks, he finally felt alive.

Tori's lips parted for him on contact. She let out the softest sigh as she pushed deeper into the kiss. There was an urgency to her body's response to him. Her hands roamed all over his chest. She was everywhere, pulling his hair, scratching his back. His tongue explored her mouth, seeking her warmth as they got reacquainted.

He slid his hand down her thigh, feeling the slick, cool fabric of her shiny leggings under his palm. He grasped her hips but then pulled back to gauge what she wanted.

"What's wrong?" she asked, breathless. She continued to run her hands over his chest and arms, working him up with just the simplest of touches. He had missed her so much.

"I really want to make you feel good before we go in there," he proposed, raising his eyebrows suggestively. "But we have to make it work right here, and we've gotta be fast. You up for it?"

"Oh, hell yes," Tori responded enthusiastically, crawling over the center console to straddle his lap. He let out a husky laugh, excited that she was just as eager as he felt right now. He reached below his seat and pulled up on the manual adjustment bar to send the seat flying back as far as it could go.

Once they were situated, his hands were back in her hair, fisting handfuls of silky-smooth strands as he pulled her face down to his. He said they had to work fast, but Rhett took his time savoring her mouth. His tongue caressed hers at an unhurried pace. When he bit down on her bottom lip, she let out the sweetest moan.

"Rhett. Please," she begged. He felt her hips jet forward as she desperately tried to make contact between her center and his body.

"I've got you, beautiful," he responded, moving one hand down in search of the waistband of her leggings. He slipped his hand between their bodies and immediately connected with her clit. She moaned appreciatively when he found his target.

Shit. She wasn't wearing any underwear. He grunted in approval as her body responded to his touch. He moved his mouth to her neck, working his thumb in slow circles against her. She was so wet, so smooth, so perfect. He knew just where to touch her, just where to graze her to send shivers down her spine.

It didn't take long for Tori to start moving her hips against his hand, demanding more from him. She didn't need to ask twice—he was there. Rhett sunk two fingers into her, never breaking pace as he kept working her clit with his thumb.

"Oh my gosh, Rhett. Yes. Please don't stop," she whispered. Her whole body was draped over him as she continued to grind against his hand.

"I know you. I've got you," he reassured her, maintaining the rhythm he had created but using his other hand to pull her body even tighter—even deeper—over him.

After a few minutes of steady pressure, he felt her thighs tense up against his legs. She was close.

"Eyes on me, beautiful. I want to watch you fall apart," he whispered into her ear. He gently coaxed her head back so he could look into her eyes.

"Come for me," he demanded.

Tori collapsed against him as she spiraled over the edge. He watched her face contort with pleasure, her forehead slick against his with a light sheen of sweat. The windows were all fogged up around them. Rhett stayed unmoving as she recovered from her orgasm; he didn't want to do anything to interrupt her pleasure. Eventually she peeled her body off his and lifted her hips up so he could move his hand.

"That was unbelievable," she praised him, grinding her hips appreciatively in his lap and kissing him deeply. Rhett accepted her praise and her kisses, but after another minute, he reluctantly pulled away.

"You know I would stay in this car with you all night, V, but I promised you a show for your birthday, and I feel like we better get in there soon."

Tori sighed in protest. "To be continued?" she asked, running her hand along the seam of his jeans in the most tantalizing way.

"To be continued."

CHAPTER 19

Rhett

"Ahhhh, I am SO excited!" She looped her arm through his after they cleared security. Rhett smiled down at her, pulling her into his body and kissing her head. She was literally glowing. He loved seeing her this happy, knowing he was responsible for making her feel like this.

"Me too," he replied softly into her hair.

"Do you want to grab some food while I go to the bathroom? Then we can swap?" she suggested.

"Yeah, that's fine. What do you want?"

"I want a pretzel, and I think I might want a beer." Tori looked up at him earnestly. Rhett stilled, trying to keep the surprise from showing on his face. "Is that okay?"

Rhett knew her question was self-assuring rather than permission-seeking. Over the years, abstaining from alcohol had become a hallmark of health. She rarely drank in an effort to stave off the cancer she swore was lurking in her body. Turning down drinks gave her some semblance of control. He always offered her a drink when they were together anyways, but he never pushed it or teased her about turning down booze. He wouldn't dare.

"You got it, beautiful," he answered with a smile. Rhett tried not to look too pleased with himself as Tori left his side to find the end of the women's bathroom line. He couldn't help feeling a smug satisfaction that she was willing to loosen her grasp on her inhibitions tonight.

The line crept along as he perused the concession menu and the merch options.

"Hey, man," he started when it was finally his turn. "Can I get two pretzels, a dozen boneless buffalo wings, a Blue Moon tallboy, and two waters?" Rhett whipped out his card and paid for the food without paying attention to the total. He added a generous tip and signed the credit card slip before grabbing their food and shifting over to the merchandise counter.

There were several people working the booth. Rhett set his sights on the closest employee, a cute girl with an eyebrow piercing and a full sleeve inked on one of her slender arms. Rhett could feel her sizing him up as he leaned over the counter.

"Can I get the black one in a large please?" he asked as soon as he caught her eye.

"That's my favorite design," the girl said coyly, scanning the price tag and calculating his total.

"It's awesome," he agreed. "My girlfriend's going to love it." He offered her a polite smile, then inserted his card into the reader before accepting the shirt and slinging it over his shoulder.

Rhett managed to balance all the concessions as he made his way to an empty high-top table. He searched the crowd for Tori, a smile taking over his whole face when he spotted her in the sea of bodies.

"I feel way better," she declared, approaching the table and eyeing everything he had ordered. He couldn't help but notice how strikingly beautiful she looked—hair loose and straight, eyes shining brightly when she smiled. There was something different about her tonight: she was comfortable and at ease, which wasn't typical for Tori.

"Ohhh, is that for me?!" She reached for the T-shirt still slung over his shoulder.

"Well, I bought it in my size, but I'm prepared to share custody." The only time Tori wore T-shirts was when she was painting or sleeping anyways.

"Fine, but I call dibs on all major holidays," she joked, opening the shirt to inspect the design.

"I'm gonna go find the bathroom," he said, brushing his hand along her hip as he moved past her. *Damn, those leggings looked so hot on her ass.* "I'll be quick, but you should start eating," he suggested, checking the time on his phone.

Rhett kept his phone out as he made his way through the crowd. Somehow the line for the men's bathroom was longer than the women's line. He played with his phone as he waited. He realized he should check in with Chandler before the concert started, so he shot off a text.

Rhett: Hey Babe, I made it to Michigan. Just wanted to tell you goodnight now in case reception is spotty at the cabin. Tell your parents hi for me.

Instead of repocketing his phone, he sent off another text, this one to his sister.

Rhett: Have fun tomorrow, Maddie Girl!! You've got this.

He couldn't help but smile as he thought about how stoked his little sister had been when she called him earlier in the week to tell him she was named lacrosse team captain. He made a mental note to get her game schedule in his calendar so he could catch a few of her home games.

Rhett's phone vibrated in his hand as their replies came in.

Chandler: Have a great time. Tell your family I said hi, too!! Miss you already and can't wait to see you.

She signed her text with two hearts.

Maddie: Thanks, Bro! Team pics tomorrow then I'm having the girls over to the house for some hot tubbin' and sunroom fun.

She punctuated her response with champagne and beer emojis. He rolled his eyes but resisted lecturing her via text. Maddie was eighteen, and she was going to do what eighteen-year-olds do when they want to impress their friends. It's not like he had set the greatest example when he was her age.

Rhett: Just be safe, Maddie. Love you.

Fifteen minutes had passed by the time he finally made it through the restroom line and back to Tori.

"You were gone for SO. LONG!" she exclaimed, wrapping her arms around his neck as soon as he was within reach. Rhett glanced down at the table and noticed that she had eaten half of everything he ordered. He went to move the tallboy away from the edge of the table and noted that it was already half gone, too.

"Do you want another one of these before we go in?" he asked, lifting the can a few inches off the table. He kept his tone neutral, afraid to scare her off with any implied judgement.

"I'm not gonna get drunk at a concert, Everhett." He didn't miss the use of his full name, but he also didn't tease her that she already seemed well on her way.

"Of course you're not," he appeased her. "But this weekend is your birthday present, and I want you to have the best time possible. I've got you if you want another."

"Okay, okay, fine," she relented with a slight eye roll. She responded as if he had been trying to convince her for hours.

"Let me just eat this real quick." Rhett set to work downing the room-temperature wings and hardened pretzel. It didn't matter that the food was cold and subpar—he hadn't eaten since that morning, and he was starving. He polished off the makeshift dinner in less than five minutes, collected all their trash, then grabbed their water bottles before taking Tori's hand.

He expertly guided her through the crowd, refusing to drop her hand now that she had at least sixteen ounces of beer in her. Thankfully most everyone had already headed to their seats. There was only one person in front of them at the concessions booth.

"Two Blue Moons, please," he ordered, inserting his card again, grabbing the cans, and pivoting. "Come on, beautiful," he directed Tori, looking for the Door C Reserved Seating entrance per their tickets.

Rhett had studied the Reserved Seating section for a week before tickets went on sale. He had keyed in on a small section of seating on a V-shaped riser to the left of the stage. He was able to snag the two seats closest to the rail, and because of the unique shape of the section, there was no one else in front of them.

"Stop," Tori gushed when Rhett led her all the way to the front row. They weren't floor seats, but they were honestly better, because no one could stand up in front of them in this section.

"Good seats?" he asked, grinning.

"You shut your face right now, Everhett Wheeler!" she squealed. "Good seats? These are fantastic!! You are fantastic. I'm so excited I could rip your clothes off your body right here."

"I really want to see this show, but I'll take you up on that as soon as we get to the cabin later," he promised as they stepped out of the aisle and into their two-person row.

He glanced around the venue, taking in the electric buzz around him, feeling the energy of the crowd in his bones. The stage set consisted of a black velvet backdrop with stars cut out and illuminated with bright spotlights. The entire venue was cast in shadow with the house lights already dimmed. Anticipation started to build in Rhett's body. For the show. For the weekend. For her.

Tori leaned back against the railing instead of sitting down right away. She tipped the can of beer all the way up, indicating the first tallboy was a goner. She cast her eyes down at Rhett, winked, and tossed him the empty can.

He loved her like this, playful and carefree. Seeing Tori enjoying herself—not working, not stressing about money, not hyper-focused on her school work—just seeing her let loose and have fun was the most satisfying rush.

"Take my picture!" she exclaimed, pulling out her phone and unlocking it before handing it over. She backed up against the rail and turned toward him, smiling with the stage in the background.

Rhett hopped up out of his seat into the aisle. He took another two steps back, making sure he got the stage in the frame, following the rule of thirds just like Chandler taught him.

"Where are you going?!" she giggled as he backed up one more step. He hit the shutter mid-laugh, catching her in motion.

"Hold still," he admonished, taking another shot. "Okay, now look over to the side like someone just called your name." Tori turned her head but bit down on her bottom lip, no doubt trying to hold in a snicker.

"Beautiful. Okay, now look right at me, and do something sexy."

She turned her head again, locking eyes with him instead of looking into the camera. She bit down harder on her bottom lip and winked.

"Got it." Rhett groaned with satisfaction, swiping through the dozen options he had just taken. He quickly AirDropped them to his own phone. She looked gorgeous in every single picture, and now he was rocking a semi from one single wink.

"Okay, okay!" she exclaimed, waving her arm and motioning him back to her. "Get over here, you. Let's take a selfie."

He shifted his body behind her in front of the railing, resting his arm low around her hips. He held out her phone with his other hand, hitting the camera button once while he gazed at her, then again after he turned his head to smile directly into the camera.

He felt the roar of the crowd rise up around them. He spun them around so they could swap positions, Tori pushed up against the rail with Rhett standing directly behind her.

He took advantage of the darkness and let his mouth find her neck. His free hand caressed the small of her back before wrapping around her waist. She pushed her ass back into his groin, her body warm and relaxed in his arms. Rhett closed his eyes and sighed, committing the moment to memory. It was nights like tonight that kindled the smallest spark of hope, that let him burn for the possibility of a future with her.

"It's always been you," he whispered into her hair as the band hit the first notes of "Universal Color." He knew she couldn't hear him. That was okay for now if it meant he got to hold her like this for a little while longer.

CHAPTER 20

Rhett

Rhett pulled the car as close to the side door as possible before putting it in park.

"Tori," he whispered softly, reaching over to place his arm on her shoulder. "Hey, Tori, wake up. We're here." She had fallen asleep after the concert before they were even out of the parking garage, making the forty-five-minute drive to his family's cabin unexpectedly quiet, save for her soft snores.

The concert was amazing. It had exceeded his high expectations for Karta Stella, and the whole experience was even sweeter because he got to see them with Tori. She was wild during the show: singing, dancing, shimmying up against him, and even slipping her hand into his pants at one point. Thankfully they had the row to themselves.

A part of him felt sad that she wouldn't let herself do that more often. Seeing her so uninhibited tonight made him resent all the ways she closed herself off because of fear. Rhett hoped he could make that same carefree feeling last for her all weekend. She loved coming up to the cabin, and they hadn't been up here alone in over a year. He was so eager to please her—in more ways than one—over the next few days.

She didn't even flinch when he gently shook her shoulders again, so he gave up and decided to let her sleep while he got things setup. She wasn't going to be any help unloading the car anyways if she was groggy or still tipsy. He kept the Prelude running so she wouldn't get cold before he popped the trunk to unload the car.

He had used an app on his phone to turn on the heat in the cabin before they left the venue. He punched the code into the deadbolt keypad to unlock the side door, then turned the handle and stepped into one of his favorite places in the world.

He flicked on just one set of lights in the kitchen before setting down the first load from the trunk. He made a few trips back and forth from the car to the cabin. On the last trip, he spent a few extra minutes inside, putting away the groceries Tori had packed them and carrying their bags into the master bedroom.

He set the bags down and looked around the room. Rhett usually slept in one of the two basement bedrooms when he was here with his family, and Tori slept with Maddie in the loft just like they had done since they were little. She always ended up sneaking down to the basement with Rhett at some point during those trips, too. He smiled to himself as he thought about all the happy, sometimes naughty, memories this place held for them.

He backtracked into the kitchen, fetching a few water bottles from the fridge and searching the cupboards for ibuprofen. He wandered back into the bedroom and opened up her bag, looking for whatever she had packed to sleep in.

"Were you going to leave me out there in the Prelude all night?"

Rhett jumped at the sound of her voice. He turned around to see her slumped against the doorframe of the master bedroom, pouting. Her eyes were still half closed as she let out an exaggerated yawn. Her hair was a tangled mess, and she had already ditched her shoes and jacket.

"Hey! You're up. No, I tried to wake you, but you were sleeping so peacefully..." Rhett started to explain.

"I'm teasing you, Wheeler." She rolled her eyes, then shut them as another yawn surprised her.

"Are you okay sleeping in here?"

The master bedroom was spacious and airy, decorated with soft white and cream linens plus a few navy and gold accents, per his mom's usual interior design style. It was like a Pottery Barn catalog exploded inside a log cabin next to Lake Erie. There was a double-sided fireplace embedded in the wall so it could be enjoyed from the bedroom and from the master bathroom. In the morning, they would wake up to amazing lake views out of the floor-to-ceiling windows.

"Oh yeah." She practically skipped over to the king-sized canopy bed.

"There's water and painkillers on your side, V. You better drink up if you want to avoid a headache tomorrow," he suggested. "I'm going to go turn off the car and lock up."

"I already turned the car off," she said, tossing the keys of the Prelude onto the nightstand.

"Thanks, beautiful." He reached for his keys, still intent on making sure the car was actually off. He trusted her, but he didn't trust the two Blue Moons she had consumed. He just wanted to make sure everything was taken care of before they turned in.

She had, in fact, turned the car off. She had closed the trunk and locked it, too. Maybe she wasn't quite as far gone as he'd thought. Rhett moved quietly back through the cabin, checking to make sure the coffeemaker had water in it before flicking off the kitchen light and finally heading to their bedroom. His body was humming at the prospect of having her all to himself for the weekend.

When he walked back in, he found Tori already under the covers, spread out in the middle of the bed, sound asleep once again. He quietly peeled off his shirt and swapped his jeans for joggers before climbing in to join her. She had managed to change into their new Karta Stella shirt—and nothing else. He also noticed that she had drank half the water bottle he left out for her and that the pills were gone. *Good*, he thought to himself. Hopefully she wouldn't feel too crappy in the morning.

As excited as he had been to sleep with Tori tonight (especially after all her antics during the show), he felt just as satisfied to cuddle up beside her and actually sleep. He moved as quietly as he could toward the center of the bed, closing the space in an effort to eliminate the distance that they had used as a safeguard for the last six weeks.

He adjusted his pillow and buried his face in her hair, inhaling the scent of peppermint and rosemary that still lingered from her shampoo. He spent several seconds just breathing her in, letting himself pretend that this was his reality, that he could have her this way, every day, forevermore. He didn't want to think about all the reasons why this couldn't be his life. He wrapped one arm around her and closed his eyes.

Although she wasn't awake, she subconsciously responded to his touch, shifting her hips backward and pulling his arm tighter around her body. The way she melted into his form scratched all the happy places in his brain. This is all he wanted, for the rest of his life: to hold her, to love her. This is where she belonged.

"It's always been you," he divulged for the second time that night.

"It'll only ever be you," she replied so quietly he almost didn't hear it.

He bristled at her words, then froze in place. An inky darkness settled in his gut as anxiety flared in his body.

"Tori?" he whispered into the darkness. His question was met with silence.

"Tori?" he tried again, his voice a little louder and a little more desperate this time.

The Tori he knew wouldn't have let his words linger—hell, he wouldn't have even said them had he thought she was awake. She would have pushed back, snapped him back to reality, and put him in his place. He so rarely found a flaw in her emotional armor. Yet here she was, in his arms, not only allowing him to share the depth of his feelings, but also reciprocating his affection.

“Tori?” he tried one more time.

Her only response came in the form of a soft snore and the stirring of her hips into his crotch. Rhett sighed, accepting that she was really asleep, and that she may not have even been awake when she replied to him moments ago. The echo of her words would have to be enough for now.

Chapter 21

Tori

Tori kept her eyes closed as her body drifted awake. She took a deep breath, testing her resolve to actually wake up. She was curious as to how she would feel after indulging the way she did last night. A quick assessment told her she had fared better than expected. The only reminder she had drank a lot came from the urge to pee.

She slinked out of bed, trying not to wake up Rhett. He had spent so much time driving in the car yesterday, first from Easton to Hampton, then from Hampton to Ann Arbor, then finally from the concert to the cabin. He could use a little extra sleep. She made her way to the en suite, desperate to relieve herself.

Tori lingered at the sink as she washed her hands. When she scanned the countertop, she spotted her toothbrush and her toiletry bag. Rhett must have unpacked for her last night.

Last night.

There weren't even words to describe the bliss she had experienced last night. The set list was better than she could have even imagined. Feeling Rhett next to her, behind her, practically on top of her as they sang along to the songs they had been listening to together for a decade... she couldn't remember ever being happier than she was last night.

Last night would live in her memories as one of the best nights of her life. Rhett had thought of everything. He had planned the perfect night. She had felt so alive. To feel so loved, to feel so cared for... it was all deeper than she usually allowed. But something about the last six weeks without Rhett had left her empty. She wanted more of him.

She needed to feel more deeply connected to him. After years of pushing him away and keeping him at arm's length, all of a sudden she couldn't get enough.

Letting her hair down and letting herself feel everything was a new experience for Tori. She felt different this morning—lighter somehow. It was like being in the front row of a roller coaster, hovering at the top of the first hill. The accompanying stomach drop was inevitable, but the anticipation of free falling was worth it.

As amazing as last night had been, she had passed out on Rhett on the drive home. She remembered making her way into the cabin, and she remembered being excited to sleep in the huge master bedroom. Beyond that, she knew she hadn't been great company. She was determined to make it up to him this morning.

Tori brushed her teeth, then swiped on the vanilla peppermint lip balm she had stashed with her toiletry bag. She quickly ran a brush through her hair and pinched her cheeks for a bit of color.

She snuck out of the bathroom and climbed back into the canopy bed they had shared last night. She shimmied to the middle and cozied up to the gorgeous man she adored. He looked so peaceful as he slept: younger, despite the dark stubble along his jaw, and totally at ease. So often these days, Rhett looked like he was holding back or worrying about something whenever he looked at her. His words were reserved, his eyes filled with trepidation. She knew he was walking on eggshells. Things had nearly unraveled the last time they were together. She felt an acute heaviness from being the cause of his pain the last time he was home.

But there was no pain between them right now. In fact, there was nothing between them at all, except for the black Karta Stella T-shirt she had slept in last night and the light grey joggers that hung low on his hips.

Tori brushed her fingertips across the planes of his chest. She loved the hardness of his body, the way it contrasted against the gentleness of how he cared for her. She had had a front row seat to the way his form had grown and hardened over the years. As much as she adored the lanky Rhett she first fell in love with, as well as the athletic Rhett from high school, it was this version of him that fueled her fantasies now. He was all man with his defined features and easy confidence. He was just so sturdy and solid and strong.

She moved her hands from his chest to his stomach, delicately outlining the etches of his muscles. She knew he was a little ticklish there. His lips turned up in a smile before he opened his eyes.

"Good morning, beautiful," he greeted her, his voice still heavy with sleep.

"Oh, did I wake you?" Tori asked innocently, placing both hands against his stomach as she hooked a leg around his lower body. She felt his erection through his joggers against her inner thigh. *Good morning, indeed.* His chest lifted under her hands when he laughed.

"Come here, you," he said as he pulled her closer. His lips found hers as they embraced.

"Rhett," she tried to get his attention in between kisses. He was ravenous this morning, though, nipping and kissing her lips like she was the air he breathed.

"Everhett," she tried again. He didn't stop kissing her, but he moved lower to kiss along the column of her neck, freeing her to keep talking.

"I just wanted to tell you that last night was amazing. It was perfect. I loved it." Rhett stilled. She felt him exhale against her neck. She had uttered the "L" word without overthinking it. She was acutely aware of his reaction to hearing it. *I said what I said,* she thought to herself, not brave enough to repeat it. "Thank you for everything," she added instead. "I'm going to remember last night for the rest of my life."

"You're welcome, V. You know I just want to make you happy." His face was still buried in her neck, his voice muffled and laced with emotion. The stubble on his chin tickled her collarbone.

A pang of guilt burrowed into the pit of her stomach as Tori held back saying anything else. Instead she pushed her body into his, forcing him to roll onto his back. She hoisted herself up and straddled his lap as she ran her tongue across the hollow of his throat.

"I wish it could always be like this." He spoke so softly she didn't know if his admission was for her or more for himself. She was well-versed in shutting down Rhett's emotional advances. She knew she should cut him off at the pass right now, but for some reason, she couldn't bring herself to do it.

Her voice trembled with vulnerability when she finally replied. "I know. Me too," she admitted.

He pulled her head back gently, meeting her gaze and reaching up to brush her hair out of her face. Neither one of them dared push the other to say anything else. Instead they drank each other in, trapped in each other's orbit, their eyes admitting the depth of their truth.

Something unspoken passed between them. Suddenly it all felt like too much. She didn't want to take back what she said, but she couldn't allow herself to say anything else either. She couldn't let him fully scale the walls she'd carefully constructed over all these years. She couldn't let him hope.

She had to do something to prevent things from escalating. Tori found his lips again, pushing her tongue into his mouth like her life depended on it. She let out a soft moan when he responded, his tongue teasing and tasting her in return.

She reached down to press her hands along the hard lines of his chest. She loved the sharpness of his body, the crevices that felt so familiar yet still so exciting. She dug her nails into his shoulders, then lowered her head to kiss the side of his throat.

He let out the sexiest noise—a mix between a sigh and a grunt. His vocalization urged her to continue trailing kisses down his chest. He shifted beneath her, adjusting himself as she worked her way down his body.

She felt the tickle of a small patch of chest hair against her lips. She licked one of his nipples and glanced up to make eye contact with him. She knew before looking that his eyes would be on her. What she wasn't expecting was the depth of his gaze. There was heat, but his blue-grey eyes also sparkled with reverence. It was a look of lust mingled with adoration. That look sent a wave of wanting right down to her core. Her clit throbbed in response.

She continued to work her way down his body, running her teeth against the solid muscle under his stomach and hooking her fingers into the waistband of his sweatpants. He tasted like ocean air and something distinctly Rhett. He smelled intoxicatingly like home.

"You ready for me, Ev? I'm about to blow your mind," she promised as she clawed at the waistband of his pants. He moaned his approval, then lifted his hips to give her easier access. She peeled his pants all the way off and discarded them on the floor. She sat back on her knees and smiled at him before pulling off her own shirt.

Tori ran her hands along the crease of his hips, right where the top of his legs met his trim waist. She admired his length standing erect and glistening with a hint of precum on the crown. She wrapped one hand around his dick and offered him one more salacious smile.

She heard his breathing hitch as she took his penis into her mouth. She felt his hips buck slightly in encouragement. She knew the sensation of her lips sealed around him drove Rhett insane. That was the goal: pleasure him to the brink, distract him from everything besides her touch. She swirled her tongue around the tip, pressing back and forth against the ridge of his head. She took in as much of him as she could throat, using her hand to rub up and down the rest of his shaft. She hollowed her cheeks around him, moaning as his length hit the back of her throat. When she felt his hips begin to move in rhythm to her mouth she doubled down: sucking harder, stroking faster.

"Tori," he groaned in exertion. She knew he was holding back, trying to make it last. She could tell by the huskiness of his voice. "I'm not gonna last long after last night," he confessed, reaching down and gently brushing a section of hair from her face.

Tori couldn't help but smile as she thought back to last night. He had made her come hard in the car before the show. Then she had worked herself into a frenzy dancing and grinding up against him. She was so hot for him by the time they left the concert. With last night top of mind, she resumed her efforts to drive him to the edge now.

"Tori," he warned again, his voice low. "I want to be inside you," he begged.

She felt the same need, recognizing her desire to physically connect with him after all the weeks they had spent apart. She released his dick from her mouth, placing a soft kiss on the head before crawling up his body.

"I need to feel you inside me, too," she admitted, peppering his neck and jaw with kisses. Rhett found her lips and kissed her with a fervor she hadn't felt since they were in high school. He flipped her over on the mattress, pressing his body into her pelvis with need. Their frantic scramble to connect reminded her of how it had been years ago.

Her mental walk down memory lane was cut short when he shifted down the bed. Her entire body snapped to attention when she unexpectedly felt the flat of his tongue press against her opening.

"Are you with me, V?" he asked as he peered up at her from between her thighs. Of course he could tell when she wasn't completely in the moment. He knew her so damn well.

"I'm with you," she promised, arching her back to close the space between Rhett's mouth and her core. He didn't need any more encouragement. He licked her from her opening to her clit, switching from soft and slow to quick, targeted flicks of his tongue. His tongue dipped in and out of her at an unhurried pace. She felt his fingers spread her open, exposing her, teasing her with what was to come.

She had missed him so much over the last six weeks. Feeling his mouth rhythmically working her over now only deepened that longing. She shifted her hips against him, matching the pace he had set. She was practically fucking his face. With each movement, she felt her body climb higher. He moved his hands under her ass, propping her up and giving him even deeper access. She glanced down at his head buried between her thighs as the promise of release started to build.

"Rhett, please," she demanded.

"I know. I've got you, V." He lined himself up and entered her in one motion. He was right there. Connecting them. Filling her. Making her whole. Completing them. He stilled, holding the position and kissing her softly as she adjusted to his girth. Her whole body went lax as he made love to her mouth.

When he finally began to move, she couldn't resist circling her hips to meet him. Their lips melded together, their bodies pressed against each other in an effort to touch each other everywhere. There was a hunger between them that was so much more than physical desire.

Rhett adjusted the angle of his hips in an effort to please her. She let out an uninhibited moan of approval when he landed on his target. She was unbelievably wet, which was exacerbated by the warmth that was starting to pool in her core. She felt his thumb connect with her clit; she felt his mouth move over her nipple and bite down. She felt everything. She felt him everywhere. She wanted to be consumed by him. She wanted it all.

"Don't stop. I'm right there," she panted, desperate to hit the crest of her orgasm.

"Fuck, Tori. I'm right there with you." Rhett drove even deeper into her without breaking pace. He fucked her harder and pushed her higher until she toppled over the edge. She couldn't make sense of the noises coming out of her, of the waves of pleasure rolling through her. Her body spasmed as her vision blurred. Seconds later she heard him let go and felt the warmth of his release inside her. He continued to gently thrust a few more times before collapsing onto the bed. He caught himself on his forearms and pressed his forehead into hers.

She felt the sheen of sweat along his hairline as he bowed his forehead in reverence. The sincerity in his voice matched the love in his eyes. "V, that was everything. You're incredible."

"It's not me, it's us. We're incredible together," she corrected without censoring herself. Rhett said nothing, instead closing his eyes and sucking in a deep breath.

Tori still didn't know what had come over her. She couldn't blame anticipation or alcohol or music or anything else she had been using as an excuse over the last twenty-four hours to justify what she was doing right now. She felt herself opening to Rhett in a way she hadn't allowed in years. And even though he hadn't called her out yet, she was sure that he could feel it happening, too.

Chapter 22

Rhett

He fell back asleep after their morning escapades, only to wake up about an hour later. Sunshine filled every corner of the master bedroom, illuminating Tori's bare back as she slept beside him. He remained motionless on the pillow next to her, soaking in the warmth he felt because of the sun on his skin and the sight before his eyes.

Last night had been a blast. He couldn't remember a better time with Tori in the last several years. There wasn't one moment that defined the night for him—it was everything. Their sweet driveway reunion after six weeks apart. The drive to Michigan. The feeling of Tori's lips on his the moment he parked the car. The not-so-innocent parking deck action before the show. The energy of the crowd's excitement all around them. Her singing, their dancing. The way she accepted his affection and even subconsciously reciprocated it last night.

He assumed last night was an anomaly: an emotionally charged night that she would be quick to move past in the light of a new day. And yet all the unspoken emotions from last night had carried over into this morning. He saw it in her gaze, he felt it in the softness of her body. He could sense it in the depth of her wanting when they'd made love that morning. She was unguarded. She was right there. And for the first time in six years, she wasn't pushing him away.

He didn't know how to handle this. Hell, he rarely knew how to handle things with her, instead relying on her to explicitly tell him how he was supposed to feel, act, and react in most scenarios. Should he try to question her about the apparent shift between them? Or would bringing it up only make her shut him out like usual?

Rhett raked his hand through his hair. He had been shut down so many damn times over the years. It was premature to assume that anything had changed between them. Tori would tell him if their arrangement was off or if she actually wanted something more. Wouldn't she?

He needed to physically move his body to make sense of all the thoughts swirling in his head. He snuck out of bed and quietly riffled through his bag, pulling out a pair of athletic shorts, a T-shirt, and a hoodie. He scooped up his running shoes and a pair of socks, then grabbed his phone and earbuds from the nightstand. He texted Tori in case she woke up while he was gone.

Ev: Going on a run. I'll make breakfast for us when I get back.

Rhett snagged a beanie from the pocket of his coat before heading out the door of the cabin.

He felt better after his run. He hadn't figured anything out or come to any revelations about what was going on between him and Tori, but just feeling the sun on his face had been cathartic. He had pushed himself for more than an hour, following the six-mile loop that jutted out along the lake before cutting back through the woods. He was dripping in sweat from his effort despite the fact that it was only in the high forties.

He entered the keypad code on the cabin door, turning the handle as quietly as possible in case Tori was still asleep. He was welcomed home by the warmth of the cabin and the smell of bacon.

His eyes scanned the kitchen, landing on Tori standing in front of the stove. He closed the door softly, not wanting to startle her. He watched her standing there, shifting her weight from hip to hip, wearing nothing but the black Karta Stella shirt he bought her last night.

"Hey, beautiful," he greeted as he kicked off his shoes at the door and pocketed his earbuds.

"How was your run?" Tori asked over the sizzle of the frying pan without turning around. She had either heard him come in or sensed his proximity.

"Cold," Rhett admitted, sauntering into the kitchen and wrapping his arms around her from behind. "And sweaty," he added, nuzzling his head down into her neck.

"Eww!! You're soaked!" she exclaimed as she tried to wiggle out of his arms. Rhett just held her tighter, laughing as he planted a loud kiss on the side of her face.

"How can you be so sweaty if it's cold outside?" she demanded, finally turning around to assess him. She had tongs in her hand, and a few pieces of hair had fallen out of her bun to frame her face. She looked so beautiful. Rhett's heart swelled with gratitude that he got to be at the cabin with her this weekend.

"I just ran six miles. Of course I'm sweaty," he defended himself, still smiling. "That smells awesome, by the way. But I was going to make *you* breakfast once I got back."

Tori shrugged. "I know. I saw your text. But I woke up hungry and figured you would be starving when you got back. You're not the only one who knows how to play house," she teased.

Playing house. Is that what they were doing this weekend? Rhett didn't have time to dwell on her choice of words. The weekend was already going too fast for his liking.

"How long until the food's ready?" he asked, lowering his head to hover just a few inches from her face.

"Ten-ish minutes?" Tori replied, reaching up to kiss him. She was acting like it was the most natural thing in the world for her to be in the kitchen making brunch, like they had an easy kind of love.

"I'm going to take a super quick shower then," he said, returning her kiss with another one, this one deeper, before gently swatting her on the ass and turning to head to the bathroom.

"Oh, you're gonna pay for that, Wheeler!" she called after him.

Rhett entered the master bathroom, adjusted the dual rain showerheads, and found a towel and washcloth under the sink.

He showered quickly, anxious to get back out to the kitchen. He really was hungry, his body craving sustenance almost as much as he was craving her. Running had cleared his mind enough to know that he didn't want to waste one more minute of the weekend worrying about where things stood between them.

Tori was just setting their plates on the table when he walked back into the kitchen. He quickly ran a hand through his still wet hair to work out the tangles as he walked past the kitchen island.

"Perfect timing." She flashed him a beaming smile as he approached the table. Rhett couldn't resist wrapping her into a hug and kissing her again. She let herself go soft in his arms. He could barely contain the grin that spread across his face as she returned his affection. This was all he ever wanted.

"Mmmmm," he hummed into her mouth. "This smells amazing."

They ate in comfortable silence for a few minutes, glancing up at each other every now and then and smiling.

He broke the silence first. "So, what are we doing today?"

Tori was quiet for a minute as she chewed. She gave him a sheepish smile before responding.

"I'm dreaming of taking a hot bath in the big tub," she confessed, "and I definitely want to go down to the lake at some point. Other than that, I just want to be with you."

Rhett stilled at the simplicity of her words. There were no teasing undertones, no sexual innuendos to distract him.

"That sounds perfect to me, V. I'll clean up so you can go take your bath." Rhett couldn't help but notice the slight tightness in his chest. He still couldn't wrap his mind around why she was acting so agreeable and docile. Why was this so easy? Why did they feel more like a real couple than they had felt in years?

He couldn't dwell on it. He wouldn't allow himself to forebode the joy of what could be, if only she'd let it be. They were here together now, and he was going to do everything in his power to make the most of it.

Chapter 23

Tori

"Hey, beautiful," Rhett greeted her as she stepped into the bedroom after her bath. He smiled as he tucked in the last corner of the duvet on the bed.

"Hi," she responded, pulling the oversized towel tighter around her body. For some reason, she felt more tense now than she had before the bath. She lingered near the bathroom door, scanning the room for her bag. She wished she would have taken her clothes into the bathroom with her. Now she had to strip down in front of him when she was already feeling unexpectedly vulnerable.

The trepidation in his voice interrupted her train of thought. "Everything okay, V?"

Tori nodded, then made the mistake of looking him in the eyes. *Damnit,* she scolded herself as she felt tears well up and spill over.

"Hey, don't cry. What's wrong?" he implored as he made his way over to meet her and folded her into a hug. She let him engulf her body in his arms, leaning into him with all her weight and forcing him to hold her up. A sob ripped through her, surprising them both.

"Tori," Rhett cautioned, genuine concern radiating off his body. "You're scaring me. Tell me what's wrong."

She sniffled and inhaled deeply, testing her lungs to make sure there weren't any more surprise sobs lingering below the surface.

"I don't even know. I was just thinking about... things... in the tub. About your graduation. About Virginia. About us."

She was telling him the truth. Why was she telling him the truth? She honestly had no idea where her candor was coming from today.

She knew Rhett would leave her alone if she told him to. But that was the problem: she didn't want him to leave her alone. Not now, and not ever if she was honest with herself.

"It's almost over," she sobbed into his chest. She couldn't control the tears that just kept coming.

Rhett stilled. She felt his body go rigid as his arms squeezed tighter around her. The energy shifted between them, and he sucked in a sharp inhale. She knew him well enough to know that a decision had just been made. He was bracing himself for something.

"It doesn't have to be almost over," he whispered. It was an offer and a suggestion and a hopeful prayer wrapped up in seven simple words.

She didn't know what to say. She knew what she wanted to say. She wanted this. She wanted him. But she wasn't allowed to feel this way. She was in no position to make a decision like this—a commitment like this—in her current state of mind. But she also couldn't bring herself to pull away and lose the possibility of what he was offering right now.

"Kiss me," she finally demanded, yanking her hands out from under his shirt to pull his head down to meet her. She didn't care if Rhett knew she was using sex to distract them from the mounting tension that was threatening to spoil their carefully crafted arrangement. He would never call her out on it, because he wouldn't risk her pulling away for good.

She was desperate to snap out of this funk, to regain control of her emotions. She pressed her mouth to his with a ferocious hunger, frantic to fill the void of everything she stood to lose when he finally moved away.

Tori woke up with a start. She wasn't sure how long she'd been asleep, but it was long enough to feel the deep cast of grogginess that set in after a really good nap. She hadn't meant to fall asleep. She didn't want to waste any of the time they had left together at the cabin, but after her emotional breakdown—and the way Rhett comforted her and made love to her and held her—she was wiped out.

Her exhaustion had been mounting for a while. She had been anxious for weeks leading up to this weekend. Then they stayed up late at the concert last night, and she drank those two beers. It made sense that she felt drained today.

"Hey," Rhett greeted her tentatively. He was sprawled out on the mattress next to her, lying on his back in just his boxers. He stretched out the arm closest to her, inviting her in.

Tori didn't say anything, but she shifted over to close the space between them. She curled her naked body into his side as he pulled her even closer. She relished the smell of his deodorant and the subtle musky scent lingering between them as she focused on him drawing little circles along her back. She let out a sigh and closed her eyes.

"I'm hungry," she confessed, eager to cut through all the heaviness of her breakdown. Rhett chuckled in response.

"Do you realize that this weekend has just been a lot of me feeding you and fucking you?" he asked before reaching down to tickle her side.

"Yeah, but those are two of your favorite pastimes, so I figured I was doing you a favor," she teased as she poked him in the stomach.

"You're not wrong." Rhett grinned as he freed his arm from under her body so he could use both hands to try and retaliate. She tried to fight back, but she was so much more ticklish than he was. It didn't help that his stomach and his arms were covered in lean muscle, creating an impenetrable armor against any sneak attacks.

"Okay, okay! ENOUGH!" she exclaimed before scouting out of bed. "I'll just starve if you don't want to feed me."

Rhett loved taking care of her, so although her words were spoken in jest, she knew they'd hit the mark. She rummaged through her bag and pulled out clean underwear, a pair of black leggings, her very best bra, and a tank top. She dressed in silence, facing the windows, acutely aware he was watching her from the bed.

She turned around to confirm her suspicions. *Shit.* Not only had she caught him looking, she also caught that look of adoration and devotion again. She knew that hazy look in his eyes, and she knew where it often lead.

"Look alive, Wheeler!" she snapped, borrowing an overused phrase they had both heard Mike shout hundreds of times in the kitchen at Clinton's. "I was serious about needing to eat." She raised an eyebrow for emphasis.

"I know you were," he responded sheepishly. "I was just teasing you, beautiful." Tori rolled her eyes. Of course she knew he was teasing. She started to circle the bed and make her way to the kitchen, but not before grabbing one of his sweatshirts and pulling it over her head.

"I brought a frozen pizza. Want to have that?" Now it was Rhett's turn to roll his eyes in response to her suggestion.

"Yeah, I know what you brought, V. Who do you think unloaded the car and unpacked all the groceries?"

"Oh, yeah. Thanks again for everything last night, Ev. For planning it. For taking care of me." She made her way over to hug him. Rhett sat up and draped his legs over the edge of the bed, spreading them wide to make room for her. "I'm so glad we got to do this."

He cupped her face in his hands before responding, "It really was an amazing night. You don't need to thank me, though. You know I love taking care of you."

It would be easy and expected for her to pull away from him right now—to make a sarcastic comment, crack a joke, or even scold him for using the "L" word in that context—but she didn't want to employ any of her tried and true defense mechanisms. Not here. Not now.

Instead she just let him hold her between his legs, his thumbs brushing over her cheeks in adoration. Neither of them said anything for a few breaths. It was Rhett who eventually broke the silence.

"You know I'll always do that for you, Tori. I will always take care of you if you let me." He let the statement stand alone for a moment before continuing, "Anytime you want to go out, or have a few drinks..."

"No way," she cut him off, pulling back to look him in the eye now that she knew the context of his offer. "I drank enough last night for the whole year, maybe for the whole decade."

He looked pained at her rejection, but he recovered quickly. He ran his hands up and down the arms of her sweatshirt and gave her a slight smile that didn't reach his eyes.

"I'm just offering, beautiful. We had so much fun last night. It wouldn't be the worst thing in the world if you wanted to do it again," he tried.

"I know we had fun last night, but that's not happening again anytime soon. I just can't be reckless," she confessed. "You know that, and you know why. I don't want to do anything to speed up the inevitable." Her words were heavy between them: a dash of reality cutting through the unbridled joy of the last two days. A reminder of all the reasons why she was determined to let him go.

Rhett didn't say anything right away. He held her at arm's length, pensively stroking up and down her arms as his eyes searched her face for something.

"I know," he finally relented. His words carried enough weight that she knew he understood the subtext of her defensiveness. She exhaled, grateful that he wasn't going to push her.

"When's your next scan?" he asked quietly.

"Last week of April," she responded automatically.

He nodded, accepting that the conversation was over. She knew he'd text her sometime next week to get the exact date and time, and she knew he'd be home for the appointment. He had driven her to her very first scans when she was sixteen years old, and he'd been with her for every one since. He knew how the anxiety of each appointment weighed on her, rolling in like the menacing clouds of an afternoon thunderstorm. The week before each round of tests—and the days afterwards as she waited for her results—felt unbearably heavy. He was the bright spot she could count on during what was always a tumultuous few weeks.

She never explicitly asked Rhett to come home for her scans, but she always scheduled the appointments on Friday afternoons or Monday mornings, and he always made a point of conveniently being home in Hampton those same weekends. It was an unspoken promise they shared: A way for him to be there for her without her feeling like she was asking too much. A way for him to love her without her feeling like she was giving him any hope for the future.

Chapter 24

Rhett

"Oh my gosh, it looks like Maddie is having *fun* at home," Tori gushed as she reached across the island for another piece of pizza. "Look at these," she insisted, passing her phone across the counter.

Rhett quickly swiped through several pictures on Instagram of his sister and her teammates posing in their Hampton Lacrosse uniforms in front of their parents' house. He zoomed in on the last picture: a selfie of Maddie and two of her friends with their Gatorade sports bottles held out.

He shook his head in disapproval and checked the clock on the stove to confirm it was only a little after six p.m. "It looks like they're starting early tonight. Damn Gatorade bottles," he muttered under his breath.

"And where do you think she learned that trick, Everhett?" she taunted him. He just shook his head again and smiled at her from across the kitchen island.

"I honestly think you get as much credit for that lesson as I do. You were her babysitter, after all," he stated matter-of-factly. "And unlike Maddie Girl, we were younger than eighteen when we started helping ourselves to my dad's bar stash."

Tori grimaced at his recollection. "We were bad," she deadpanned.

"We were so bad," he replied with a flirtatious edge to his voice.

"But I wouldn't change a thing about it." Her words carried a level of sincerity that he wasn't expecting. Sincerity, nostalgia, and a little sadness, too. As much as he loved to reminisce about their high school antics, it was hard to talk about that time without getting into the details of their breakup before college.

Not wanting to taint the moment, he swiftly changed the subject. "I have an idea," he declared, pulling out his phone to check the Weather app. "If we head out right now, we can make it down to the swing for sunset."

"Ohhh yes! Good thinking. Let's go." Tori bit off one more mouthful of pizza before hopping off the bar stool.

He reached for her hand as they walked out the door. She easily accepted, letting him lead her out of the cabin and down toward the water.

The lakeshore was less than fifty yards away from the cabin. There was a pebble path that led from the house right down to the water of Lake Erie. Thankfully the evening air was warmer than it should be for March in Michigan. He had forgotten to grab a layer in his hurry to get her out of the house.

"Did you come down here on your run?" she asked, dropping his hand so she could link her arm through his as they walked side by side.

"I did. I ran along the lakeshore for almost three miles before cutting through to the trail in the woods and circling back."

Tori slipped her phone out of her pocket and slowed her pace. They stopped walking so she could take a few pictures of the hazy March clouds hovering low over the lake. He felt the pebbles through the soles of his shoes as he waited for her to line up her shot.

"I'm sort of jealous," she admitted. "Not about the running, but I wish I would have come down here earlier today. This is one of my favorite places in the world." She sighed, pulling his arm tighter against hers as they continued down the path.

"We'll come back down tomorrow morning as soon as we wake up," Rhett vowed, quick, as always, to try and please her any way he could. She squeezed his bicep in response.

"Do you think I should post this?" She held up her phone to show him one of the pictures she had just taken. The way the clouds reflected in the water during golden hour made the lake look ethereal.

He squinted to look closer at how she had framed the picture. "Yeah, definitely. That's an awesome shot."

They veered off the pebble path toward the wooden bench swing that sat just a few feet from the edge of the water. Rhett let Tori sit down first, then he positioned his body at an angle beside her so she could lean back on him. She finished adding a few hashtags to her post, then slid her phone back into the pouch pocket of his hoodie.

"Damn I love it here." Tori sighed, dropping her head back to peer up at him. Rhett smiled down at her, brushing the hair out of her face. Her eyes stayed locked on him as he continued to play with her hair. Between the familiarity of the bench swing and the sound of the soft swells of water lapping onto the shore, a sense of calm settled around them. This was their spot. And for the first time in a long time, this was them. They weren't sneaking around. They weren't holding back. There were no gears turning, no tempering of their chemistry, no roles to play. Rhett felt more present and in his own body than he had in a very long time.

The difference was Tori. She hadn't made any effort to push him away over the last twenty-four hours. More than that, she had shocked him over and over again by her openness this weekend, by her willingness to connect. For the first time in a long time, she had let him in and let him stay.

"You're different this weekend, V." He tried so hard not to put any sort of infliction to his tone.

"I know," she admitted, gazing up at him. "I *feel* different." She ran her hand down the side of his jaw. She let one finger caress his lower lip, teasing him. Her touch was tender yet brazen.

"Wait, could I still be drunk from last night?!" she mocked, lightening the mood as quickly as she had intensified it.

Rhett shook his head and smirked before placing his arm across the front of her shoulders.

"I mean it," he tried again. "This weekend just feels... different." He let the word linger between them, refusing to fill in the blanks for her. Her response would be the greatest tell.

She stilled in his arms, her face turned toward the orange and purple clouds reflected in the water. He twirled a strand of her hair but didn't say anything else. He wanted to give her time to formulate a response. He wasn't going to force the conversation, as desperate as he was to have it.

"I know. I feel it, too. I don't know what it is. I don't know why I can't fight it. But I feel it, too."

Rhett's heart practically leapt out of his chest at her admission. If things *felt* different, did that mean things were different? A rush of fear coursed through his veins. A warning bell was tolling deep inside him. The uncomfortable tightness of his throat was almost enough to stop him from pushing any further, but he knew he would never forgive himself if he didn't at least try.

"Tori?" he asked, unsure of what he was even going to say next.

"Yeah?" She looked up at him again, this time reaching all the way up to run her fingers through his hair. She kept her arm raised, resting her hand on the nape of his neck. Her touch gave him the courage to continue.

"Do you think we can try this for real?" he whispered with unabashed hope.

A pause.

A breath.

And then, a response.

"Try..."

"Us. Try us. Do you think we could try being together again?" he clarified.

Tori said nothing. Rhett could feel his lungs protesting from the surplus of carbon dioxide, but he couldn't bring himself to exhale. Every moment that she didn't respond was weighed down by equal parts torture and anticipation. She hadn't given him any indication this was going to end well... but she hadn't said no yet, either.

"I don't even know what that would look like."

Her response was timid and reserved, but it wasn't a no.

His mind faltered. His heart skipped a beat. He was desperate to find the right words.

"It would look just like this, V," he vowed, panic-stricken as he waded into uncharted territory. He hadn't expected to have this conversation this weekend. For a guy who loved a plan, he felt foolishly unprepared.

"It would look like this, but with everything out in the open. We would be official, and we would be exclusive," he added, letting the last word linger for emphasis. "It would be me kissing you in public. It would be you telling your dad that I'm your boyfriend. It would be true and beautiful and real. It would be us just being us, now and when I move to Virginia, and I think it would honestly be easier than what we've been doing for the last three years."

Another pause.

Another breath.

"It would be so complicated to explain..."

Holy shit. It still wasn't a no.

"Yeah, you're not wrong. But I don't think it would be unexpected by anyone, and who cares what they think anyways?" Rhett sat up straighter. He was desperate to make her feel his sincerity, for her to take this seriously and give it her full consideration. "I know what I want. I know what I'm asking. I know you're scared. But I swear I'll be there for you and follow your lead. We don't have to figure it all out tonight. If you're telling me there's a real chance for you and me, if there's a glimmer of hope that we could be together for real, that's what I want. I want you, Tori."

Rhett let the offer linger between them. A shiver rippled through his body. He wasn't cold. In fact, he could feel the flush rising in his face as he waited for her to respond. He felt like he had just ran another six miles. His heart was beating too fast. He took a steadying breath, willing his body to release some of the fear, desire, and adrenaline blasting through his veins.

They had been here before. In fact, they had been here (or at least in some twisted version of here) just six weeks ago. Rhett propositioning her, wanting all of her; Tori denying him, keeping him at arm's length. Rhett eventually accepting—settling, really—for whatever she was willing to give him, per usual. He knew this song and dance all too well, but this whole weekend felt different. Tori had just admitted it felt different for her, too. Was there hope that the conversation they seemed to have over and over again would end differently tonight?

Her silence fed the anxiety chewing into his confidence. And yet... she still hadn't shot him down.

"Just say yes!" he exclaimed, frustrated and frantic. They were so close.

"Rhett, I can't let..."

"Fine. Don't say yes," he interrupted her. "Not tonight, at least. We don't have to figure it all out tonight. Tori, please. Just tell me that it's not no," he begged.

She sat up on the bench swing and turned around to face him. Was this it? Was this how it ended?

Inhaling, she used both hands to tuck her hair behind her ears.

"It's not no."

It's not no.

"Tori," he breathed, reaching out and pulling her into his arms. He couldn't form thoughts, let alone full sentences. He pulled back slightly, seeking reassurance in her face that this was really, truly happening.

"It's not no?" he questioned again, giving her a chance to confirm or deny where things stood between them.

She peered up at him and bit down on her lower lip. Then a small smile crept onto her face.

"It's not no," she confirmed, nodding as she spoke the three words that were quickly becoming the sweetest thing she had ever said to him. That was all the confirmation he needed.

He bowed his head to kiss her, seeking assurance that this was real. That he wasn't dreaming. She responded immediately, opening her mouth at the urging of his tongue and letting out a soft whimper against his mouth.

He had thought last night had been one of the best nights of his entire life. And yet here they were, here she was, topping that experience and taking it all to the next level.

CHAPTER 25

Rhett

He woke up with Tori in his arms. *Right where she belongs*, he thought to himself as he reveled in the memories of last night. He laid perfectly still as not to wake her and stared at the ceiling fan hanging from the rafters of his family's cabin. He almost couldn't believe everything that had transpired between them this weekend. How had they gone from the relationship turmoil at the Ledges last month to Tori agreeing to be with him again last night?

A tightness found its way to Rhett's chest as he thought about all the things they needed to discuss. There was so much to figure out. He knew he would have to be the one to bring up most of it, and he knew he had to be strategic about it. He felt an uneasiness about trying to force Tori to figure things out too quickly, fearful she could still change her mind. But he also worried about leaving things undefined and falling back into old habits.

He took comfort in the fact that a lot of the logistics would just fall into place. They had already been doing long distance for the last several years. Hampton was twice as far from Norfolk as it was from Easton, but there were plenty of nonstop flights between Norfolk International and the local airports. It would be easy to fly home on the weekends and to fly Tori to him when her schedule allowed.

He knew they were going to talk about money, and he wasn't looking forward to that face off. He would be making a six-figure salary in a few months, and he had no student loans or debt to worry about. He knew she would still resist accepting financial help from him, at least at first. But if they were together, he was going to take care of her.

He wondered what he could get away with paying for without her putting up too much of a fight. He would cover all her travel expenses, of course. He chewed on the inside of his cheek as he considered that he could add her as an account holder on his credit card. If he asked her to use the card so that he earned points, she would probably be okay with that. Then she'd have the card with her at home in case of emergencies.

He could also get her and Paul both added on NorfolkStar's company cell phone plan. They would have to change their numbers, and Tori would be pissed to give up her 330 area code, but it didn't make sense for them to be on different networks.

He tried to rein in his racing thoughts. There was no longer an expiration date on their relationship. They had time to figure things out. He didn't have to figure everything out on his own, either. *Tori wants this, too.* Years of rejection had conditioned him to tread lightly, but he didn't have to worry about that anymore.

The first light of dawn was starting to creep into the room. He had only slept for a few hours, but he felt wide awake now. He decided to get up and start the coffee. He had promised Tori they would go down to the lake early this morning before they had to drive back to Hampton for her shift at Clinton's, and he intended to make good on that promise.

Rhett located and pulled on his joggers as quietly as possible. He padded over to the bathroom, feeling the weight of his phone in his pocket when he pushed down his pants to relieve himself.

He washed his hands, then pulled his phone out to check the time. He had four texts and three missed calls. His heart caught in his throat as he hit the Messages app and saw that they were all from his sister.

Shit. He and Tori had joked about all the trouble Maddie was apparently getting into last night, but things must have escalated. But why would she call him? She knew he wasn't anywhere near Hampton if she needed help.

The first text had come through at 11:06 p.m. last night:

Maddie: Hey, can you call me real quick?

Then again at 11:54 p.m.:

Maddie: I need to talk to you ASAP.

12:02 a.m.:

Maddie: Rhett, I think I messed up. Call me as soon as you see this.

Finally, 12:07 a.m.:

Maddie: RHETT. Answer your phone. I don't know what to do. It's about Chandler.

Chandler?

Rhett felt his shoulders tense as he reread the last message. He swallowed hard and shook his head, refusing to let the sight of his soon-to-be-ex-girlfriend's name make him panic.

Chandler had been the last thing on his mind this weekend. He had texted her from the concert venue on Friday, but that was the last time he'd talked to her. He'd told her that he didn't get reception at the cabin, so he assumed he was off the hook for messaging her again until he arrived back in Hampton.

Rhett steadied himself against the double vanity, then splashed water in his mouth from the sink.

"Get a grip, Wheeler," he muttered under his breath. There was no way Chandler (or anyone, for that matter) knew he was officially back with Tori. It had happened less than twelve hours ago. He was so keyed up from this weekend, he was letting his mind get ahead of itself.

Rhett reached for his phone again, this time looking at the timestamps of the missed calls from Maddie. 11:04 p.m. 12:05 a.m. The last one snapped his thoughts to attention: 6:42 a.m. Less than twenty minutes ago.

The panic started to rise in his chest again. Something had to be really wrong for Maddie to still be trying to call him this morning. He looked again to make sure he didn't have any other missed calls. There was nothing from Chandler, his parents, or any unknown numbers.

If Maddie had tried to call him this morning, he assumed she was already up or still up from last night. He walked over to the bathroom door and closed it, not wanting to disturb Tori. He sat on the edge of the tub before hitting his sister's name on the screen.

She picked up on the second ring.

"Hey, Maddie," he started, trying to keep his voice low even though the door was closed.

"Rhett," she sighed into the phone, "I think I messed up." Her voice was raspy in his ear. She was either still drunk, or she'd been up all night crying. He didn't know which scenario was worse.

"Hey hey," he tried to soothe her over the phone. "You're okay, Maddie Girl. Just tell me what's going on."

"I'm so, so sorry, Rhett," she cried into the phone.

Fuck. This couldn't be good.

"Maddie," he said her name sternly, trying to calm her down and steady himself for whatever was about to be revealed. "Tell me what's going on right now."

The line was silent for several beats. Rhett pulled the phone away from his ear to make sure the call was still connected.

"I'm so stupid..." she started again. She was audibly crying now.

What he had intended to sound like a sigh came out as more of a growl. She went silent on the other end of the line. If she didn't start talking, he was going to lose it.

"I posted pictures from my lacrosse party on Instagram last night." Rhett exhaled. He had seen the pictures, and now he at least had some context for what they were dealing with. She must have gotten busted for drinking with her teammates. Although that still didn't explain how Chandler was involved.

"I had a lot to drink," she confessed, calming Rhett's nerves that this wasn't really about him after all. Underage drinking and dodging trouble? That he could handle.

"I wasn't really thinking, Rhett. We took a lot of pictures outside the house, then there were a few in the sunroom, too."

"Yeah, I know, Maddie. I saw the pictures on Instagram last night." He didn't need a play-by-play of everything she had posted on social media for the world to see.

"Oh," she hiccupped. "So you already saw her comments?"

Rhett felt his spine stiffen. He didn't have to ask to know who she was talking about.

"Whose comments?" he implored anyway. He wouldn't believe it until he heard her say it.

"Chandler. Chandler's comments. First she asked if the pictures were from this weekend. Then she asked why I wasn't with you at the cabin." Maddie let out a soft sniffle.

"Hang on," he mumbled, pulling the phone away from his ear to open the Instagram app. He quickly searched for Maddie's username and clicked through to her profile.

It was right there on the screen. The pictures Maddie posted that he and Tori had looked at together last night. Then two separate comments Chandler had posted around ten p.m.

"Fuck," he muttered to himself before bringing the phone back to his ear.

"Rhett, it gets worse," she confessed. He balled his free hand into a fist. He calculatedly set his gaze on the cedarwood infrared sauna. That would cause the least amount of damage if he needed to punch something before this call was over.

"Spill it, Madison." He could hear the rage in his own voice, seething and desperate, but he was too focused on not hitting something to control his tone.

"She called me."

Rhett barked out a laugh. Ten seconds ago, he honestly couldn't imagine how the situation could get any worse, but she was right. This was worse.

"I shouldn't have answered. I didn't even mean to answer. But I was drunk, and it was late, and I panicked."

Rhett dragged his hand down across his face. He couldn't remember ever being this pissed at his little sister. She couldn't even claim ignorance. She was one of the few people who knew what Tori meant to him. She knew exactly what they were doing in Michigan this weekend.

"Tell me exactly what she said, Maddie. Word for word. I'm not fucking around here," he whispered into the phone. His voice was sinister and unfamiliar even to him.

Maddie hiccupped before she replied. "It started okay. She asked me about the team and told me congratulations for making captain. I tried not to say much because I was so afraid of saying the wrong thing. After a few minutes, she asked if I was already back from Michigan."

Maddie paused. Rhett held his breath.

"I told her I hadn't gone yet—that I was leaving tomorrow. Then she asked if you were already there. I didn't know what to say, Rhett. I told her I didn't know your exact plans for the weekend."

Rhett exhaled. This wasn't as bad as he had thought. If she had kept it ambiguous, he could easily smooth things over with Chandler.

"Then she asked me if I knew where Tori was this weekend."

"Goddamnit!" he barked into the phone. This was not okay. He was breathing heavier now, no doubt from holding his breath on and off for the last several minutes.

“I don’t remember what I said. I don’t think I actually said anything because she just kept talking. I didn’t even have a chance to respond.”

That sounded like Chandler. He had been at the receiving end of enough of her tangents to know it was hard to get a word in edgewise once she was on a roll.

“She said she saw a picture Tori had posted on Instagram, so she was just curious. She didn’t sound mad. She seemed composed and calm, actually.”

Rhett froze in place. The picture of the sunset last night. The picture Tori had taken just minutes before she agreed to be with him again. The picture he had encouraged her to post, even after she double-checked to make sure it was okay.

“How did it end, Maddie?” He felt like an ass for freaking out on his sister. This wasn’t her fault. He had no one to blame for this mess but himself.

“She said goodnight and hung up like it was no big deal. She’s never called me before, we’ve only ever texted, but she acted like we were friends catching up at eleven on a Saturday night. I tried to call you last night, Rhett. I tried to warn you...” She broke off into another sob.

“Shhh, hey, hey. Listen to me, Maddie. You’re okay. This isn’t your fault. I’m sorry I lost my cool. You didn’t do anything wrong,” he soothed her.

He dragged his hand through his hair and sat back down on the edge of the tub. From this angle, he could see Tori’s form through the double-sided glass fireplace. She was still lying in the bed they had shared all weekend, blissfully unaware of the mess that was unfolding.

“I’m so sorry.”

"I know. It's going to be okay." The reassurance was for her as much as it was for himself.

"What should I do if she calls again?"

Rhett considered his options. He didn't want his little sister stuck in the middle of this mess. This was his problem, and it was his responsibility to make it right.

"Just send her to voicemail. I'm going to call her later anyways. She won't bother you again," he stated with finality.

"Okay. I love you," Maddie sniffled.

"Love you, too, kiddo. I feel bad you had to deal with this, Maddie Girl. I'm sorry I didn't answer last night when you tried to call me."

"It's okay, Rhett," she responded, accepting his apology without reservation.

"No, it's not. But it's going to be. Go get some sleep," he instructed as he hung up the phone.

He lingered in the bathroom after ending the call and contemplated all the different ways he could proceed. Calling Chandler was out—the timing would be too suspicious. Texting her might be an option, albeit still risky. She would question why he was up so early on a Sunday.

Part of him was tempted to just say screw it and let it come undone however it was going to unravel. After last night, his relationship with Chandler was over anyways; she just didn't know it yet. But as tempting as it was, he couldn't let it happen like that. Although their relationship had always been surface-level, he still felt like he had to do right by Chandler. He wouldn't deny her the closure she deserved. His racing thoughts were interrupted when the phone vibrated in his hand.

He glanced down and nearly dropped the device when Chandler's picture illuminated the screen. Had he accidentally called her? No, that didn't make sense. Why would his phone be vibrating if he called her? She was calling him.

Problem solved. He was too relieved to even question why she was calling him so early. Chandler's impatience was about to take care of itself.

"Hello?" he asked as he brought the phone to his ear.

"Rhett!" She sounded genuinely surprised for someone who had initiated the phone call. "I was just trying to leave you a voicemail! I didn't realize you would answer. It's so good to hear your voice. Why are you up this early?"

He scrubbed his face with his free hand, trying to find his calm before he proceeded to do what he knew he was about to do.

"Yeah, I know it's early. I... I had some things to take care of this morning before my trip with Jake." Technically that wasn't a lie. "Look, Chandler, I'm glad you called."

"What sort of errands could you possibly be doing at seven a.m. on a Sunday?" Chandler interrupted him through the line. Her question came out huffy—he knew that tone. He mentally scrambled for an adequate response. *Shit.* He shouldn't have answered the phone without a plan.

"Jake had to go into Clinton's early this morning, so I figured I might as well make myself useful while he's at work."

"So you're in Hampton?"

He couldn't discern whether her question carried a weight to it or if he was just being paranoid.

"Well, not at this exact moment, but I will be later today." He maneuvered around the truth while still trying his best not to lie to her. Why was he trying to save face with Chandler anyways? It was over. He needed to tell her it was over.

But she was relentless. "So you'll be in Hampton later today?"

"Yes, babe," he replied out of habit. "I'll be in Hampton later today."

"Perfect. I gotta go, but I'll talk to you soon!!"

Chandler hung up the phone before he could respond. He felt blindsided by her call. He was relieved that it was over, minus the fact that they were technically still dating. That was okay for now—it's not like he wouldn't have to see her multiple times once he was back at school. They shared all the same friends, and they practically lived together.

He also felt a small wave of relief. It wasn't lost on him that breaking up with Chandler over the phone this morning might put a damper on the rest of the weekend with Tori. She had just finally agreed to not push him away less than twelve hours ago. How would she react if he dumped Chandler before she even woke up?

He knew he couldn't push for too much too soon when it came to Tori. This was it—this was everything he wanted, and the last time he was ever going to have to fight for it. He was determined to play his cards right.

He made sure his phone was on vibrate as he repocketed it and headed to the kitchen. He wanted to make this morning as memorable as possible before they had to go home. Coffee and a breakfast picnic down by the lake would be the perfect endcap to what was turning out to be the best weekend of his life.

--

"It's almost eleven thirty, Rhett. We have to get ready to go." Her words said one thing, but the little moan she just let out told him he better not pull away just yet as he continued to nuzzle into the sweet spot right below her ear.

They had spent the last several hours down by the lake. The grass had still been dewy when they first arrived. They cuddled on the swing and ate breakfast before spreading out their blanket on a little hill between the house and the shore.

"I know, I know. But I can't stop kissing you. You taste like cinnamon sugar. I want to lay here and kiss you by this lake for at least a few more hours."

"Yeah, well, you seem to have more time on your hands than me," Tori said as she placed her hands on either side of his face. He gave her one more kiss and reluctantly rolled to his side.

He hadn't known what to expect this morning, but nothing had changed since last night. She was still right there: so open to him and willing to commit. He hadn't bothered burdening her with any of the things he had been stressing about that morning. There would be time to talk about long distance and money and all the moving pieces later. For now, he wanted to honor the moment. To savor her softness. To revel in the new and improved definition of their relationship.

"Hey, whatcha thinking over there, Mr. Logistics? I see your wheels turning," she teased as she ruffled his hair. Of course she could tell when he dipped into planning mode. Rhett realized he was going to have to make a shift of his own: He needed to be more open with her now. There was no longer any reason to worry about saying too much or saying the wrong thing at the wrong time. He needed to give as good as he got in this new version of their relationship.

He smiled softly before responding. "Honestly? Everything. My mind has been racing since last night. Mostly I'm just trying to convince myself that this is real. That this is happening. That this—that us—isn't just all in my imagination."

"Oh, Rhett." His name was gentle on her lips, her eyes gleaming with sincerity and the faint traces of heartache. She leaned forward again and ran her hand down his jawline. "This is really happening. I know I said it wasn't a no last night, but that wasn't a fair response. It's not a no—it's a yes please. I know we have a lot to figure out, but

I'm in it. I'm with you." She pushed off his chest and sat up, gathering up the leftover food and their coffee mugs. "But we still have to go. Not even your love could save me from the wrath of Lia if I'm late for my shift."

He knew she was right about getting on the road soon. He shook out their picnic blanket before folding it, trying to hide how deeply her words had affected him. *It wasn't a no—it was a yes please.*

"Hey, do you have an alarm set or something?" Tori asked, cutting into his wandering thoughts. "I keep hearing a phone vibrate and thinking it's mine."

Rhett reached into his back pocket and held his breath, worried that Maddie or Chandler was trying to call him again. His worry turned to annoyance as he scrolled through the notifications on the screen. He had two texts and a whopping six missed calls from Jake, all within the last ten minutes.

"It's just Jake. He knows we're coming home today. I'm surprised he waited until after eleven to start harassing me." He blew out a long breath as he flashed the screen so she could see all the alerts.

"That's weird," she responded. "I was sure he was scheduled to work today."

Worry nudged Rhett's subconscious. "Huh. Yeah. I figured he would work all weekend, too, since we'll be in Buffalo most of next week... Hey, you know all about the party tonight and then our trip next week, right? We were planning to be gone from Tuesday to Sunday. I don't know what you have going on this week though. Is it okay..."

"Rhett," she scoffed. "I'm your girlfriend, not your mother. I want you to go and have fun on your stupid Spring Break Bros Trip with Jake. Just promise me I get to see you again before you go back to school?"

He stopped listening the moment she uttered the word "girlfriend." It was going to take a long time for him to get used to that. And even if he eventually got used to it, he was sure he would never tire of hearing her say it.

"Come on, girlfriend," he declared triumphantly as he wrapped his arm around her shoulders. "Let's get you to work."

CHAPTER 26

Tori

An unexpected yawn caught Tori by surprise as she watched the houses pass in quick succession out the car window. They were just a few

minutes away from downtown Hampton.

"Do you want me to stop so you can get some coffee, beautiful?"

"No, I'm good," she insisted. "Plus, it's Sunday. There will be fresh coffee at work if I need it."

She hadn't slept much last night, her body anxious to connect with Rhett while her mind struggled to make sense of what she had agreed to. She had told him it wasn't a no last night when he asked her to be his girlfriend again, but she may as well have hired a skywriter and painted "Hell yes!" above Lake Erie. She wanted to be with him. And she wanted him to only be with her.

She was happy, and she was sure of herself, but there were still a lot of conflicting feelings she needed to work through. Tori felt an undertone of guilt as she thought about all the time they had wasted not together. Well, that wasn't exactly right. They had been together-ish for the last three years. But knowing how much she had hurt Rhett—how she had pushed him away and distanced herself from him—made her feel incredibly selfish now. There was also a small voice in her head questioning if this was the right call. She knew what she wanted. She trusted Rhett knew what he wanted, too. But could she live with the very likely consequences of her change of heart?

They still had so much to figure out. Rhett was moving in a few months. She wouldn't graduate for a few years. She didn't know how they would manage long distance or for how long they'd have to do it. And what about the less-immediate future? What was the plan when boyfriend and girlfriend wasn't enough? How could she give in to being with him now after all the years of keeping him at arm's length?

And yet the expanse of time ahead of them now that they didn't have a self-imposed expiration date on their relationship gave her hope. Navigating the new version of their relationship wasn't going to be easy. But it wasn't going to be as hard as going their separate ways and leaving a decade of love by the wayside.

As they approached the overpass that segmented downtown Hampton from the residential streets, a train horn blasted off in the distance. Tori smacked the ceiling of the Prelude before Rhett could even react. "Train time!" she exclaimed. The train came into view just as they drove under the overpass and felt the vibrations from the tracks.

He chuckled and shook his head. "I swear you have the schedule memorized."

"You're just mad that I always beat you." She smirked, reaching over and pinching his bicep.

Rhett stopped the car at the main intersection before edging through the blinking red lights. "Time check?"

"We've still got a little time. Why don't you park over by the clock tower?"

He slowly drove past the parking lot behind Clinton's. Jake's black Jeep was in one of the far spots at the end, so he was working today, just like she thought. Rhett turned right at the clock tower that stood guard on the edge of downtown and pulled into a parallel parking spot at its base.

Tori made her way around the car and met him at the trunk. She reached out and laced her arm through his. She knew the significance of the gesture wouldn't be lost on him. She used to try so hard to keep any affection or contact to a minimum when they were together in public. But she didn't have to think like that anymore. She moved her arm down and intertwined her fingers with his as they started walking toward Clinton's. Just the feel of him next to her felt like peace.

"Hey." He paused, gently pulling on her arm so they both came to a stop.

"Hmmm?" she asked, turning her face up to look at him. They were in the middle of downtown, standing below one of the evergreens that rose at least eighty feet into the sky.

Rhett bent down to kiss her. He started soft, barely touching his lips against her mouth. When Tori leaned into him, he deepened the kiss. They obviously weren't building to sex, but the passion and fervor in their lip-lock sizzled right at the surface. It was like all the restraint they had both shown over the last several years had carbonated and was finally being released. She couldn't remember the last time they kissed in public. She contemplated ditching her shift and just staying out here with Rhett all afternoon. She never wanted this feeling to end. Eventually he pulled away with a frustrated groan that Tori felt deep in her core.

"I just wanted to kiss my girlfriend one more time before we go in there." He grinned. "I'm going to go in with you and see what Jake wants, but then I'll probably head home to get ready for the party tonight. Do you want me to drop your bag off at your house?"

Tori shook her head. "Nope. It'll be nice to have my stuff with me if I decide to sleepover at my boyfriend's house tonight."

He cocked an eyebrow. "If?"

"If... When... You know what I mean," she told him breezily. "Come on, Wheeler. Don't make me late. The sooner I get in there, the sooner I get to leave and come home to you."

CHAPTER 27

Rhett

He couldn't contain his smile as they walked into the side entrance of Clinton's hand-in-hand. Everything about the morning had felt like it was unfolding in high definition. His feelings were unfiltered. His heart felt like it was finally playing full out. He was just so damn happy. But as he turned to kiss Tori one more time before her shift, he heard it.

A shrill laugh that sounded like it belonged in a sorority house opposed to Clinton's on a Sunday afternoon.

His head snapped toward the sound as his eyes grew wide in recognition. A high-pitched exclamation followed the laugh, and although he couldn't make out the words, a deep sense of knowing settled in his gut. As soon as the voice registered, he looked back at Tori. He had unknowingly dropped her hand. Or had she pulled away first? He met her gaze, searching.

Searching for what, exactly, he didn't know. It's not like she would have recognized Chandler's voice the way he just did.

Tori's brow furrowed in response to his visceral reaction. She knew something was suddenly wrong. He wished more than anything he didn't have to be the one to tell her what that something was.

Lia pushed through the kitchen doors with four plates in her arms before he could say anything. She nodded at both of them in greeting. Rhett moved ahead of her to hold open the door to the main dining room.

"Thanks," she responded, a sad smile barely reaching her eyes when she met his gaze. "You better get in there," she added quietly, but not quietly enough. She glanced past Rhett to Tori before walking deeper into the restaurant.

"Rhett?"

Fuck. He dragged in a choppy breath before turning to Tori.

"What's going on?"

He took two strides back to her, desperate to close the space between them. "I don't know what's going on for sure. But it sounds like Chandler might be in there."

"Wait, what? Chandler? Here?" Each word came out as a question. He felt as blindsided as Tori sounded.

"I don't know, but I think I heard her voice just now. Shit... I'm so sorry, beautiful. This is stupid. But I'll figure it out. Why don't you go clock in on the kitchen computer? I'll come find you once I know what's going on for sure." His voice sounded calm, but the confusion and the edges of anger were already swirling into a tornado of fury in his mind.

Tori's brow furrowed even deeper. Her green eyes assessed him for a few tense seconds before she lowered her chin once in agreement and turned toward the kitchen. A nervous energy spread through his body, fueled by the anxiety of Chandler possibly being at Clinton's and the realization that he had no idea what to do or say if his suspicions were correct. He reached out toward Tori for comfort, but he was too late. She had already turned and pushed through the kitchen doors.

Rhett walked into the restaurant and spotted her immediately. Chandler's shiny blond hair cascaded in curls down her back. She wore a hot pink, fitted sweater and her usual dark jeans. Her back was to him as he stalked toward the bar. Her loud, high-pitched laughter carried over all the other sounds in the restaurant, sending a chill down his spine.

"Chandler. Hi." He plastered a fake smile on his face as he came to stand next to where she was seated.

"RHETT!!!" she exclaimed about four octaves higher than necessary. She attempted to turn her body toward him and stand up at the same time, resulting in a sort of awkward crash off the barstool into his arms.

Rhett's whole body tensed as he locked in on Chandler's eyes. *Godamnit, Jake*. Before he could even help her back onto the barstool, her lips were on him. He felt the slickness of her shiny lip gloss as her mouth moved against his. He smelled the tomato juice and vodka on her breath, confirming his suspicions.

"Hey there," he responded tersely, gripping Chandler by the hips to steady her as he helped her back onto the barstool.

"Surprise!" she exclaimed, giddy as she looked up at him. Rhett shook his head in disbelief. Chandler was tipsy, borderline drunk. Jake had let her get drunk. Chandler was drunk, in Clinton's, and Tori was just about to start her shift. Bottomless Bloody Marys would be the death of him.

"Are you so surprised to see me? Did I surprise you, Rhett?" she probed, running her hand up and down his arm as she spoke. He shifted away from her touch, leaning into the wood while trying to subtly discourage any additional physical contact.

"Yeah, I'm definitely surprised."

"I thought for sure you would be on to me when we talked this morning!" she continued, her voice still louder than necessary.

Tori had emerged from the kitchen and strode toward the main dining room. Rhett felt her pass him before he even looked up. The tension radiating off her body was palpable. He was so attuned to her, especially after this weekend. What he wouldn't give to reach out and pull her into a hug right now. He needed to get this situation under control.

Rhett shot daggers at the back of Jake's head, willing his best friend to turn around and notice him standing there. "I can't believe you're here. It looks like you've been having *lots* of fun with Jake," he accused, nodding toward the empty glass in front of Chandler.

Jake spun around at the sound of his name. His expression was a combination of exasperation and dread. *Good.* Rhett wanted him to squirm. What the hell was he thinking letting Chandler hang out here and get drunk?

"Jake is like, the BEST bartender ever," Chandler declared, swiveling her hips to make the barstool spin from side to side. "He's been telling me all sorts of funny stories, and he makes such good Bloody Marys. I've been here for hours, but it feels like just minutes! Why haven't we ever come here for brunch? I love this place!"

Rhett didn't take his eyes off Jake as Chandler blabbered on. He shook his head in disbelief.

"... Jake was giving me the rundown about everyone I'll meet at the party tonight," he heard Chandler say. THAT got his attention.

"Jake told you about the party?" he asked, still not looking at her. He could feel the heat rising up his neck. Jake shot him an exaggerated grimace before turning to refill water glasses on the other side of the bar.

"Wheeler." Rhett's head snapped to attention when Mike called his name. He watched as the man set his plate down at his usual corner seat before hoisting himself up onto the barstool.

"I see we have a visitor," he inquired. His tone was softer than normal, his eyes squinting in question. *Was there going to be a problem?* Rhett wondered the same thing himself.

"Yeah, let me introduce you," he sighed. "Mike, this is Chandler Cunningham. Chandler, this is the owner of Clinton's, Mike Hobbs. He gave me my first job here back in high school."

Chandler flashed a huge smile in Mike's direction. "It's a pleasure to meet you, Mr. Hobbs. You have such a lovely restaurant." Not even Bottomless Bloody Marys could make her forget her manners. "I can't believe Everhett hasn't brought me here on a date before now."

Rhett shot Mike a desperate look, silently begging him to wrap up the conversation before it could go any further.

"The pleasure is mine," Mike responded curtly. "I'm glad you're enjoying yourself." He nodded to her once to indicate the conversation was over, then started in on his lunch.

Chandler turned back to Rhett. "I've gotta pee! I think I've had at least five of these things." She giggled, holding up her empty Bloody Mary glass. He rolled his eyes at how quickly she could transition from well-mannered socialite to tipsy sorority girl.

"The bathroom is around the corner." He pointed in the general direction. "Do you need me to go with you?" He honestly wasn't sure what was worse: a drunk Chandler wandering around Clinton's and possibly running into Tori or escorting a drunk Chandler through the restaurant in front of all their friends and regular customers.

Chandler stood on her tiptoes and kissed him again, this time on the cheek. "You're so sweet Rhett, but I'm good," she insisted, steadying herself and smoothing out her sweater. "I'll be right back."

He waited until she was out of site to stalk around the bar.

"Wheeler," Mike warned from his place at the bar.

"I'm fine," Rhett snapped in response. He knew better than to test his boss' patience. It wasn't his fault that his best friend was a Bloody Mary-mixing Judas. "I'm not going to cause a scene," he promised. Mike returned his gaze and nodded once.

"What. The. Hell," he hissed into Jake's ear as the other man stacked glasses in the cooler.

"Hey, man, don't even start with me right now," Jake shot back. He turned around and made himself look busy wiping down the back bar. "This whole situation is fucked up."

Rhett raked his hand through his hair before leaning against the back bar and crossing his arms. "How long has she been here?"

"Since before noon. I tried calling you a million times, bro. I didn't know what to do!"

"So you took it upon yourself to plow her with drinks and invite her to the party tonight?" Rhett fired back. "The party, I might add, that's not happening." He watched as Jake's expression transformed from frustrated to enraged.

"Honestly, bro? I did the best I fucking could. She's been here for almost *four hours*. She kept trying to leave to go to your parents' house and surprise you. Do you know how hard I've been working to keep her here?" He chucked his rag into the sink with a flourish.

Rhett could feel the tension coursing off his best friend. Four freaking hours. His anger started to dissolve as he realized just how far Jake had gone to try to help him today.

"She's a real piece of work, ya know. I'm not sure I've ever seen someone carry on a full conversation with themselves like that." Jake shook his head, anger rolling off him in waves. "But hey, at least she's hot. Now I know why you keep her around."

Rhett pinched the bridge of his nose and shook his head. Just when he was starting to feel bad for the position he had put him in today, the guy goes and shoots his mouth off with bullshit that he knew would dig under his skin.

"Fuck off, Jake. You have no idea what you're talking about."

"You're right," he shrugged, "I don't. Maybe it's time you finally enlighten me? I'm sick of all your pretending. I know you, bro. *That's* not your girl. Why the hell won't you talk to me about any of this?!"

Rhett stayed silent and tried to steady his breath. He hadn't been prepared to deal with a drunk Chandler. He felt even less prepared to face off with a combative Jake.

"Where is she?" The soft voice startled Rhett. Lia had made her way behind the bar to clock out.

"She's in the bathroom," he replied automatically, running his hand through his hair again.

"No, Rhett. I mean where's *Tori*?" she clarified, shooting him a knowing glance. "I have two tables I need to turn over to her before I leave, and I've only seen her once since you guys got here."

Tori. He had promised her he'd find her once he knew what was going on, but she had come out from the back first and seen Chandler with her own eyes. Rhett was almost certain she had heard Chandler when she walked past the bar earlier. She probably didn't realize the other woman was drunk, though. He needed to talk to Tori right away. He needed to make sure she was okay, and he needed to come up with a new plan for dealing with Chandler.

"You coming to our party tonight, Lia?" Jake asked.

Goddamnit. He just wouldn't quit about the stupid party. Never mind the fact that Rhett felt like everything was unraveling around him.

"That depends," she replied flirtatiously. "Who's gonna be there?"

Jake started listing off the guest list: a few of the other servers from Clinton's, some of the valet guys he hung out with on the weekends. Realization converted to acceptance as Rhett listened to the longer-than-expected guest list. It was clear that the party was happening tonight, whether he participated or not.

"I'll be right back," he muttered, defeated. He headed back into the kitchen while avoiding Mike's gaze. "Keep her here once she gets back from the bathroom, Jake," he shot over his shoulder before he pushed through the kitchen doors.

CHAPTER 28

Tori

Who the hell let the decaf coffee run out in the middle of Sunday brunch? Tori let out a long sigh and picked at a thread on her apron while she waited for the coffee to brew. At least glaring at the slow-drip percolator was buying her a few extra minutes to process what was happening at the bar.

Chandler at Clinton's—sitting at the bar, interacting with her friends—felt like a grotesque invasion of privacy. This was her workplace. Those friends were her family. That would all be a lot to process on its own. But then there was what she heard Chandler say to Rhett as she walked past them. She had no context for the comment, but that didn't matter. She knew what she heard.

"...when we talked this morning..."

He had talked to Chandler that morning. When, though? While she was sleeping? Before they went down to the lake? After she had assured him that they were really, truly together? She felt like such a fool.

It didn't actually matter when he had talked to her, Tori realized. Rhett had talked to Chandler earlier, and now she was here. Chandler's presence was an invasion, but Rhett's secrecy was a betrayal.

The coffee maker sputtered its final glugs as Tori reached for two navy and white speckled coffee cups with the Clinton's logo printed on them.

"Tori, I'm so sorry." She hadn't heard him come into the kitchen. He reached the beverage station in three strides. He extended an arm in her direction, but she shifted on the balls of her feet to block him out. He must have noticed the subtle snub because he took a step back and put a bit more space between them. "Tori?"

She let him sweat it for another few seconds before responding, "What is she doing here, Ev?"

"I honestly have no idea. I didn't even know she was here until we walked in the door, beautiful."

Tori assessed him out of the corner of her eye, then turned to face him head on. She had seen the shock register on his face when they first arrived. She had felt the tension crest in his body right before he dropped her hand. She believed him that he didn't know Chandler was here. But there was more to the story he was trying to leave out.

"So you had no idea Chandler was coming to Hampton today? She's been here at Clinton's— hanging out with Jake, sitting next to our regular Sunday customers—since when, exactly? Since Jake tried to call you this morning?" She shook her head in disbelief as she listed the offenses.

"Fuck." Rhett raked his hand through his hair again. "I didn't even put that together. Yeah, Jake said she's been here for a while. That's what I needed to talk to you about, V. She's drunk. I know I said I'd get her out of here, but there's no way I can send her home like this," he explained.

Tori's eyes widened as she started to connect the dots. Chandler wasn't going home anytime soon. She tried to keep her tone even as she asked her next question. "I heard part of what she said to you. Out at the bar. Did you really talk to her this morning?"

Rhett grimaced. Tori knew he was more agitated with the situation than with her, but still. How dare he get defensive. He had a lot of pluck for a guy who technically had two girlfriends in the same restaurant right now.

"Yeah, Chandler called me this morning, right after I talked to Maddie. I talked to her for, like, two minutes. She said nothing about coming to Hampton."

"Wait, you talked to Maddie this morning, too?" Her mind was reeling with all the half-truths that were unraveling between them.

Lia pushed through the kitchen partition then, interrupting their standoff.

"Tor, do you need me to stay?"

Tori glanced over at her best friend, grateful she was willing to stay to help her out. "Yes, please. These go to table eight," she instructed, sliding the coffees across the counter, "and table eleven hasn't put their order in yet."

"Got it. I'll stay as long as you need. But Mike asked me to come check on you guys, so you might want to wrap things up before he comes back here to check on you himself."

"Thanks for covering me, Lia." Tori turned back to Rhett before she dismissed her. "You won't have to stay too late. This isn't going to take long."

Rhett returned her glare, clearly agitated by her comment. They stood in silence, each one staring at the other in frustration, as Lia loaded the mugs onto a tray and walked out the door.

"We need to figure this out," Rhett huffed as he grabbed her by the arm and started marching to the walk-in cooler. His grip was tight on her elbow as he pulled on the silver handle and stepped inside.

Tori recoiled at his handling. Did he really think he could pull shit like this? Did he think he could keep things from her, then just say sorry and make it all better? *Screw this.* Tori refused to be complacent in her own steamrolling.

"What the hell is your problem, Wheeler?" she practically screamed. They both knew from experience that sound didn't travel from the walk-in cooler, so she wasn't worried about anyone overhearing them.

"You talked to Maddie *and* Chandler this morning while we were at the cabin and just forgot to mention it to me?!"

"Yes. But I didn't realize it was a big deal! Maddie called me to tell me Chandler called her last night. She was freaking out because Chandler commented on her Instagram, then asked about you." Rhett ran his hands through his hair as he tried to explain the overly complicated game of telephone.

The information sent her reeling. So a whole dramatic scene had occurred at some point that morning, and he didn't even think to mention it to her. When would he get it through his thick head that keeping things from her was the same damn thing as lying? Chandler probably hadn't even decided to come to Hampton until they got off the phone. If he had been upfront with Tori this morning, she would have suspected something was up, and they may have been able to stop Chandler from coming to Hampton altogether. This whole shitshow could have been avoided if he had just included her. But he didn't. He chose to try to handle it on his own and box her out.

"What did Chandler say this morning? Don't leave anything out," she added. He owed her an explanation and an apology.

Rhett leaned forward into her space, looking down at her for a few breaths before responding. Each exhale transformed into a hazy little cloud between them as his breath hit the refrigerated air.

"It was early, V. She called me around seven a.m. She said she didn't even expect me to answer... She was calling to leave me a voicemail. She asked if I was in Hampton or not. I told her I wasn't. I didn't tell her where I was. Just that I wasn't in Hampton at the moment but that I'd be there later today. That was the extent of the conversation, I swear. Listen, Tori, don't freak out. This is okay. I can figure this out," he insisted, his eyes searching her face. She knew he was trying to gauge her reaction, but she wasn't willing to give him the reassurance he wanted just yet.

"Why didn't you tell her it was over when you talked to her this morning?" She kept her tone cool and clipped. Rhett always insisted Chandler was nothing more than a distraction, so it shouldn't have been hard to break up with her as soon as her call came through.

"Tori."

He said her name the way her dad would say it when she was little and she had just done something she knew better than to do.

Wrong move, Wheeler. She was not going to be scolded when he was the one who had messed up.

"Don't 'Tori' me, Rhett. Like I'm a child. Like it's outrageous to think that after years of you begging me to be with you, and me finally agreeing, that you would actually break things off with your other girlfriend! I didn't realize I needed to make that apparent to you last night!!" She was full-out yelling at this point. She wondered if she was loud enough that maybe someone *could* hear them in here. She inhaled the frigid air through her nose to try and calm her nerves.

"It's not that simple, V," Rhett tried again. "I was so unsure about everything this morning—about Maddie's call and about what Chandler knew and didn't know—I wasn't thinking clearly. I thought about breaking up with her this morning, but the call was so short, and then I felt like I owed her a proper break up."

"So are you saying you're unsure about us?" she pushed harder.

She spoke the words before she thought them through. She felt so small and pathetic when she heard the doubt in her own voice. She didn't even know where that question came from. But now that she said it, she needed to hear the answer.

Pain and annoyance flashed in Rhett's eyes. She knew she was being immature, but she couldn't stop the insecure word vomit from coming out of her mouth.

"Tori, stop. Please don't do this right now." He lifted his hand to his neck, massaging the back of his shoulder as he closed his eyes. "I'm not unsure about us. I've never been unsure about us. Don't try to piss me off and push me away. Look, I know I messed this one up. I'm sorry. Let's just get through the afternoon and the party tonight..."

"The party?!" Tori interrupted him in disbelief. "You're still having a party?"

"I don't think I'm having a party as much as I think Jake is forcing me to participate in a party he's throwing at my house... but yeah. The party is happening. I have to take Chandler home with me when I leave here. Jake invited her to stay for the party, so I think it's best if we tread lightly for the rest of the night."

Bile rose up in Tori's throat as she realized what he was asking her to do. He wanted her to keep playing pretend in front of everyone at the party tonight. To put on a show. She had performed the role for almost three years, so it wouldn't be hard to do for one more night. But the principal of what he was asking her to do sliced through every hopeful thread they had woven together that weekend.

"Please don't ask me to do that, Rhett. There has to be another way." She couldn't imagine having to go back to pretending now that she knew how good it felt to love him out loud.

"I'm sorry. I know it sucks. But I don't want to upset Chandler and risk her trying to drive home drunk... You know I can't do that. Please just go along with this. Come to the party for at least a little while tonight," Rhett begged.

"Why?" she asked too quickly. She hoped he couldn't hear the pain in her voice.

"I think it'll look suspicious if you don't show up."

All the air left Tori's lungs in a harsh exhale. The chilly air of the cooler crept into the deepest part of her heart. Rhett didn't want her at the party because he actually wanted her there or because he needed to make sure she was okay. He was only worried about what their friends would say if Tori skipped out tonight. Maybe he cared more about Chandler than he admitted to her. Maybe he cared more about Chandler than he even admitted to himself.

"How dare you try to convince me to come over tonight to make you look better," she hissed through gritted teeth. "What's the plan, Rhett? Huh? What am I going to do? Sit around pretending to be your bestie while you and Chandler get cozy in the hot tub?!" She knew what a Jake and Rhett Party typically entailed.

"Tori, you know it's not like that. As soon as Chandler sobers up tomorrow..."

"Save your breath, Wheeler. You don't owe me any excuses. I'm not coming over tonight. We're not doing any of this. Have fun at your party." She tried to shove past him, but Rhett shifted in front of the door and cut her off.

"We're not doing what, exactly?" he snarled.

"We're not doing *any* of this. We're not going to be together the way you said you wanted, Everhett. I'm not willing to be a laughingstock so you can save face. How dare you even ask me to do that? We're. Not. Doing. This."

"You don't mean that," Rhett challenged her, his eyes seething and despondent.

"Yeah, I really do." She shrugged indifferently. She didn't, of course, but she had learned a few things herself while playing pretend over the last three years. She stared at him, unblinking, until a single tear slipped out. She silently cursed her body's betrayal. She doubted the tear would have even formed if they weren't standing in a giant forty-degree cooler.

"Don't cry, beautiful," Rhett begged as he wrapped his arms around her. "Please, Tori, don't cry. It's okay. We'll get through this. I'm going to fix this," he insisted.

She let him pull her into a hug, but she shook her head when he tried to lift her chin and kiss her.

"It's too late," she whispered. It was all too much. Too complicated. Too embarrassing. Too contrived. Too dramatic. "Please just leave and get her out of here. Don't try to come back to pick me up tonight. I'll get a ride home with Jake or one of the other servers."

She pulled out of Rhett's arms then, scrubbing away any stray tears that threatened to spill over and straightening her apron. She didn't look back as she walked out of the walk-in cooler, but he didn't try to come after her, either.

CHAPTER 29

Tori

"Tori?" her dad's voice startled her awake.

"What? What is it? I'm up, what's wrong?" She sat up in her bed faster than intended. She instinctively clicked on the lamp on her bedside table, then immediately regretted it. A sharp pain surged behind her temple on the side of her head, reminding her of the two beers she drank as soon as she got home from work before she gave up on the day and put herself to bed.

"Fun weekend?" Her dad chuckled. He was standing in the doorway of her bedroom, wearing an oversized flannel jacket. Now that she was awake, she could hear Penny barking downstairs.

"Something like that," she replied vaguely, still not fully awake.

"Well, you seem to have some gentlemen callers in the backyard, and Penny's going crazy. I'm surprised she didn't wake you up."

She blinked a few times, trying to make sense of what her dad had just said.

"Tell him to go away, please," she whispered. She hoped her dad would be willing to do her dirty work for her without asking too many questions.

"Uh, it's not Rhett. It appears to be an intoxicated Jake and another kid I don't recognize. I don't think they're gonna leave until someone goes out there. Want me to tell them to shove off?"

Tori pulled her comforter up to her shoulders as she considered her options. Why the hell was Jake in her backyard? She reached for her phone to check her messages, then remembered she had turned it off as soon as she got home. She held the power button down and waited for the screen to illuminate. Things clicked into place as she let out a huge yawn.

10:20 p.m. Everyone was at Rhett's house, and the party was probably just getting started.

"No, it's okay, Dad. I'll go out and talk to them. Rhett's having a party tonight, and I thought I could just stay in and get a good night's sleep. Guess I was wrong..."

"Is everything okay, sweetheart?" He ran a socked foot back and forth across the hallway carpet, staring at it intently instead of looking at her when he spoke. "I'm surprised you're home if Rhett's having people over..." he trailed off, trying to guide the conversation without overstepping.

"I'm fine, Dad. I'm just tired. I spent all weekend with Rhett, remember? I just didn't feel like partying tonight."

"Understandable." He nodded, dropping the conversation as quickly as it had started. "I'm going to bed soon, so just take your keys if you end up going over there for the night."

"Thanks, Daddy," Tori whispered as he turned and left her room.

"TORI!! TORI THOMPSON!"

"VICTORIA!!!"

She could hear them before she even opened the door off the back of the kitchen. No wonder Penny was going crazy—they were obnoxiously loud. Tori stepped into the backyard, trying to avoid the muddier spots of the lawn. She moved slower than intended. She was still feeling the beer she had drank earlier that night.

"Dude, we did it. Look! There she is! We freakin' manifested her into reality!"

Oh boy. If Jake was already talking about manifesting things, he was a special level of wasted. And possibly high. She took a few more steps toward them, squinting to see who was standing next to Jake.

"What are you jackasses doing out here?" she called out. She should be annoyed because they had woken her up, but they were both wearing the biggest little-boy-grins on their faces. They were clearly proud of their efforts to draw her out of the house.

"Tori! Baby! You're alive!!" Jake exclaimed instead of answering her question. He spun around once for emphasis. She was surprised he could pull that off without swaying.

"I'm alive. Why wouldn't I be?" She stopped five feet in front of them and crossed her arms over her chest. She was wearing a pair of leggings and an Archway sweatshirt, but the late March air was still chilly without a real coat.

"Tori!" Jake held his hands in front of his face, repeating her name again. "*No one* can get a hold of you. Not me. Not Rhett. Not even Cory or Lia!! We volunteered to come over here on a recon mission," he declared, ribbing the guy standing next to him.

Tori rolled her eyes, then turned her attention to his companion. He was taller than Jake and extremely good looking. He had broad shoulders and an unseasonably dark tan. A mess of blond curls crowned his head, and even in the dark, she could tell he had deep-blue swimming pools for eyes. The stranger returned her gaze, cocking his head slightly and smirking. Of course he had perfectly straight white teeth behind his full lips.

"Did you ever think I turned my phone off because I didn't want anyone to get a hold of me?" she replied to Jake before turning back to his friend. "Do I know you?" she asked, biting down on her lip as she continued to size him up. She was sure she recognized him from somewhere.

"I went to Arch, too," the stranger replied, pointing at the logo on her sweatshirt.

"Oh, no, I didn't go to Archway Prep. I went to Hampton High. I just..."

"Fielding Haas," the man interrupted, outstretching his hand to her. Tori took two steps forward and shook it. "But my friends call me Field," he added as their hands touched. "And you're Victoria Thompson, which I only know because I've been down here screaming your name for the last ten minutes with this jackass."

"You can call me Tori," she corrected him. "Haas..." she repeated his name out loud as she finally placed him. "Oh, that's right. You played lacrosse with Rhett."

"Close. That was my brother, Dempsey," Fielding replied with a smile. "I played hockey. But we both graduated with Wheeler."

No one said anything for a few beats, then Jake broke the silence.

"Are you going to change first?"

"What makes you think I'm going over there?" she shot back.

"Because it's a party, Tori. A Jake and Rhett Party. And you know damn well this may be one of the last times we get to do this," he stated matter-of-factly.

She heard the melancholy and nostalgia in his justification. He was right. Rhett would be moving to Virginia in less than two months. She almost let herself consider the invitation before snapping back to reality.

"Jake, I can't. Today was a mess. Things aren't good right now," she said into the ground. She glanced up at him and met his eyes, silently imploring him to take pity on the situation and leave her alone.

"Tori!! PLEASE! It's not a party without you!" he begged. "You're breaking my heart, baby!"

Tori rolled her eyes. Jake's declaration couldn't be further from the truth. She rarely drank and she never smoked. She spent most of her time at their notorious Jake and Rhett Parties following everyone around and cleaning up after them. Still, it was sweet that he wanted her there tonight.

"Is she over there?" Tori asked softly, directing her question at Jake while trying to ignore Fielding's puzzled expression.

"Yeah, Queen Buzzkill is over there. She was asleep when we all arrived, but I guess we were too loud, so now she's pouting in the living room. She's hungover from all the Bloody Marys she pounded this afternoon, and she refuses to go in the hot tub even though Rhett told her she could borrow a bathing suit from Maddie."

Tori physically recoiled at the idea of coming face to face with Chandler. It wasn't going to happen. She needed to get these guys out of her yard so she could crawl back into bed.

"What's wrong?" Fielding asked sincerely. "Do you not like Wheeler's girlfriend or something?"

Wheeler's girlfriend.

Tori's expression hardened at his word choice. It stood to reason that Fielding had just met Chandler tonight. The fact that he knew her relationship status meant that Rhett had kept up with his charade exactly as planned. He was introducing Chandler as his girlfriend. Even after Tori had made it clear how painful and disrespectful it was. Even after she broke down at the idea of him trying to save face in front of all their friends. Even though she begged him not to do it this way.

Fury replaced reluctance, and revenge trumped trepidation as she reconsidered her options. Maybe she *could* crash the party. A sly smile crept on her face as she acknowledged the itch to do something reckless. She may have broken down earlier in the walk-in cooler at Clinton's, but she refused to stay broken.

"Please come over," Fielding urged, pulling her out of her own thoughts. "I've never been to one of these parties, and it sounds like I'm not going to get the full experience unless you're there."

Oh, this guy was good. He was smooth and charming, and she knew damn well that Rhett would be fuming the moment he saw the way Fielding looked at her. She could work with this.

Jake must have sensed her fading hesitation. "I'll be your buffer if you come over. You won't even know she's there," he promised.

Tori closed her eyes and let out a long exhale, already disappointed in herself for what she was about to do. Maybe it was the beer from earlier, or maybe it was her desire to hurt Rhett as deeply as he had hurt her today.

"Fine," she relented. "But I have to change, and I am *not* walking across the yard by myself. Stay here and I'll be back down in five," she instructed, looking first at Fielding, then over to Jake to make sure they knew she was serious.

"YES!!" Jake let out a holler as he punched the air. "I knew we could do it, man!"

Tori turned around and hurried back into the house, hoping her bravery would outlast her consciousness.

She took the stairs two at a time back up to her room.

"Yahtzee," she muttered to herself as she pulled out the navy bikini she wore last time she and Rhett were in the hot tub. That had been the weekend that everything had shifted between them. The memories from that night were too much for her to think about right now. He had made his decision. And now she was making hers.

Once she had changed into her swimsuit, she threw on a dress as a cover-up and headed to the bathroom. She pulled her hair out of its messy bun and quickly brushed through the waves. She braided the front along her hairline and pinned it back. Then she added a bit of concealer under her eyes and swiped on two coats of waterproof mascara. She finished the look with a perfect application of bright red Super Stay lipstick. She was wearing more makeup than she had worn in months, but she refused to show up to this party looking like a mess, even if that's how she felt on the inside.

Satisfied she was as ready as she would ever be, Tori quietly made her way back downstairs. She detoured to the fridge and grabbed three cans of her dad's favorite beer. She made a mental note to restock the beer supply this week when she went to the store. She had put a considerable dent in his stash today.

Next, she grabbed her cell phone and keys, then slipped on a pair of sandals before heading back outside.

"Ready!" she called out to the two men waiting for her. "Catch," she added to Fielding, tossing him a can of beer once she was within tossing distance.

Fielding smiled as he pulled the can effortlessly from the air. "What's this? She comes bearing gifts? I think I'm in love."

"It's a roadie for our commute," she explained as she handed a can to Jake and cracked open her own.

"Oh, nice, Tori. You didn't think I could catch it?" He sounded personally offended by her actions.

"Correct." Tori smirked before taking a big swig. Fielding let out a loud laugh before turning to Jake.

"She's not wrong, man," he gloated as he shoved Jake in the side.

"Let's go, boys," Tori instructed, sounding more confident than she actually felt. She led the way since she knew the exact spot in the broken fence that connected her yard to the Wheelers', even in the dark.

"Tori, you look like a whole damn meal right now," Jake announced as both men trailed behind her. Fielding hummed in agreement.

She was used to Jake's shameless teasing, but now that there was someone else with them, she felt a little uneasy. If they both noticed the extra effort she had put forth tonight, Rhett certainly would, too. She hoped she knew what she was doing.

"That was kind of the point." She glanced over her shoulder in time to see a new layer of understanding blossom on Jake's face.

He groaned as he took a long sip of his beer. "Why do I have the feeling that I didn't think this through? Rhett's about to freak out, isn't he? He is already so pissed at me."

"Why do you think I agreed to come over in the first place?" She caught Fielding's eye and smiled, trying to reassure him as much as herself that this was a good idea.

"No turning back now." Jake turned the can up and chugged the rest of his beer.

CHAPTER 30

Rhett

He heard her before he saw her. He was genuinely surprised—he figured there was no way Jake would be successful in convincing Tori to join the party. He set his gaze on the broken spot in the fence and sank lower into the hot tub, reaching for his Gatorade bottle while he waited for the first sight of her. He took a swig of whiskey and swished it around his mouth before swallowing, reveling in the burning sensation as it slipped down his throat. The burn was a good enough distraction from the ache he felt in his gut.

He watched as Tori traversed over the broken part of the fence between their yards and stepped into his orbit. Jake and Fielding Haas followed. They were too far away for him to hear what they were talking about, but his spine stiffened when he heard Haas laugh in response to something she said.

Rhett sat up straighter, willing her to look at him. If he could just catch her eye...

But it was Jake who glanced at him first. Even from across the yard, Rhett could read the expressions on his best friend's face: first a warning, then an apology. He raised a wet hand out of the water and ran it through his hair. This day just kept getting better and better.

"Look who decided to finally join the party," Dempsey shouted as the trio circled the pool deck and made their way over to the hot tub.

"Tori!" Cole called out to her from his spot near the waterfall. "I haven't seen you in forever!! Get in here, girl!"

Rhett shot a warning in Cole's direction, but it didn't land. Cole hadn't taken his eyes off Tori. A quick scan of the other hot tub occupants confirmed what he already knew: all eyes were on her as she made her way toward them.

Rhett scanned her body from head to toe, possessively doing inventory of the woman he had woken up next to that morning. She was wearing flip flops and a short, thin dress, probably a cover-up for whatever she had on underneath. Her hair was down and wavy, the way it got whenever she let it air dry, with a little braid trailing across the front. Her green eyes looked gorgeous, and she was wearing bright red lipstick that was guaranteed to command everyone's attention.

He took another swig from his bottle as he tried to catch her eye. There was no way she didn't know he was staring at her at this point. She was avoiding him on purpose.

"Hello, boys," she greeted the group as the newcomers congregated around the steps of the hot tub. The same steps where he had made her come and she had sucked him off the last time they were in here together. Rhett let out a long sigh, but he knew no one heard him. It was drowned out by the guys' response to her.

She smirked, looking around at the all-male occupants of the hot tub. "Mind if I join this sausage fest?"

"Come on in, gorgeous!" Cole replied. She walked over to one of the pool loungers and set down her cell phone and key ring. She made quick work of pulling off her dress and slipping out of her sandals before walking back toward them.

Of-fucking-course. She was wearing the same blue bikini she had been wearing last time they were in the hot tub together, the one that came completely undone when you pulled the strings at the sides. One of the other guys let out a wolf whistle. He felt his blood pressure rise to match the temperature of the water as she carefully lowered one foot into the hot tub.

"It's not a total sausage fest. There's more people in the house," Fielding explained to her as he shed his own shirt and folded it next to Tori's. He followed closely behind her, not leaving nearly enough space for Rhett's liking.

"Oh yeah?" Tori asked innocently, slowly sinking her body below the water and floating toward the middle as she looked around. "Who else is here?"

Jake was the last one in. He lifted his chin at Fielding to indicate the other man should move down a spot so he could take his usual place at the left side of the steps.

"Lia, Tiff, and Cory are all in the sunroom," Jake explained, reaching behind him for the Gatorade bottle he had mixed before he went on his self-proclaimed Tori Recon Mission.

"Yeah, and Wheeler's girlfriend is in the living room watching TV," Fielding shared. The idiot thought he was being helpful. He had no idea he had just tipped off a landmine.

Rhett had hoped Chandler would fall asleep and stay asleep when he brought her back to his house that afternoon. Things were going according to plan until Jake started blasting music through the sunroom speakers around nine. Chandler appeared downstairs and introduced herself as "Rhett's longtime girlfriend" to each and every person at the party.

Tori smiled at Fielding as she bobbed up and down in the water, still floating around the middle of the hot tub instead of taking a seat along the perimeter. She finally turned her attention to Rhett, looking directly at him for the first time that night.

"Hi, Rhett." A ripple of emotion coursed through him as he swallowed hard. Their bodies were always so attuned to one another, and tonight was no different, even if they were surrounded by six other dudes. Her gaze cut him deeper than normal. He knew she wasn't here with good intentions.

Tori kept her eyes locked on him as she slowly moved through the water. It took him another breath to realize she was swimming toward him. He felt his dick twitch with the recollection of the last time they were in these same positions. What he wouldn't give to reach out and possessively pull her body into his now...

"Whatcha drinking?" she asked flirtatiously, lifting her chin toward the Gatorade bottle in his hand. Rhett didn't respond to her question. He was desperate not to give in to her games.

Now that she was in his space, he could see the glassiness in her eyes. By the looks of it, she had already had a drink or two. He silently cursed himself for not handling things better today. If Tori had been drinking, it was because of him. He did this to her.

"Are you gonna offer me some?" She pouted, sticking out her lower lip for emphasis. Rhett pushed down every urge in his body to pull her face toward his and bite down on that pouty red lip. She may have been tipsy, but she knew exactly what she was doing.

When he didn't respond, she moved even closer. She reached out one hand and rested it on his leg, right above his knee. Her fingers ran back and forth along his thigh, teasing the hem of his swim trunks. Rhett flinched at her underwater touch, but he didn't push her hand away. Instead, he shook his head slightly, sending her a silent but desperate warning. He was trying not to react to her. He couldn't let anyone else see just how affected he was by her. He felt his heartbeat in his throat as he swallowed hard and opened his mouth to finally respond.

"I'd be happy to go inside and make you a drink, Tori," Fielding offered, snapping them both out of the spell they were under. He had obviously been watching the scene unfold.

"No, she's fine," he growled toward Fielding while maintaining eye contact with Tori.

Rhett knew the valet guys well enough. He had gone to school with Teddy, Anwar, and the Haas brothers, and he remembered Cole was in all the same art classes as Tori at Hampton High. It wasn't that he didn't trust them to not pull something. It was more like he didn't trust *her* not to lead one of them on in her current frame of mind. Tori knew the power she could have over men—the power she had over him—and Rhett knew she was angry enough tonight to flex that power. Fielding was transfixed by her every move, but he didn't realize he was just a pawn in her game.

"I'm fine? But I don't have a drink in my hand, and I thought this was a party?" She tilted her head slightly so the ends of her hair dipped into the water. Rhett's nostrils flared at her challenge. He had spent the entire day trying to navigate through this convoluted situation, and he just kept fucking it up. Why had he expected tonight to be any different?

"Fine. Here." He thrusted the bottle into her hand, pissed at himself that it was still half full. "But you're not going to like it," he added. Giving her his drink was better than trusting Fielding or anyone else to give her something.

"Thanks, Ev." She smiled at him again before closing her teeth around the tip of the bottle to pull it open. She took a long draw and swallowed, her face expressionless as the whiskey slid down her throat.

"So it's a Jameson kind of night." She sneered at him before taking the bottle and retreating back toward the waterfall across from the stairs.

Rhett glanced over at Jake, curious to see if he had witnessed their exchange. Jake met his eyes, and the look they shared told him that his best friend hadn't missed a damn thing. Tori wasn't herself; she was reckless, and she was looking for trouble tonight, whether that meant making it, finding it, or being it.

He looked back at Tori and studied her. Why had she come over here after all? Where was her head at? She still wasn't sitting down, instead bobbing in front of the stone waterfall in the most enchanting way. She was shifting her weight from leg to leg in the water and taking regular sips from Rhett's bottle. Every few seconds, she would move or laugh hard enough to rise up above the bubbles and expose the peaks of the bathing suit triangles stretched her over breasts.

She was engrossed in conversation with Teddy and Cole, but that didn't stop her from glancing over at Fielding every so often. Haas hadn't taken his eyes off of her since they'd gotten into the goddamn hot tub. If only that asshat knew Rhett had been inside of her less than twenty-four hours ago.

"Everhett," a high-pitched voice carried from the door of the sunroom to the hot tub.

Fuck.

He closed his eyes and lowered his head back against the cement. He had been so wrapped up in watching and worrying about Tori that he had forgotten Chandler was even there.

"We're still out here," he called back to her reluctantly, not bothering to lift his head.

He heard her heels click against the patio bricks as she approached. *Here we go.* Rhett felt utterly helpless as he opened his eyes. Chandler was squatting above him. She leaned down and greeted him with a surprise upside-down kiss.

"Hey, you," she murmured, running her nails through his semi-wet hair. "I think I'm going to get ready for bed. Care to join me?"

"Tempting," he whispered back to her, acutely aware of Tori's gaze boring into him from across the hot tub. "But I don't think I can abandon ship this early after inviting everyone over." There was no way he could go inside and leave Tori out here now. He was desperate to buy himself more time.

"Okay," Chandler conceded before rising to her feet. "Oh!" he heard her surprise once she stood up. This was the moment he had been dreading: the love of his life coming face-to-face with the girlfriend he had only started dating at her insistence.

"Uh, Chandler," Rhett fumbled, "you met most of the guys earlier, but Tori just got here." He pointed to Tori like she wasn't the only woman in the hot tub.

"Well, well, well," Chandler clucked, "if it isn't the infamous best friend. It's sooo nice to finally meet you, Tori. I've heard so much about you!" Her voice was sticky-sweet. He noticed she was standing tall with her shoulders back and one hand on her hip. She didn't look tired anymore.

"It's nice to meet you, too, Chandler," Tori replied coolly. She lifted Rhett's water bottle toward the other woman in a pseudo-toast before taking a long pull from it.

"Honestly I wasn't sure if we were ever going to meet. It's like Rhett keeps you hidden away whenever I'm in town! I've tried to get him to introduce us for ages, but it just never works out. But that's okay. You're here now. I'm thrilled! Honestly, Maddie tells me all the time how great you are. I can't believe it's taken us..."

"I need a refill," Tori interrupted the other woman mid-sentence as she moved through the water.

Chandler barely let the disruption register before shifting gears.

"Oh, perfect! Let's have a drink together! Just nothing with vodka. Jake made me the most amazing Bloody Marys earlier today, and I guess they were buy one, get one free or something at Clint's. I think I drank enough vodka to last a lifetime."

"Clinton's," Tori corrected her sharply.

"Oh, right. Clint's, Clinton's... whatever it's called."

Rhett knew Tori's anger was rising. Chandler's dismissal wasn't going to land well. He needed to intervene.

He gazed up at Chandler and forced a smile. "Babe, would you mind grabbing us some waters from the mini fridge behind the bar? I think everyone could use an alternate right now."

"Yes! Of course!" she chirped in response to his request before scurrying back into the sunroom.

"I need a real refill," Tori deadpanned, shooting a sharp glare in Rhett's direction. She stood up when she got to the first step. Water cascaded down her body in rivulets. Rhett was certain all eyes were on her: her shapely legs and tight ass were on near-full display in her navy bikini as she climbed the stairs.

He didn't have time to glance around at the other guys and confirm his suspicions. Tori misstepped and slipped on the second to last stair. Rhett's reaction was immediate; he was up and out of the water in an instant, steadying her body against his before anyone else even registered that she had tripped.

Their contact was electric. His body tingled with recognition and desire. It took all his willpower not to nuzzle into her neck, audience be damned. He inhaled sharply as she regained her footing.

"Tori," he growl-whispered into her ear. It was a warning and a plea. He could hear the pain in his own voice. She had to know what she was doing to him—to them—right now.

"I'm fine, Wheeler," she huffed, spinning her head around to shoot daggers with her eyes. "I don't need you," she added sharply as she tried to brush him off.

Rhett dropped his hands at her dismissal and sank back into the water. He knew better than to push her. He watched her stumble twice more as she made her way across the patio to the sunroom.

He reached for the Gatorade bottle she had dropped and turned it over, confirming what he already knew: It was empty. She had just slammed back at least four shots of Jameson mixed with very little ice. Rhett pinched the bridge of his nose and closed his eyes again, debating whether he should follow Tori into the house or play it cool and try to keep Fielding in the hot tub, away from his girl.

"I've got her," Jake muttered as he got up to follow Tori inside. He clasped his hand on Rhett's shoulder as he hoisted himself out of the water. Rhett cast a somber glance in his best friend's direction, wishing more than anything that they could trade places and it could be him to go after her instead.

CHAPTER 31

Tori

Babe. He calls her babe. Of course he calls her babe. She's gorgeous. She's everything he could possibly want in a girlfriend, in a wife, in a mother for his children. She's everything he could want for his future.

Tori ripped open the door of the sunroom, stumbling back slightly from the momentum as it swung out. She felt a hand find the small of her back and steady her in place. She whipped her head around, ready to tell Rhett off again, only to find Jake looking down at her instead.

"Cool it, baby. It's just me." He assessed her up and down. His hand was splayed across her bare back. It was then that she remembered she wasn't wearing anything except a bathing suit. She pushed off Jake's body and stalked over to the storage cabinet in search of a robe.

"Alright, Chandler, you ready for round two of Jake School?"

What the hell... Jake was supposed to be *her* friend. Why was he paying so much attention to Chandler? Tori hadn't realized she'd have to compete for everyone's attention tonight. Rhett, yes. He had proven to be spineless all day. She knew his angle before she even crossed over that fence. He was still playing pretend, trying to make everyone believe he had things under control, acting like he was in a committed relationship with Chandler. But Tori was surprised by Jake's abandonment.

"Tori, come sit with me," Cory called from across the room. She sulked over to the couch and plopped down next to him, leaning her body against his and closing her eyes. She opened them quickly when she felt someone sit down on the other side of her, but exhaled in relief when she saw it was just Lia.

"You're in rare form tonight, Tor." Lia laughed as she reached over to adjust Tori's robe. She closed it around her front then pulled the sash tighter. "What made you decide to come over here after all?" Her tone wasn't accusatory, just curious.

Tori huffed out another sigh. Why had she come over here? She was drunk and tired and cranky. She was having a hard time remembering why she had left her bed in the first place.

"Honestly? I think I needed to see it for myself," she admitted, nodding her head toward Chandler and Jake behind the bar. As if on cue, Chandler let out a shrill laugh, wrapping her manicured hand around Jake's bare bicep in response to something he said. Tori winced.

No one said anything, so she took it upon herself to keep talking.

"I mean, I've seen pictures of her, and he talks about her, but this is the first time I've met her in person. For the first time in three years, Easton Barbie actually seems real."

"Why do you care so much?" Cory asked.

Tori considered his question and contemplated how much she wanted to share. She felt far less filtered than normal as the warmth of the Jameson continued to spread through her limbs. She probably had another five or ten minutes before she would succumb to the haze of her indulgence. It was now or never.

"Rhett and I have been... together-ish... for the last three years," she whispered, her eyes fixed on Chandler as she spoke. Cory gasped. Lia stayed silent.

"That's why he comes home so often. That's why he picks up shifts at Clinton's. Even though Easton is four hours away. And he has a sizable trust fund. He doesn't need the shifts. He doesn't need the money. He comes home to be with me."

She felt Cory sit up straighter, but he stayed quiet, so she continued.

"We were together this weekend. In Michigan," she clarified. "Rhett asked me to be with him for real, and he said he was going to break up with Chandler."

Understanding passed through Lia's eyes.

"Then what is she doing here?!" Cory exclaimed. He put his own hands to his mouth when he realized how loud he had been. Thankfully Jake had turned up the sound system so loud that the windows behind them were vibrating to the bass. There was no way their voices could carry all the way across the room over the Machine Gun Kelly song blasting through the speakers.

"My question exactly," Tori retorted. She felt like she could use another drink, but she wasn't about to approach the bar with Chandler behind it. Instead, she slumped back into the couch between her friends. "I believed him when he said he wanted to be with me and only me. But when we got to Clinton's this afternoon, Chandler was there. Rhett admitted to talking to her this morning without telling me."

Cory sighed dramatically. "You know Rhett could have anyone he wanted. If he wants you..."

"He clearly doesn't know what he wants."

"Tori," Lia scolded from the other side, "I saw you both when you walked into Clinton's this afternoon. Rhett definitely wasn't expecting things to happen the way they did. He was really upset with Jake."

"So? What is that even supposed to mean? Of course he was upset. He was in the process of getting caught."

"Oh, come on, we both know..."

"Please don't try to defend him, Lia. You don't know what's going through his head."

"And you do?"

She had her there. Tori quieted, glancing around to make sure their conversation was still private. "I thought I did," she admitted.

"Who are you really mad at right now?" Leave it to Lia to hit the nail on the head. Tori let her silence serve as her answer.

"That's what I thought. You and Rhett need to talk. Really talk. Sober talk."

She rolled her eyes at her best friend's scolding.

"Don't push him away just to make him hurt the way you're hurting, Tor," Lia tried again, softer this time. "I know you. I know what you're doing right now. Don't self-destruct tonight to avoid having to deal with him tomorrow."

Tori let Lia's words sink in as she sunk further into the couch. She closed her eyes again, wishing she was still in her bed, wishing she hadn't taken the bait, wishing she wasn't so determined to do what she knew she was going to do. But just like Jake had said earlier: there was no turning back now.

CHAPTER 32

Rhett

Rhett looked around at the other guys in the hot tub. He wondered how much longer he'd have to stay out here with them, pretending to care as they shot the shit and drank his liquor.

"So, what's her story?" Fielding asked as he moved over into Jake's abandoned seat. Rhett's defenses went up instantly. He took a steadying breath before turning to respond.

"Whose story?" he asked blankly, like he didn't know exactly who was on Fielding's mind.

"Tori, man. You guys dated back in high school, right? Do you know if she's seeing anyone now?"

Rhett didn't know Fielding as well as he knew his brother. Dempsey and Rhett had played lacrosse together all four years at Archway Prep. They were two of the only three freshmen to play varsity their first year. Dempsey was a good guy, or at least he had been in high school. The Haas brothers had gone on to graduate from an Ivy, but they were both back in Hampton for some reason now, working valet for a few of the restaurants in town. Rhett didn't know their full story, but he knew their family had money, so he assumed they were just drawing from their trust funds and shooting the shit for as long as possible before joining the real world.

The valet boys were notorious for their partying. They all lived together in a big house right on the edge of Hampton. They were known for being nondiscriminatory in their pursuit of any woman with a pulse: they hooked up with drunk sorority girls just as often as they pursued the older women they met while parking their expensive cars.

"No story, but she's off limits," he replied with a shrug.

Fielding smirked and took a long drink. "She wasn't acting off limits."

Rhett felt his spine stiffen and his cheeks flush. He hadn't considered having to fend off advances from these guys on Tori's behalf tonight. The fact that he couldn't just come out and say she was his girlfriend killed him. He had to try and find a workaround.

"She's clearly drunk, Haas. Off. Limits. Or do things like consciousness and consent not matter to you?" Rhett's voice dripped with disgust. He realized all eyes were on him now, watching curiously as he and Fielding went back and forth.

"She's drunk *tonight*," Fielding stipulated. "She won't be later this week, though, and spring break has just begun."

Rhett visualized his feet encased in cement blocks, anchoring him in place in the hot tub. It was the only way he could stop himself from jumping out of the water and putting the other man in a chokehold for suggesting he was going to pursue Tori.

"You callin' dibs, Field?" Anwar asked from across the way.

"Yeah, she's mine," Fielding announced, looking around the hot tub to confirm his roommates heard him.

"You guys are something else. She's wasted, and you're really trying to call 'dibs' on getting with her? I should send all you sickos home right now," Rhett threatened.

"Chill, Wheeler. I'm not putting any moves on her tonight," Fielding promised, his arms raised in defense. "Too easy," he declared with another smirk.

"Play nice, Fielding," Dempsey warned his brother. At least one of the Haas brothers had the decency to read the room.

"Oh Dem—you always underestimate me." Fielding smiled slyly at his twin. "You didn't see how she was looking at me before we came over here. She'll be in my bed within seventy-two hours, tops."

"Care to put your money where your mouth is, Field?" Anwar challenged from across the water.

Rhett growled his disapproval as the other men placed bets on how quickly Fielding could get Tori into bed. Without another word, he stood up and exited the hot tub, pulling a towel off the pile from one of the pool chairs. Dempsey also got out and wordlessly dried off beside him before heading inside. Rhett ran a towel over his hair, then noticed Tori's things were still sitting on the chair outside. He picked up her phone, keys, and dress, hoping she had enough whereabouts to at least grab a robe when she went inside.

Relief washed over him when he pulled open the sunroom door and his eyes landed on her, fully robed and squished between Cory and Lia on the couch.

"Rhett!" Chandler greeted him loudly, calling everyone's attention to his entrance. "Come taste this! Jake is teaching me how to make an old-fashioned. He said it's one of your favorites." She slid a full tumbler across the bar in his direction.

"Huh," he heard Tori start from her spot on the couch. "I didn't know you liked anything besides straight whiskey, Wheeler."

Rhett glared at her. He saw Cory gently pinch her lips together and try to shush her. *Good man.*

"I think most of us have had enough to drink tonight," he replied to Chandler, but glanced over at Tori with a pointed look. "Can I get one of those instead?" he asked, cocking his head toward the water bottles before taking a seat on one of the barstools.

"Oh shoot! I'm sorry, Rhett! I totally forgot to bring the waters you asked for. Jake came in and distracted me with all his smooth bartending skills." Chandler smiled as she nudged Jake in the side.

Jake looked up at Rhett, his eyes laced with frustration. He was back on babysitting duty and trying to keep the peace. Rhett owed him big time.

"No worries, babe. I'm pretty sure those guys don't give a shit about feeling hungover tomorrow anyways." He shrugged as he accepted the water bottle from her.

"Can I get one of those water bottles, too, babe?" Tori heckled from the couch.

Guilt rose inside him when he heard her tone. The word "babe" had just slipped out. She probably sounded like a bitch to everyone else, but Rhett could hear the sadness in her voice through the Jameson-laced slurs. She was hurting. He was hurting her. He knew he couldn't fix everything tonight, but he owed it to Tori to at least try and smooth things over as much as possible.

He hopped off his barstool, grabbed another water bottle, and slowly approached the couch. Cory wordlessly stood up and moved out of his way, giving him a clear path to Tori.

Rather than sit, he chose to squat in front of her. He felt Lia shift uncomfortably next to them. He glanced up and offered what he hoped was a reassuring smile: he came in peace.

He tried to speak calmly as he uncapped the water bottle and handed it to her. "Here you go." He gently set both hands on her robe-covered knees for balance. She looked at him but said nothing as she took a long drink of water. Rhett searched her face to try and gauge his next move. Where was her head at right now?

"You look tired, V. Can I take you home?" he inquired, silently pleading with her to not fight him anymore tonight. If he could just get her out of here...

"I didn't come to this party with you or for you, Everhett, so no, you can't take me home," she replied loudly before she shoved the open water bottle back into his hands. He didn't know if she was intentionally making sure Chandler heard her from across the room or if her volume was just fueled by the whiskey coursing through her veins. Either way, Rhett knew she was unfiltered and nowhere near done fighting tonight.

"You could always ask Jake to take me home." Tori sat up straighter and shifted to the edge of the couch before parting her legs. "I heard he's a really good babysitter."

He didn't break eye contact as she gave him a clear visual of her bikini bottoms. When her first attempt didn't garner a reaction, Tori spread her knees even wider, testing him. They both knew he couldn't react to her body in front of everyone without giving himself away. She leaned forward and wrapped one of her hands around Rhett's wrist, pressing her fingers into his pulse point as she used him as an anchor for balance.

"Or better yet," she leaned in even closer, stopping just a few inches from his face, "I should ask Fielding to take me home," she mused, biting down on her bottom lip and arching one eyebrow.

Rhett jerked back and rose to his feet. She had no idea the conversation that had just taken place in the hot tub. She had no idea what was at stake. He raked his hand through his hair, desperate to get her far away from Fielding and everyone else at this party.

He glanced around the room to confirm what he already knew: They had a full audience. Jake and Chandler were eyeing him wearily from behind the bar. Lia hadn't taken her eyes off the two of them, and Cory and Tiff were desperately trying to look anywhere but the couch. Everyone knew he was on edge, and at least half the people in the room knew they were witnessing a dispute between lovers, not just a fight between friends.

Fuck it. He was done playing games. Nothing was worth losing her over, even if it meant other people got hurt in the process. He decided at that moment that protecting her—that protecting them—was his only priority for the rest of the night. He had to get Tori away from this scene before things escalated any further. He knew he was about to leave carnage in his wake, but he didn't care. Jake could deal with Chandler and hold her off until morning.

Rhett locked eyes with Tori, singularly focused on making her listen to him. He needed to stop her downward spiral now that he had given up on keeping up appearances. He had to get this night under control.

"Tori, I need to talk to you alone. Upstairs. Now," he barked. He didn't even glance toward Chandler behind the bar as he made his way across the sunroom and into the house.

"Uh-oh," he heard Tori taunt from behind him. "I think I made Daddy mad." She obviously knew they had an audience, too. She was just putting on a show. He didn't need to turn around to know she would follow him inside.

CHAPTER 33

Rhett

"Up," he ordered. Rhett was legitimately concerned she wasn't going to be able to make it up the stairs in her inebriated state. The Jameson must have fueled her, though, because she took the stairs two at a time before turning toward his bedroom.

His weight made the squeaky stair groan in protest when he stepped on it. He turned into his bedroom and scanned the space for her. *She must have ducked into the bathroom.* He flopped onto his bed and exhaled. He was exhausted and despondent. The last eighteen hours had just been a long string of wrong calls on his part. How had he fucked this all up so quickly?

The woman he loved was locked in his bathroom after embarrassing him in front of the girlfriend she had required him to date. She was lowkey threatening to hook up with another guy, and that guy was eager and willing to get into her pants so he could win a bet. The whole situation was a twisted mess.

When he sat up, he noticed Chandler's overnight bag on the floor by Tori's side of the bed. He grabbed it and tossed it into his closet.

After a few minutes with his own thoughts, Rhett felt considerably calmer. They were alone now. It would be easier to get through to her. He was confident he could get everything straightened out. He just needed Tori to come out and talk to him. He stood up and approached the bathroom door, worried she was getting sick but didn't want to tell him.

"Hey, V," he called softly through the door. "Everything okay in there?"

When she didn't respond, he tried the handle, but the door was locked.

"Tori," he called again. Silence. "Tori, are you okay? Answer me, or I'm using the key to open the door. We need to talk."

"Go away, Rhett," she finally responded. Her voice was muffled. She sounded so far away.

"Open the door and let me in, please."

"I said, GO AWAY!" she screamed, her voice cracking on the last word. She was crying and trying to hide. Rhett inhaled slowly. He could handle this. Sad, crying Tori was easier for him to connect with that angry, spiteful Tori.

"Please just let me in, beautiful," he tried again, rattling the door handle a few times to get her attention. He felt more desperate with each passing second.

"I'm not opening the door for you, Wheeler." He heard the determination in her voice when she spat out his last name. He knew he was running out of options.

"Tori. Please."

"No means no, Everhett. Go downstairs. Send up Lia. Or better yet, send up Fielding."

Fucking Fielding.

She had obviously found her mark. Maybe Fielding wasn't exaggerating—maybe something had happened between them earlier tonight. He shuddered as he thought about how the other man had staked his claim in the hot tub.

"Unlock this door right now," Rhett demanded, breathless from a surge of anger inspired by the thought of Fielding Haas. He felt white-hot panic rise in his chest when she didn't respond.

"Goddamnit, Tori!" he hollered, smashing his fist into the door before resting his forehead against the barrier between them. A stinging warmth pooled in his hand from the force of impact. He immediately regretted raising his voice, but the fury that had built up in his body throughout the day had nowhere else to go. Now that he unleashed his rage all the words he had held back all night started to pour out of him. "Stop acting like you're innocent in all of this! I didn't do this by myself! The only reason Chandler is even in my life is because you insisted on it. She's only here because of you! Did you really think no one would get hurt? Did you think we'd come out of this unscathed? Your shitty arrangement has consequences, Victoria."

A muffled sob carried through the door and snapped him out of his tirade.

Fuck. What was he doing? He had to make sure that she was okay; he had to make sure that they were okay. He was willing to do anything—to try anything—to just get through this night. He reached up above the door in search of the key. His fingers connected with the small metal ring as a puff of dust released from the doorframe. He fumbled once to insert the key into the hole before he felt it catch.

"I'm coming in," he warned.

Tori was attempting to scramble to her feet as he opened the door. She gave up when she laid eyes on him. She was a defenseless animal trapped in a corner, her body out of fight. She sank back down in his walk-in shower and let her head rest against the wall.

"Damnit," he muttered under his breath, rushing over to be by her side. He resisted the urge to gather her up in his arms and instead forced himself to sit down across from her on the tiles of the shower. He was afraid to get any closer. They sat in silence for almost a minute before he couldn't take it any longer.

"Hey, look at me, beautiful," he prompted.

Tori lifted her gaze without raising her head. Her hair was wild around her, her eyes red and swollen as tears continued to fall. He could tell she was seething: mad at him for how everything had gone down that day, pissed at herself for being out of fight. Rhett was feeling the whiskey he had drank before she took the bottle from him. He could only imagine the thick fog that must have a hold on her by now.

"What do you want?" she hissed.

You. But Rhett didn't speak his answer out loud. He had no idea what to say or how to make any of this better. He cursed himself again for not standing his ground earlier—he never should have handed her that Gatorade bottle. He shouldn't have let her get in the hot tub. Hell, there shouldn't have even been a party at his house tonight. The weight of every wrong decision he had made throughout the day crushed him. He felt so hopeless—but he needed to hang on for her.

"Why are we up here, Rhett?" Her words were heavy, laced with exhaustion and whiskey.

She shifted onto her knees, clumsily closing the small area between them and pressing her hands into his chest. She pressed into him with her full body weight, leaning into the space he was trying to give her. "Need me to rub one out for you?" she taunted. Her bright red lips slanted toward his mouth but then changed course and landed near the shell of his ear. "Were you hoping for a quickie before you go back downstairs to your girlfriend?"

Rhett's whole body recoiled at her jab. "Tori," he scolded, placing his hands on her robe-clad arms and trying to create more space between them.

"Answer me, Everhett. Why are we up here?" she demanded as she sat back on her heels.

"I just wanted to talk. Things felt too intense down there. I thought if we could come up here alone, we could figure this out together."

"I'm not in the mood to hear anything you have to say to me," she snarled.

"Today just needs to be done," he declared. "This has all been too much. I can't even begin to tell you how sorry I am for how everything went down today, beautiful."

"You don't owe me an explanation. It was over the moment we walked into Clinton's, and we both know it."

"Damnit, Tori!" He sighed, running his hand through his hair. "Stop saying it's over. You were mine twelve hours ago!" He felt the end of his nerves begin to fray. He was so close to unraveling.

"Don't kid yourself, Rhett," she replied coldly before leaning toward him again. "I was never yours."

He knew she was drunk, angry, and desperate to hurt him, but her words still stung. There was no hope of getting through to her. He needed to put her to bed and put this whole night to rest. They needed to be done trying to destroy each other tonight.

Although he knew better than to try to fight her anymore tonight, he couldn't resist putting a final stake in the ground.

He leaned forward to match her posture, desperate to make her hear him. "Tori, why would I believe you right now? It's never been over between us," he hissed. "You're drunk, and you're angry. I'm not about to let you throw away everything we have and everything we're going to have because of one bump in the road. There's literally nothing you could say to me right now to convince me otherwise."

Tori tried to scrub the moisture out of her eyes. "You're right," she croaked, tears silently rolling down her cheeks. She nodded solemnly. "There's nothing I could say to make you believe me." Acceptance passed over her expression. She pulled her knees into her chest and lowered her head, letting out a muffled cry.

"What can I do for you?" he implored. He wanted so badly to pull her into his arms, to close the space between them and take care of her like he had all weekend. But he also knew she was hurting right now, and he was the cause of her pain.

"Just help me up. I'm ready for this day to be done, too."

Rhett nodded, pushing off the shower bench to rise up before offering his hand. It had to be a good sign if she was willing to accept his help.

"I brought up your things," he told her, pointing to where he'd left her phone, keys and cover-up on the nightstand. "Maybe just stay here tonight?" He couldn't stand the thought of her trying to walk downstairs past everyone in the sunroom and hot tub.

She nodded wordlessly, already pulling back the sheets on her side of his bed.

"Do you want a shirt to sleep in, V?" he asked as he walked into his closet to find something more comfortable for her to wear. When she didn't respond, he glanced over to find her already lying in his bed, turned on her side.

He reached into the closet for Chandler's overnight bag and slung it over his shoulder before turning off the lamp. The day was finally done.

"Goodnight, beautiful," he whispered even though he knew she was already asleep. "Tomorrow will be better," he promised out loud for his own sake.

CHAPTER 34

Rhett

Rhett placed Chandler's bag in the guest bedroom before heading back downstairs. He was serious about what he had said to Tori: this night needed to be done.

He strode into the sunroom, ready to give out directions and wrap things up. The hot tub had cleared out, and Jake had gotten out the plywood panel they kept under the couch for beer pong. Fielding and Dempsey were boisterously facing off against Teddy and Tiff. Lia and Cory were huddled together on the couch, deep in conversation. Chandler, Jake, Cole, and Anwar were all lined up at the bar.

There was an awkward charge in the air as he made his way over to Cory and Lia first. He could feel all eyes on him, no doubt because of the scene he had caused before he demanded Tori follow him upstairs.

"Hey," he greeted them cautiously. "Are you guys staying over?" They knew the party rules—stay over or get a ride home—but he still wanted to make sure they were safe.

"I haven't been drinking," Cory replied. "I'll drop Lia off on my way home." Rhett nodded curtly and walked away, anxious to put distance between himself and Tori's two best friends.

He let out a sigh as he walked behind the bar. He stretched his arms long against the familiar wood, leaning forward before looking up at the people seated before him.

Their looks ranged from curious to annoyed to sad. He focused on Cole and Anwar first, choosing his words carefully. They had both eagerly wagered in on Fielding's bet. He couldn't wait to get them out of his house.

"We don't fuck around with drunk driving. Are you all staying here tonight?" he asked, waving his hand in the general direction of the beer pong match to indicate he meant everyone in their crew.

"That's the plan," Anwar confirmed before downing the rest of his drink, "although I can't make any promises about Teddy and that waitress."

Rhett glanced over to the game and saw Teddy wrap his arm around Tiff's shoulders. He watched for another moment as Tiff stood up on her tiptoes to whisper something to him. She looked just as into him as he was her.

"Okay. Make sure someone calls them a car if they want to leave. For anyone staying, there's a couch out here, but it gets really bright in the morning. There are also two couches in the living room, another one in the den, and a huge sectional down in the basement. There are tons of blankets plus a full bathroom in the basement, so that's your best bet."

"Sweet." Anwar nodded appreciatively before reaching over the bar and helping himself to the bottle of vodka.

"Hey, Rhett, listen," Cole started. "I know we haven't hung out that many times, but I wanted you to know that we were just joking in the hot tub about Tori. I didn't realize..."

"We're not talking about that now," Rhett cut him off, glaring at the other man.

"It just seemed like..." Cole tried again.

"Leave it alone, Cole," Rhett replied through gritted teeth. He felt Chandler's eyes on him from the end of the bar, but he was relying on her impeccable manners not to ask what they were talking about.

Rhett moved over to stand in front of Jake. "I need to be done for tonight."

"You and me both, man," Jake responded as he blew out a long breath. "Hot tub is off and covered. I'll crash down here once these goons wrap it up."

"I'll make sure the house is locked up and the alarm system is set. Just turn it on before you pass out for the night. I don't want to set it now in case anyone decides to leave." They had thrown enough Jake and Rhett Parties over the years to know the routine. A lot of things may have spiraled out of control tonight, but they had this part down to a science.

"And Jake?"

"Yeah, bro?"

"No one goes upstairs." The words came out crystal clear, sounding more like a threat than a suggestion. He needed to make sure Anwar and Cole heard him, too.

"Agreed."

He finally turned to Chandler. He knew he was responsible for how so many things had unfolded over the course of the day, but he couldn't help but think about how much shit wouldn't have hit the fan if she just hadn't shown up in Hampton unannounced.

"I'm sorry today sucked," he grumbled. He was exhausted, defeated, and completely out of fucks. That was the best he could do right now. "I'll walk you upstairs if you're ready for bed?" he asked, running his hand against the stubble on his jaw.

Chandler said nothing but nodded and gave him a small smile that didn't reach her eyes. She hopped off the barstool and turned to Jake. "Thanks for putting up with me all day," she said, wrapping her arms around him in a side hug and kissing him on the cheek. Jake looked surprised by her unexpected affection.

"I'm glad we finally got to meet," he responded.

Chandler made her way around the bar, waving to Cory and Lia on the couch. "Goodnight, everyone," she called to the group playing beer bong before turning to smile at Cole and Anwar. "It was nice to meet you guys, too."

Chandler's heels clicked across the sunroom tiles as she made her way toward the door. Rhett began to follow her into the house, but he paused to issue one more warning to the group congregated around the beer pong table.

"Hey, Cole and Anwar know the deal for sleeping arrangements tonight for anyone who's staying. The house has an alarm system so just tell Jake if you're heading out so you don't trip it. Upstairs is completely off limits," he finished, raising his arm to wave goodnight.

"You and your stupid limits," Fielding muttered just loud enough for him to hear before sinking a ball into the cup he was aiming for.

Rhett didn't take the bait, instead walking into the house and toward the stairs. Chandler had her foot on the first step when he caught up with her.

"Hey, so I moved your bag to the guest bedroom down the hall," he whispered.

"What? Why?" she asked, glancing back at him with a look of panic in her eyes.

"It's not a big deal," he reassured her. "Tori passed out in my bed, and I didn't want you to have to go in there to get your things."

"Why didn't she pass out in the guest room?" Chandler hissed as the second-to-last stair from the top squeaked in protest. She stopped on the landing and turned to face him.

"I honestly don't know, babe," Rhett lied. "My room's the first door off the stairs, so maybe that's as far as she got?"

Chandler glanced toward his bedroom. The door was open, the outline of Tori's body clearly visible under the covers. She let out a long, dramatic sigh.

"It's weird that she's in your bed right now, Rhett. This whole night has been off. I'm trying not to freak out, but I just get this bad feeling about Tori."

He was desperate to make her shut her up. He couldn't do this right now. He needed to be done. He decided to take the path of least resistance, just one more time tonight.

"Shhh," he soothed, willing Chandler to lower her voice and actually stop talking. "I know. I'm sorry. Honestly? Tori doesn't drink much, so I'm pretty sure she doesn't know whose bed she's in right now. Do you want me to try and move her?"

She bristled at his suggestion, just like he knew she would.

"No, of course not. It's just... You know what, never mind. I don't care where your ex-girlfriend from high school sleeps tonight, as long as you're climbing in bed with me," she stated triumphantly, running a perfectly polished nail along the stubble on his jaw.

It was Rhett's turn to bristle toward her. After everything she had just witnessed, how in the world was she still interested in sleeping next to him, let alone sleeping with him? She clearly hadn't been paying attention tonight. That, or she was willing to stay in denial if it meant staying with him. Rhett felt his stomach clench with pity as he realized just how much she was willing to tolerate.

"Babe, I'm exhausted. I'm not going to be any fun tonight."

"Then where do you plan to sleep, Everhett?" He knew that look in her eyes, and he knew he didn't have another fight left in him tonight.

"I'll sleep in the guest room with you," he insisted as if it was obvious. "I'm just falling asleep on my feet right now and didn't want to disappoint you."

"I'm exhausted, too," she responded, smiling and leaning into his body. Rhett instinctively wrapped an arm around her. "Let's go to bed."

He casually walked over to his bedroom and pulled the door shut. Then he followed Chandler into the guest room, accepting his fate for the night. He left the door cracked open and claimed the side closest to it, confident he'd be able to hear anyone hit the squeaky step if they tried to come upstairs.

CHAPTER 35

Rhett

He didn't wake up as much as he decided to stop trying to sleep. He had tossed and turned all night despite the utter exhaustion he had carried to bed. He felt like a sponge that had been wrung out over and over again—he was spent and useless.

He grabbed his phone and checked the clock for the hundredth time. 6:30 a.m. He didn't need to lie in bed next to Chandler any longer. He slinked out from beneath the covers and made his way out of the room. He shut the guest bedroom door behind him, then turned to confirm the door to his room was still closed, too.

He ventured downstairs in pursuit of coffee and painkillers. He hadn't drank in excess last night, but between the lack of sleep and the stress of the last twenty-four hours, his head was killing him. He also knew Tori would need something to take the edge off this morning, if her stomach could handle the pills.

Rhett started to take inventory of who was where as he moved through the house. Jake was snoring on one of the couches in the living room. Dempsey was stretched out and half falling off the couch opposite of him. No one was in the sunroom, and a quick peek into the den confirmed it was empty as well.

He started the coffeemaker and quietly padded down the basement stairs. He only had to go about halfway down to get a good view of the oversized sectional across the room. He was surprised to see Teddy and Tiff in the middle section of the couch, Tiff's body draped over Teddy's under a blanket. Cole and Anwar had each claimed a side of the couch as well.

Rhett made his way back to the kitchen. He knew Cory and Lia wouldn't still be around this morning, but he was pleasantly surprised to only find one Haas brother in his house.

He pulled down two travel mugs from the cabinet and pocketed the bottle of ibuprofen he found next to the sink. He grabbed the cream from the fridge as well as a water bottle. Once he had prepped Tori's coffee the way she liked it, he carefully balanced the mugs and water and made his ascent up the stairs.

He slowly turned the knob of his bedroom door. The room was illuminated by soft morning light; he had forgotten to lower the blinds last night after Tori had climbed into his bed. He balanced everything in one hand before turning around and locking the door behind him.

He made his way over to her, unsure exactly how to proceed. He knew he had to do things differently today. He was committed to breaking up with Chandler as soon as she woke up. He was just as committed to proving to Tori that he was in this with her; they were in this together. He couldn't defer to her completely, and he couldn't try to control everything. They needed to work together as a team if they were going to move forward as a couple.

Still unsure how to proceed, Rhett decided to try the only thing he could think of to bring her back to him.

She was in the middle of the bed, per usual, so it was easy for him to fit his body under the covers without waking her. She subconsciously shifted in her sleep when he laid down.

Rhett savored the contentment that settled in his body from just lying beside her. When he finally reached out to touch her arm, he realized it was bare. She must have ditched the pool robe during the night. He pulled the duvet up higher to cover her as he felt her melt her body into the mold of his frame. She was right there. They were going to be okay.

"Hmmm," he heard her hum quietly some time later. Rhett shook the fog from his head and yawned. He hadn't meant to fall asleep, but he wasn't surprised he had finally succumbed to closing his eyes now that he was with her.

Tori rolled back into him unexpectedly. He stilled as he felt her press against him. She was completely naked under the covers. He remained perfectly still as she continued to stir. The way she subconsciously rolled her ass back into his groin... he couldn't wait for this fight to be over.

She finally let out a loud yawn, indicating she was awake. He felt her body freeze before she wordlessly shimmied away from him.

"Hey, it's just me, V," he whispered in her direction. "I brought you coffee."

Tori didn't say anything in response. Rhett pulled her back toward him, and when she didn't push him away, he brought his head to rest behind hers on the pillow.

"How's your head?" he asked softly as he ran his hand over her hair.

"How's your girlfriend?" she shot back, her voice low and gravelly with sleep.

Rhett continued to caress her hair, trying not to let her words affect him. He had her alone right now, and he needed to make sure they were okay. After a few minutes of silence, he moved his hand to the nape of her neck, rubbing gently along her hairline, trying to massage away the tension between them. She sighed again but still said nothing.

"Do you want to talk?"

"I don't want to talk," she replied. She didn't expand or give any reasoning. She was still in total shutdown mode.

"Okay. I'll talk. You can listen."

Tori made no objections, so he continued.

"Yesterday was the worst day of my life, V. It was worse than when you broke up with me before college. It was worse than the car crash. It was worse than driving you home from the clinic after you got your test results," he confessed.

"I fucked up yesterday morning by not telling you about the Maddie and Chandler drama right away, and then I just kept messing up all day long. I'm so sorry for how everything went down. I panicked and I played my cards all wrong. I never meant to hurt you —I just didn't want to hurt anyone. But somehow by trying not to hurt anyone, I think I hurt everyone," he rambled on. He felt like he just couldn't find the right words to explain how he was feeling, to make her understand what lengths he would go to never feel this way again.

"I'm not used to you being completely mine. Not yet, at least. I think all the years of keeping secrets and operating on a need-to-know basis has messed with my head. That's not an excuse. I know I have to do better. I *will* do better. I'll be better for you," he promised.

"Today is a new day," he continued, "and today I need you to forgive me. I need you to tell me we're okay or at least tell me that we're going to be okay. I'm going to end things with Chandler as soon as she wakes up. She'll be out of our lives forever, and I'll spend the rest of forever making sure you know you're the only one for me."

Rhett hoped his groveling was hitting the mark. She hadn't said a word since he started talking. He wrapped his arm around her and placed his lips to the back of her neck. When she still didn't respond, he hugged her even tighter.

"Tori? Please say something..." he trailed off, kissing her shoulder and rubbing his hand up and down her bare arm.

"Don't get any ideas, Wheeler," she finally whispered. Rhett stilled and moved his hand off her arm. He wouldn't dare touch her if she didn't want to be touched.

"You're gonna have to go find a condom if you want things to go any further."

Rhett froze as his mind tried to process what she was saying. He told her he had just been tested last week. They didn't need condoms. They had been together—condomless—all weekend. That had been part of their arrangement from the start.

She wasn't making sense. Condoms were for people having casual sex. This wasn't casual—nothing about them was casual anymore. Why would she tell him to use a condom? Unless...

No fucking way. Bile rose in his throat as his body jerked involuntarily away from her.

"What did you just say to me?" he growled.

"You heard me," she replied. Cold. Calculated. She didn't need to repeat the words with a tone like that. He knew what she said. He knew what she meant. His heart felt it in its deepest depths. He was bleeding out from the inside.

"Who?" he demanded, his vision blurring as rage built up in his body.

"It's none of your business, but I'm sure you could figure it out if you thought hard enough about last night." She was still facing the windows, her naked body unmoving under his sheets. "I told you last night that we were over. I tried to tell you so many times... Maybe now you'll finally believe me."

He let out a guttural groan. His eyes burned with rage—no, not just rage. Those were tears. He couldn't believe what he was hearing. He couldn't process how any of this had happened. He had laid awake all night in the guest room. He would have heard if someone had come upstairs and opened the door to his room. Wouldn't he?

But Tori had gone to bed wearing a bathing suit and a robe, and she was completely naked under the covers now. Apparently there was a reason Fielding was nowhere to be found this morning. He had fled.

Fucking Fielding.

Rhett couldn't lie next to her for another second. He shot up in bed and threw his legs over the side. He looked over at her, desperate for her to say something, to say anything, to deny it or take it all back. But she didn't speak. She didn't turn to face him. He could barely hear her breathing.

"So this is it?" he hissed, scrubbing the tears from his eyes before he turned around to look back at the wall. "You're so determined to push me away that you had sex with someone else in my bed last night?"

Tori didn't answer him, but at this point, he hadn't expected her to.

"Message received, Tori. Message fucking received. Congratulations," he declared. "You don't need to worry about pushing me away anymore or ever again. I'm gone."

Rhett rose out of bed and stalked to the door. He cast one last glance at her in his bed. She had rolled over to lie flat on her back with the covers pulled up all the way up to her chin and her hands resting on her forehead. Her eyes were cast up toward the ceiling. She didn't even acknowledge he was leaving.

CHAPTER 36

Tori

"Oh, baby. Yikes. You were hot last night, but you're just a hot mess this morning," Jake greeted her when she finally dragged herself down the stairs. She had laid in Rhett's bed for hours after he stormed off. She hoped that if she just stayed there long enough the mattress would consume her and she wouldn't have to face the reality of what she had done.

She glanced at the couch where Jake lounged, scrolling on his phone. He looked freshly showered and not all that hungover. How was that possible after last night?

"Are we..." Tori started to ask, casting her eyes toward the sunroom.

"We're alone," he answered before she even finished her question.

"Where did he..." Her voice came out an unfamiliar whisper. She was wrecked, emotionally drained, and more pissed at herself than she had even been at him. Tori was grateful when Jake filled in the blanks.

"He came down here raging before eight. He woke me up, told me I was in charge, and demanded that I get everyone out of the house as soon as possible. He and Chandler left shortly after that. He said he'd be back sometime tomorrow." Jake shrugged and shook his head as he eyed her up and down. "I have no idea what set him off."

"That would have been me," she confessed, plopping down onto the couch next to him. Her head was pounding. No, it was swimming. She was having a hard time deciding whether she was hungover or still drunk. Was it possible to be both?

"I figured as much. Come on," he instructed, reaching his hand out to her.

"I don't think I can go anywhere right now," she moaned, rejecting his invitation and curling her knees up under her body instead.

"Stop being dramatic. That's my job around here," he reminded her. "We're just going to the sunroom. I'll get you water and some painkillers. You probably need a little hair of the dog, too, before the interrogation begins."

"Ugh," she moaned in protest, but she let him pull her to her feet.

Tori settled into the couch in the sunroom while Jake took his position behind the Wheelers' bar. She watched as he worked, mixing and stirring with the ease of an experienced bartender. Jake was the same age as Tori and Rhett, yet right now he looked so much older than she felt at the moment. He had been through a lot in life, especially in high school, and then again with the death of his dad and the fallout with his brothers.

Tori sometimes forgot how sweet and decent Jake really was underneath his bad boy, no-shits-given exterior. He looked over at her then and caught her watching him. His eyes held hers for a moment, sizing her up. They had been friends for more than fifteen years. Their friendship ebbed and flowed, always seeming to cool off a bit whenever Rhett was home. Sometimes she missed the closeness she and Jake had shared in high school after he transferred from Arch to Hampton High, but she had accepted long ago that his greatest loyalty was and always would be to Rhett.

Jake poured two drinks from a mixer with a flourish. "So here's the deal, Thompson. First, we drink. Then, you talk."

Tori reached for her drink and accepted his terms. She was in no position to argue, and she felt like she needed someone to talk to right now. Normally that someone would be Rhett, but seeing as he was the person she had just emotionally ravaged a few hours ago... She took a slow sip and relished the taste of the tart tomato juice and tabasco burning her throat.

"You know, I think I like your spicy Bloody Marys better than his."

Jake made an exasperated noise as he sat down. "Don't try to butter me up, baby. You're still in the hot seat." He settled into the couch next to her and took a sip from his own glass before continuing. "Also, you don't need to tell me what I already know. Everyone seems to like my spicy Bloody Marys just fine when Wheeler's not around."

"Oh, Jake. Don't be so naive," she teased. "Rhett could literally serve tomato juice straight from the can, and everyone at Clinton's would declare it was the best thing they'd ever put in their mouth."

"You're not wrong. He's golden, Tori. We know it. He knows it. This whole goddamn town knows it." His words were soft but candid. "I've played second fiddle to him for most of my life, and I don't even care. He's the best friend I've ever had. He's just so steady."

Tori sucked in a sharp breath. She didn't need Jake to regale her with all of Rhett's best qualities. She knew there was no one better.

"You didn't make mine too strong, did you?" she asked, wrinkling up her nose. She realized she had drank more in the past three days than she had in the past three years combined. She had enough to deal with right now without letting herself start to freak out about her alcohol consumption before next month's scans.

"Not yours, baby. Just a splash for you," Jake reassured her, giving her knee a quick squeeze.

She couldn't remember exactly when he started calling her "baby," but he'd been doing it since high school. He had started using the nickname just to make Rhett mad. Now, years later, it really did feel like a term of endearment. She was grateful Jake cared enough to hang back and be with her today.

She took another sip of her drink, then reached for the water bottle and painkillers he had brought out to the sunroom. She swallowed two pills before turning to face him. He was looking at her with a mix of pity and curiosity.

"So?" he asked.

"So," she responded, still negotiating with herself about how much she was going to tell him.

"Let's not make this harder than it needs to be. I think you should just tell me everything."

Tori pursed her lips and tried not to roll her eyes. Jake was Rhett's best friend—she knew everything she said could and would be held against her eventually.

"You don't have to worry," he addressed her concern before she even vocalized it. "I'm in the dog house big time. Maybe even more than you. He's pissed at me for about ten different reasons right now. And I'm so mad at him for how he handled things yesterday. I doubt we're even going on our trip this week..." Jake trailed off, the sadness evident in his voice. "Your secrets are safe with me."

"Fine," she relented.

"Yeah?" He sounded cautiously optimistic.

"Yeah. You go first, though. Tell me what you already know."

Jake cocked one eyebrow in her direction before he began to speak.

"I know that you and Rhett have been playing some twisted game for a while now. You were both obsessed with each other in high school. You dumped him before college. You broke his heart, and he was a mess. You weren't around for a lot of the mess, Tori. It wasn't good... Over the last few years, he hasn't been so mopey. He hasn't seemed so broken. He started dating Chandler. He also started coming home more often and picking up weekend shifts at Clinton's. That part never made sense to me. You two seem to be closer than ever now, or at least you did before this weekend, yet he's still with her?"

She felt the tears well up in her eyes as she listened to his shrewd assessment of her love life. But Jake wasn't done.

"He won't tell me anything about your relationship now. And I know you have some sort of relationship, and that there are things to tell. We used to talk all the time, but now he's so goddamn protective of you that he shuts me down at every pass. I'm barely allowed to mention your name in conversation," Jake confessed. He glanced at Tori, and she saw the pain behind his eyes. A pang of guilt cut through her as she realized how her arrangement with Rhett had affected his friendship with Jake.

"But I've watched you two together over the last few years," he continued. "The looks across Clinton's. The touches when you think no one is paying attention. The way he acts like a giddy, horny high schooler whenever he comes back to town. I know Everhett loves you. He has loved you since the summer before eighth grade. I don't think he ever stopped loving you, and I don't think he ever will."

Tori blinked as the tears fell. Then she blinked again, keeping her eyes closed this time.

"How'd I do?" he deadpanned.

"You nailed it. Well, most of it anyway..."

"Okay, what did I miss?" He took a long sip of his drink, watching her over the rim of his glass.

Tori paused before replying.

"Rhett and I have been... more than friends... since spring break of his junior year." She gave Jake a knowing look. He nodded but stayed quiet, waiting for her to continue.

"He didn't get over us like I thought he would when he went to Easton. I broke up with him before college for the same reason I won't be with him now—he deserves better than me."

Jake's eyes narrowed at her self-deprecation.

"He deserves more than me and what I have to offer," she clarified. "I came up with the idea. We could be... together," she chose her words carefully, "when he's home if and only if he dated other people at school. Enter Chandler."

Jake's mouth was wide open now, but he still didn't make a sound.

"I actually set them up," she confessed. "I downloaded the dating apps on his phone, and I created his profiles. I did all the swiping."

"That's fucked up, Tori." *There it was*. She knew the judgement was coming, and now her hackles were raised.

"I just wanted him to have a distraction back at Easton. It was a way to casually keep things going until he graduated and moved away for good. I wanted it just as much as he did, and it worked out well enough over the last three years. It's more than just sex," she added, "for both of us. I know I can't let him get too close or too attached... but I'm not strong enough to keep him away, either."

She gazed over at Jake, trying to gauge his response.

"So then what happened this weekend?" he implored. His voice was gentler now. "Why did you fly off the handle when she showed up? You know about her. You literally hand-picked her."

She stilled at his jab. She could feel her body tense up defensively at the thought of Chandler.

"Everything has been amped up since he came home unexpectedly in February. All my resolve to keep him at arm's length has disappeared. I feel like I'm on a Ferris wheel that I can't get off. This thing isn't stopping, but I'm enjoying the ride too much to care. I've been having a hard time remembering why I can't be with him..."

"And why is that, exactly?"

Tori shook her head. Jake knew this part. Did she really have to repeat it? If he needed a reminder, he was about to get a reminder.

"Do you want to help your best friend pick out a coffin for me in the next ten years, Jake? You guys do almost everything together. I'm sure he'd let you tag along."

Jake recoiled at the dark place she had gone so quickly.

"Tori," he scolded her. "Baby. Just because your mom..."

"No." She cut him off. "You don't get to talk about her. You don't get to offer your prediction for what my future holds. I'm not sick yet, but I will be someday, Jake. It's not an if. It's a when. I have test results to prove it. While other women my age will be having babies, I'll be having a hysterectomy. And even then I'm probably just buying myself some extra time. My life cannot be his life. I'm never leaving this town. I'm never moving out of that house. Rhett will want to get married. He'll want to have kids. He deserves those things, and I can't..."

"Okay, okay. Stop, Tori. I get it. I'm sorry. I didn't realize you were going to go nuclear on me like that. Give me some sort of warning next time, okay? So this weekend..." Jake tried to steer her back to where they had left off.

"Right, sorry. This weekend. We went to a concert on Friday night, then we went to the cabin. It was amazing. It felt so good to be together, no secrets, no hiding. It was all so easy." Tori sighed.

"Rhett asked me to try again this weekend. To try us again. All those things I just said about my future? I let myself pretend that wasn't my reality. He asked if we could be together, and I didn't say no."

Jake's eyes grew wide with comprehension.

"So you guys were, like, officially together when Chandler showed up at Clinton's yesterday?"

Tori groaned. "Technically yes. We didn't talk everything through at the cabin, but he called me his girlfriend, and I knew he was planning to end things with Chandler. I let myself get swept up in all of it. You know how he is. He's smooth and charming and..."

"He's golden."

"Exactly. He's golden. We hadn't figured everything out, but we had agreed to try. But then things started to unravel. Maddie called. Chandler called. He didn't tell me about any of that as it was happening. Once we got to Clinton's and I found out that he had talked to her that morning without telling me, I picked a fight and freaked out on him," she confessed to herself as much as to Jake.

"Part of me knew he was just trying to protect everyone involved, but when I saw them together, I lost it. Being with someone like Chandler is what Rhett deserves. I couldn't help but wonder if part of him really does want to be with her. They've been together for a while now... He's going to be the CEO of a huge company one day. It makes sense that he would want a supportive housewife, a big house in the suburbs for his kids, the whole nine yards. Those are things I can't give him, but she can. We got in a fight in the walk-in cooler, and I told him that we weren't going to be together after all."

Understanding passed through Jake's expression. Rhett might have been golden, but he was also stubborn to a fault, relentless in the pursuit of whatever he wanted.

"Then he told me the party was still on. And he asked me to come over and pretend like nothing had changed. 'Just get through the night' was his reasoning. That threw me over the edge, but he couldn't see past his own plan. No matter what I said, he just kept trying to brush it off, to assure me he had it under control. I felt like I was talking to a wall. It might have been okay if he would have left me alone and let me cool down. But he just. Kept. Pushing."

Tori reached for her drink and turned the glass upside down, finishing it in two gulps.

"So when you and Fielding showed up in my yard last night..."

Jake was silent for two beats. He sat as still as a statue beside her, sizing her up through squinted eyes.

"Honestly, Tori? I underestimated you." He rose to his feet and headed back to the bar, grabbing her glass in the process. Of course he couldn't just let an empty glass sit on the table. Mike had trained him well.

"Another?" he asked.

"Yeah. Might as well make mine full-strength this time." *Scans be damned.*

"So I will tell you this. I know you might not want to believe it, but just hear me out. I really do think he thought he had it under control yesterday. But Chandler was a mess by the time you guys got to Clinton's. There's no way he could have sent her packing. She couldn't drive. And I didn't make the situation any easier by insisting we still partied last night. I was so pissed at him for not answering any of my calls. I spent hours talking about the party in front of Chandler, because I knew he'd have to go through with it once she knew about it." Jake gave her an apologetic look as he got to work making another round of drinks.

"You're not the only one desperate to spend as much time as possible with him before everything changes in May," he confessed.

She couldn't help but feel for him. He may have contributed to some of the fallout yesterday, but she knew he hadn't meant to hurt her or Rhett. The whole situation was just a mess.

Jake changed the subject as he finished making their drinks. "He literally wants to murder Fielding, you know. I guess something happened between them in the hot tub when we came inside last night." He returned to the couch with two full Bloody Mary glasses balanced in his hands.

"What do you mean?"

"I don't know the details yet. As soon as you got out of the hot tub, I made sure you were okay, then I spent the rest of the night babysitting Chandler. Once you guys went upstairs, Cole told me that Rhett was really riding Fielding about you being off limits. I didn't have a chance to ask Field about it, though, because he got a ride home with Cory and Lia last night."

Tori's eyes grew wide.

"What?"

"Shit," she muttered. "Fielding didn't stay here last night?"

Jake shook his head.

"Shit, shit, shit..." She groaned as a new level of awareness started to surface.

"What's wrong? What is happening right now? You're freaking me out, Tori..."

"I think I messed up," she groaned before explaining. "So I realized last night that I wasn't going to be able to get through to Rhett. He was suffocating me, and I just couldn't bear to deal with it with her still here. I knew I needed to change my approach because obviously he wasn't going to listen to anything I said."

"Okay..." he nodded, urging her to continue.

"So when he brought me coffee this morning I miiiiight havemadehimthinkIhadsexwithFieldinglastnight," she blurted out, horrified with herself as she spoke the words out loud for the first time.

"WHAT?"

She was pretty sure he had heard her. "I made Rhett think I had sex with Fielding last night."

There it was. The words hung in the air between them while Jake's mouth hung agape.

"I had fallen asleep in one of the big pool robes and my bathing suit. I woke up in the middle of the night sweaty and damp, so I took it all off, but then I fell back asleep before I could get up and find anything else to wear. Whiskey is obviously not my friend," she grimaced.

"This morning Rhett tried to get in bed with me." Tori's cheeks blushed as she confessed more of their secrets. "He noticed I didn't have any clothes on. I'm sure of it. I didn't plan it in advance, but once I knew he knew I was naked, I took my shot. I didn't think it through. I just decided to see if it would work."

"Shit, baby. You slept in his bed last night, didn't you?"

Tori nodded. She should have wondered why Rhett had so easily accepted the lies she told him. Or why he didn't come back upstairs and call her on her bullshit after he confronted Fielding. But she had still been a little drunk, and then she was so happy she had finally won a round against him that she didn't even question why it worked. She hadn't realized that her victory round was actually a total knockout.

If Rhett and Fielding had already butted heads the night before... and Rhett found her naked in his bed... and Fielding had left the house before Rhett could confront him... She almost couldn't believe how well all the pieces had come together.

Jake finally broke the silence between them. "Fuck, Tori. He was so upset this morning. You may have actually destroyed him." Jake ran his hand through his short, cropped hair in a very Rhett-inspired motion. Tori's heart ached at the reminder. She knew he was right. What he didn't know was that she may have actually destroyed herself in the process, too.

Tears streamed down her cheeks as she sat in the pain of what she had done. Jake pulled her into a side hug, and Tori rested her head on his shoulder. She knew he had every right to be mad at her, but she was still grateful for his comfort. They sat in companionable silence for several minutes, both heartsick for their golden boy.

"It's probably better this way," she finally muttered. Jake pulled away and looked down at her like she was crazy.

"Something had to end it, Jake," she said before he could argue, growing more sure of her declaration as she spoke. "It's the end of March. He's leaving in May. I have no intention of being with him long term, especially not after this wake-up call, and we both know he would have held on for too long."

They sat quietly for a few more moments.

"I know things are rocky between you guys right now, but promise me you'll make sure he's okay," she whispered.

"I promise," Jake swore to her.

Tori felt emotionally decimated but fortified in her decision. It was time to be done thinking, time to be done feeling. She needed to pick herself up and move on. Or maybe not on, but at least forward. She knew she would never really be able to move on from Rhett, but she couldn't just sit on his couch all day, either.

"Give me your phone, please," she instructed, holding out her hand. "I need Fielding's number."

"Why?"

"I feel like I need to give him a heads-up that Rhett might be on a rampage," she explained. She didn't think Everhett would go after the other man, but she also knew better than to test his temper. Especially if he had been drinking, and especially if he felt betrayed.

Jake nodded in understanding before taking out his phone, unlocking the home screen, and passing it to her.

She texted herself the number, then pulled out her own phone and sent off a quick message as Jake rose from the couch and headed into the house.

Tori: Hey, it's Tori from last night. I got your number from Jake.

He responded to her message a few minutes later:

Fielding: Hey you. I was hoping I'd hear from you again.

She rolled her eyes. Fielding was obviously into her, or at least the idea of her, but she was not in the mood for flirting right now.

Tori: So don't freak out, but you need to know about something that happened this morning.

Tori waited a few breaths for his reply.

Fielding: Let me guess? You woke up and realized you were in love with me, too?

Tori shook her head. If she wasn't so worried about Rhett confronting him, she would have been amused by his cockiness.

Tori: Not quite. Rhett thinks you and I had sex last night, and he's pissed. I don't know if he'll be around Hampton this week or not. I don't think he'll do anything, but I just wanted to give you a heads up.

Her phone vibrated within ten seconds of sending the last text. When she glanced down, she realized Fielding was actually calling her.

"Hello?" she answered hesitantly.

"Tori! Hey. You just couldn't stay away, huh?"

"Um, yeah. I guess not. I didn't expect you to call me." She glanced through the doorway to where Jake was making himself useful in the living room. She really should help clean up, too. She moved toward the makeshift beer pong table and started stacking empty cups.

"So why does Wheeler think we slept together?" Fielding asked. She could picture the smirk on his face even through the phone.

"I... may have said some things to try and make him mad."

"Victoria! You used me?! And here I thought we had a real connection!"

Now it was her turn to smirk. This guy. He was light and playful. Everything was a joke to him, and he didn't seem bothered by Tori's confession. He was the antithesis of her serious golden boy in so many ways.

"I think you owe me, Tori," he continued.

"What do you mean?"

"I mean, if I have to walk around this town worried that Wheeler is going to put a hit on me, it needs to be worth it. Go on a date with me tonight."

"I, no, you don't understand, I..."

"What's wrong? Doesn't Wheeler have a girlfriend? I literally met her last night."

He had her there.

"I don't really date, Fielding."

"Fine. We can just hookup if you don't want me to buy you dinner first."

"I don't date, and I'm not going to have sex with you, either. But nice try. Goodbye, Fielding." She didn't make any moves to hang up the phone.

"Oh, shit. No! Don't go! I was teasing. Look, I like you, Tori. I would love a chance to spend time with you and get to know you better without having to worry about what Daddy Wheeler thinks." He scoffed. "Maybe we could just hang out sometime?"

"Fielding, I don't want to lead you on."

"I know—I heard you, you don't date, and I respect that. I'm pretty sure we could hang out as friends, no expectations. In case you didn't pick up on it last night, I'm a pretty good time."

She couldn't help but smile. "I'm starting to get that impression." Was she actually letting herself be talked into this? "I'm off on Tuesday and Thursday this week. Maybe Jake could hang out with us, too?"

"Tuesday works for me," Fielding confirmed. "We can hang at my house. Text me your address so I don't have to cut through Wheeler's backyard to pick you up again, okay?"

Once they hung up, Tori finished cleaning the sunroom and contemplated her next move. She knew she and Rhett needed distance to get over everything that had transpired over the weekend. Physical distance. Emotional distance. She obviously couldn't be trusted not to hurt him again. She tied off the garbage bag of empties as she made her decision. She pulled out her phone and scrolled through her contacts.

"Please don't hate me because of this," she whispered out loud, blinking back tears as her eyes landed on his name. "I would love you forever if I could, Everhett Wheeler. But I don't have forever to give. That's why I have to let you go."

She clicked on his contact information, scrolled down, and pressed the red "Block this Caller" button. *There. Done*. She felt a foreign sense of finality wash over her. Blocking him was just symbolic: She'd had his cell phone number memorized for the last ten years. But deep down Tori knew this was it. Now that she had made this decision for them she really did have to let him go.

Chapter 37

3.5 Weeks Later

"Tori!" Jake yelled at her back as she passed through the bar area of Clinton's while balancing a full tray. He was lucky she didn't startle easily.

"Hmm?" She turned her head to see what he wanted without breaking pace on her way to her table.

"We've got company, baby!"

Tori glanced past Jake and spotted Fielding sitting at the bar, grinning at her. She returned his easy smile as she made her way further into the restaurant.

This was how it had been for the last few weeks. Anytime Tori and Jake were at Clinton's and Fielding wasn't working his valet job, he would show up and drink at the bar. He didn't mind just hanging out while they worked. Then the trio would inevitably end up at Jake's condo or Fielding's house later that night.

She was glad for their company. It was easier to not overthink things when she spent most of her free time with them. She had rarely been alone since the now-infamous Jake and Rhett Party. She knew Jake had been coordinating their work schedules for the last few weeks so they were on all the same shifts.

She made her way over to a family of four and presented them with their fish dinners. Clinton's was always busy on the weekends, but it was especially packed on the Friday before Easter. She checked on the rest of her section before circling back around to the bar.

"Can you make me two more gin and tonics?" she called out to Jake as she got to work filling up a pint of beer.

"You got it, baby."

"So Tori," Fielding started from across the bar, "what do I have to say to convince you to come to our party tomorrow night?"

Tori rolled her eyes. Fielding had been asking her to come to their Saturday night house party for the last three days. She was anxious for the party to actually happen so it would be over and he could stop talking about it.

It wasn't that she didn't want to hang out with Fielding. She was actually disappointed she wouldn't see him much this weekend. They had been spending afternoons together at his house on Mondays and Wednesdays in between her classes in addition to hanging out at night with Jake. She made them sandwiches, he made her laugh. She felt lighter when they were together, and it was nice to have a new friend who wasn't connected to Rhett.

"I'm pretty sure I partied so hard last month that I'm still buzzed."

"No way! I refuse to accept that," Fielding protested. "I think you've got a lot more potential in you. What I saw last month was just the warm-up. I can't wait to see how wild you get once you really let loose."

"It's not gonna happen, Field," she replied curtly as she loaded up the beers and mixed drinks onto her tray.

"Ah, come on. I'm just teasing, Tori. No pressure. You know I wouldn't let anything happen to you if you wanted to party. Everyone at the house knows we're friends, so you're cool."

Tori shook her head. It was sweet that Fielding thought she was worried about drinking too much, or that she was nervous to drink in front of his roommates. Is that what normal twenty-four-year-olds got to worry about?

"You're wasting your breath, Haas. It's not going to happen." She raised her eyebrows and shot Jake a pointed "handle it" look before walking back into the dining room.

"Sheesh, she's full of piss and vinegar tonight, huh?" Fielding mused, turning up his drink before sliding it across the bar for a refill.

"Tori really isn't a party girl," Jake explained. "What you saw over spring break... that wasn't typical for her. Honestly, she's never like that. I don't think I've seen her drink that much since high school."

Fielding nodded. "Good to know. I was starting to worry it was just me."

"Don't stress, Field. You'd know if Tori didn't like you." He shot him a pointed glance. "The fact that you're sitting here and she wants to hang out with you all the time... that's something. That's a lot of something. I'm sort of amazed you two clicked so quickly."

Fielding was silent at first, then spoke just above a whisper, "Wheeler really did a number on her, didn't he?" He accepted the new drink Jake extended his way and swallowed half of it down in one gulp.

"They really did a number on each other," Jake clarified.

"Are you guys cool again? You and Wheeler? I know things were weird when his girlfriend was in town."

"We'll be fine. Rhett and I have been friends for twenty years. We rarely fight, but when we do, we go hard. We know exactly how to push each other's buttons and piss each other off."

"Ha!" Fielding shouted. "Dude, I'm a twin. You don't have to explain shit like that to me."

"I need these G&Ts remade," Tori clipped out, coming around the corner and setting her tray down on the back bar. "They're supposed to be Beefeater."

"Oh shit, I forgot that from earlier," Jake apologized.

"No worries. I forgot to remind you."

The rest of the shift flew by. Clinton's closed at ten p.m. and was cleared out by eleven. Tori hoisted herself onto a bar stool after she closed out her section. Jake was almost always the last person to leave besides Mike, and since they had driven together tonight, she needed to wait for him to close out the bar. She didn't mind. She would rather be here with her friends than sitting around at home by herself.

She had mastered keeping busy to the point of exhaustion over the last few weeks. She had also made a point of trying to be as social as possible. If she wasn't hanging out with Jake or Fielding, she made plans with Lia, hung out with Cory at his apartment, or took Penny for a walk. She was going to great lengths to not let herself think too much about what she had done and what she had lost as a result of her actions.

"Oh shit, I didn't realize you guys drove together tonight," Fielding said when he saw her waiting for Jake. He was absentmindedly twirling his keys around a long finger. "I would have had a few less if I knew you needed a ride home, Tori."

That got their friend's attention.

Tori held her breath as Jake looked up from all the tickets he had spread out across the back bar. He turned his head first toward Fielding, then back to her. He gave her a strained look, but she didn't need to see the pain in his eyes to know what he was thinking. She knew the trigger; She could read his body language. She spoke up to save Fielding from a potential fight he didn't even know he just initiated.

"It's fine, Jake," Tori insisted. "I'm sure Fielding's not going to drive tonight, and I would never get in the car with him if he had been drinking." She tried to keep her tone gentle and reassuring. Jake stared at her for a few more seconds before nodding once and returning to his work, his face still screwed up in anger.

Jake and Rhett had very strong opinions about drunk driving. They had since high school, since the night of the accident when Rhett totaled his Audi. Rhett had been tipsy, Jake was unknowingly inebriated, and they were almost certain the guy who ran them off the road had been totally wasted. The accident changed so many things. It was one of the reasons they had started hosting Jake and Rhett Parties at the Wheeler house, and it was why they both liked bartending at Clinton's. They could call the shots, and they could order rides for anyone who wasn't okay to drive. They liked having complete control.

Fielding stayed quiet throughout their whole exchange. He must have picked up on the tension because he stopped playing with the keys and set them down on the bar before joining the conversation.

"She's right, man. I'm not driving. Dem is picking me up on his way home from work."

Jake nodded once, his eyes focused on the receipts in front of him.

"Speak of the devil..." Fielding held up his phone and plastered a big grin across his face. "Dem's here, so I'm out. See ya tomorrow night at the house, Jake."

He hopped off his bar stool and made his way over to Tori. He wrapped his arms around her from behind and gave her a hug, resting his chin on her shoulder. She smiled but didn't turn around to look at him. That would have felt just a little *too* intimate. He moved to lower his head toward her neck, and she swore she heard him inhale. She swatted at his arm, but his affection didn't bother her. She knew he was just messing with her like he always did, and she smelled like French fries and fried fish anyways.

"Fielding!" she scolded him when he didn't let go after a few more seconds.

"Goodnight, Victoria," he teased before releasing her. "And hey, if you change your mind about the party tomorrow, just call me. I'll pick you up, and I'm more than happy to be your DD so you don't have to sleep over at the house. Open invitation."

He gave her a dazzling smile and held her eyes with his for a few seconds before his phone vibrated again.

"I'll be right out," he barked into the phone before turning on his heel and walking toward the front door. "Good night, kids! Don't do anything I wouldn't do!" Fielding called behind him as he pushed out of Clinton's.

"Does that guy work here now and I just don't know it?"

Tori hadn't heard Mike come out from the kitchen. How much had he just seen? She took a deep breath and chastised herself—it didn't matter if he saw Fielding's arms around her. She was free to do what she pleased with whomever she pleased.

"No, sir," Jake answered, stacking up his receipts and turning around to the computer. "That's Fielding Haas. He works valet at Mama Maria's and The Grille, and he spends a lot of money at the bar here." He held up the receipts in his hand for emphasis. "Tori and I have been hanging out with him lately. He's good people."

Mike surveyed them for a moment, then nodded. "Speaking of good people..."

Tori braced herself. She knew what was coming next. She had been anticipating it all week. Rhett hadn't been back to Hampton since the first part of spring break, and that had been almost four weeks ago. Easter was just a few days away, so it made sense that he was due home this weekend. It was inevitable that Mike would ask about him.

"I'm surprised Wheeler isn't on the schedule this weekend."

Jake glanced over and tried to catch Tori's eye. She refused to look at him, not willing to show an ounce of emotion, instead scrutinizing the beer tap handles in front of her.

She hadn't talked to Rhett since the morning after the party. She kept waiting for the pain of what she had done to start to fade, but the same intense sharpness rose up in her chest anytime she thought about her golden boy. He had hurt her, yes, but she had struck back so viciously and with such finality. Part of her regretted everything about that morning: about how she responded when he tried to apologize for mishandling the Chandler situation, about what she made him believe about Fielding. But then she reminded herself why she did what she did.

It was better this way. Maybe not better for her, but it was better for him this way. She couldn't give Rhett what he wanted—what he deserved—in the future. Being with someone else would make him happier in the long run. Even if that someone else was Chandler.

"He's in Virginia this weekend," Jake finally replied when he realized Tori wasn't going to contribute to the conversation. "He had to go down to find an apartment and meet with his grandfather since he's moving next month."

Tori's breath stilled in her chest. She knew Rhett was in Virginia—Anne had mentioned it when she had called to invite Tori and her dad over for Easter dinner—but hearing the words out of Jake's mouth made the situation more real. Was he apartment hunting with Chandler? Was she going to move to Virginia? Tori knew enough about the other woman to know that she was graduating next month, too. It had only taken her four years to earn her degree, opposed to Tori's eight-year track. Chandler would be able to follow him if he asked her to.

"That makes sense. Well, I know you guys are both off tomorrow, and we're closed on Sunday, so have a nice weekend."

"I'll be around if it gets busy and you need me to come in," Tori offered as Mike turned to head back to the kitchen. "Just call me." She wouldn't mind having a distraction from everything going on this weekend. Jake and Fielding would be in party mode tomorrow, then she would be spending Sunday with her dad and Rhett's family. She also had her bi-annual scans on Monday. She always felt keyed up and anxious before those appointments, but this time there was an extra layer of sadness to contend with. The scans reminded her of Rhett's absence and the reason for his absence.

Mike smiled at her and nodded before turning to head back to the kitchen.

"I will not be available tomorrow night Mike, so don't call me," Jake shouted after their boss.

Tori saw Mike's shoulders shake with laughter.

"Go home, Jake!" he hollered back to him.

"Yes, sir." Jake circled the bar, grabbed Tori's hand, and pulled her behind him.

"You okay, baby?"

She knew she was a sucky actor. Jake saw right through her.

She gave him a sad smile and nodded but quickly turned her head away. She couldn't deal with Jake being nice to her right now on top of the heartache she was already feeling.

"You did good," he whispered, giving her a once-over to assess if she was going to be able to hold it together on the ride home.

She steeled herself and stood a little taller before she replied with a false sense of confidence, "Just like ripping off a Band-Aid."

CHAPTER 38

Rhett

"Well, Everhett, it seems like just about everything is in order here." Rhett's granddad smiled at him from behind the large desk. "You've done well, son, and NorfolkStar is lucky to have you on board. *I'm* happy to have you on board," he emphasized.

Rhett felt a surge of warmth toward his mother's father. Jonathan Ashton was a powerful man: the CEO of one of the largest transportation logistics companies on the east coast. He was also kind, fair, loving, and steady: everything Rhett aimed to be himself.

He had fond memories from his childhood of spending two weeks each summer in Virginia with his grandparents. His grandma would dote on him and Maddie, feeding them, spoiling them, and showing them off around the neighborhood. But it was his granddad's attention that Rhett was always after. He loved touring NorfolkStar Transport headquarters, staring at the maps and charts hanging on his granddad's office walls, going down to the shipyard, and watching the cargo come in.

Securing this job and impressing this man was important to him. Getting to spend more time with his granddad as he aged was just icing on the cake.

Rhett nodded as he accepted the praise. "Thank you, sir. I'm looking forward to the opportunity to prove myself."

"Okay, Everhett, enough shop talk. How are things at home? I feel like we always talk about work and school, but I miss catching up with my grandson."

Jonathan pushed away from his desk then, rising leisurely to make his way over to the bar cart near the window of his office. Rhett watched him, noting that his gait was slower now than it had been when they walked the halls of NorfolkStar earlier in the day.

"Neat?" his granddad confirmed, already pouring the deep amber liquid into a tumbler.

"Yes, sir," Rhett replied.

His granddad made his way back to the desk, handed over one of the glasses he had just poured, and settled back in across from him. "To new beginnings," he toasted, raising his glass before taking a slow sip.

Rhett mirrored his actions and returned his granddad's easy smile.

"Go on, then. Start talking. I want to know what's going on with you."

Rhett took another sip of his drink, buying a few more seconds before he had to respond.

"Well," he started, avoiding looking his granddad in the eyes as he spoke, "things are okay. It's been a bit chaotic this semester, trying to finish up school and wrap my head around moving. I've been at Easton for six years now..." he trailed off before shifting gears.

"Mom is good. She's involved with Maddie's lacrosse team and the after prom committee, so she's as busy as ever. Dad's been traveling just as much as usual, so I haven't seen him since the holidays, but we have plans to go to a few baseball games before I move down here."

"And your friends at home? How are Jake and Tori?"

Rhett continued avoiding his grandad's gaze. He knew there wasn't anything to the question beyond general curiosity, but he didn't want to show any reaction at the mention of Tori's name.

"Both good, both good," he repeated nervously while nodding. "I saw them last month at the beginning of spring break."

"And how about Chandler? How's she doing?"

"She's good, too." Rhett smiled assuredly. "She's graduating next month, but she's not planning to get her master's right away. She's waiting to hear back from a few internships she applied to in Columbus and New York."

"I'm surprised she didn't tag along with you on this trip." Rhett stilled. He knew this strategy far too well from years of subtle interrogation from his mom.

"Not this time," he explained. "We're going to spend Easter with her folks on Sunday, though."

Jonathan nodded, pausing to sip his drink before he spoke again. "Do you think she'll join you here eventually?"

"I'm not sure. We've been together for a while now, but we haven't talked about her moving here or anything like that."

His granddad nodded again.

"I'm surprised to hear you two haven't discussed it."

His granddad said nothing more, letting the words linger between them. It was fair for Jonathan to question where things stood between Rhett and his girlfriend. He had the business to think about: would Rhett be distracted by going back and forth to Ohio on a regular basis? He knew his granddad's concern probably ran deeper, too. Was he going to be happy in Virginia?

"That's probably a conversation we'll be having soon. It's overdue."

"You know I only care about your happiness, Everhett. I don't mean to pry. I just don't want to see you give up on something you want—or hold onto something for too long that isn't meant for you—because of this new role. If I learned anything after fifty-nine years of marriage to your grandma, it was to prioritize family above all else. This is a job. It's our family business, sure, but at the end of the day, it's just a job." He gave Rhett a pointed look.

Rhett responded with a curt nod before turning his glass back and finishing his drink. The advice landed differently than he knew his granddad intended. He had been settling back into his relationship with Chandler over the last several weeks, but that didn't mean he wasn't still reeling from his breakup with Tori. None of that was relevant to his position at NorfolkStar, though. He needed to keep his head on straight for the rest of this trip.

"Tell me more about that final project brief you sent me for your practicum last week. I have to admit that I didn't understand half of it, but I was impressed by the cost-savings projections for next fiscal year."

Rhett was grateful for the change in subject. Back to business.

"So all those numbers are based on real data I had Tonya send over at the end of Q4. The ability to combine satellite weather technology with our own data will allow us to adjust the dock staffing schedules to a cost-savings of more than $20,000 a week."

This was safer territory. He could talk logistics with his granddad all day. He couldn't wait to graduate next month and finally work for NorfolkStar Transport full-time. He was ready to move here. He was ready to move forward.

"Rhett, did you bring the leftovers in from the car?" Chandler yelled from the bedroom of the apartment. They had just returned from Easter dinner at her parents' house in Wetherington. They had a nice meal, and Chandler's dad had offered him a glass of expensive Cognac after dinner. All in all, it should have been a good night.

But then Maddie had told him it was okay to call home. He just wanted to say hi to his family, but things unraveled when Maddie stepped outside with him still on FaceTime. Rhett didn't think his sister had intentionally tried to set him up, but he had watched the look of determination come over her when she stumbled upon Tori in the sunroom. Maddie saw her shot, and she took it. Tori looked unaffected when Maddie tried to force interaction between them on the phone. Rhett was gutted when he saw her just sitting in his family's sunroom by herself.

Under any other circumstances, he would have been there. He would have been home. They would have been sneaking little touches as they did the dishes together. They would have been plotting what time Rhett would sneak into her bedroom that night. They would have been together.

But he wasn't there. He had gone to Virginia, then came back to Easton and spent the holiday with Chandler and her family. This was his life now. Tori wasn't part of it anymore.

"Yeah, I got them, babe," he replied listlessly to Chandler's question, pulling open the fridge door to make sure he had actually put them away.

"Today was such a good day, Rhett." Chandler sighed as she walked into the kitchen. She pulled the fridge open and grabbed a water bottle before turning around to face him. "And last night was pretty great, too." Rhett's memories from last night were fuzzy, thanks to all the gin and tonics he had downed at Chippy's, but her salacious smile implied they had both enjoyed themselves. "Thank you for changing your travel plans so you could be with me and my family this weekend."

"You're welcome," he replied, returning her smile. "I like spending time with your parents. You're a priority to me, babe."

She wrapped her arms around his waist and rested her head against his chest. He raised his arms to return her embrace. Thankfully Chandler hadn't been in the room with him when Maddie pulled her little stunt. She had no idea he had interacted with Tori that day. *It doesn't matter anymore*. Rhett shook his head in frustration. He was usually good at burying his feelings, but he just felt so raw tonight.

"Hey," Chandler called him back to the moment. She pulled away slightly and glanced up. "Are you okay?"

"Yeah, I'm okay. I'm just tired from traveling this week, and I'm starting to stress about everything I have to do before moving."

Chandler nodded. She always accepted his responses, regardless of how much truth they held. Something irked him about how willing she was to go along with whatever he said. But that was a different conversation for a different day.

"I'm going to go take a shower. Are you coming to bed soon?"

He shook his head. "No, not yet. I might watch a show or listen to music. I'll be in there in a bit."

Rhett made his way into the living room and flopped down on the couch. He mindlessly reached for the remote just to occupy his hands. He didn't actually want to watch anything. He also didn't want to lie in bed and scroll on his phone for hours while he tried to fall asleep. He hadn't been sleeping well at all.

When Maddie went out onto the porch to talk to him away from their parents, it was because she wanted to ask him to hook her up with supplies for after prom at the cabin. The dance was the weekend before Memorial Day—just four weeks away.

Rhett pulled out his phone and opened his calendar app. He needed to set a reminder now before it slipped his mind. As he scrolled past the current date, one of the notes for the upcoming week caught his attention.

Tori—scans??

He had entered the note quickly while they were at the cabin last month. Everything had unraveled later that weekend, though, so he had no idea the actual date and time of her appointment.

He didn't feel right not being home when she had to go for scans. But he also had no damn idea when her appointment was scheduled. Tori usually scheduled her scans right before or after a weekend, making it easy for him to be in Hampton. More than once, he had contemplated just showing up at home. He couldn't shake the feeling that he needed to be there. But appearing in Hampton unannounced wasn't going to magically fix things between them. Seeing her in person would be like pouring salt into a wound, and that was if she was even amicable toward seeing him.

He entered Maddie's prom date into his calendar, then let the phone drop onto his chest.

After four weeks apart, he wished his feelings for Tori had ebbed enough to take the edge off. But after seeing her on FaceTime tonight, after being more connected to her through Maddie's phone than he had been for a month, the heartbreak felt as fresh as it did the morning after the party.

She had gone to such great lengths to push him away and hurt him. He still couldn't wrap his mind around her sleeping with Fielding in his bed. He couldn't process that level of betrayal. Most days he let himself forget about it out of self-preservation, but every now and then, the truth crept back in like a vise squeezing him from the inside.

Rhett puffed out his cheeks and let out a long sigh of acceptance. He wasn't going to go home to Hampton this week. He needed to stop torturing himself by continuing to entertain the idea. He didn't have enough information about her appointment, and he didn't have enough gumption to believe she wanted him there. Besides, he really did have a lot to do for school before the semester ended. He would just stay in Easton until graduation, move home the following weekend, then make the big move to Virginia the last week of May.

He told himself it was better this way. He knew this was how it had to be for them to move on, to really get over the ten years of ups and downs and everything they had put each other through.

He knew better, and yet that didn't stop him from picking his phone back up and doing the same thing he had done every single night, at least once a night, for the last four weeks.

He unlocked the screen. He found her contact information. His thumb hovered over her name, pausing for a few seconds as he reveled in the hope of "maybe" before he clicked on her number. Then he lifted the phone to his ear.

And just like every other night for the last four weeks, the call went straight to voicemail. She had blocked him, which he discovered the very first night after the party. Rhett closed his eyes and listened to her recorded message all the way through, picturing her face in his mind's eye. When the recording prompted him to leave a message after the tone, he ended the call.

"Goodnight, V," he whispered before pocketing his phone and peeling himself off the couch.

Chapter 39

Tori

She had been searching for a pot with a fitted lid when she came across an electric skillet and inspiration struck. "Hey, do you guys have a waffle maker?" she called from the spot where she sat on the kitchen floor.

"Wait, you know how to make waffles?" Fielding sauntered into the kitchen. He was wearing dark jeans and a fitted powder blue T-shirt that clung to his arms and chest. The fabric was looser around his waist, and when he moved, Tori could see the tippy-top of the dip of his hips. She wasn't interested in Fielding that way, but she couldn't totally ignore the fact that he could rock a pair of jeans and a T-shirt. "Why did I not know this? And why are you on the floor?"

"I'm on the floor because I wanted to make stir-fry for lunch, so I was looking for a pot with a lid. And yes, I do in fact know how to make waffles. I'm in charge of Waffle Wednesday at Camp New Hope each year. I make the best waffles you've ever tasted. But step one is having a waffle iron, which I'm guessing you don't have. Maybe I could bring mine from home this weekend?"

Fielding looked down at her with a grin. "You're so cute. You're already thinking about what to feed me this weekend. Have I professed my love to you yet today, Tori Thompson?" He offered his hand to help her off the floor.

"Oh, stop. Go take a cold shower or something." She rolled her eyes but let him help her up anyway. "I feel like I have to plan ahead to keep up with your appetite."

She bumped the cupboard closed with her hip. No pot with a fitted lid meant they were having sandwiches for lunch again. Oh well. She didn't mind. Making sandwiches with Fielding at his house trumped eating a sad to-go salad by herself on campus.

"Damn. Waffles sound so good. Now I'm starving. What can I help with?"

"See if there are any of those good sub buns left that we used on Monday." She turned toward the fridge to start digging out the rest of the ingredients.

"Hey, wait, so if you're already meal planning for this weekend, can I assume we've got plans?"

Tori considered his question. She knew the boys were having a get-together on Friday night. Not a full-fledged party, Fielding assured her, because Dempsey and Teddy had to work that night, but Jake was coming over, and Anwar and Cole would be home, too.

"Perhaps," she teased. "But we're going to need a grocery run if we're feeding everyone this weekend." She pulled out the nearly empty bags of lunch meat and held them up for emphasis.

"Agreed. Will you go shopping with me? We can go on Friday since you don't have class. What's your work schedule this weekend anyways?"

"I'm only scheduled for Sunday, open to three."

"I've got to work on Saturday night, then again on Sunday morning. That gives us Friday night to party, and all of Saturday to eat waffles."

"Wait—I thought Friday *wasn't* a party?" she countered.

Fielding rolled his eyes and reached over her head to pull out two glasses from the cupboard. She moved out of his way as she finished making their sandwiches. They moved around the kitchen in sync, a comfortable vibe between them.

"I meant 'party' as in the verb—to party. You know... to hang out, to have a few laughs, to have a good time? I already promised you it wouldn't be a rager. I meant it. You can trust me, Tori."

"Did you really just provide a dictionary definition for the word party?" she joked. She hated it when he tried to be gentle with her. She much preferred his witty banter and smart mouth. "They really did provide an exceptional education at Archway Preparatory Academy."

"Shove off," he laughed. Tori plated their sandwiches, then carried them over to the little table in the kitchen's eating area. Fielding followed with their water glasses, a few napkins tucked under his arm.

Before she could sit down, Tori felt her phone vibrate in her back pocket. She glanced at the screen. The number was calling from Akron, Ohio.

"Oh, hang on, I want to take this," Tori muttered, taking a few steps out of the kitchen into the living room. "Don't wait for me to start," she told Fielding over her shoulder. "I'll just be two minutes."

She stepped another few feet into the living room and perched herself on the edge of a couch as she swiped to accept the call.

"Hello?" she answered.

"Hello. This is the nurse calling from Dr. Ritter's office for Ms. Thompson."

"That's me," she confirmed, picking a few crumbs off the leg of her jeans from the sub buns she had just cut. She had been waiting for this call since she walked out of the clinic nine days ago. She always stressed herself out unnecessarily about her results. She tried to steady her breathing. It would all be over in just a few minutes.

"Can you please provide me with your birth month and date for security purposes?"

"March 15," she confirmed.

"Great, thank you for that. The reason for my call today Ms. Thompson is because the results of your blood work just came back from your appointment on April 22," the nurse explained.

Tori stopped breathing. Her finger and thumb froze into a pinched position, holding onto one last crumb she had meant to swipe away to the floor.

"My blood work?"

"Yes. We're showing abnormal results from your CA-125 blood test last week. Now, the CA-125 is not typically viewed as a diagnostic test, but for the research study, we run it on an annual basis because of its link to ovarian cancer. Abnormal results don't mean there's any cause for concern; abnormal just means the results were out of range and more testing is required."

"I know what abnormal means," Tori hissed into the phone.

Her right leg was bouncing up and down without conscious thought. She had lost all feeling in her left leg because of how she had it tucked under her body on the edge of the couch.

"Right. So the next step is to come back in for a pelvic exam and ultrasound. Typically with someone your age, there's no urgency to come in for follow-up testing, and some patients opt to wait until their next scheduled wellness visit. But given your family's medical history, Dr. Ritter asked me to call you right away and get you scheduled to come back in for the exam and ultrasound on Monday."

"What time?" she demanded.

"Three p.m."

She closed her eyes in an attempt to shutter herself from the reality of what was happening right now. She had always anticipated this call, but she wasn't prepared for how the news would swirl up inside her like disturbed silt.

"What about the mammogram?" she thought suddenly, speaking the words out loud.

"Hold on, let me pull up the rest of your chart. The mammogram was all clear," the nurse replied on the end of the line. "The results will be uploaded into your online profile for you. I'm also going to send over some information about the appointment on Monday. What to expect, what to do and not do beforehand, that kind of thing. Be sure to avoid penetrative intercourse forty-eight hours beforehand, and please arrive at least fifteen minutes prior to the start of the appointment."

Tori heard nothing else.

She didn't even remember ending the call.

Her mammogram was clear.

Her blood work wasn't.

The genetic research study only required a blood draw once a year, not every six months like the other screening protocols. That should have been enough, but right now it didn't feel like enough. Whatever was there—whatever was in her—it could have been there for an entire year prior.

Her mammogram was clear.

Her blood work wasn't.

Her mom had breast cancer first. She had breast cancer in her twenties, more than ten years before she got the ovarian cancer that killed her. This wasn't how she had expected it to happen.

A buzzing grew louder in the distance. It was muffled but persistent. It sounded like the summer cicadas all emerging from the depths of earth in unison. She could feel the vibrations in her body, she could practically hear it in her bones.

She needed to sit down. No, she was already sitting down.

She needed to stand up.

She needed to go.

She needed to get out of here.

"Tori?"

She heard her name being called from far away. She would worry about that later. Right now she had to go.

"Tori?"

She felt fingertips wrap around her arms. She was being lifted. Lifted up? No, lifted down. Her left leg was still numb, and now that she had changed positions, a million needles pricked her from the inside. She was on the floor. She wasn't going to be able to stand up, let alone get out of here. Her body always betrayed her.

There were hands on her face. She blinked twice, then squinted her eyes. Fielding's face came into focus.

"Tori, what the hell is going on? Are you okay?"

He was kneeling before her. He had her face in his hands. She noticed he had a few small freckles across the bridge of his nose. Were those new? She had never noticed those before...

Fielding's freckles were cute, and she thought about teasing him, but then she remembered she didn't want to be here. She could feel herself slipping away. Away was safe. Away was good. She had to get away from here.

"Tori!" he practically screamed. She could feel his hostility bubbling up. She didn't want to be here when he lost his cool. Fielding wouldn't hurt her, but she was tired of dealing with angry boys. Fielding wasn't supposed to be the angry one. That special honor was reserved for her sad, angsty golden boy. Her golden boy. Yes, that's who she needed right now.

"Call Rhett," she whispered. She shook off his hands, letting her forehead rest against her knees. She hugged her legs closer to her chest. Her left leg still felt like it wasn't even a part of her body. She was jealous—she didn't want to be part of her body, either.

"What the hell are you talking about? What's going on?" His words registered, but she didn't know who he was talking to. She waited, listening closely for their answer.

"Did you fall? Are you hurt?" Fielding sounded panicked. She glanced around the room. Who was he talking to?

"Tori, I'm about to call 9-1-1..." he threatened. She let her head lift up slightly but kept her chin firmly planted on her knees. She locked eyes with Fielding.

"Call Rhett."

Tori closed her eyes again. She was so damn tired. She felt Fielding pry something from her hands. He could have whatever he wanted. She didn't care.

Her breathing had picked up considerably now that she was crumbled on the floor. Her lungs were fighting to suck in enough air, to turn oxygen into carbon dioxide. No, wait. Maybe her lungs wanted the carbon dioxide to get out? Did she always have to think this hard about breathing? She felt herself try to inhale. Nothing came in. Then she tried to exhale. Nothing came out.

"Goddamnit, I can't find his number in your phone," Fielding snapped.

That got her attention. Tori lifted her head and sat up straighter. Her body automatically—finally—pulled in a shaky breath. Fielding locked eyes with her again. She saw the panic in his face. Did he know what the nurse had just called to tell her?

He couldn't know. No one knew yet. This wasn't how it was supposed to happen. She didn't expect it to be like this.

She heard a sad noise come from Fielding's direction. It sounded like an injured animal. Did one of his roommates have a pet she didn't know about? It sounded like it was in pain. She decided she should try and help it. She shifted her weight, attempting to stand up on her own. She felt her body rise slightly off the floor, then reconnect with the ground three seconds later. She glared at Fielding—had he just pushed her?

"Call Rhett," she heard herself demand again. Yes. She nodded. That was a good idea. Rhett wouldn't push her down. Rhett wouldn't let Fielding push her down, either.

"Tori, I'm trying, I swear. You gotta help me out here. I can't find Wheeler's number in your phone. I sure as hell don't have it. Do you know his phone number?" He had the saddest look in his eyes. She wanted to reach out and comfort him, to take care of him and to help him, just like she wanted to help that poor animal.

Focus.

Did she know Rhett's number? Of course she knew his number. She watched herself from above: thirteen-year-old Tori splayed out on her purple bedspread, Nokia cell phone in hand. As soon as the clock hit nine, she dialed the phone number she knew by heart. She held her breath as the phone rang once, then a second time. She hadn't seen him since they got off the bus that afternoon. She couldn't wait to talk to him now...

"Hey, Jake, I'm sorry to call you at work, man."

She heard Fielding talking again. He talked a lot.

"Tori is here and she's freaking me out. She's sitting on the floor, and she can barely speak. She just keeps telling me to call Wheeler, but I can't find..."

"No, of course not. No. I've been with her all afternoon!" he bellowed. Talking and yelling. He sure did like to hear his own voice.

"She came over between classes. We were about to eat lunch when she got a phone call. It was taking a long time, and when I came in to check on her, I found her on the floor in the living room. It's like she can't hear me. I can't get through to her. She just keeps telling me to call Rhett."

A pause.

"Yeah. Yeah, that should work." Fielding sounded so defeated.

"Tori, hey, look at me. Can you hear me?" He had put one hand on her face and gently lifted her chin. "Tori, I've got Jake on the phone. I'm going to put him on speaker phone now so you can hear him, okay?"

"Baby, what's going on?"

Another voice had entered the room. When did Jake get here? Tori looked around before glancing back down at the phone Fielding was holding out in front of her. She blinked twice, trying to gain enough clarity to respond to his question. She heard Fielding let out a growl of frustration.

"She can hear you, man, or at least I think she can, but she's still not talking."

"Tori, baby, you gotta talk to me. What's going on? Field said you got a phone call. Is it about your dad?" A pause.

"Is it about school?" Another pause.

"Is it about Lia or Cory or Maddie?"

Maddie, Tori thought to herself. Yes, Maddie. No, no, not Maddie. *Rhett*.

"Call Rhett," she croaked out again, desperate for someone to actually hear her, to listen to her. How many times was she going to have to say it before they understood?

"Dude, just text me Wheeler's number. I'll call him. I don't know what else to do for her."

"Fuck. You know that's not going to go well, man. Let me call him instead. You're at the house, right?" Jake confirmed. "I'm at Clinton's, but I can be there in fifteen minutes, twenty minutes, tops. Keep your phone on you. I'll be there as soon as I can."

CHAPTER 40

Rhett

He had been on campus studying for a few hours when he decided to finally head over to the business building for his final. He had half an hour until go time, and he was feeling good about the exam.

He only had to sit for two finals this week: one today, then one more tomorrow morning. The rest of his degree requirements were met through his practicum and final project for the semester. It was wild to think that just two tests and eighteen hours stood between him and the end of his college career.

As he stepped into the shadows of the business building, Rhett felt his phone vibrate in his pocket. He reached for it absentmindedly, his thoughts still on graduation.

It was Jake. He hit the button on the side of his phone to ignore the call. He'd call him back that night or the following day. He took a few more steps forward before his phone started vibrating again. He knew who it was without looking. The man was relentless. He sent the call to voicemail once again but then opened up his Messages app to shoot him a quick text.

Rhett: *About to walk into a final. I'll call you tonight.*

The little dialogue bubble popped up on the screen, indicating he was already replying.

Jake: *Call me as soon as you can. It's Tori.*

Rhett stopped in his tracks. He stared at the screen of his phone and reread the message. Jake knew where things stood between him and Tori. His best friend may have a flare for drama, but he wouldn't mess around with something like this. If he told him to call ASAP, he meant it. He hit Jake's name on the screen without giving it another thought. There was nothing to think about. His gut told him this couldn't wait.

The phone only rang once before he answered.

"Bro, I'm so sorry to do this to you right before a final," he lamented.

Rhett gripped the phone tighter to his ear. "What's going on, Jake?"

"I don't know for sure, but something's up with Tori. Something's wrong. She's freaking out."

"What do you mean she's freaking out?" he fumed. He made an effort to unclench his jaw.

"I told you I don't know yet. I'll be with her in ten minutes. I was at Clinton's when Fielding called me. She's with him right now at..."

"Fucking Fielding," he growled into the phone.

"No, man, I don't think this is because of Fielding. They were hanging out, and he's the one that called me to tell me something was wrong. It sounds like she's having a panic attack. She just keeps saying 'call Rhett,' but Fielding couldn't find your number so he called me."

He saw red as he thought about Haas with Tori. What had he done to her?

"Where are you now?"

"I'm on Stone Road, heading to the valet guys' house. They live right on the edge of town."

He felt like he'd been sucker punched in the stomach. Tori was with Fielding. She was alone with Fielding. Tori was at Fielding's house. Something happened to her at Fielding's house.

"Goddamnit, what did Haas say when he called you? Do you think he did something to her?"

"No, Rhett. Listen to me. Tori and Fielding are friends. They've been hanging out a lot lately. I'm positive Field didn't do anything to her," Jake tried to reassure him.

"I'm not," he shot back. Since when were Tori and Fielding friends, anyways? She had fucked him in his bed, but they were still hanging out now? Was there something going on between them?

Rhett pulled the phone away from his ear to check the time again. Twenty-two minutes until his final.

"Field said they were having lunch and Tori got a phone call. She went to the other room to answer it, but then she didn't come back to the kitchen. He found her sitting on the floor. He doesn't know who called. He doesn't know what they said. All she keeps saying is 'call Rhett,' but Fielding couldn't find your phone number in her phone for some reason."

"She blocked me last month," Rhett confessed as things started to click into place, "and her scans were last week..."

That had to be it. Someone called with her test results, and they weren't good. He closed his eyes and tried to think through his options. He had to take a final exam in twenty minutes. Even when he got through that one, he had to take another final tomorrow morning at ten. He had to sit for these finals to graduate.

He raked his free hand through his hair, pulling on the ends and closing his eyes in concentration. "Jake," he croaked out, emotion clouding his voice. He didn't even know what to say. He was four hours away. He was useless. It wasn't supposed to be like this.

"I know, bro, I know. I'm so sorry. I'm trying to get there as fast as I can, but I'm at least ten minutes away, maybe fifteen if there's a train."

That meant Tori only had Fielding with her for the next ten to fifteen minutes. Rhett couldn't let himself think about the injustice of Haas comforting her while he was four hours away.

But Tori had asked for him. That was all he needed to hear. He knew what he was going to do. He would have to suck up his pride and forget all the anger he felt over spring break when she betrayed him. This wasn't about him. This was about her, and she needed him right now.

After a few more silent beats, Jake interrupted his train of thought.

"What's the plan, Rhett? I'm eight minutes away now. Your final is at three o'clock?"

Rhett pulled the phone away from his ear, checking the time again. He had sixteen minutes.

"Get there as quickly and safely as you can. I have this final at three, then I have another final tomorrow morning. I can't come home until tomorrow afternoon at the earliest. Fuck. Jake..." his voice cracked with emotion. "Please take care of her. Stay with her. Tell her I'll be there as soon as I can."

"I've got you covered. I'll be there for her."

Rhett hung his head, defeated by the admission that he couldn't give Tori what she needed right now. Why did it feel like she was always just out of reach?

"Wait, I've still got fifteen minutes until my test. Send me Haas' phone number," Rhett commanded. He might not be able to be with her right now, but he still had a way to reach her.

"You sure that's a good idea?" Jake questioned.

"Yes," he replied without hesitation.

"Okay, yeah. I'll text it to you right now, and I'll text Fielding a heads-up to answer."

"Thanks, Jake," Rhett muttered before ending the call. He looked around campus while waiting for the text to come through. A stream of bodies filled the green space now, with a steady line of students walking into the business building to take their finals.

He had thirteen minutes... or more like ten minutes, because he had to get up to the third floor and into his seat by three.

The phone vibrated in his hand. He opened the text and hit the number on the screen. It rang once. Then again. Rhett started to shake his head as the phone rang a third time. *Fucking Fielding.*

"Hello?"

He exhaled. He could somehow feel her through the phone already. She was right there.

"Haas—it's Wheeler. Put her on the phone," he barked.

"Hey, man, listen, she can't even hold the phone," Fielding tried to explain.

"Fine," Rhett conceded. "Put me on speakerphone, and you hold the phone for her."

Rhett heard rustling in the background. A few seconds later, Fielding's voice came through the line again. "Tori? Tori, can you hear me? Rhett's on the phone." Then, louder: "Okay, you're good, she can hear you now."

"V, it's me. Jake just called me and said you got a phone call. Was it about your scans?"

Silence.

"She's... she's nodding," Fielding confirmed. Rhett closed his eyes in frustration. He hadn't been there for her when she went to her appointment, and he couldn't be there for her now. On top of that, he was dependent on Fielding to translate this conversation between them.

He felt the anger rise inside him. A tremor caught him by surprise as he tried to bury down his rage. All of that would have to wait for later. This wasn't about him. This wasn't about Fielding. This was about Tori. Whatever she needed, whatever he could offer her right now, that was his primary focus.

"V, listen to me. I know you can hear me. What did they say? Can you remember?"

More rustling on the end of the line. Rhett thought he heard footsteps. He silently cursed to himself as he remembered that Fielding lived with a bunch of other guys. He was sure Haas hadn't thought to take Tori somewhere private so she didn't have to have a goddamn panic attack in the middle of his house for everyone to see. Of course he wouldn't have thought of that. He didn't know how to take care of her.

"Sorry, we're back. Jake just got here," Fielding explained.

Rhett let out a long breath he didn't know he was holding.

"Rhett, you there?" Jake questioned.

"Yeah, man. I'm here."

"Hey, baby, hey, come here..."

Rhett listened intently as he heard his best friend go to Tori. His shoulders dropped slightly. Jake was there. Jake would be there until he could get there. Relief flooded his body, but panic started to rise again as he saw one of his buddies from class enter the business building. He didn't have much time left. He had to get through to her.

"Tori." Her name came out strong and clear even though that was the opposite of how he felt. "Tell me what the doctor said so I can figure out what we need to do," he insisted.

"Abnormal blood work," she whispered through the phone. Her voice was low and gravelly. She didn't sound like herself at all. "I have a follow-up appointment on Monday."

It was the worst possible news, coming at the worst possible time, but at least he knew the cause of her pain. Now he could make a plan.

"Okay, beautiful, listen to me. I have to take a final right now. I'm so sorry, but it starts in a few minutes. Then I have to take another one tomorrow morning." Rhett heard the frustration in his own voice. He inhaled, trying to calm down, trying not to let her know he was seething. He could do this. He needed to do this for her.

"As soon as I'm done tomorrow, I'm there. I'll be back in Hampton by late afternoon, dinner time at the latest. We can do this."

Silence.

"She's nodding," Jake assured him. Rhett knew Fielding was probably still in the room, too, but he didn't give a damn right now. There was only her.

"Tori, listen to me. You're going to be okay. We will get through. I'm going to be there as soon as I can. I've got you, beautiful."

"Okay," she finally mumbled. Her voice still didn't sound like her own, but that one single word was all the confirmation he needed.

"Jake?" he asked, turning his attention to his best friend.

"Yeah, bro, I'm here."

"Take her home. Make her eat something. Don't leave her alone until Paul gets home, and make sure you talk to him before you leave her house. If she can't tell him what's going on, then you tell him to call me," Rhett ordered, commanding the situation the best he could from so far away.

"Got it. Go take your test. I've got you."

Rhett glanced at the screen of his phone again. He had four minutes until his final. He started jogging toward the business building, desperate to get this first obstacle out of the way.

"One more thing, man," he added.

"What do you need?"

"Unblock my number from her goddamn phone."

"Done."

CHAPTER 41

Tori

"Dude, I'm so glad to see you," Fielding confessed to Jake. "That was intense. I don't even know what's going on." He glanced down to where Tori still sat on the floor. She saw the storm of emotions in his eyes: worry, sadness, stress. If she had more energy to process anything besides her own shock, she would have felt bad for what she had just put Fielding through.

Tori looked up at Jake, who had been by her side since he arrived. He hadn't taken his eyes off of her, even when Fielding spoke. He held her gaze for another moment, a question rising between them that he didn't want to speak out loud.

"You can tell him," she replied to his silent question. She was okay with Fielding knowing. He deserved to understand what was going on after what he had just witnessed.

"Tell me what?" Fielding looked between the two of them on the floor. She felt Jake rest his hand on her shoulder.

"Tori's mom was sick when she was little," he started. "She had cancer when Tori was just a baby, then it came back, and she died when Tori was eleven." Jake paused, but she didn't have anything to add. She kept her forehead pressed into her knees as he continued.

"It's all genetic. Tori goes for scans twice a year because of it. She's in a special research study that covers the costs. It sounds like the results from the latest scans weren't good."

She looked up at Jake then. She knew her eyes were emotionless. Everything was raging inside her, but she didn't have the energy to share what she was feeling or to deal with anyone else's reactions.

She was so disappointed in how she had responded to the phone call. She never expected to be sitting on Fielding's floor, begging him to call Rhett. She had no right to want for him anymore, to rely on him as her emotional support person. She felt like she had betrayed herself. But now that she knew he was on his way, her physical and emotional need for him felt inevitable. That realization shocked her as much as it comforted her.

"Tori..." Fielding hesitated, moving to sit in front of her as he reached for her hands. She let him hold her hands, but she refused to meet his gaze. She didn't want his pity. She didn't want his comfort. "Tell me what I can do to help. I want to be here for you. I'm sure everything will be..."

"No." Tori cut him off with one word. He didn't get to reassure her. He didn't get a say in this. This was really happening, and there was nothing anyone could say to stop it. Fielding was a good friend, but he'd only been her friend for a few weeks. She didn't want him to think he was going to be around for any of this.

"Don't, Fielding," she chastised, finally looking up. "There's nothing you can do." She glanced over at Jake, giving him a weary look to let him know that she was done.

"That's bullshit," Fielding shot back. "We're friends, Tori. You can't just shut me out. I want to support you. Let me be here for you." His anger didn't surprise her. Fielding never treated her like she was something that could break. That was one of the things she liked most about him, honestly. Unfortunately, this wasn't the right time to try and put his stake in the ground.

Tori looked over at Jake again, shook her head once, and buried her face back in her hands.

"Leave it, Fielding," Jake ordered.

That was the exact response she had been hoping for. She knew he would take control of the situation and handle it the way Rhett would have if he were here.

"I want to help!" Fielding exclaimed as he raised a fist to his mouth in frustration.

"Look, there's nothing you can do. I know it sucks to feel powerless, but that's what we are here. There's nothing I can do, there's nothing you can do, and Tori hates when people pretend otherwise," he explained. That was true. Jake knew her well.

Fielding let out a huff. He was so rarely frazzled. This was a different side to the playful, flirtatious man she'd gotten to know over the last month.

"If you're serious and you really want to help, you can help me make sure she's not alone until Rhett gets home," Jake challenged.

She could feel the tension spike at the mention of Rhett's name. There was an unspoken battle waging between them. Fielding knew so little about her history with Rhett. He probably thought it was weird that she wanted him to be here.

Tori peeked up at the two men, curious as to who would end the standoff first. She already knew who was going to win. But how would Fielding handle losing? Whatever passed through his eyes told the other man what he needed to know. "That's what I thought," Jake muttered under his breath before turning back to her.

"Come on, baby. You heard Rhett. I've got to get you home, then I'll stay with you until your dad gets there." He reached for her arm and gently pulled her up to her feet.

"Shit. Fine. I can come over tomorrow and stay with her if you have to work," Fielding relented through gritted teeth.

Jake studied the other man for a moment before responding. "Thanks, man. I have to be at Clinton's at eleven, so if you can show up at ten thirty, that'll help."

Fielding nodded once before turning to her. "I really am sorry, Victoria," he offered again, this time his pity mixed with a tinge of guilt. "But I'm not going anywhere. You'll see. I'm going to be here for you, anyway you'll let me. I'll see you tomorrow."

Fielding pulled her in for a brief side hug, kissed the side of her head, then released his hold. Jake didn't drop her hand the entire time.

"Hey, Tori? We're here."

Jake's words interrupted her racing thoughts. She glanced up and recognized the blooming lilac bushes in front of her house on Sunset Drive. "I'm going to go in with you and hang out until your dad gets home, okay?"

She felt tears begin to form in her eyes as she thought about telling her dad about the bloodwork. He had already lost a wife. Now he'd have to grapple with the very real possibility of losing a daughter, too.

"Come here," Jake insisted, reaching across the middle console of his Jeep and pulling her into a suffocatingly tight hug. Tori let him engulf her body. She didn't need the comfort, she couldn't feel it anyways, but she knew it would make him feel better.

A sob rippled through her chest unexpectedly. She hadn't cried yet. She hadn't let herself cry on the phone or in front of Fielding. There would be plenty of time for crying. The sob surprised her, but she knew it came from a place of appreciation. She was so grateful for Jake's friendship, for the way he showed up for her and subbed in when his best friend wasn't around.

"I can't do this alone," she cried into his shoulder. Her tears mixed with her mascara and left inky black stains on his T-shirt.

"I know, baby. I know." Jake tried to comfort her by running his hand up and down her back and squeezing her even tighter. He was trying his best, but she knew she wouldn't feel any semblance of true comfort until Rhett was the one holding her.

She had always planned to cut out the cancer from her body just like she had planned to cut out Rhett from her life: to remove them both before either one could change her forever. But now nothing was going according to plan. The feeling of powerlessness consumed her. She wasn't surprised when Rhett told her he was coming home. She knew he wouldn't hesitate. But she hated herself for asking so much of him. She felt equal parts ashamed and angry that she had put so much effort into pushing him away for so long, only to cave this easily.

"I can't do this without him," Tori clarified as the tears continued to fall.

"He'll be here soon," Jake assured her. All she could do was nod into his chest.

Rhett would be there soon.

CHAPTER 42

Rhett

Rhett's phone was in his hand before he even stepped foot outside the business building. The last two and a half hours had gone by in a blur; he couldn't recall a single question from his final exam, but he was confident he had prepared well enough that he had at least passed the test.

He hit Jake's name on the screen. He wanted a full report of everything that had gone down today.

"How is she?" he asked in greeting.

"It's not good, Rhett." He knew Jake wouldn't bullshit him. He knew it wasn't good, and yet he still felt something cold pass through him upon hearing his response.

"I think she's in shock," Jake explained. "When I first got to Fielding's house, she was having a panic attack. She keeps going in and out of it. It's like she's been in a trance all afternoon."

Rhett growled his frustration into the phone but said nothing else, allowing Jake to continue.

"I couldn't get her to eat. Don't get pissed at me about that. I swear I tried," he defended before Rhett could lecture him. "Her dad got home about half an hour ago, so I just left. I talked to him for a few minutes. He got the drift of what's going on. He has to work tomorrow, so I'm going back in the morning. I'll stay with her until I have to leave for my eleven a.m. shift, then Field's gonna take over..."

"No!" Rhett barked into the phone. "Fielding can't be part of this."

"Rhett..." Jake said his name with hesitation. "Look, we might as well get into this right now. There are things you need to know about Tori and Fielding."

He made his way toward an empty bench on the path to the Quad. He needed to have something sturdy to hold onto to keep his cool.

"Tori and Fielding are friends. We've been hanging out a lot together, the three of us. They hang out separately, too. Field has been there for Tori since spring break, but not in the way you might think. She hasn't been having the easiest time with your absence, but she's happier when she's with him."

A sick feeling rose up in his chest. He hated that his best friend was defending Haas right now. He felt even more despondent as he realized how blind Jake was to the other man's true colors. He wouldn't be singing his praises once he told him what he knew.

Honestly, he hadn't expected Fielding to still be around. The fact that he was meant that the other man was obviously trying to weasel his way into Tori's life. Rhett knew his intentions. Fielding had made them loud and clear that night in the hot tub. He also knew that Fielding had scored the night of the party, although part of him hoped it would have been a one-time thing. If Rhett was coming home for Tori, whatever Fielding and Tori had going on was over. He knew himself well enough to know he couldn't keep his cool and be her calm with Haas breathing down his neck.

"Jake, I know you like partying with the guy, but Fielding Haas is not good people. I didn't have any right to say anything before, but now that I'm coming home for her, I'm standing my ground. He can't be involved with this. Keep him away from Tori," he commanded.

"Rhett, I'm telling you, he's fine. If I say he's good, you've gotta believe..."

"No," Rhett cut him off. "You don't know what I know."

Jake sighed through the phone.

"Listen, bro, I know what you think happened. I know what Tori made you *believe* happened the night of the party. She told me everything the next morning. But what you think happened between them? That didn't happen."

Rhett stilled. Why would Jake say that? What was he playing at?

"Jake, don't try to protect her or Haas right now. I'm coming home for Tori regardless. It doesn't matter what they did..."

"Oh, it matters. I never intended to get involved in this cluster. I figured you two would work it out on your own eventually, but you've gotta understand this. Tori didn't sleep with Fielding. She only said she did to hurt you. I swear on our friendship that she never slept with Fielding. Not that night and not since. They're just friends. I swear."

Rhett stood up from the bench and started pacing in front of it. The confession ping-ponged around his mind as he let the new information sink in. Tori hadn't slept with Fielding in his bed. That felt like the truth. Rhett believed the words as soon as Jake spoke them out loud. The idea that she would ever do that seemed ludicrous now that he thought about it out of context.

"Rhett?" Jake asked at the end of the line. He had no idea how much time had just passed as he grappled with this new information.

"Yeah, I'm here."

"You believe me, right?"

"Yeah, I do. I'm just trying to figure out why I still feel like I want to punch Fielding in his fucking face," he spat out.

"Because this whole situation is messed up, bro. I would be just as mad if I was you," Jake admitted. "But Fielding's not the bad guy here. He didn't know there was anything between you and Tori, which honestly is on you. He wasn't the one that made you think anything happened between him and Tori. That one's on her. She hurt you, Rhett. That's why you want to hurt someone right now."

"I would never hurt her," Rhett growled into the phone. But again, the truth of the situation resonated deep in his bones.

"I know that, bro. And I get why you're pissed. You don't think I know what's at stake right now? I've had a front row seat to how Tori's tried to push you away and hold you at arm's length all these years. I've watched her hurt you, sometimes intentionally, sometimes not. Yet as soon as things start to fall apart for her, she's begging us to call you."

"It's not like that," Rhett defended. "There's more to it. Our connection... what we share... for me, it's always been her. I never stopped pursuing her, and I probably never will. Even though she doesn't say it, I know Tori loves me, too."

"I know that," Jake relented. "She did everything she did because she loves you. She did it all to protect you from her and to protect you from yourself. But I think today proved to all of us that there's no protecting either of you from each other. If you're going to come home to her, you two better figure things out for real, for all our sakes. It's time to cut the shit and be done pretending."

He nodded in agreement. He didn't have time to wonder why Jake hadn't told him any of this until now. Now that he knew the truth, there was only one way forward. He was going home tomorrow because Tori asked him to, and he was going home as more than her friend.

"Listen, Jake, I can't begin to tell you how sorry I am and how much I..."

"Rhett? Let's not do this right now. I know what you're about to say, and we both know you would have done the same for me. We're good. It's all good. I'll be here for her until you get here."

Rhett exhaled. A sense of calm came over him, accompanied by an certainty that he had all the support he needed to get through whatever the next few days would bring.

"I love you, bro," was all he could muster to say before hanging up. He sank back down onto the bench and ran his hand down his face. A few hours ago, he had been nostalgic for this place, already missing Easton and the whole college experience. Now, all he wanted to do was get through the next day and get home to his girl.

CHAPTER 43

Rhett

He let the door slam behind him as he entered his apartment. He was hyper-focused on everything he had to do, and he knew he didn't have a lot of time to make it all happen. First, he had to pack. He needed enough things for at least a few weeks in Hampton until he'd be able to come back and properly pack up the apartment. He also needed to try and study for tomorrow's final exam.

"Hey, babe! How was your final?"

Rhett froze in the kitchen at the sound of Chandler's voice. Some level of his consciousness knew she was here because he had seen her car in the parking lot, but he hadn't had time to think through how he was going to handle her.

"I'm just getting ready to head out. Grace texted me and said the shirts for EastonFest just arrived, so I'm going to head over there and help her sort them," Chandler explained as she stepped out of the bedroom and into the main living space.

Rhett stood in the kitchen and weighed his options. If Chandler left now, he might not have another chance to talk to her before he left. Things needed to be over with her before he arrived in Hampton tomorrow.

"Listen, Chandler, I need to talk to you before you leave." She looked at him curiously, then sat down at the small table in the kitchen.

"What's up?"

Rhett eyed her where she sat. He willed himself to be diplomatic, to try to speak kindly and ease into what he was about to say. But all he could think about was Tori. He didn't have time to bullshit or tiptoe around things now. This needed to be done.

"Something's going on at home. I have to go. I'm packing up tonight, taking my final in the morning, then heading back to Hampton as soon as it's over."

"What do you mean something's going on at home?" she scowled. "Is someone hurt? Are your parents okay?"

Rhett turned to fully face her but made no move to sit down. Instead, he stood in the kitchen with his arms folded across his chest. "I got a call this afternoon. I'm needed at home."

"What the hell, Rhett? EastonFest is this weekend. Will you be back for Saturday?"

He shook his head slowly.

Chandler's body tensed up defensively. He saw the color of her eyes darken as realization hit.

"It's her, isn't it?" she hissed, rising to her feet and stalking toward him. She pointed a perfectly-polished nail at his chest. "You're running home to Tori."

Rhett said nothing. He didn't need to. He knew his lack of denial would be confirmation enough.

"When will you be back?" she demanded, crossing her arms across her own chest to match his stance. Rhett exhaled. He didn't have enough energy to have a full-out fight with Chandler right now. *Tie up the loose ends, get home to Tori,* he reminded himself of his priorities. He needed to end this as quickly and efficiently as possible.

"It's probably best if you don't expect me back at any certain time."

Chandler's eyes grew wider at his admission.

"What do you think you're doing right now? This isn't right. It's not going to end like this." She scoffed. She took two steps toward him, her hands now planted on her hips. She wanted to fight for them. He wanted her to disappear.

"That's where you're wrong, Chandler. This is exactly how it's going to end."

"No. I refuse to accept this. I've let you do this plenty of times before. Run away from me. Run to her. It's been three years, Rhett. You don't think I know your patterns by now? I don't care about any of that. I've stuck around through worse. We're not done here."

"Chandler," Rhett cautioned, softer this time. He had spent so much effort trying to shield her from the truth. He had not expected her to push back like this when it was so blatantly obvious his priority was Tori. "Hey, listen to me. I'm sorry to end things like this, but that's exactly what I'm doing. We're over. I'll always think fondly on the time we spent together. But you deserve someone who's going to pick you first, every time."

"And that's not you?"

"No." Rhett shook his head. "I'm sorry, but that's not me. It never was me, and it never will be me."

He watched her deflate before his eyes as his words sank in. She looked so defeated.

"But we're so close to you moving to Virginia," she whispered so softly he almost didn't hear it. "I've held out for so long..."

Her expression transitioned from frustration to hurt to rage as they faced off in silence. She blinked first, then said nothing else as she turned on her heel to storm into the bedroom.

"I'm leaving. Text me when you're gone tomorrow so I know I can come back and get my things," she hissed over her shoulder. She disappeared for a few minutes, then reemerged into the main living area with a tote bag slung over her shoulder.

"And screw you, Everhett. You don't know what you're giving up. I never asked you for anything. I never tried to change you. I was willing to put up with all your non-committal bullshit and just wait it out while you got her out of your system. Who else is going to do that for you? You don't even know how good you had it."

Chandler slammed the door behind her. He let out a long sigh of relief. It was over. Her words were true, but they didn't hurt. Rhett knew he didn't need to find anyone else to wait around for him: Tori would never be out of his system.

He spent the rest of the night trying to distract himself. He packed up what he needed for home. He texted Maddie to bring her up to speed with what was going on and what he was planning to do once he got home to Hampton. He tried to read over his review guide for his final. Eventually he ordered food and ran out to pick it up, gassing up the Prelude while he was out. He felt as ready as he was going to be for whatever the next day would bring.

By the time he showered and lay down for bed that night, he decided to face what he had avoided doing all day. He ran his hand through his hair over and over again, pulling on the ends as he worked up the nerve to make the call.

Tori had asked for him repeatedly. He knew she wanted him there, but he still felt so unsettled. All their interactions that day had been orchestrated. He had talked to Jake about her. He had talked through Fielding's phone to her. He had yet to just talk to Tori without someone else in the mix.

He felt no hesitation about breaking up with Chandler or about driving home to Hampton the next day. So why was he so worried about reconnecting with her?

Ev: Hey Beautiful, are you awake?

He wanted to put the ball in her court, to let her decide if she wanted to hear from him tonight or if she wasn't ready for that yet.

V: Yes. Call me?

Rhett held his breath as he scrolled through his contacts and found her name. He had tried to reach her so many times over the last four weeks. He knew she had blocked him the Monday after the party. He knew it before he had even tried to call her that first night his call went straight to voicemail. Something in his gut knew it was her way of protecting him. And yet he had still attempted to call her again and again over the last four weeks. He had listened to her voicemail every night for a month. When he clicked on her name tonight, he knew with certainty the call would finally go through.

She answered on the first ring.

"Hi," she whispered.

There she was. Any doubts that had been lingering in Rhett's mind dissipated with the sound of her voice. He felt a part of himself settle back into his body. She was home, and tomorrow, he'd be there with her.

"Tori, this sucks so hard," he groaned into the phone. Relief. Desperation. Sadness. Love. It was all there.

"I know. I know," she repeated, her voice breaking on the last word and confirming all the spiraling worries in his mind. She was hurting, and he couldn't be there now. It was killing him to not be with her tonight. But he would be there soon.

"Hey, don't cry, beautiful. Tomorrow, I'm there. We're going to figure this out together." When Tori didn't reply, he kept talking. "We don't have to talk tonight. You don't have to say a thing. I just need to be with you, and this is the best I can do right now. Is your phone plugged in?"

"Yeah," she whispered softly through the phone.

"Good." Rhett nodded to himself. He could see her in his mind's eye, lying in her bed huddled under a pile of blankets, Penny snuggled up at her feet. "I'm going to stay on the phone with you all night if you'll let me, V. Just pretend I'm lying right there next to you. And tomorrow, I'll be there for real," he promised.

Rhett continued to talk—to comfort her, to distract her, to just be with her—until he heard her softly snoring a few hours later. Even then he kept his promise and stayed on the phone all night long.

CHAPTER 44

Rhett

The whole morning felt hazy. Rhett remembered packing up the car. He got himself to the business building for his last final. He remembered putting pen to paper and feeling okay about the exam. He even recalled merging onto I-71 toward Hampton. But nothing could hold his attention for long. He was just so desperate to get to her. It wasn't until he was on Route 8, less than ten minutes away, that things started to come back into focus.

Jake had texted him around ten thirty that morning while he was taking his final to let him know he was headed into work, but that Fielding was there in his place. Rhett reached for his cell phone as he took the exit toward Hampton. He hadn't really thought about how he'd handle coming face-to-face with Fielding once he got to Tori's house, but the reality of that situation was starting to sink in. Maybe if he gave him a heads-up...

Ev: 10 minutes out

Rhett shot off a text first to Tori, then separately to Fielding's phone. There. That should be enough time for the other man to vacate the premises so they could avoid a confrontation.

He checked the parking lot behind Clinton's and spotted Jake's Jeep as he drove slowly through downtown, stuck behind afternoon traffic. He made a mental note to text his best friend later once he knew the plans for the weekend.

By the time he pulled in front of the Thompsons' house, he was keyed up and anxious. He had to park in the street because a massive Infiniti SUV was parked in the center of the driveway.

Fucking Fielding. Of course he hadn't taken the hint. It would have been too decent for him to excuse himself and not be here when Rhett finally arrived.

None of it mattered, though. He was here. She was in there. He couldn't move up the driveway fast enough.

He let himself in through the side garage door, then pushed into the door that led into the laundry room. Wafts of fabric softener and Tori filled his nostrils as he quietly kicked off his shoes.

The quiet didn't keep. A scurrying of paws tore across the kitchen, and a few seconds later, Penny was yapping at his feet. Rhett knew better than to try to ignore the pug mix, so he squatted down and gave her a few good scratches behind the ears.

"Hey, girl. Hi, Penny. Ohhh you're such a good girl. I bet you've been taking good care of your mama, huh?" With Penny temporarily satisfied, he rose to full height. He walked cautiously through the lower level of the house, just in case someone was downstairs. He knew where he'd most likely find her though.

If Rhett stopped to think for too long, he would realize that it felt like his insides were trying to come out. Stress, anxiety, and anticipation bubbled up as he became acutely aware of his own breathing. Muscle memory took over as he rounded the stairs and climbed them with purpose. All he had to do was put one foot in front of the other and keep moving forward.

He turned left at the top of the stairs. Her bedroom door was wide open. The first thing he saw was Fielding's long body sitting at her desk. The man looked at ease in her pink swivel chair, leaning back with his legs outstretched wide in front of him. He had a smile on his face, obviously amused by whatever Tori was saying to him from across the room.

Rhett stepped from the hallway into Tori's bedroom for what may have been the thousandth time in his life, but today, everything was different. He didn't knock. He didn't pause. He didn't hesitate. He barely registered Fielding sitting up and addressing him from his perch at her desk. The other man was an afterthought. Everything was background noise. His sole purpose was her.

"Tori," he breathed out as soon as his gaze locked on her sitting up in bed, back straight against the headboard. He was across the room in three strides. He was sitting on the bed two seconds later. She was in his arms just one moment after that.

"You're here," she exhaled into his chest. He felt her body give in. She was soft in his arms, totally malleable to his touch.

"I'm here, beautiful. I'm here," he assured her as he squeezed her tighter and ran his hand up and down her back. It felt so damn good to finally hold her. "Let me see you," he insisted, loosening his grasp and shifting away from her.

She peered up at him with swollen, bloodshot eyes, but there was no resistance in her gaze. She was open to him. She was fully present with him. She was right there.

"I'm here now," he repeated, looking her in the eyes and gently resting his forehead against hers. He wove a hand into the hair at the nape of her neck, just like he'd done so many times before. What he wouldn't give to kiss her right now, just to deepen the connection and let her know he wasn't going anywhere. "I'm here for you," he promised before closing his eyes.

A noise from across the room caught Rhett's attention. He had forgotten they weren't alone.

"I'm gonna go downstairs and grab something to drink," Fielding muttered as he rose to his feet. "You want anything, Tor?"

"No. Thanks, Field," she mumbled, dismissing him without breaking eye contact with Rhett.

Fielding left the room and pulled the door closed behind him. They were finally alone.

Rhett took another moment to breathe her in. To smell her hair. To feel her body in such close proximity to his. To be in her orbit. Their bond was still there. Of course it was still there. What they shared was unshakable.

"What can I do for you right now, beautiful?" he asked, eager to do whatever he could to ease some of her burden.

"I don't even know..." Tori trailed off, scooching back from him so she could pull her knees into her chest. Rhett nodded toward the headboard, indicating he wanted her to keep moving over. She made more room on the bed, then he joined her, pulling her into his arms once again. He knew in his bones this was where he was meant to be.

"When were your scans?" He felt guilty bringing up the appointment he hadn't been home for, but he needed to know.

"The Monday after Easter." Her voice was shallow, her words hollow.

Rhett stilled at her response. He didn't need to tell her how much he regretted not being there for her. He could hear the pain in her voice. It mirrored the pain he felt in his gut.

"I don't understand what you told me about the bloodwork." He kept a firm grasp on her body as she leaned against him.

"I don't know much about it, either," she confessed, burying her head deeper into the crease of his arm. "They only do bloodwork once a year, not twice a year like the other tests. The bloodwork has to do with ovarian cancer, not breast cancer."

Rhett nodded. He had spent enough time Googling CA-125 blood draws last night to know where this was headed.

"You said you have another appointment on Monday?"

Tori nodded.

"In Akron? What does that entail?"

"Yes, in Akron, at three o'clock. I think it's an exam and an ultrasound. The nurse said they'd send over instructions about it, but

I haven't even checked my email since I got the call yesterday..."

Rhett let her fade out. He wasn't going to push her right now. They didn't need to discuss all the what-ifs about Monday. He knew why he was here: to support her. To distract her. To love her. All those things came as naturally as breathing, and that's what he needed to focus on now. There would be time for everything else later.

"I feel stupid for how this all happened," she confessed, tearing Rhett away from his own train of thought. "I had a full-blown panic attack at Fielding's house. I made Jake leave work yesterday, and I screwed over Mike and the rest of the staff. You stayed on the phone with me all night and probably didn't even sleep or study for your exam. Then today everyone has dropped everything to..."

"Hey," he interrupted her. "You don't have anything to feel bad about."

"But it's just abnormal blood work. And I've been expecting it for the last ten years! I honestly feel embarrassed by how I reacted."

Rhett tried to keep his cool as he pulled her back into him. "Stop, Tori. You have nothing to be embarrassed about. Your feelings and your reaction to all this is completely legitimate. Hell, you should have seen how I reacted when I found out."

"I'm sorry you had to come back for me. I'm sorry I wasn't stronger."

"Don't you dare try to apologize for that. The only thing I'm upset about is the fact that I wasn't here when you went to your appointment. I'm so sorry I wasn't here for you," he lamented, resting his chin on top of her head. She didn't say anything, but she reached up and laced her fingers with his, forgiveness flowing between them for everything they had put each other through over the last four weeks.

"I'm sorry, too," she whispered, squeezing his hand for emphasis.

Rhett nodded, accepting her apology and promising himself that was all he needed. He didn't want to hash out all the highs and lows of the last month. The words Jake had said to him last night resonated: They needed to be done trying to hurt each other. It was the only way forward.

"I know, beautiful. It's over. I'm here now," he assured her. "So listen, I have an idea, but I want to make sure we're on the same page first. I don't want to push you or make you feel like you have to do something you're not comfortable doing. You have to be 100% on board for this to happen. I am here because you asked me to be here and because I want to be here. I don't think it's a good idea for us to sit around Hampton all weekend worrying about all the what-ifs. There's literally nothing we can do between now and Monday, right?"

"Right." Her response was low and drawn out.

"That's what I thought. Let's get your work and school schedule sorted out, then I want to take you away for the weekend."

"What do you mean?"

"I mean we're going away. Leaving Hampton. Just the two of us, if you want to go. Do you have finals this week? Do you have anything else you have to do for school?"

"I already turned in all my final projects for the semester. I just have a take-home final I need to submit, but it's already done. I was supposed to work tonight and Sunday."

"Perfect. I can text Jake and Lia right now and get your shifts covered. I'm sure your dad will take care of Penny. I want to get you out of here, and I want to be alone with you. But only if that's what you want, too."

She ran the pad of her thumb over his knuckles. "That's what I want, too."

He was equal parts relieved and excited she was willing to trust him and go along with his plan. "Why don't you take a shower and start packing? You won't need much. Just bring comfy clothes. We'll be gone until Monday, if that's okay with you?"

Tori shifted in his arms, leaning forward and turning her head to catch his gaze.

"That sounds perfect," she confirmed, biting down on her bottom lip. Her face had a bit more color to it now. She placed a hand on his arm. "Where are we going?"

Rhett smiled down at her. "Where do you think we're going?" he asked, resting his forehead against hers. Recognition flared in her eyes as a content smile crossed her face. Rhett placed a gentle kiss on her forehead before pulling away.

"I'm going to give you some privacy and make a few calls. I assume your dad will be home soon, so we can talk to him before we go. Let's try to leave here in the next hour if possible. We can be at the cabin by dark."

Tori smiled up at him and nodded. He rolled out his shoulders, encouraging the tension of the last twenty-four hours to melt away now that he was here. He made his way to the door, already thinking through everything he needed to take care of before they could leave for Michigan.

"Everhett," Tori whispered just as he reached for the handle of her bedroom door.

"Yeah, beautiful?" he asked as he turned back toward her.

"Thank you for coming home. I know it might seem silly since it's just bloodwork, and I have my Dad and my friends here... but as soon as I got the call, the only person I wanted was you."

CHAPTER 45

Rhett

"So you and Tori, huh?"

Rhett's head snapped in response when he heard Fielding address him from across the living room. The other man was sitting on the floor, legs stretched out in front of him, Penny wiggling and squirming between them. He hadn't expected Fielding to still be here when he came downstairs. His presence was almost as surprising as his question.

"You're still here," Rhett accused, making his way into the kitchen and leaning back against the counter by the sink.

"Of course I'm still here. I've literally been here for six hours. I wasn't going to just take off without saying anything." Fielding refused to make eye contact as he talked, instead smirking down at Penny as she rolled back and forth in front of him.

Rhett wanted to smack the smirk right off his face. He was comforted by the fact that he had walked in on Fielding at Tori's desk when he arrived. That told him two things: Tori and Fielding's friendship was strictly platonic, just like Jake had claimed, and Fielding knew where things stood, whether he liked it or not.

Rhett chose his next words carefully. He wanted to communicate the seriousness of their relationship to the other man without oversharing.

"Yeah, me and Tori. We've been together on and off for the last ten years. For me, it's always been her."

Rhett kept his eyes locked on Fielding, willing him to look up and see the sincerity in his gaze. Fielding finally turned his attention away from Penny and shoved up to his feet in a quick, fluid motion.

"Good to know," he said, brushing off his pant legs and giving Rhett a curt nod.

He couldn't help but notice the skepticism on the other man's face. This wasn't last month, though. There would be no back and forth, no defiant banter between them. Rhett wouldn't stand to be challenged on Tori this time or ever again.

"You don't believe me?" he retorted. Fielding must have picked up on the gravity in his tone. The other man took two steps toward the kitchen and closed some of the space between them. He rested an arm on the back of one of the kitchen chairs, then methodically opened and closed his fist. There was an uneasiness to the room now.

"Oh, I believe you. I just witnessed it with my own eyes up there." Fielding tilted his chin toward the stairs for emphasis. "But it's still news to me. I've spent more time with Tori over the last month than I've spent with my own brother. That's saying something because I live with that guy. I guess you could say we've gotten pretty close." Another smirk.

"She hasn't mentioned you once. She doesn't talk about you. She doesn't call you. Your number wasn't even in her phone when I tried to find it yesterday." Fielding looked directly at him then. "I'm just surprised by how things have played out. Like I said: news to me."

Rhett analyzed the man challenging him as he debated how he wanted to proceed. No, that wasn't right. He knew exactly how he *wanted* to proceed. He wanted to throw down, to stake his claim, and to make sure this guy never tried to contact Tori again. But ramming horns with Fielding wasn't going to do anything except make Tori mad and spur Fielding on. He needed to think about how she would want him to proceed.

This wasn't a fight. This wasn't a game. Rhett couldn't let things escalate. He had to be the adult in this situation for all their sakes.

"Look, man, I appreciate you being there for Tori over the last few weeks. And I really appreciate you helping out yesterday and today. Jake told me you've been a good friend to her. I appreciate that more than you know. Things might get spotty because of everything going on with her health, so don't feel bad if you don't hear from her in the coming weeks," he divulged, hoping Fielding would finally take a hint and take his leave.

"I'm cool with that, as long as it's Tori's choice," he countered.

"Obviously it would be her choice," Rhett shot back.

"I'm just saying, Wheeler... You haven't been here. I have. What Jake told you is true. We've gotten close. I'm cool with her dropping our friendship if that's what she chooses to do. I guess I don't really see her making that choice though." Fielding shrugged as he finished his statement, but Rhett saw the declaration for what it was.

"Noted," he clipped in response. He realized at that moment that this guy was going to be a problem. Maybe not today, maybe not this month, but he knew now that he couldn't underestimate Fielding Haas. Rhett started walking toward the front door, intent on showing the other man out. "Thanks again for your help. Maybe I'll see you around some time," he said with finality.

Fielding stalked out the front door without saying another word.

Chapter 46

Rhett

"Ready to go?" he asked, glancing over at Tori in the passenger seat of the Prelude. He had been so sure about his plan up until this moment. Now that they were on their way to the cabin, he couldn't help but question if this was the right move.

"I'm ready." She reached over to squeeze his hand before he put the car in reverse.

"And you're sure about this?" he asked as he backed out of the driveway. It was all so abrupt. He felt like he was holding his breath, waiting for her to change her mind. They hadn't been on speaking terms two days ago. Now, they were leaving for a long weekend away at the cabin, just the two of them. So little time had passed since the concert and that trip, yet so much had changed during the last four weeks.

"Yes, I'm sure," Tori confirmed. "This just feels right." She looked over and smiled at him again, easing some of the uncertainty that had started to circulate in his gut. "Are *you* okay with all this?" Her question came out soft and timid. "I know it wasn't fair of me to call you after everything that happened last month. Once I realized you were going to come home for me... I probably should have told you not to come, but I couldn't bring myself to push you away."

Rhett gave himself a moment to process what she was asking. He wanted to be candid with her without trudging too deeply into the details of everything that was still unresolved.

"I couldn't imagine not being here for you right now, V. I'm glad that you called me. I know things got messy there for a bit. We both know we have a lot to talk about. But this feels right for me, too." He found her gaze and focused on her gorgeous green eyes.

"Do you want to talk about it now?" he hesitated. They needed to talk about so many things. They needed to talk about everything. He was eager to get it all out in the open, but he also didn't want to overwhelm her or make her feel trapped by forcing a hard conversation in the car.

"I don't even know where to start..."

"Let's wait until we get to the cabin then," he insisted. "No pressure. But I'm ready when you are. I'm not putting things off or hiding this time." He looked over at her earnestly, willing her to feel his love and believe that they'd be okay.

She yawned, a deep, full-body yawn that reminded Rhett he was tired, too. Listening to music would help keep him awake and keep his mind from wandering during the drive.

"I bet you're exhausted, beautiful. Why don't you put on that playlist you made us for the concert, then you can close your eyes and rest."

Tori pulled out her phone and synced up the Bluetooth to his head unit. "Yikes," she muttered to herself. "I have so many missed calls and messages." She sighed before the first sounds of Thirty Seconds to Mars came through the speakers. Then worry etched on her face hit deep. He couldn't stand to see her like this. He couldn't stand to let her think she was in this alone.

"Wait. I have something I need to say," Rhett declared, reaching over to turn down the volume. They didn't need to talk about everything if she wasn't ready to talk, but he didn't think he could last another minute with this weighing on his chest.

"Promise me we're in this together. It's you and me now, V. I'm done pretending. I'm done trying to control things. I want to be your partner, to be with you through everything. Just tell me what you need, let me help make it happen, and cut out all the rest of the noise."

Tori was silent. He started to doubt the boldness of his declaration. He knew he was taking a risk by putting it all out there so early in their trip, but he needed her to know he was all in.

"I promise. It's you and me now, Ev. I love you," she finally replied.

Rhett blinked, then blinked again, then remembered he was driving and needed to stay focused on the road. Had she really just said that? He waited for her to admit she was just teasing him, but she returned his stare with a totally serious face. He gaped. What the hell was she playing at?

"Oh my gosh, stop looking at me like that! Am I in the car with Jake right now? You're being so dramatic. It's not like I've never said that to you before," she mumbled.

Rhett realized she was deflating because of his reaction, but he felt too raw to try to save the moment.

"I, I just haven't heard it in a really long time," he stammered. He reached over and took her hand.

"But you had to know," she insisted. "Don't pretend like you didn't feel it, too, like you don't feel it still."

"Oh, I've felt it, beautiful. I've hoped for it. But the only way I was allowed to love you over the last six years was to keep my distance when you broke up with me, then to not get too close once you set the terms for our arrangement." He shrugged, trying not to let the weight of his sadness come through his words.

"I thought I was doing the right thing by you at the time," Tori muttered, picking at invisible lint on her leggings.

"And now?" he asked as he tightened his hold on her hand. They were in it now, whether she liked it or not. He wasn't letting her pull away so easily this time.

She didn't respond.

"What's different now, Tori? I need to hear you say it to believe this is real." He didn't want to push her too hard, but he couldn't resist giving her a little nudge.

She waited a few more moments before responding.

"I always thought I was protecting you. Protecting you from me, protecting you from my future. Nothing is different now, but everything is different now, too. As soon as I got the call, my brain and my body went on autopilot. I couldn't have stopped myself from calling you, Rhett. It was beyond me. I don't have the strength to keep you away and go through this alone. But I didn't know that until I was finally staring down the barrel of a diagnosis. This is bigger than both of us. I was just trying to do right by you before..."

"The only thing that's right for me is being with you, beautiful. Plain and simple. There's only you."

"That's sweet of you to say, but we both know it's not only me."

"Tori," he interrupted her, his tone serious and unwavering. He glanced at her through his peripheral but kept his eyes on the road. "Chandler is out of the picture. I broke up with her, finally. It's only you."

He felt the air shift between them. *So much for keeping things light on the drive up.*

She finally broke the silence. "I have to tell you something."

He was almost certain he knew what she was going to say, but he made no effort to stop her. He needed to hear the words from her mouth.

"I didn't sleep with Fielding at the party."

There it was. Rhett dropped his shoulders and unclenched his jaw. He felt the darkness that had overshadowed his world for the last four weeks finally begin to dissipate.

"I'm so sorry I made you think I had sex with someone else in your bed. It was thoughtless and selfish. I wanted to hurt you. I just wanted to break you down and piss you off, but it backfired and worked too well. You believed me so easily..."

"I didn't believe you at first, but so many other things clicked into place that morning. I know you're sorry. I forgive you. We don't have to talk about it anymore if you don't want to."

Tori whipped her head around to stare at him. "Wait, why aren't you more upset with me right now? Just because I might be sick doesn't mean I get a free pass," she scoffed.

"Tori..."

"No, answer me. I just confessed that I lied to you and caused a huge fight between us that lasted over a month. I almost destroyed us, Rhett. If I hadn't gotten that call, you wouldn't be here now. We wouldn't even be speaking. Why aren't you more upset with me?"

"I've had some time to think about it. Jake told me the truth yesterday."

"Oh."

"Don't be mad at him, beautiful. I had him talked into a corner, and he had no choice."

"What do you mean?"

"He told me you were with Fielding when you got the call. I was adamant that if I was coming home for you, that guy couldn't be around. Jake told me the truth about that night because that was the only way to get me to calm down."

"I'm sorry for what I made you think," she apologized.

"Yeah. About that. I don't think I've ever been more pissed off in my life, Tori. The last month has been torture. We can't do that to each other ever again."

"I know. It was so low. To be honest, I was shocked when it worked and you actually believed me. I've never wanted anyone else, Ev. I know I always acted like our arrangement was to keep you from getting too attached, but I needed it as a constant reminder not to fall too hard, too."

Rhett gripped the steering wheel until his knuckles paled.

"Fuck, Tori. I've spent the last six years wanting more. Wishing it was only you and me, hoping you loved me the same way I loved you... It was there all along, wasn't it?"

"I'm so sorry, Ev," she offered again as she wrung her hands together in her lap.

"I'm sorry too, beautiful. Over the last few years I convinced myself the best way to love you was to stick to the arrangement and just do what you said you wanted me to do. I should have tried harder. There's nothing I regret more than not fighting harder for us," he professed.

"Why did you let me get away with it for so long?"

Because I love you. He knew he owed her a better explanation though.

"That night you came across the fence? The night we started this whole arrangement? You gave me the smallest glimmer of hope that night. I've held onto it for years. I told myself that if I could just be patient, if I could just play the game well enough, that maybe we'd get here one day."

"You held on for maybe?"

"I held on for you. I never gave up on us, Tori. And I never will," he promised. "But we can't keep living in the past. We have a hell of a lot of time to make up for, and I plan to start right now." He squeezed her hand gently. He considered pulling over at the next rest stop to show her exactly what he meant, but his desire to get her to the cabin before dark outweighed the physical lust building between them in his tiny car.

Tori squeezed his hand in return, then let out a muffled yawn, bringing her hand to her mouth and scrunching her eyes closed.

"Why don't you try to close your eyes and rest? We've got another two hours until we get to the cabin, and I can only imagine how exhausted you probably feel right now."

She smiled and nodded before pulling her legs up under her body and curling into the seat.

She loved him. She had never wanted anyone else.

He loved her too. He had loved for every second of every damn day for the last ten years, if not longer, and now he was finally allowed to admit it.

It was almost dark by the time they pulled up the driveway of the cabin, but there was still a lightness to their surroundings thanks to the later sunset. Tori had slept for most of the drive after their talk, which was okay with Rhett. He needed that time to think.

She had woken up when they crossed the bridge into town, but they hadn't spoken much over the last fifteen minutes. The silence wasn't awkward, but it still felt heavy. He wondered for the dozenth time that day if bringing her to the cabin had been the right move.

Tori unbuckled her seatbelt and wordlessly opened the door, pulling his Arch sweatshirt sleeves down and crossing her arms in front of her as she stepped out of the car. Rhett watched her in the mirror as she circled around to the trunk. She moved slowly but with intention. He wasn't sure if she was still tired or just feeling weighed down by all she was carrying. Either way, he was determined to make her feel lighter this weekend.

Rhett exited the car and stretched his arms over his head, letting his back and arms crack a few times before following her.

She was leaning against the bumper of the Prelude. A bright smile illuminated her face and reached up to her eyes.

"You look happy," he observed, tilting his head toward her and spinning his keys on his finger. Tori read his intentions and pushed off the back of the car, taking a few steps down the pebbled path toward the lake. It took all Rhett's restraint not to follow her, to wrap his arms around her, to pull her body into his. But even though they had talked through their biggest issues on the drive, he didn't want to get ahead of himself.

"I am happy," she confirmed, turning to smile at him over her shoulder. "This is the first time I've felt fully inside my own body since yesterday afternoon."

"Do you want to go down there now?" he asked, lifting his chin toward the bench swing at the lake's edge.

Tori shook her head.

"We're staying until Monday, right? I'll get plenty of lake time this weekend. Right now I've got to pee, and I'm finally hungry. I haven't eaten much since yesterday morning," she admitted. She hadn't eaten anything at all over the last thirty hours, according to Jake. Bringing her here had definitely been the right choice.

"Let me just grab the bags. Do you remember the code to get in?"

Tori nodded, then proceeded to walk up to the side entrance and punch the numbers into the keypad. She opened the cabin door and disappeared inside as Rhett popped the trunk of the car.

He got everything inside the cabin in just two trips. He would need to go to the store tomorrow since they hadn't made a grocery run in advance, but Maddie had assured him there was plenty of food in the freezer to hold them over tonight.

He locked his car and quietly entered the kitchen. He grabbed their bags but stalled. They were here. They were alone. That usually meant they shared the master bedroom. But Rhett didn't want to presume anything, and he sure as hell wasn't going to pressure her to confirm their relationship status tonight.

His mind made up, he dropped her bag near the master bedroom, then pivoted to head downstairs to one of the basement bedrooms with his own belongings. His foot had just hit the first step when he heard her voice.

"Where are you going?" she demanded as she emerged from the bedroom.

"Uh," Rhett faltered, "I'm just running my bag downstairs. I'll be right back up, then I'll make dinner for us."

"Why are you putting your stuff downstairs?" Her tone was clipped, almost accusing. Realization passed on her face as she looked from the basement stairs to his bag.

Rhett toed the basement step before responding. "I didn't want to assume that just because we were here together, it meant that we were actually together, officially..."

"Everhett." His name sounded sharp on her tongue. "I literally just told you I love you in the car, which you didn't reply to, by the way. I admitted I didn't sleep with Fielding. You said you dumped Chandler for me. We're alone at the cabin, which means we are both sleeping in the master bedroom. We are officially together now, so get used to it."

Relief washed over him as he backed up onto the main level and dropped his bag. He was over to her in four strides, both hands tangled into her hair.

"I love you, Victoria Thompson. I'm sorry I didn't say it earlier in the car. I was just caught off guard. I love you so damn much. I'm going to tell you that at least a hundred more times this weekend." His lips crashed into hers, desperate to reignite their connection after all the time apart. Kissing her now felt like a spiritual awakening deep inside his core. It wasn't just his body responding to hers: it was his heart, it was his soul, it was everything he was and everything he hoped they would be.

CHAPTER 47

Tori

Tori woke up slowly, allowing the sunlight pouring in from the floor-to-ceiling windows to warm her face before she actually opened her eyes. She reveled in the deep satisfaction of a good night's sleep as peace settled over her.

Rhett had come home for her. He had brought her to the cabin. And although the reason for their reunion was her literal worst nightmare, she couldn't help but feel grateful for how it all came together.

When he had finally kissed her last night, it was with a white-hot passion fueled by all the heartache of the last month. It was the kind of kiss meant to make her feel his yearning, the kind of kiss that made her feel loved and seen and cherished. He had guided her into the master bedroom, not stopping until she was backed up against the bed. He made love to her mouth, savoring her with his tongue as his hands worked through her hair.

She could feel every ounce of his love in the connection between them. She wasn't upset that he hadn't said "I love you" back to her right away in the car. She knew she had surprised him with her words, and she understood that her golden boy was too analytical to respond to something like that without thinking it through. She didn't need to hear it, because he made sure she felt it in his kiss. She was breathless when she finally pulled away.

They didn't end up having sex last night. Between Tori's underlying anxiety about her appointment on Monday and the fact that Rhett came home unexpectedly without stopping by the health center, they agreed they were making the responsible choice. They had used sex as a crutch so many times before. There would be plenty of opportunities to make up for lost time soon enough.

After making out on the bed like horny teenagers, Rhett had insisted on cooking a huge dinner. Taking care of her had always been his way of loving her. Her appetite had returned, surprisingly, so she had no problem eating two servings of pasta plus the full bowl of ice cream he scooped out for dessert.

They had spent the rest of the night lying in the big canopy bed, cuddling and talking. It wasn't like the talk in the car or earlier in the week: The hardest conversations were behind them. They talked about everything and nothing. It was an opportunity to fill each other in on everything that had happened over the last month, a chance to get reacquainted.

She told him about all the planning meetings for Camp New Hope and about how his dad had offered to help her find an internship next year. She filled him in on the progress Mike had made on the renovations for the Oak Barrel Room and how Jake was going to be the general manager once it opened later that summer. She told him about spending time with Jake and Fielding, too. He went quiet whenever she mentioned Fielding, but he didn't object to hearing about it, so she didn't leave anything out. After years of sneaking around and tiptoeing the line, she wanted to tell him everything. There would be no more secrets between them now.

When it was his turn, Rhett told her about his trip to Virginia. He had signed a lease on a two-bedroom apartment that started June 1. He showed her pictures of the outdoor pool and the complex's gym, and he talked about the projects he was already working on in preparation of going full-time at NorfolkStar Transport. He was in the process of hiring an assistant, and he needed to go back to Virginia in a few weeks for the final round of interviews. He gave her the briefest of rundowns about his breakup with Chandler. She didn't love the idea that he had been with Chandler exclusively for more than a month, but she also recognized the role she had played in driving them closer together. He finished his recap by telling her that he planned to telecommute throughout the summer between Norfolk and Hampton, and that he was committed to being home with her as often as possible in the coming months.

Acceptance washed over Tori as she lay in bed next to the man she loved. Rhett was hers and only hers—finally. She had fought him long enough. Now, it was time to be with him and to allow herself to be happy, for however long that may be. She knew he didn't completely understand the extreme measures she planned to take when it came to the preventative (or now potentially necessary) surgeries. But those were a certainty in her mind, just like he was a certainty to her now.

She felt a strange sense of relief that cancer had finally reared its ugly head. She had spent the last ten years in a tortuous cycle of anticipatory grief, thinking about cancer, worrying about her next set of scans, trying to do everything she could to stave off the inevitable. Now all the anticipation was over, and that was oddly freeing.

For the first time in a very long time, she felt hopeful. The cancer was here, or at least close enough to the surface that she had proof it wasn't all in her head. The acceptance she felt now was what had been missing for the last ten years. Knowing with certainty what would come next, and knowing who would be with her through it all, galvanized her for the future.

She felt Rhett stir behind her before he spoke.

"Hey, beautiful. Are you awake?"

Tori rolled over to face him, moving to close the space between them. "I'm awake." She smiled, resting her hands on the tops of his collarbone.

"How'd you sleep?" he asked, placing a chaste kiss on her forehead. She felt his fingers move down her body and find the small of her back. He worked his hand up under the shirt she was wearing, brushing his fingertips along the curve of her ass before landing on her hip.

"I slept great, actually." She smiled wider then, shimmying her body up against him and swinging one of her legs over his. The feeling of his hand on the bare skin of her thigh awakened something in her core. She always felt insatiable around this man, but after a month apart, her desire to connect with him was stronger than ever.

She could feel his warmth and hardness through his boxers. She worked a hand between their bodies and closed her fist around his erection. He was so solid, so steady. She savored the length of him in her palm. She watched Rhett's eyes go dark as he continued to caress her hip with feather-light touches. She matched his pace as she stroked him through the fabric of his underwear.

She arched her back and offered her mouth while simultaneously pressing her breasts and hips into his body. He caught her lips with his, matching the rhythm of his kiss to the stroking of his hand. Tori felt desire percolate through her core.

She broke the kiss and moved her mouth along the column of his neck, feeling the stubble on his jawline scratch against her lips. Rhett moaned when she landed on her favorite spot: the hollow of his throat, right below his Adam's apple. She could feel the vibrations of his wanting as another sound escaped him. She kissed his pulse point, then used her tongue to outline the little V at the base of his throat.

"Tori," he pleaded. She heard the restraint in his voice. He was holding back, begging her not to tempt him. His fingers skirted along the top of her inner thigh, right along the hem of her underwear.

"I want you so badly," she groaned in response, moving up to nip at his ear. She rolled her hips toward him with enough force that his hand dislodged and brushed against her center. Oh yes. She wanted him, and she wanted him right there. The ache between her legs had her practically panting, but nothing had changed since last night. Rhett hadn't been tested, and he also disclosed that he hadn't thought to grab condoms when he raced home to Hampton. They had to reel it in, at least a little, at least for now.

"I know," he acknowledged, lowering his forehead to rest it against hers, "and I know we can't. But would this be okay?" he asked as he rested the palm of his hand between her thighs. He applied the slightest pressure against her clit as he waited for permission.

"Yes." She shimmied out of her underwear, scrambling to unhook them from around her ankle and throw them on the floor. "Yes, please."

"Chill, woman," he scolded her playfully. "I've got you. But we're in this together now, remember? So you're gonna help me."

Before she could even process his words, Rhett had taken her hand in his and moved it down between her legs. She shuddered on contact. He cupped her hand and guided her fingers up and down. They moved together, completely in sync. She felt her own arousal slick between her fingers. She was so warm. So wet. So desperate for him. So desperate for them.

He repositioned her hand right above her clit. He wrapped his hand around just two of her fingers, guiding them in a circular rhythm that matched the pace of her breathing.

"You promised me we were in this together," he reminded her, his mouth moving against hers before he bit down on her lower lip. "Are you with me, V?"

"I'm with you," she panted.

"Then keep going," he whispered into the shell of her ear as he moved his hand lower and pushed one teasing finger inside of her. He dipped in and out of her a few times, but he didn't try to draw it out.

She was already so wet for him, turned on by the intimate way he knew exactly what she needed. She felt a second finger press into her. She braced down against him, riding his hand, rubbing her own clit, and losing herself to every sensation he was inspiring in her body. After just a few minutes the base of her spine started to tingle. Her climax was imminent, and she knew he could feel it rising inside her, too.

Tori locked eyes with him as her insides clenched around his skillful fingers. She was just seconds from coming. "I love you," she gushed.

"And I love you," he replied, his eyes dark, his breathing elevated as he held her gaze. Her climax ripped through her as she let out a long moan. Rhett crashed his mouth into hers, kissing and licking as they both rode out her release.

He held her for a few minutes, one arm wrapped around her, his face buried into her hair, his hand still buried deep inside her. When he finally pulled back, he kissed her again, but this time it was soft and sweet.

"That was okay, right?" he questioned, letting his hand settle at the base of her neck as he gently rubbed the muscles there.

"That was more than okay, Ev."

"You know what I mean," he smirked. "We're here. We're together. But this is new territory for us in a lot of ways. I don't want you to feel any pressure this weekend."

"I know, and I love you for saying that, but this is us. We haven't been able to keep our hands off each other since eighth grade. I'm not sure what you thought was going to happen when you brought me to the cabin all alone and told me you loved me," she teased.

"I didn't have any expectations, V. Honestly. I've been on autopilot for the last two days, desperate to just get to you and take care of you any way I could," he confessed.

Tori let his words sink in. The gravity of his admission wasn't lost on her. The fact that he was willing to drop everything—that he dumped Chandler and raced home to Hampton when he wasn't even sure if she was interested in being with him—was significant. She marveled at his devotion, at his unwavering love and selflessness in light of everything that had transpired between them.

"Will you come take a bath with me?" she asked, smiling at him and resting her chin between his neck and shoulder as they continued to embrace.

Rhett groaned. "Are you kidding me right now? I thought if I got you off, you'd give me at least an hour before tempting me again. What kind of bath are we talking about here? Just a PG dip in the tub?"

"What do you think about a PG-13 rating?" she countered. "You didn't come yet."

Rhett cleared his throat. She knew she had him now.

"And you've only gotten off once," he stated, trying to keep his cool as he sat up on his side of the bed. Tori felt her body reignite in anticipation.

"Let's go, Wheeler," she commanded, raising her arms and lifting her T-shirt up over her head. She stood up then, circling the bed and extending her hand to him.

He stood up to meet her, pushed down his boxers, and accepted her hand. Yep, she definitely had him now.

CHAPTER 48

Rhett

He promised it would be a quick trip. He just wanted to run into the local grocery store and grab a few more supplies. Maddie had been right—there were a ton of snacks and pantry staples in the cupboard, plus meat in the freezer—but they could really use some fresh produce, and he wanted to get cream for Tori's coffee.

He hadn't planned to call his mom when he first left the house, but as he pulled into a parking spot toward the back of the lot, he found himself reaching for his phone.

He texted his mom on a regular basis, and he always called her on Sundays if he wasn't already home that weekend, but they didn't usually have spontaneous phone conversations during the week. He knew he was going to catch her by surprise, so he shot off a text first.

Rhett: Hey Mom-- busy right now? I want to call you.

His phone was vibrating in his hand thirty seconds later.

"Hello?" he answered, suddenly feeling anxious.

"Hi, Everhett," she replied.

"Hey, Mom, thanks for calling."

"Is everything all right?"

Rhett let her question sink in. How much did he want to tell her?

"No, it's not." His response surprised him, and it also answered his own question: he really was going to lay it all out for her now.

"Oh, honey, what's wrong? I saw your text about the cabin. Maddie said you were there with Tori?"

"Yeah, yeah, I am," he confirmed, exhaling and running his free hand up through his hair. He knew Tori would be okay with him telling his mom the details about her bloodwork. "Tori got bad news this week. She went for one of her regular scans a few weeks ago, and the results came back abnormal. Her blood work is off, so now she has to get more testing done. She thinks it's ovarian cancer."

His mom let out a soft gasp on the other end of the line. Rhett hated gutting her like this, especially over the phone.

"She called me on Wednesday when she got the news. I came home yesterday and brought her up to the cabin. You know how much she loves it up here. I wanted to help take her mind off everything. We're just here for the weekend. We have to come home on Monday so she can go get more tests done."

"Oh, Everhett." His mom exhaled softly. "I am so, so sorry. Is Tori with you now? Can I talk to her?"

"No. She's back at the cabin napping. I just ran out to pick up a few things."

"Oh, sweetheart. I don't even know what to say. Carla didn't have ovarian cancer until she was in her late thirties... I can't imagine how Tori's feeling right now."

"It's not good," Rhett confessed, letting his head sink back against the headrest. "She had a panic attack when they called her with the results. Jake had to go pick her up and bring her home. I hated not being there."

"Everhett, didn't you have finals this week?" his mother questioned.

"I did, and I got them all done before I came home. That's one of the reasons I couldn't come back until Thursday. Jake really helped me out."

"He is such a good friend. You're lucky to have people like him and Tori in your life." She paused. "I know you and Tori have a special connection, so I understand you wanting to be there for her, but what does Chandler think about all this?"

It was a fair question, but he still didn't feel prepared for it. His mom rarely brought up Chandler. He used to think it was because she loved Tori and would always hold a flame for their relationship. But lately, as he neared graduation, he felt her curiosity begin to peek through more often. It felt like she was watching him for hints about what would happen when he moved to Virginia.

"I broke up with Chandler before I came back to Hampton yesterday. Honestly, it was long overdue..." Rhett trailed off, not wanting to get into the details about his relationship with his ex right now.

"My heart is just breaking for you both right now." He knew she meant him and Tori, and he was grateful for the quick pivot away from the topic of Chandler. "Does Tori know you called me? Would it be okay if I texted her?"

"I'll tell her we talked when I get back to the cabin. Just give it a few hours, then you can text her. I'm sure she'd love to hear from you."

"Everhett, do you think you need to call your grandad?"

Another loaded question. Rhett knew that his plans may very well need to change in the next few weeks. He was going to be there for Tori whatever came next. There was no doubt in his mind that she wouldn't be going through any of this alone. Not anymore and not ever again.

"Not yet," he decided as he answered her question. "There's nothing to tell yet. I feel like I need to have more information and to come up with a concrete game plan before I call him."

"You put a lot of pressure on yourself, honey. You don't have to carry the burden of all of this alone, you know. I'm sure if you just talk to your granddad, he'll be okay with whatever you need to do to support Tori."

"I know he will. I just want to have more answers than questions ready when I call," he explained.

"I understand. I hate that you are going through this, Everhett. I hate it for both of you."

Rhett stayed silent for a few breaths.

"Mom?" he asked softly, closing his eyes as he felt the first hints of moisture starting to form behind them.

"Yes, honey?"

"I don't know what to do," he confessed. The tears fell quietly down his face, but he knew his mom could hear them in his voice. "You know I love her. I think she's finally ready to love me back. All I want to do is take care of her. But now it feels like I could lose her right as we're finally about to be together."

"Oh Everhett," she sighed, her own tears muffling her voice as she began to cry, too.

"At her appointment on Monday, they're either going to tell her she has cancer, or they're going to tell her it was a false alarm and they will just keep monitoring things. This is it, though. I know what she's going to want to do after this, regardless of the diagnosis."

His mom was aware of Tori's preventative surgery plans. He knew Tori would be ready, desperate even, to move forward with the surgeries after this, regardless of what the follow up tests revealed.

"If she needs more tests, or surgery, or other treatments... she only has student health insurance," Rhett whispered, segueing into the real reason he had called his mom.

Anne let out another muffled sob. Rhett listened to her sniffle through the phone before she finally blew her nose and broke the silence.

"I would never want you to make a decision like this under pressure, honey. You two haven't been together since high school. You haven't even had a chance to have a real relationship as adults."

She was right. He knew she was right. And yet, Rhett already knew what he was going to do.

"That said," her tone softened, "I have loved Tori like my own daughter for years, and I know in my heart that whether you propose to her tomorrow or five years from now, the outcome will be the same. You two were made for each other. There has never been anyone else for you, Everhett, even though I know you both tried your hardest to prove otherwise."

He exhaled, grateful for his mom's words that confirmed what he had been thinking about all day.

"Do you want me to drive up and bring the ring to you?" she offered.

The ring. Her mother's ring, soon to be Tori's ring. The ring that he had stashed away in the lockbox in his closet when his grandma gave it to him before she died. They weren't even together when he received the ring, but Rhett knew even then that the ring belonged to the girl he had loved his whole life. It had always been Tori's ring.

"I love you, Mom. Thank you for listening to me and supporting me." It was her love and her unwavering faith in their relationship that made Rhett feel like everything was going to work out. "You don't need to bring me the ring. That won't matter to Tori."

"I'm so glad you called me, Everhett. I am always here for you. I know what sort of man I raised, so I already know what you're going to do, and you have my blessing."

CHAPTER 49

Rhett

He stepped quietly into the cabin, trying his best not to rustle the grocery bags in his hands. He wasn't sure if Tori was still sleeping or not, but if she was resting, he didn't want to wake her.

He had quickly grabbed what he needed at the store, anxious to get back to her after spending so much time on the phone with his mom. He set down all the bags, then set to work putting things away. Once done, he crept into the bedroom, thinking he could crawl into bed next to her if she was still napping.

The bed was empty, though, and Rhett didn't hear any signs of her anywhere else in the cabin. He started to pull out his phone to text her as a sneaking suspicion presented itself in his mind. He walked across the bedroom to the floor-to-ceiling windows that looked out over the lake. With each step, he was more confident he knew where he would find her. When he looked out the windows, he saw her down by the lake, spread out on the bench swing with a pillow cushioned under her head.

She was facing the lake, and the sun made her hair look extra shiny in the light. She looked so beautiful. It was hard for him to believe that she was finally his.

He nervously ran a hand through his hair as he chewed on the inside of his cheek. He was coming to terms with what he had told his mom on the phone less than an hour earlier. He knew without a shadow of a doubt that he was going to marry Tori. It wasn't so much of a realization about what was next for them as much as it was a return to a deep sense of knowing.

He knew in his core they were going to be together. He knew in his heart it was only ever going to be her. And now that they were here, he knew he was going to propose to her today.

The only thing he didn't know was which excuse Tori would grab for first. He felt no hesitation about what he was planning to do, but he did wish he had more time to think through and prepare counterarguments.

It was important he asked her to marry him this weekend. If he waited until after her appointment on Monday, she would think his proposal was conditional. There was literally nothing conditional about his love for her, but he knew her well enough to know that she would let those kinds of thoughts eat away at their relationship. There was no room for doubt. This wasn't a pity proposal. This was the real deal, all he'd ever wanted, and his one shot to lock things down before both their lives changed forever.

The other reason it needed to be now was because this time had to be different. He deeply regretted not ending things with Chandler a long time ago, especially during the showdown over spring break. He wanted Tori to have unwavering confidence in them and in the fact that their relationship would be different and more than anything he'd ever shared with anyone else. He was so sure about her. He needed her to know that he wasn't going anywhere for any reason, this time or ever again.

Rhett inhaled, mustering up the confidence he needed. He let himself watch her for a few more moments before he turned around and left the bedroom to join her down by the lake.

They were too young.

They had only been back together for a day.

She was still in school.

He was moving.

Rhett ran through the laundry list of excuses he knew Tori was going to assault him with when he asked her to marry him. A new one popped into his consciousness with each stride as he made his way down the pebbled path toward the bench swing.

She was sick.

She didn't want kids.

She didn't want to leave her dad.

Her dad couldn't afford the house without her.

He tried to slow his breathing. He felt himself getting agitated and defensive already. He needed to reign it in. He couldn't do this from a place of anger or frustration. After everything they had been through together, the only way to do this was to do it from a place of love.

She must have heard him approaching because she sat up and turned her head toward him. The most sincere smile lit up her whole face.

"Hey, beautiful," he called to her casually. "No, no, stay there," he insisted as she moved to sit up and make room on the swing.

"Hi," she greeted him, still smiling as he approached.

"Whatcha got there?" he asked, nodding down to the small black notebook in her lap. He didn't really need to ask what she was doing. He knew that the notebook was filled with sketches and doodles. She'd been filling up those little notebooks since middle school. He had even punched Colin McKew on the bus in seventh grade when he tried to snatch one of the notebooks out of Tori's hands.

"Just journaling a bit," she admitted, holding up the notebook for emphasis. "Do you want to sit with me?"

"I'm not going to sit," he replied, shaking his head and inhaling. This was it. He was really doing it.

"Hmph." She made the cutest disgruntled noise. "So are you just going to stand in front of me and block my view?" she teased, reaching out to playfully swat at the side of his body.

"I'm not going to stand in front of you, either..." Rhett trailed off as he took Tori's hand in his. Slowly, confidently, he began to kneel in front of her.

"Holy shit," she muttered to herself, sitting up to full height, her spine stick-straight against the back of the swing.

"Tori," he started, as butterflies and heartburn churned in his stomach. He cleared his throat, but it didn't help.

"I have loved you since the first time I felt you press up against me in the pool while we were supposed to be babysitting Maddie the summer before eighth grade."

Her face lit up with a smirk that transformed into a grin. Her smile spurred him on. He knew he was on the right track.

"I have loved you since the day I watched you paint your first canvas. I have loved you since the first time you reached through the broken spot in the fence and held my hand as we said goodnight. I have loved you since the night you spent two hours riding city buses to get to downtown Akron so you could be with me at the hospital after the accident." He was done reminiscing. It was time to move forward.

"I have loved you for every moment of every day for the last ten years of my life. Every. Single. Moment, Tori. Every. Single. Day. For me, it's always been you. And if you'll let me—if you'll have me—I want to keep loving you for every moment of every day for the rest of our lives together."

He swallowed. It was on the tip of his tongue. The words needed to come out. He had to say it now.

"V, will you marry me?"

He felt the pebbles dig into his kneecap as he held his breath. He could see the reflection of the water in the irises of her eyes. He waited for the objections to start tumbling out of her mouth. He looked her directly in the eye, silently begging her not to fight him too hard on this. Another beat passed. He started to wonder if he should stand up. He may be able to put up a better fight if they were sitting next to each other as equals...

"Yes."

Rhett blinked. He hadn't been paying attention as he worried about all the arguments she was about to sling his way.

"Yes?" he questioned, doubt apparent in his own voice.

"Yes, I'll marry you."

Shock and awe flooded his mind as he processed what he had just asked and what she had just said. She said yes. Without hesitation, without a fight, with total confidence, Tori had just agreed to marry him.

"You said yes?" he stated, although it came out as more of a question as he rose to his feet. In one fluid motion, Rhett sat down on the bench swing beside her and pulled her into his lap.

"I said yes." She laughed, wrapping her arms around his neck and nuzzling up to kiss him.

For the first time in weeks, in months, in years, everything made sense. There would be no more hiding, no more sneaking around. No more arrangements, no more secrets to keep. During a week when everything else seemed to be crashing down around them, he was sure of this. He loved Tori. She loved him. And for the last and final time, he had asked her to be with him, and she said yes.

Chapter 50

Tori

There was no point in delaying the inevitable. Everything over the last forty-eight hours had come into focus, so when Rhett asked her to marry him, she simply said yes.

She was amused that he was so surprised by her response. She realized that he had probably been prepared for her to fight him on this, for her to mount a whole campaign about why they couldn't get married after just finally agreeing to being back in a relationship last night. But so many of her fears and concerns were already staring her straight in the face. She didn't have the bandwidth to fight with him just to delay the inevitable. She was truly, madly, deeply in love with the man who had just proposed to her, so she said yes. It was honestly the easiest decision she had made in a long time.

"Um, any chance you're forgetting something?" she prompted, pulling away from Rhett's lips to look him in the eye.

"Yeah, about that..."

"Everhett! Did you seriously just propose to me without a ring?!"

She wasn't really upset, but she couldn't pass up the opportunity to tease him. Mr. Logistics was so damn good at planning everything, at setting up a strategy and following through. She was genuinely curious as to why he didn't have the ring with him right now.

"I'm sorry, beautiful. I didn't know where things stood between us when we came up here yesterday. I didn't even go to my house when I got to Hampton. I came straight to you, then we drove here," he explained. "I already have the ring... It was my grandma's. She gave it to me before she died. Mom and Maddie got all her other jewelry, but she wanted me to have her ring. If it makes you feel any better, I knew the second she gave it to me that the ring would be yours one day."

"That does make me feel better," she assured him as she cupped his face in her hands. Rhett's selflessness when she was at her lowest of lows was the definition of devotion. She hadn't known love could feel like this until he dropped everything to be by her side. "But I think it's going to be a long time before you live down forgetting condoms *and* my engagement ring in the same weekend."

"My mom offered to drive it up to me, but I told her you wouldn't mind waiting."

"Wait, your mom knows?"

"I called her when I went to the store. I sort of already knew what I was planning to do, but I just felt like I needed to talk it through. You'll get your ring as soon as we get home," he promised.

"You were right with what you told Anne. I don't mind." She breathed him in, savoring the quiet and the calm she felt from being in his arms. She didn't want to ever forget this moment.

"I love you," she added earnestly.

Rhett smiled back at her. "I have always loved you, Victoria. I will keep loving you for the rest of forever." He interlaced their fingers and bent down to kiss the top of her head.

She felt a sense of peace settle between them. There wouldn't be any more pushing after this. Rhett knew what he was getting into, and he had made his choice. She couldn't keep protecting him from her, not anymore, not now that they were promising each other forever, or as long as they had together.

"What are you thinking right now, Mrs. Wheeler?" he teased, loosening his grip on one of her hands so he could rub up and down her arm.

"Hpmh." Tori snorted. "I'm thinking you're crazy if you think I'm going to change my last name when we get married," she retorted.

"Do you know how many pieces I've created that I've signed Tori Thompson on?"

"Yeah, but I'm pretty sure I could find several of these little things," he tilted his head to the notebook on her lap, "that say 'Mrs. Victoria Wheeler' in them from middle school."

Tori smiled up at him but shook her head.

"You know I don't care," he clarified before she could get a word in. "Keep your name or change your name, it doesn't matter to me. All that matters is that you're mine, now and forever."

Chapter 51

Tori

Her shoulders tensed up around her ears as Rhett pulled into the parking lot of the clinic and found a spot near the front door. He had timed everything perfectly. They had left the cabin after lunch and had arrived with twenty minutes to spare before her appointment at three.

"Okay, beautiful." He turned toward her as he put the car in park. "We're here. What can I do for you right now?"

Tori swallowed down the lump in her throat. She didn't know what to say; she didn't know how to ask for support. She was so used to doing all of this alone, to being strong and just powering through. She had no idea what she needed. She glanced up and met his eyes, shaking her head slightly and offering him a sad smile.

"Hey, don't do that," he whispered, reaching over for her hand. "You can't shut me out, V. Not anymore. We're in this together now, remember?"

"I know. And I'm not trying to shut you out," she promised. "It's just a lot..."

"I know, beautiful. Just remember that you're not alone." He used his grasp on her hand to pull her toward him and place a gentle kiss on her forehead. "I'm here for you," he swore to her.

Rhett's words didn't ease the tightness in her chest, but they gave her the strength to keep going. She unbuckled her seatbelt and reached for the door before she realized he was mirroring her actions.

"What are you doing?"

"I'm going in with you," he countered as if it was obvious.

Her heart skipped a beat. She'd had no expectation for Rhett to come in with her. She knew there was nothing he could really do once they got inside. But his eagerness to be there for her was palpable. It solidified in her mind that no matter what came next, they would be okay.

"They probably won't let you come back with me for the exam," she explained, giving him one more chance to just wait in the car instead.

"I don't care," Rhett asserted. "I'll sit with you until they call you back, and I'll be the first thing you see when it's over. It's you and me now, V. You're not doing any of this alone, so get used to it."

Tears welled up as she nodded her head in agreement.

"Hey, listen, one more thing before we go in there," he mumbled. He wasn't looking directly at her, and she could sense his uncertainty. "I know what's probably coming next after this appointment. We both do," he stated with more confidence. "While we're here, I want you to get a list of the best oncologists and surgeons available for what's next. You should get a copy of all your records, too. This will probably be one of your last appointments at this office."

Tori narrowed her gaze as she processed what he was saying. Understanding washed over her as she realized the deeper meaning of his request. He wanted her to transition out of the clinic and start seeing more specialized care providers for treatment and surgery. That made sense. She wanted that, too. But it also meant she would need more than the paltry student health insurance she had through the school, and she would need it as soon as possible.

"Okay," she accepted after a few more seconds had passed.

"Okay?" he questioned, his voice laced with disbelief. It was like the proposal part two as she watched him try to process her response.

"Yes, okay," she confirmed. "I know what you're saying. I didn't really think it through before, but if we're going to get married, we should do it soon so I can be on your health insurance with NorfolkStar."

The look on his face confirmed she had hit the mark.

"That means things are going to have to happen really fast, Rhett," she asserted, trying to read his expression as she continued. "It probably makes the most sense for me to have the first surgery this summer, so I have plenty of time to recover before school starts back up in the fall. You're okay with that?"

"Yes. I would marry you tomorrow if I could, V," he admitted.

She smiled at his eagerness. "Well, I don't think tomorrow's going to work for me. Plus, I'm still ringless," she reminded him, holding up her left hand for emphasis.

"Not for long. I'm taking you home as soon as we're done here, beautiful. That ring will be on your finger before dinner tonight."

"Wait," she added as a bitter realization came to the forefront of her mind. "You know I didn't say yes for the health insurance, right?" She looked up at him sheepishly. The painful truth was that even if she was using him, Rhett would never call her out on it.

"I do," he replied instantly. "And you know I didn't ask you to marry me just because of the health insurance, right?"

"I do," Tori confirmed, nodding in relief.

"I love you. I want you. I can't wait to marry you." Rhett leaned across the center console of the Prelude one more time to kiss her. "This is all I ever wanted, V, and I'm going to keep reminding you of that for a very long time. Now let's get this over with so I can take you home."

She had been right. They wouldn't let Rhett come back into the procedure room with her. He said he was fine sitting in the waiting room, but she didn't miss the deep concern on his face when she was called back.

She changed into the thin blue disposable gown as instructed. Somehow, a sheen of sweat had formed over her body even though the exam room was freezing cold. She studied the ultrasound machine that sat idly beside her. She knew that machine would be beeping and whirring soon enough, confirming to the technician everything Tori assumed was already happening inside her.

All of the comfort and relief she had felt at the cabin evaporated as the minutes ticked by. She wondered how much longer this was going to take. The waiting had been going on for close to ten years. She was ready for answers now. She was ready for what was next.

The door finally opened, but it was only the nurse who had brought her back and taken her vitals at the start of the appointment.

"It's going to be a few minutes still, dear. Dr. Ritter wants to come in for the appointment since the tech can't answer questions during the procedure," she explained.

Tori felt a lump form in her throat.

"I can let your boyfriend know what's going on so he doesn't worry," she offered, interrupting the panic that threatened to rise up in Tori's body. She teared up at the reminder that Rhett was here with her, just outside in the waiting room. She wasn't alone. She didn't have to do any of this alone.

"That would be great. And he's my fiancé, actually," she added, saying the word out loud for the first time since he had proposed. *Don't get too used to it*, she reminded herself. Based on the conversation they had just had in the parking lot, he wasn't going to be her fiancé for long. Husband would be the word she would need to get used to in the very near future.

A wave of calm washed over Tori as the nurse left the room. She was where she had dreaded being for the last ten years. But Rhett was here, too. They would be getting married sometime in the next few months, if not sooner. A tiny thrill surged through her as she thought about the prospect of planning a wedding. She pictured Rhett in a tux at the end of the aisle, smiling at her, holding her steady and never letting her go.

Tori was ready to surrender now, to give up the fight against the fear and anxiety that had felt like a vice grip on her heart for so long. It might not be okay in the end, but they would be together until then. For the first time in a long time, Tori was willing to admit that being together with Rhett was all she had ever really wanted anyways.

WOW! Thank you so much for reading When You're Home. I hope you loved this story, and are already craving more from Rhett and Tori and the whole Hampton gang. Please consider leaving a review for When You're Home on GoodReads, Amazon and other retailer websites, or social media. Providing a great review is one of the best ways you can support an independent author. Thank you for sharing the love!!

UP NEXT FROM ABBY MILLSAPS

Tori and Rhett's journey continues in the follow up novel to When You're Home...

While You're There

Coming Fall 2021

Available for Preorder NOW!

Acknowledgments

At 12 years old I knew I'd be an author some day. At 22 years old I was much too concerned with doing everything right to even entertain the idea of being a writer. And now at 32, I am astounded that this journey has led me here: to Hampton, to Tori and Rhett, and to you, dear readers. I loved writing When You're Home. It is the privilege of a lifetime to share this story with you. Thank you for joining me on this journey.

This book would not have been possible without the following people:

David, who always sees me, and who always likes what he sees. Thank you for supporting this dream, for loving these characters, and for believing in this book even when I didn't. I love you so damn much.

My daughters, who clapped and cheered and celebrated this accomplishment with me, then promptly asked me to make them a snack. I love you, and I hope I've set a good example for how I want you to passionately and relentlessly pursue your dreams.

Ethan, who never questioned Rhett and Tori's love (but always questioned Rhett's diet), and Bonnie, who was the very first person to read this book in its entirety.

Kimberly, my amazing critique partner, pen pal, and friend. We may not have started beta reading the "right way," but I wouldn't want it any other way. Thank you for writing fabulous letters and making the suggestions that shaped this story.

My amazing ARC Readers who took a chance on a brand new author, and who fell in love with the gang from Hampton, Ohio. You have made this book launch a joyful experience. I'm so lucky to have found you, and I appreciate every moment you've spent reading and talking about this story.

Mrs. B, for knowing I was a writer a few decades before I knew it myself, and for writing love notes in purple pen in the margins of my work. I have carried around the books you gave me and the encouragement you bestowed upon me for the last 20 years.

My family, for pretending like they didn't know I was writing a book, and for letting me do this on my terms.

And finally, every creative soul who dreams of writing or painting or drawing or composing or playing or acting or dancing or... anything. You're not floundering. You're in progress. Don't ever give up on the magic that's inside you.

About The Author

Abby Millsaps is an author and storyteller who writes steamy contemporary romance. She loves to write about the big feelings that surface when people grow up, grow apart, fall in love, and discover what they're made of. Her characters are relatable, lovable, and occasionally confused about the distinction between right and wrong. Her books are set in picturesque small towns that feel like home.

Abby started writing romance in 7th grade. Sure, it was Newsies-inspired fanfic and short stories about slow dancing to 'This I Promise You' at the middle school dance, but like all good love stories, they always ended in happily ever after. She met her husband at a house party the summer before her freshman year of college. He had a secret pizza stashed in the trunk of his car that he was saving for a midnight snack— how was she supposed to resist a meet cute like that? When she's not writing Abby enjoys dancing with her two young daughters, spending time with her family, and traveling to her favorite theme park destinations.

Connect with Abby Online

Website: www.authorabbymillsaps.com

Instagram: @abbymillsaps

Twitter: @abbymillsaps

Facebook: Author Abby Millsaps

Made in the USA
Middletown, DE
29 March 2022